TROUBLE ISLAND

TROUBLE ISLAND

A Novel

SHARON SHORT

MINOTAUR BOOKS
NEW YORK

First published in the United States by Minotaur Books, an imprint of St. Martin's Publishing Group

TROUBLE ISLAND. Copyright © 2024 by Sharon Short. All rights reserved. Printed in the United States of America. For information, address St. Martin's Publishing Group, 120 Broadway, New York, NY 10271.

www.minotaurbooks.com

Design by Meryl Sussman Levavi

Library of Congress Cataloging-in-Publication Data

Names: Short, Sharon Gwyn, author.
Title: Trouble island : a novel / Sharon Short.
Description: First edition. | New York : Minotaur Books, 2024.
Identifiers: LCCN 2024028212 | ISBN 9781250292841 (hardcover) | ISBN 9781250292834 (ebook)
Subjects: LCGFT: Detective and mystery fiction. | Thrillers (Fiction) | Novels.
Classification: LCC PS3569.H594 T76 2024 | DDC 813/.54—dc23/eng/20240702
LC record available at https://lccn.loc.gov/2024028212

Our books may be purchased in bulk for promotional, educational, or business use. Please contact your local bookseller or the Macmillan Corporate and Premium Sales Department at 1-800-221-7945, extension 5442, or by email at MacmillanSpecialMarkets@macmillan.com.

First Edition: 2024

1   3   5   7   9   10   8   6   4   2

In memory of Great Aunt Ruth.
And to all the women who've survived
their versions of Pony.

TROUBLE ISLAND

℘ROLOGUE

LOONS AND GULLS arc in the vast, blue-gray sky over the island below.

Yet even wheeling far above it, the birds are tethered to Trouble Island. No matter how high they soar, how far south they fly later in winter, or how far north come spring, they will never be able to truly break free.

Instinct draws them to this stretch of forty-six limestone acres flatly topping the lake's surface, one of many islands in the archipelago dotting the waters of Lake Erie.

On this morning, the birds dive into the lake, seeking whitefish that resurface in November's cooler water. Intent on their prey, they seem not to notice the purple sandpipers—here on a stopover in their migration from the Arctic Ocean to the Atlantic—running in and out to the rhythm of the waves' slow reach and retreat.

Away from the shore, platoons of waterfowl bob up and down on the frigid waves.

Inland, owls nest in forests of hackberry, chinquapin oak, blue ash, sugar maple—trees that thrive in shallow soil. Woodland birds rustle around in swatches of poison ivy for the vine's winter crop of red berries, just now coming on, or glean insects from tree bark.

Of course, none of these birds know about the small blue-and-yellow macaw that lives in a cage in the mansion on the southern shore of the island, though if the macaw were to be set free, some among them might note it as easy prey. Perhaps the northern goshawk, now swooping among the airborne birds whose ancient warbling cries turn frantically warning, but too late. Midair, the goshawk snatches a gull.

The wheeling birds barely notice as I emerge from the woods, running past the old lighthouse and the hulking remains of an ice-boat, abandoned alongside it.

Though bundled up in my coat, hat, and boots, I'm shivering.

Not just from spotting the goshawk kill its prey.

Or from the cold.

Or from the anticipation of what I'm about to do.

But from the fear that's lived in the pit of my stomach ever since I landed on Trouble Island, a fear that claws through my heart, making it pound, and into my throat, making it hard to breathe. The fear that I, like the birds, will remain tethered to the island.

As I let myself into the unlocked, abandoned lighthouse keeper's cottage, I tell myself *no*.

I am not like the birds.

This morning, I am finally breaking free.

I set aside my glasses and disrobe down to my homemade full-body swimsuit, swimming cap, and the goggles I keep stowed away in the cottage.

I pick up a fishing knife.

I go back out into the cold. At the edge of the dock, I stare down at the frigid, rollicking waters of Lake Erie. I hesitate just a moment. *Free.*

With that promise thrumming in my mind, I plunge into the lake.

The shock is brutal.

I've swum in this lake before. I have about two minutes before I'll need to come up for air, about ten—maybe twelve—before cold will numb my limbs and hypothermia will begin setting in. I also know that here, on this island, especially in the lake, two minutes is an eternity—and so is even one second. Here, eternity can fit into any sliver of measured time.

Though frigid, the water feels good sluicing over my face. I revel in the feeling of strength as my arms stroke to pull me downward, my legs kick to propel me on. I need just a minute to locate what I'm searching for . . .

But instead what comes into view is a figure.

Face bloated. Arms floating out as if grasping for fish, for water snakes, for *me*.

Reflexively, I gasp.

Swallow water.

Flail.

Swim back, back, back . . .

CHAPTER 1

I'LL ALWAYS REMEMBER my first sighting of Trouble Island.

I believe it shall appear in my dreams and nightmares for the rest of my life, emerge before me in odd moments, just as it first materialized through the fog as I stood on the prow of the McGees' small yacht nearly two years ago.

I'd only just distinguished the shore when Rosita McGee's mansion emerged, as if it floated there on its own, created of mist and water and sky.

Rosita's descriptions drifted across my mind.

From the veranda I can see for miles across Lake Erie!

The library—so many books! Not that anyone besides me uses it. But you *would.*

The roses out front are so lush that I can smell them from the tennis courts.

Such were the wistful descriptions that once spurred visions of what my first trip to the island would be like: swirling images of lightness and laughter and joy and ease.

But as it turned out, my first—my only—trip was no such visit.

It was for my imprisonment.

AFTER MY FIRST few days on the island I discovered that there was no angle from which to see the full façade of the mansion. Trouble Island is too small and flat and forested, the mansion too big. No matter how I approached—emerging out of the woods on the singular gravel path that semicircles the southern edge of the island, returning from serving guests at the pool or on the tennis courts, coming back from the small cemetery—I could only glimpse Rosita's mansion in small bits, like puzzle pieces.

Fitting, as although I once thought I knew her, Rosita herself had become a puzzle.

After that, every time I glimpsed a fragment of the mansion, my first view from the yacht's prow would flash before my eyes. The only time I had seen the façade of the mansion whole.

Until an early morning last November 1931, when everything changed.

AT FIRST, I thought I'd finally found my means to escape the island.

I was taking my last swim of the year in the early morning around the island, which normally took me an hour, but a half hour in, I was too cold, even in my flippers, goggles, and the full swimsuit I'd made. I came out on a patch of grassy beach along the northern edge of the island, just before the shoreline became challengingly rocky. I knew if I kept going, I'd have to swim past the rock-ridden stretch to the north dock, and there was no path from that dock—used for private business—back to the mansion.

As I staggered out of the lake, something glinted under the morning sun in the shore grass, catching my attention even with my poor eyesight. Curious, I went to it, and found a rectangular lockbox.

I picked up the box, too heavy to easily swim with, so I made my way to the semicircular path, which traced from the southwest dock—where guests launched fishing boats or visited the old lighthouse—to the main dock in front of the mansion.

I hurried as quickly as I could along the path to the lightkeeper's old cottage. Inside the dark, dank abode, I rushed to the derelict rolltop desk, rolled back the broken cover where I stowed my glasses and clothes while I was swimming to protect them from mice and other critters. I was so curious that, though I shivered, I didn't peel out of my suit, but quickly took off my goggles and put on my glasses.

I studied the box; it was in good shape, not corroded or rusted. So it had not been in the lake, at least not for long. Was it a box that belonged to a recent visitor? A box from one of the many ship-wrecks on Trouble Island's shore thirty, forty, even fifty years before? Maybe the box had fallen into the tangled roots reaching from the trees and shrubs that grew on the very edge of the shoreline. Maybe a ferocious Lake Erie storm had stirred up the box, and in a great crashing wave, deposited it in the tall grass, where it had remained, waiting, a gift from the lake to me. A reward for all my months of swimming. Of coming to appreciate the lake and island's natural life, as our visitors never seemed to. They, instead, focused on the delights of the island's mansion, the headiness of being a guest of the island's notorious owner.

The story I wove for the box pleased me, and so, after I spotted a hammer carelessly left on a side table—the cottage was used as a storage and toolshed—I was careful as I used the tool's claw end to pry open the box.

I stared in shock at the contents: three bars of gold bullion. Jewels—a diamond necklace, cuff links, earrings.

I considered taking the box back to my room at the mansion, but I didn't want to face my workmates' curiosity and questions. I thought about stashing it in the rolltop desk, but the top didn't lock.

I spotted an old fishing net and had what I thought, at the time, was a brilliant idea: I'd bind the box in the net and tie up the box under the southwest dock. I took a moment to consider how the fitful lake and its creatures might affect the box. It should be fine for a week, even two, and by then I hoped—prayed—I'd have concocted a plan for leaving the island before icy winter weather locked us all down. I closed it, bound it with twine, and tied it up securely in the net. I carried my odd package of loot out to the southwest dock.

Before I could have second thoughts, I donned my goggles, grabbed the net-bound lockbox, and jumped back into the frigid, rollicking water. Under the dock, I held my breath so long that my chest was on the verge of convulsing, but eventually I tied up the net.

And then I surfaced, gasping for air, yet giddy. I laughed aloud with joy. The contents of that box were worth at least five hundred dollars, enough for me to start my life over—once again.

But my delight and hope were short-lived. For I spotted a boat coming from the south toward Trouble Island.

Even with my blurry vision, I could see the blue flag flying from the boat's stern.

I knew what that meant.

That I had to get to Rosita as quickly as possible.

So I pulled myself out of the lake and onto the island's southwest dock. I did not even pause to change from my swimsuit back into my dry clothes or slip on my shoes.

I ran from the shore along the island's graveled path, not expecting to encounter any of my workmates. We were supposed to be closing down the mansion for the winter, and because of my escapades with the lockbox, I was late.

But around the curve, one of them—the new bodyguard—was walking toward me. He looked alarmed, stopped me, took off his hunting jacket and offered it to me. I accepted it, gratefully, but did not pause or, through my chattering teeth, answer his question about what I was doing, nor did I turn back when he called after me.

I ran on and finally emerged from the woods onto the mansion's grand skirt of lawn. I rushed up the limestone pathway between the main dock and the porticoed front entrance, not sparing a single glance at the boxwood topiaries of exotic animals—bear, elephant, giraffe—that always charmed visitors. I ran past the multi-tiered fountain topped with a glorious goddess perpetually pouring water. That morning her water was off, a canvas crumpled at the base of the fountain as if she had tossed aside her cape.

Where is the groundskeeper?

I brushed aside the thought, kept running, and finally stopped before the mahogany front door. I panted, my lungs burning. As I was technically deemed staff, I almost always came and went by the basement kitchen door. But that morning, I yanked the front door open, hurried inside, then skidded on my bare, wet feet across the black-and-white marble entry floor, nearly crashing into a ladder below the chandelier, its cut crystals glinting in the morning's spare sunlight. Wood polish and a pile of cleaning cloths lay on the bottom step of the sweeping central staircase.

Where is the housekeeper?

It was better that my fellow domestics did not see me. They'd think I'd gone mad if they saw my disheveled state: dripping wet, shivering, barefoot, wearing only my swimsuit and a man's jacket, my knees and hands scraped and bloody because I'd fallen on the path. I rushed up the stairs, grabbing the curved mahogany banister, fearful of slipping, falling again, cracking my head open.

From the gallery, I veered down a long hall, passing the door to my own bedroom. No time to change into respectable clothing, or to run a comb through my snarled hair. I yanked open the door to the stairwell to the third floor and ran up to Rosita. Always to Rosita.

For that was why I'd been sent to Trouble Island. My punishment for what I'd done in Toledo was to come here in servitude to the McGees, a servitude that was meant to be a life sentence.

A sentence that at first I thought I deserved.

Now, looking back, I realize that from the moment I first spotted Trouble Island and Rosita's mansion, deep down I knew that only a small part of me would remain forever on this island.

But the rest of me—the best of me—would find a way to break free.

CHAPTER 2

Rosita's door was ajar.

Alarming.

For since Rosita permanently came to Trouble Island six months after my arrival, and ensconced herself in the third-floor suite, she always kept it closed. Locked.

Soon after, she ordered me to get a suite key from the groundskeeper, to keep the key safe, and to use it only in an emergency, though Rosita never defined what "emergency" might mean. Sometimes, especially in the middle of long, dark nights, my imagination conjured possibilities: fire, a horrific storm, Rosita falling or dying.

Our routine since Rosita's withdrawal to the suite was simple: I knocked on Rosita's door, she opened it, I entered. Everyone else knew never to come to the third-floor suite. Only I was to ascend those stairs. Only I was to attend to Rosita.

But that morning, I panicked and rushed in, crying out her name.

Her expansive suite filled the whole of the third floor. A master bedroom with a bathroom on the west end of the suite, mirrored by another bedroom on the east end that had once been a nursery and playroom but that was now shut off; shortly after Rosita arrived, she'd had a lock added to the door. She was the only one with a key.

In between the bedrooms, a sitting room that was larger than the main floor of the two-bedroom house I'd once shared with my husband in Toledo.

As I stood in that room, breathless, my gaze skimmed over ornate red velvet love seats, leather chairs, mahogany tables, Persian rugs. Then finally rested on Rosita, standing before the French door to the veranda, her slim back to me.

As always, Rosita wore a black mourning dress and veil and mules, her attire revealing only her slender ankles, her delicate hands and wrists, peeks of alabaster skin that evoked the white quartz headstone in the graveyard. Beside that headstone was a berobed, bronze angel, wings spread wide, gazing heavenward, a dove just starting to take flight from the palm of an outreached hand. Rosita stood just as still as that angel. As if perpetual mourning would somehow resurrect her son.

On the dining table just to her right, I spotted the tray I'd brought up much earlier, bearing her usual coffee and poached egg and dry toast—all untouched, by now cold. My own empty stomach flipped—guilt rather than hunger. Was Rosita's disdain for her usual breakfast in response to my betrayal?

I scanned the table for the note I'd slid under Rosita's door.

Dear Rosita, I'd written in the wee hours, *I've become ill this morning and must take to my bed. However, I've prepared your breakfast and left it outside the door. My apologies for the coolness of the coffee. Ever faithfully yours, Aurelia.*

I did not spot my note, but her red leather-bound diary caught my eye. Not having seen it since she came here, I'd assumed it had been left behind with so much else in her Toledo mansion. My eyes prickled at a brief flash of memory. She never let me read her diary, of course, nor did I try to get a peek. But she'd give a coy smile before closing it and putting it aside, and say, *Just recording Oliver's antics today!* And then recount something cute or new or funny that the McGees' son Oliver had done.

I hadn't been aware that she'd brought the diary with her to Trouble Island. Why had she brought it out that morning?

But I didn't spot the note. Maybe, in a moment of pique, she'd torn it up or burned it in the fireplace. I shook aside my fretfulness over how Rosita might judge me for breaking our routine and blurted out: "Eddie's boat—it's coming!"

"Rather late in the season." Rosita's voice dripped with bitter amusement. We were well out of the season for visitors.

"Not the speedboats." Those brought legal whisky to this southernmost dot in Canada's territory. Sometimes the bootleg bounty was deposited at the hidden dock in a cove on the island's northern edge, the section of the island where the gravel path did not extend; other times, the speedboats came to the southwest dock, and the cases were stored in the old lighthouse cottage. Sometimes it was directly transferred onto one of the island's two speedboats, which then sped off to the north shore of Ohio. There never seemed to be a pattern or set schedule other than that these operations took place at dusk or in the dark.

"The *Myra*," I clarified, half whispering.

The *Myra* was Eddie McGee's personal yacht, named for his mother, though Rosita had told me that Eddie was orphaned at a young age and barely knew his mother. Sometimes, though, we revere those who have gone before us, imagine we know who they would have been, how they would have felt about us, had they lived. May through October, the *Myra* brought people either indebted to Eddie, or those he was indebted to. People eager for a stay on Trouble Island. Or people like me.

"The blue flag is up," I added through my chattering teeth.

Rosita stiffened further. "Well, then."

The blue flag signified that one or both McGees were on board. It had not flown since the last time the McGees arrived on the island, thirteen months before, in October 1930, when Rosita made it clear she was staying for good. The hoisted flag could only mean one thing—Eddie was back.

Rosita turned. I could feel her gaze, even through the black veil. She gestured at me. Asked with only impatience—no concern or surprise—"Why?"

She meant why was I wet, shivering, barefoot, in my swimsuit and a man's jacket? I wished I could see Rosita's eyes, decipher why this, given my news, was of concern. Once, I could easily read her—or, at least, so I thought.

But I doubted I'd be able to read her expression. The last time I'd seen her face, I'd observed only a slack, dull canvas. Flat, deadened eyes.

I pushed up my glasses, sliding as cold water rolled down my forehead. In the warm mansion, my lenses fogged, and I longed to give them a good swipe with the hem of the jacket, but that would have exposed too much. My swimsuit was modest enough for being in the water, but vulgar in the mansion.

Instead, I carefully composed my face, certain that Rosita could still read me. That was one of Rosita's greatest talents, reading in others what they thought they had hidden behind a careful smile, a forced laugh, an arched eyebrow. She'd taught me much of that art, but I will never become the master that she so naturally was, of showing little but seeing all.

I offered the whole truth with the fewest possible words. "I went down to the dock by the lighthouse. To swim." Suddenly, my nose dripped.

Rosita retrieved a handkerchief—clean, neatly pressed, and folded, as I always ensured—from her dress's cuff, and tossed it onto the table. It landed on the red leather diary.

"On such a cold morning? A man's jacket as your only cover-up? Were you with Liam?"

I grabbed the hankie and shook my head as I wiped my glasses. I nearly laughed at the suggestion. Dear, glib Liam, who rarely spoke except to monologue about his archaeological explorations between his work duties, who otherwise whistled tunelessly. Then I patted my nose. I crumpled the hankie in my fist. I'd launder and press it later before returning it.

"Surely not Henry?"

"What? No!" I said. Henry was old enough to be my grandfather. Then I realized she'd shifted from shaming to teasing me—almost like she did in the old days. Before—everything.

"Oh, then Seamus, of course."

My first reaction was to blush.

Seamus Grover, the newest bodyguard. He'd come to the island mid-September, a little more than two months before. We'd flirted from a distance ever since: lingering glances, quick smiles that hinted at possibilities.

But then, as I further considered Rosita's suggestion, my eyebrows rose. Ensconced in her suite for the past year, seeing only me, Rosita could not have met the new bodyguard. I'd had no reason to mention him, and so I had not.

From the veranda, Rosita watched people, heard them call to one another. If only they would look up, they'd spot her standing there. People rarely did.

Maybe she'd noticed Seamus. Been drawn to his casual confidence, his relaxed good looks.

A flash of jealousy deepened my blush. Rosita moved swiftly to me, drew her forefinger down my cheek in a slow graze. "Oh, my dear. We've discussed this. Haven't you learned not to put your stock in men?"

"I crossed his path on the way back from— Oh, what does that matter now? Eddie will be here in minutes! What do we do, Rosita?"

"First, get on a robe, lest you catch a cold." Rosita impatiently waved toward her bedroom.

I hesitated. We were long past the days of sharing clothes. But she shooed me on.

In the bedroom, I took off Seamus's black-and-red-checked wool hunting jacket and put it on the bed. I tossed the handkerchief into the laundry hamper, then stripped off my odd one-piece swimsuit.

I certainly didn't pack a swimsuit before my rushed, last-minute transfer to Trouble Island. I'd found the black ribbed-wool suit left behind in the women's bathhouse and took it for myself. I modified it so I could swim in colder months, treating the suit with linseed oil to make it stiffer and more water resistant, adding tight-fitting sleeves and legs from a black oilcloth table covering I'd found in the old lighthouse keeper's cottage by the southwest dock.

That morning was meant to be my last swim of the year in the frigid lake water. The suit pulled at my skin, leaving red marks around my chest and at the top of my shoulders, and my skin itched miserably from having kept it on so long in the cold.

As I wrung the suit out as best I could in the sink, I glimpsed myself in the bathroom mirror—my wavy shoulder-length hair now in dark straggly strands grazing my collarbone, my brown eyes so wide they seemed to fill my black-framed, thick round lenses, my face pale from the cold, yet my neck and cheeks flushed bright red. I looked like a strange bird who'd fallen from the sky into the lake, then pulled itself out and flopped, bedraggled, onto the rocky shore.

I was tempted to grab Rosita's brush to pull through my hair, or the bottle of Veronal, a sleeping sedative, to take one of the pills to calm my jangling nerves.

But Rosita had only given me leave to wear one of her robes. From the wardrobe, I selected an olive-green floor-length velvet. As I pulled it on, my body immediately took to its warmth, my skin remembering what such fabrics felt like during my brief years in Toledo. Fabrics I'd never known in my youth on a farm in southeast Ohio, which had offered up only rough cotton and burlap flour sacks, stiff and scratchy like my childhood itself.

I knew I should hasten back to Rosita, but as I rolled up my swimsuit in a towel, the frantic morning caught up with me. I deposited the swimsuit and towel next to Seamus's jacket and then I wearily sank into the chair by the window and stared down at the cemetery, which held only two headstones. A shared one for Rosita's grandmother and grandfather. A small one for little Oliver, the angel statue overlooking the spot where he'd been laid to rest at just five years old.

I'd never caught Rosita sitting there, but as I sat I realized that the rough-hewn spare chair from the kitchen was perfectly positioned for a view of the cemetery. How often had she sat there? I wondered. Why had she demanded a spare kitchen chair, though there were so many comfortably upholstered chairs to choose from? Did she prefer discomfort as she stared down at the cemetery? Was it enough for her to gaze at his grave? Or, I wondered for the first time, did she ever leave her suite to visit?

As far as I knew, she'd never deviated from the plan she'd put in place thirteen months before: she would remain in her suite, and only I was to attend to her.

With Eddie nearly upon us, I pushed aside those concerns. I rushed out to the sitting area. Rosita had flung open the French doors and stood out on the veranda. Cold air swirled into the suite, portending a bitter winter.

I jumped at a sudden caw—Largo, a lovely blue-and-yellow Hahn's macaw who doesn't like the cold.

I grabbed a throw from the divan and tossed it over Largo's cage. I whispered, *"I will bring you water and food later, good girl."*

"Good girl, good girl," she mimicked.

Despite the fraught situation, I smiled. Largo is the only creature who has ever called me a "good girl."

I went out onto the veranda beside Rosita. I nearly yelped from the cold of the floor against the soles of my feet. I stared past the fountain, down to the dock, and then beyond to Lake Erie, vast and sparkling under the midmorning sun.

For a moment, Rosita and I stood side by side, equals as we had once been.

No, that's not quite right. We were never truly equals. But we had been something better. We had been friends. And then I'd fallen from my status as Rosita's best friend and taken on the role of domestic servant nearly two years before. Yet, even after all that time, how easily, how foolishly, I fell back into that feeling of friendship.

"Rosita, let's go to the north dock, take the speedboat up to Canada. Henry hasn't put the boats in storage just yet. We'll take Largo, of course," I went on, assuming Rosita would want the bird that had been her son's pet.

"I'm not running. Why would I? This is my island. My home."

Indeed it was. Though Eddie used it for his own purposes, the island and the mansion were legally Rosita's.

But the last time he'd been here, I'd overheard him say to her: *I will give you time to return to me. But don't try my patience. If I have to force you to come back to me, you'll be sorry . . .* "Tell Maxine and the others of Eddie's arrival," she said. "Do as Maxine instructs to prepare for his stay. Find out who Eddie has brought with him and report back to me."

I said, "Yes, ma'am," again the domestic servant.

"Inform Maxine that Eddie will not be staying in my suite. Make up a guest room."

I shuddered, anticipating what it would be like to see Eddie again—the hard lines around his mouth, his stony eyes. How furious he'd be at this spurning.

"Eddie will demand to see me," Rosita went on. "Tell him that I'm incapacitated."

She'd been "incapacitated" for thirteen months. Eddie would not believe she still needed such tender consideration.

"He'll be furious, but you must be resolute. When the time is right, I will come down."

At last the *Myra* came into view. Such a lovely yacht. Modestly sized yet pristine and majestic. Riding high in the waters of Lake Erie, as if blissfully unaware of how quickly those waters could turn into icy, jagged danger.

Together we watched it slide alongside the dock. A man I couldn't place—his hat was pulled low over his face—came onto the boat's deck, then jumped out to the dock and tied up the yacht. He lowered the ramp.

Eddie emerged, alone. He strolled casually down the ramp as if on a lazy pleasure trip. He took a drag from his cigarette, then tossed it into the lake.

Then he looked up. Shoved his hands in his pockets.

Even at that distance, with his fedora cocked to one side, shading his eyes, I knew he didn't see me. That he had eyes only for Rosita. That his eyes lit up at seeing her, even as his mouth curled into a cruel grin.

CHAPTER 3

AFTER LEAVING ROSITA, I rushed to my room and changed into one of my black-and-white maid's dresses. I'd stowed them away—eager to wear pants and sweaters for the winter—but Eddie would expect his staff to be properly attired. Quickly, I hung Seamus's jacket and Rosita's robe in my wardrobe and draped my damp suit—which I usually stowed in the old lighthouse keeper's cottage—over the back of the desk chair. Then I raced down to the large kitchen in the basement hoping to find the housekeeper, Maxine Carmichael.

She was hunkered down before a floor-level cabinet, making a racket as she frantically tugged at something, grunting and cursing.

"Oh, thank God you're here! We were so worried about you."

I turned at the voice of Henry, Maxine's husband, the island's groundskeeper. The two of them together made all the meals for staff and guests, with Maxine focusing on baking and desserts, and Henry on cooking. A plump man, Henry hefted himself up from the wooden chair at the long butcher-block table that served as both staff dining table and worktable. Henry's ebony face, usually relaxed, was pinched. His head was mostly bald, but his eyebrows pushed his forehead up into what was left of his gray, grizzled hairline. Pain, worry, or both? I wondered. He had a maimed left hand, his pinkie and ring finger missing, his range of motion limited. He never complained, just oversaw the grounds and did much of the caretaking himself.

"What? I'm fine," I started. That morning, I was supposed to help them with closing down portions of the mansion for the winter. I hadn't shown up. I couldn't help but smile, touched by their concern. I wasn't used to people caring about me. Perhaps I never will be.

"But listen—I've spotted the *Myra*. Blue flag up. Eddie will be here any minute!"

No need to tell them I'd been swimming in the lake by the southwest dock when I spotted the yacht.

Maxine gave another tug. Smaller pots fell out, clanking at her feet, and she fell back on her rump, grunting. Her headscarf had come loose. As she reknotted it at the nape of her neck, she looked up at me with relief. "Oh, thank goodness!"

I hurried to Maxine. She was stick slender, but had a tender lower back, so I held her elbow and helped her up gently. Even so, she winced and clutched at her back, muttering, "Who put the stockpot all the way to the rear?"

"Me." She'd told me to do so the month before, after the last guests left, because during winter she'd just need the smaller pots and pans to cook for the six of us: me, the Carmichaels, Rosita, Seamus, and the other bodyguard, Liam. "But that doesn't matter right now. Did you hear me? Eddie is coming, and he's probably bringing others—"

"I know," Maxine said flatly. "That's why I'm looking for the big stockpot. Mr. McGee will want Henry to make Irish stew. It's always the first meal he wants." She gave a small harrumph. "No matter the season." Then she frowned. "But we only have beef, no lamb."

I stared at her. That was her concern? Eddie's arrival meant danger, and she was fussing over Irish stew?

Henry laughed at my incredulous expression. "Oh, Aurelia, it will be fine." He shrugged. "Or it won't. There's no predicting with Eddie, so there's no use worrying."

"Seamus came to tell us," Maxine said. "Then he rushed off to find Liam. I guess he found you first."

As my face started to redden—guilt at keeping the truth from them that I'd seen the *Myra* before Seamus could have—I knelt to the floor and stuck my head into the cabinet, rustling about for the big stockpot. Getting the pot for Maxine would spare her back and give my face a chance to lose its flush.

As I put the stockpot on the stove, I looked from Maxine's sweet face to Henry's unusually taut demeanor. Images of the fountain, its cover dropped on the pathway, and the cleaning supplies abandoned in the foyer, flitted across my mind. Unlike me, the Carmichaels never neglected their duties. And usually, Henry would have gotten down on the floor to dig in the cabinet for the pot, rather than have his wife do so.

"Are you all right?" I asked Henry.

"It's nothing for you to worry over," Henry said. He patted his round belly. "Just a little . . . indigestion."

"He complained, I made tea," Maxine said. "He's fine, just needs to rest."

The pair exchanged a look. They were hiding something, and I was alarmed. As a child, I'd seen that pinched look of Henry's before, on my grandfather's face before his stroke. Tears welled in my eyes. I had only guesses about the Carmichaels: that they were in their sixties, had been here for years when I arrived early in the morning in mid-April 1930.

But I did know that as I stepped off the yacht onto the dock—tears blurring my vision, my future seeming as unreal and hazy as the mansion cloaked in fog—the Carmichaels appeared before me.

Henry took my suitcase, and Maxine gently nudged me toward my new home while tutting something about toast and tea to settle my stomach after a choppy boat ride.

Ever since, they'd treated me with only kindness, doting on me like a beloved granddaughter. Setting aside treats—a bit of nice cheese, a slice of cream cake—leftover from lavish parties; *You've earned it, dear!* Maxine would say. Or slipping me pretty items left behind from guests. Nothing too extravagant—a half-used bottle of perfume, an intricately embroidered handkerchief, that kind of thing. *You deserve nice things,* Henry would say.

Oh, but I hadn't *earned,* and didn't *deserve.* If the Carmichaels only knew what had landed me on Trouble Island, surely they wouldn't treat me so kindly.

I turned to Henry. "Are you sure you're all right? With the *Myra* here, if you need to get to the mainland, to a doctor, we could ask Eddie—"

"No, no," Henry said. "Don't you worry about me." He straightened his wide shoulders, pinched his lips in a stubborn line. He pulled a cigarette packet from his pocket along with his one vanity—a gold, embossed Banjo lighter. He lit his cigarette, took a long drag as he returned the lighter to his pocket. I was always captivated by how elegantly Henry moved his hands, though one was maimed and offered little assistance to the other one. "You'll need to let Mrs. McGee know her husband is here—"

"She knows. I went to her straightaway. She told me that Eddie is to have a guest room. Not the suite."

Maxine looked concerned. "She didn't indicate why he might be coming—or why she's denying him his rightful place in their suite?"

I pushed a loose strand of hair behind my ear. I'd not taken the time to properly dry and pin up my dark mop when I dressed again. I wanted to argue against Eddie's *rightful* place alongside Rosita. *Lawful,* yes; they were still married. But not *rightful,* not after the way he'd left, the things he'd said shortly after their only child's burial.

But there was no point in arguing with Maxine. "No," I said. "How would she know he was coming?"

Maxine dropped her gaze. Oh. They thought that I might have played messenger, passing information from Rosita to Eddie through one of his visitors, or vice versa.

But I had not. I'd never been asked. So she couldn't have known . . . except, now that I thought about it, Rosita hadn't been surprised to hear my news. She'd been calm. Composed.

My stomach flipped. Rosita had had at least an inkling that Eddie was coming.

That meant that *someone* had played messenger.

"All the luggage is in the entry. For Mr. McGee, and six others."

I turned toward the deep voice that made goose bumps rise on my arms. Seamus.

He stood in the entry to the kitchen. Having insisted I take his hunting jacket, he'd switched into his gray overcoat. It hung open, revealing he still wore his work shirt and pants. A tuft of chest hair peeked out of his collar, the top button undone. A slight sheen of sweat glazed his face; a swatch of dark brown hair fell below his cap across his forehead.

My heart quickened at the sight of him, just as it had when he arrived in September, replacing one of the bodyguards. They rotated frequently, and I usually paid them little mind. Young toughs, trying to look stronger than they really were, like little boys trying to take on the swagger of big brothers. Like my former husband.

Seamus Grover was different. Calm, relaxed. Always quietly observing. Confident without saunter. Handsome without knowing it—or maybe he did know it, but didn't care, which only made him more appealing. Intelligent deep brown eyes.

The first male, besides my brother, who'd ever made me laugh.

We all turned at the sound of tuneless whistling—the giveaway that Liam was right behind Seamus. "What should we do with the luggage now?" he asked. Liam was the other bodyguard on the island, and the only one who remained year-round, for reasons I had yet to understand. He pulled off his cap, repeatedly ran his hands through his blond hair. Once he understood a schedule, a routine, any deviation seemed to make him nervous.

His hands shook as he messed with his hair. This unexpected arrival, out of the order of the rhythm of our lives on the island, was by itself enough to rattle poor Liam—never mind the purpose of the visit.

I turned back to Seamus. "You said there are six others, besides Eddie? Do you know who they are?"

"A bodyguard, I guess," Seamus said. He looked away. "I'm not sure about the others."

That glance away made me think, *He's lying.* He did know who the others were, at least some of them. Why lie?

But of course I didn't know anything about him, other than how he made me feel. And in that moment, I still believed he didn't know anything about me.

"Well, we need to know who the guests are first, before sorting out the rooms," Maxine said.

"I can take care of that," I said quickly. After all, Rosita's orders to me had been to inform Maxine of Eddie's arrival and then learn the identities of the guests and report back.

For a moment, before hurrying out to fulfill the task, I looked from face to face of my fellow staff. The dear, steady Carmichaels. Awkward yet likable Liam. And Seamus, the newest of us.

I knew only bits and hints of their pasts, dropped into casual conversations while we toiled away: cooking and serving meals, cleaning, tending gardens, toting luggage, maintaining the mansion—all the labor that made it easy for everyone else to reside on Trouble Island.

But the five of us, well, we all lived on Trouble Island as if we were broken-winged birds tumbling from the sky to this unlikely bit of earth, our only consideration after landing being to respond to the McGees' every demand.

I had no idea why my fellow fallen birds were *really* here. I hoped they didn't know why I was.

CHAPTER 4

WHEN ROSITA MADE Trouble Island her permanent residence, she tasked me with observing guests and reporting back. Sometimes she was indifferent, other times she'd grill me on every detail.

While I could never make out a pattern of what interested her, I soon became adept at finding tucked-away spots from which to spy on visitors: in corners, behind statues or topiaries, by the pool bathhouse. I came to know every inch of Rosita's mansion.

Evocative of a French country manor, the mansion crowns a man-made mound of earth—it took thirty barge trips, Rosita once told me, to bring in that much dirt. It's a three-story butter-yellow confection of porticos and verandas and tall windows and gray stone chimneys. Views from the front: the lake, immaculate lawn and gardens, a fountain pinned in place by a stone goddess, and on clear days, other islands in the Lake Erie archipelago plus the northern shore of Ohio. From the back: the pool and tennis courts and more gardens and then the rolling woods that make up the rest of the island. The small water tower that services the mansion is cleverly hidden by the trees from spring through fall.

The second-floor veranda wraps around the whole of the mansion, with access from all eight of the second-floor bedrooms. From the front, I could take in the labyrinth as well as the topiary- and rosebush-lined path from the dock to the mansion's entrance, the croquet grounds. From the back, the pool and tennis courts and, less charmingly, the water tower. On the west side, the small cemetery and on the east, the kitchen garden.

After rushing away from my workmates, I grabbed my coat from my bedroom. Then I hurried down the hallway to the bedroom on the southwest corner and went out the sliding doors to the veranda. I hunkered down on the floor, conjecturing that Eddie would want to show off the grounds before his guests came into the warmth of the mansion and wouldn't want to go out into the cold again.

It was an educated guess, for in the summer and early fall after my arrival, the McGees had visited several times, and I observed that Eddie couldn't resist giving guests the same grand tour, always ending by the labyrinth, where he'd point out the statues of nude figures by the entrance, grinning smugly when women gasped and men chuckled. *Imported from Italy,* he'd say. *Michelangelo's* David. *And Botticelli's* Birth of Venus. He said the names carefully, as if afraid of mispronunciation. *Reproductions, but aren't they fine?*

As I waited that morning, I stared up at common loons and elegant red-throated ones. Herring gulls and ring-billed ones.

I'd learned their proper names from books in the mansion's library, and slowly fallen in love with bird-watching. The preoccupation helped keep me sane since I'd arrived.

I'd come to delight in the mergansers and goldeneye ducks—so goofy—and tundra swans—so elegant. I especially liked the long-tailed ducks, who dive as deeply as two hundred feet into the lake. Oh, and the purple sandpipers, nibbling up freshwater mollusks from the break wall around the decommissioned lighthouse and the adjacent cottage.

Each night in my bedroom, I made note of birds I'd observed, along with the weather conditions.

It had taken me a while to notice, what's more, start to catalog, the island's birds.

When I'd first come to Trouble Island, I didn't think I deserved to live. Not on the island, not anywhere at all. It didn't matter that Rosita had assured me that my stay on the island would only be temporary, a few months at most, that Eddie was working on a way for me to start over elsewhere with a new identity. I sought death by swimming too long, too far out, for I thought that was all I deserved after what I'd done.

But somehow, I always found my way back to shore, and as time passed, the island healed me of such dismal desire. Like a timid woodland creature, I began sniffing the air, became curious about the island itself, its deep, quiet nature, and about the island's history. I wanted, after all, to live.

After a summer season of swimming and hiking and breathing in the deep, loamy scents of the island's woods, I came to long for what Rosita had promised before sending me here: that my island stay would only be a stopover before a new life, a new identity.

But by then, I realized Rosita had no intention of helping me leave. I was to stay on Trouble Island, serving her, being her island confidante, indefinitely. I began to plan my own escape: slowly pilfer from guests a watch here, money there, a few pieces of jewelry. I had Henry show me how to use the boats, planning to eventually steal one of them and dash to the north coast of Ohio.

But then, Oliver died, and everything changed . . .

Suddenly Eddie's booming voice—surprisingly big for such a slender man—carried up to me as he rounded the mansion's corner. I hunkered down, hoping no one would look up and see me. I'd just say I'd been opening up the sliding doors to air out the rooms, if someone did.

"Imported from Italy . . . Reproductions, but aren't they fine?"

"Sure, sure," said another man, impatient.

It took me a moment to identify him, in his heavy coat and fedora: Marco Guiffre.

I recognized him from the newspapers, the leader of a rival gang. He'd been arrested a few times for violating Prohibition laws, his picture splashed across front pages as an example of the evils of boot-legging gang leaders. Suspected of being behind several gang shoot-ings, but never arrested. Now, even from a distance, I could see he looked slightly green. The boat ride over must have been choppy.

Another man, scrawny and young, followed close behind him, a tommy gun slung over his shoulder. One of Marco's bodyguards, I assumed. I didn't recognize him, yet I shuddered, for his cocky, self-important swagger reminded me of my husband.

I wondered why Eddie would bring his biggest rival to his pri-vate island. Had they declared a temporary truce for some money-making scheme? But truces weren't Eddie's way—in business or in his personal life.

Two more men came into view. I shuddered at the sight of the ruddy face of Dr. Timothy Aldridge under his fur hat. The doctor not only knew me, he'd seen me in all my worst moments. Dr. Aldridge was quiet, harmless if you only read his surface, but nothing like the truly kind doctor I'd known back home in southeastern Ohio.

Ever since Rosita had ensconced herself in the third-floor suite, Dr. Aldridge had been coming to the island once a month from spring through fall, sent by Eddie to check on her. Rosita allowed him to attend to her, though she always insisted that I would be in the suite with them, and she never lifted her veil for him. *You'll just have to assume my temperature, vision, and teeth are fine,* she'd snap at him.

Meanwhile, I avoided his curious gaze, answering the one time he'd inquired, *How are you doing, my dear?* with cold silence. He never attempted discourse with me after that, just trudged breathlessly up and down the stairs behind me.

I frowned. He'd just been to the island a month before. Why would Eddie bother bringing him? His shaking hands rose to adjust his cap, then his old-fashioned burgundy bow tie peeking above his coat collar. The tremor was always there, so this was not an effect of the cold or nerves, and yet, I sensed his unease, almost as noticeable as the white puffs of air as he exhaled.

Enough of Dr. Aldridge; my gaze next went to the man behind him, a fellow who was so relaxed as to seem almost bored. He was dashingly handsome—broad-shouldered, athletic, square-jawed. I gasped, recognizing him, too, though, as with Marco, only from photos. His mostly appeared in entertainment magazines. He was Douglas Johnson, yes, *the* Douglas Johnson, the actor and screenwriter, who, Rosita had told me, once played the piano for her and her cousin Claire Byrne when they sang in nightclubs. That was before he'd become famous, before I met Rosita and Claire.

Then, as if I'd summoned her with the thought, Claire herself appeared. She, too, looked bored by the tour, which she certainly didn't need. After Oliver's death, she'd returned from Hollywood to Ohio, probably living on an allowance from Eddie at Rosita's insistence, and coming more often than the doctor to the island, but though she asked every time, she never received an audience with Rosita—and never failed to appear crestfallen by the denial. Maybe, I thought, she just wanted to be near her old friend, Douglas. Indeed, she trotted up alongside him, and looped her arm through his. He didn't shake her off, but the flinch of his expression from bored to annoyed suggested he would've liked like to.

Claire looked so much like Rosita once had. Oh, there were differences; Claire was slightly taller and she did not have the distinctive beauty mark above the left side of her lip that on many women would seem a blemish but that on Rosita was alluring. They were first cousins whose fathers had been identical twins.

That morning, Claire was elegant in a bright blue wool coat with a fox collar, the creature's mouth clamped onto its tail. A cloche hat, festooned with a sweeping macaw feather, covered her head. Disgust at the use of the fox's body and the macaw's feather made my face contort as if I'd bitten into a bitter lemon. How had I ever thought such ornamentation beautiful—or longed for it myself?

I wondered if Eddie saw his estranged wife in Claire's features, and how doing so might make him feel.

More importantly, I wondered what the doctor, the loyal cousin, a famous actor, a rival gangster all had in common? And why Eddie had brought them here, at such a dangerous time for lake travel?

That accounted for five of the people in Eddie's entourage. What about the sixth? Surely Eddie had brought his own bodyguard . . .

My stomach flipped. I swallowed back the hot spit rising in my throat at the realization of who that would likely be. The man in the hat on the dock when the *Myra* first arrived that morning. I'd been so caught up in the shock of Eddie's arrival that I hadn't fathomed the obvious.

I leapt up, heedless of whether anyone below would see me, for *he* was here. The man who loathed me more than anyone in the world. Who'd whispered in my ear on the morning he deposited me on the shore of Trouble Island: *I wanted to kill you and have it over with. But the McGees are too soft. If I ever see you again, I'll make sure you end up at the bottom of the lake.*

My heart thrummed as I imagined going to my bedroom down the hall, grabbing a few things, racing down to the speedboat on the southwest dock, retrieving the treasure I'd only found right before spotting the *Myra*. Then I would . . . *run.*

I rushed inside the guest bedroom, slid the door shut behind me.

And when I turned, there he was, the remaining member of Eddie's entourage.

Former cop-on-the-take.

Now Eddie's right-hand man.

Cormac Herlihy.

CHAPTER 5

IN THE GUEST bedroom, Cormac stood between me and the door to the hallway. Like Marco's bodyguard, he had a tommy gun slung over his shoulder and a holstered revolver.

"Excuse me." I hated how the squeak in my voice made him grin. I hated even more that he ran his thumb down a jagged, deep scar in his right cheek. He swayed to block me each time, his jack-o'-lantern grin ever widening.

If I jumped from the veranda, and landed just so in the bushes, I might get away with only a broken arm or a mild ankle sprain. I backed up, grabbed at the veranda door's handle.

"Don't," he said. "I won't kill you—unless Eddie tells me to."

I slumped against the door, momentarily defeated. "I must go to help Rosita. She expects me. She's still the mistress of the house."

Cormac shrugged. "You can go to her—but with Eddie. Get her to open her door."

"She doesn't want to see him."

"She's made that clear."

Eddie must have rushed straight up to their suite, shortly after his arrival, while I was down in the kitchen. I suddenly yearned to talk with Rosita, hear the details from her in the girlish sharing of confidences we'd once had.

"This is her property. She can send you—him—away—"

Cormac's laugh conveyed the sad truth: if Eddie wanted to see Rosita, he would. No one could stop him. Not even Rosita. The island and mansion were Rosita's property, but Rosita was Eddie's so long as they were married. It didn't matter how she felt about him.

"You're feistier than the last time I saw you," Cormac said. His voice, as always, was rough but flat, the sound of tires slowly grinding over gravel. But his eyes flashed with disgust—the message that I didn't deserve to be alive, let alone be *feisty*.

Why the McGees had him bring me—the only passenger that morning—on the yacht rather than on a skiff, I never quite figured out. Maybe because a skiff would be too dangerous in early April, when there could still be icy spots in the lake.

Or maybe it was because I'd sobbed, *I should drown myself, it's what I deserve,* as Rosita held me and murmured, *No, no, that's nonsense . . .*

In any case, at some point early that morning, Cormac Herlihy—still a cop, still wearing his police uniform and badge—had come into the McGees' home in the swanky West End of Toledo and roughly pulled me from Rosita's arms, saying, *Boss says get this over with. We got plenty to do tonight.*

Cormac had hustled me into a Model T in the circular driveway, driven me across the city to the working-class Onyx neighborhood. The night was cloudless, the moon full, the gas streetlamp for once not sputtering, and I stared through the windshield at the narrow brick bungalow that was my home. It wasn't lavish or posh like the McGees', but even that night, for a moment my heart swelled with pride as I stared at the front porch, the pots with the pansies I'd just planted, the pineapple plaque on the front door, which I'd put there because the old German woman next door told me that meant "welcome," the lace curtains I'd sewn, hanging in the upstairs window to the room that had been meant to be a nursery. My first house since leaving my childhood home, the house and my life so much nicer—or so I'd thought—than what I'd left behind . . .

Cormac had roughly pulled me from the automobile, snarling, *You've got ten minutes. You can stare like a whipped puppy, or pack whatever the hell you want.* I'd hurried inside, the front door still unlocked from earlier, and tried not to look in the parlor as I rushed past—but I did anyway.

I packed in five minutes.

Now, Cormac lurched toward me. I pressed my back into the glass door. He grinned, taking pleasure in my fear. I'd known men like him. I'd been married to a man like him. Pony.

Well, Anthony Walker. But he went by Pony.

But I straightened my shoulders, gave him a hard look, and a small, cold smile.

His expression collapsed into annoyance. He wasn't used to people not quaking before him. His hard, hateful eyes that morning accused me as they had on that awful night just over a year and a half before:

Murderess.

A murderess who killed her husband.

CHAPTER 6

ROSITA'S DOOR WAS locked once more.

I knocked, though I knew Rosita wouldn't come to the door. It was only 11:00 A.M., an hour and a half before her usual time for lunch. Next to me, Eddie exhaled down my neck, reeking of cigar smoke and whisky. Cormac was close behind.

"She's incapacitated." I'd already tried Rosita's lame excuse on Eddie after he'd blustered into the guest bedroom. Then he and Cormac forced me up the stairs. But I tried the excuse again.

"Bullshit," Eddie said. "Get her to open the door! She always used to listen to you."

His gaze was dark, resentful. Yes, Rosita *had* listened to me, followed my advice even when it went against Eddie's desires—but that was before I killed my husband. Before she intervened on my behalf, convincing Eddie to hide my crime and shuttle me off to this island—a far better alternative than either spending the rest of my days in prison or dying by electric chair. Or being disposed of by Cormac.

Only Rosita, Eddie, and Cormac knew what I'd done. At least, that's what I believed at the time.

I knocked again. "Rosita," I said, "I need to take care of Largo."

"Who the hell is Largo?" Eddie hissed.

I stared at him, incredulous. "The macaw that was your son's pet." Rosita had brought Largo with them when they came to bury Oliver.

Eddie flinched, then looked outraged. I'd reminded Eddie of his son's beloved pet in a way that made him seem stupid for forgetting. I'd seen him order his thugs to hurt men for lesser infractions than that.

I knocked again. Eddie grabbed my wrist, squeezed hard. "Don't you have a key?"

"I'm to use it only in an emergency," I said.

Cormac poked me in my back with his gun. "Eddie wants in. That's enough of a goddamned emergency."

My heart beat wildly in my chest like a trapped bird. I hoped Eddie might remember better times, might tell Cormac to ease off. But Eddie's perpetual frown only deepened.

"Rosita," I said, hating how my voice shook her name into a tumble of syllables. "Eddie's here. If you don't let us in, I'll have to get my key, and they'll just be angrier—"

I stumbled as the door suddenly opened.

Before us stood Rosita, her face veiled, her body swathed in a heavy black dress, her alabaster hands clasped.

As if she'd been waiting for us—for this moment—all along.

LARGO SAT QUIETLY on my shoulder while I cleaned her cage, nudging my cheek, a sign that she wanted affection. I gently stroked her head.

"You're a pretty girl, a good girl, Largo," I whispered.

Over the past year, Largo and I had bonded. I loved her lush yellow feathers, a hue that made me think of another bird, a canary Rosita had once given me, that I'd named Dahlia. When the yellow brought up memories that were too sad, I'd focus on the flash of blue and turquoise in Largo's wings. I'd trained her to respond to several commands—"pretty wings" meant she'd fluff out her wings; "say hello, say hello" elicited two excited squawks; "kisses" resulted in her giving me a gentle peck on my hand or shoulder or cheek.

That morning, I wished I'd taught Largo the trick of "hush." Her squawks were anxious. She didn't like the tension that had swept into the room with Eddie, who sat on the love seat and stared at Rosita, still standing. Cormac waited just outside the door.

As I put a fresh dish of water in Largo's cage, I ventured a glance at Eddie. He stared at his wife with longing and tenderness, as if this were years ago. I'd caught glimpses of that expression when she sang in the club where Pony and I first met Eddie and Rosita and Claire.

"Rosita," he said softly, "enough. It's time for you to come home."

"With you?" Rosita's question was tinged with bitter amusement.

"Yes! We can start over. You can have a career on the screen like you always wanted—"

"You mean what you always wanted—"

"*For* you! So wouldn't it be enough? To make up for ..." His voice trailed off. Surely he couldn't mean "make up for" the loss of sweet Oliver?

But he did. And Rosita knew it. She turned to me. "I asked you to bring me a report of who has come to the island. I assume you were on your way with it before you were waylaid?" She unclasped her hands long enough to dismissively wave toward Eddie and Cormac.

I answered over Largo's squawks, "Claire is here. Douglas Johnson—the actor and screenwriter," I said, as if Eddie would bring a random man with the same name. I immediately felt like a rube. Of course she knew who Douglas was; she'd told me once that they were childhood friends. "Dr. Aldridge. And Marco Guiffre and a bodyguard, whose name I don't yet know—"

Rosita pivoted back to Eddie, growled her next words: "You brought Marco Guiffre?"

Cormac turned so he could now see into the suite as well as down the stairs.

"I can explain," Eddie said. "If you'll agree to come back, we can get rid of Marco."

My blood ran cold. I knew what he meant by "get rid of."

"Oh, and start another war with their organization?"

Eddie shrugged. "Marco's told his men that our crews are gonna work together. His bodyguard is stupid and young—reminds me of a bagman who use-ta work for me." He sneered at me, and I knew he meant Pony. He turned back to Rosita. "We can give 'em each a nice pair of cement shoes and just tell everyone a storm suddenly blew up on the lake. Tried to save them. Who could argue that?"

Other than the obvious convenience of only Marco and his bodyguard going overboard, no one could. Lake Erie was known for its sudden, violent storms, especially at this time of year.

Eddie's cavalier attitude toward life and death did not shock me. What pinged in my mind were the words "another war with them." There had been rivalry, but not bloodshed, between Eddie's and Marco's gangs when I was in Toledo.

"You bring the man who murdered our son," Rosita said, her words cold as nails driving into a coffin, "offer to kill him when you've had more than a year to do so, and want to make some kind of deal with me?"

My chest constricted, my breath expelling as forcefully as if Cormac had crushed me. Rosita had never told me how Oliver died. I'd heard murmurings of an accident among guests, but no details. Oliver's death was deeply mourned by the Carmichaels, Liam, and me, but none of us ever talked about it.

Once, when it felt as though at least in the privacy of her suite we were returning to being friends as we'd been before, I'd asked Rosita how Oliver died. She didn't say a word. But she slapped me, hard enough to jam my glasses' earpiece into the side of my temple.

I never again asked the details of Oliver's death.

"Why are you really here, Eddie? Why did you bring Marco? Bringing him makes you just as much Oliver's killer—"

Eddie lunged toward Rosita. "How dare you say that when it's your fault—"

Suddenly, Largo flew from my shoulder toward Eddie's face.

Eddie threw his hands up. "Goddamned bird! I'll kill that thing!"

"No!" I cried. "Largo! Here, here pretty girl!"

Largo swooped around Eddie's head but quickly returned to me, landing on my outstretched hand. Her wings were clipped and she could only fly in brief bursts. I eased Largo back into her cage and threw the scarf over the top.

Rosita stood up and strode toward her bedroom.

"You can't avoid me forever!" Eddie shouted after her. "Wanna know what I'm up to? I want everyone to gather in the music room, after dinner. You will come downstairs tonight if you know what's good for you."

As Rosita stepped into her bedroom and shut the door behind her, it occurred to me that she'd known that Eddie wouldn't heed my message that she was indisposed. That she'd known he'd come up and would become emotional. And that that was just what she wanted.

Eddie stormed away. I followed, closing the suite's door behind me, eager to get out of that suffocating space, frustrated that I was again caught in the McGees' drama, bouncing between them like a ball on the tennis court.

Rashly, I thought again that I should go back to the southwest dock, retrieve the lockbox of treasure I'd stashed away, get in the speedboat . . .

As I turned, Cormac was suddenly towering over me. "You'd better make sure Rosita gets downstairs tonight."

"I can't force her to do anything."

"Find a way—or I'll tell Marco who you really are."

I frowned. While I didn't want people to know my past, this seemed a lame threat. After all, he was a criminal, too. How many people had Marco killed—or ordered killed? Why would he care about what had happened between me and my husband almost two years ago?

"So?" I said.

Cormac chuckled grimly. "Trust me. If you value your life, you won't want Marco to know who you really are. So get her down to the music room tonight."

CHAPTER 7

FOR THE REST of the day, I was tortured by Rosita's revelation that
Marco Guiffre was somehow responsible for Oliver's death. And by
Cormac's declaration that I'd better hope Marco didn't find out who
I really was. Was there some connection between him and Pony?

I kept to the mansion's basement, helping Maxine prepare dinner.
We carried trays upstairs from which she could serve the salads, Irish
stew, and fresh rolls and butter. Then I took a tray up to Rosita's door,
went back downstairs and served the staff, cleaned up the kitchen,
and kept an eye on Henry, who'd remained breathless and ashen
throughout the day.

He'd insisted, though, on making his vanilla pound cake. Once,
I'd commented that it seemed unusual for a man to cook, and he'd
laughed and said he'd been the second cook and porter on a Lake
Erie freighter. That night, I helped him slice his pound cake and
scoop on ice cream, a small quantity leftover from the summer and
put aside in the deep freezer, meant for us year-rounders as a special
treat come Christmas. We topped it with Henry's delicious butterscotch sauce. When we finished the task, we stared mournfully at
the desserts.

It seems, now, such a silly thing to lament—our ice cream being gobbled up by gangsters unlikely to appreciate the treat.

As Henry and I entered the dining room with trays of the desserts, I felt Claire staring at me. She daintily patted her lips, leaving a lipstick outline on the white napkin that she well knew I'd have to bleach out later, and gave me a sneering glance, the feather topper on her head bobbing ridiculously. I took some satisfaction on seeing that her bare arms were goose bumped. We'd turned up the radiant heat throughout the mansion, but it took hours to fully warm the mammoth home, and she had to be cold in her sleeveless, sparkling drop-waist dress. It served her right, I thought, for dressing as if this were a swanky party on Prohibition's eve. She'd whined at me earlier to please convince Rosita to meet with her—*It's been over a year,* she'd said, nearly sobbing—and I'd ignored her.

But then my satisfaction at Claire's discomfort faded as the image of my own ridiculous dress, buried at the back of my bedroom's wardrobe, flashed across my mind: sleeveless, sequined, apricot drop-waist. The only impractical clothing I'd brought with me that last horrible night in Toledo. I'd grabbed it as if I might be included in the parties on Trouble Island, the reality of what I'd done not yet penetrating my agonized, fearful haze.

Eddie's booming voice jolted me from my brief reverie.

"What the hell is wrong with this stew?" He tossed his spoon, causing it to hit his bowl with an alarming clink before splattering the thick brown broth on the white tablecloth. His behavior plus the slushiness of his voice meant that once again, he'd drunk too much.

Other spoons dutifully clattered into their bowls, as if the spoon-holders had just discovered a bug floating in the stew.

Dr. Aldridge stared woefully into his bowl, still holding a piece of bread in his trembling hand, about to sop up the last of the broth. But he dropped the bread, while Claire's pretense of superiority gave way to an expression of acute nervousness, something I'd never seen before in her face. Douglas gave a small sigh and took a long sip from his wineglass. Marco held his spoon in his chubby fist even as his fleshy face folded into layers of dismay. His bowl was nearly empty.

"Tastes off to me," said Dr. Aldridge.

Eddie turned his angry attention to Maxine. "Are you trying to poison us all? At Rosita's bidding?"

Maxine's hands trembled and I feared she'd drop the crystal water decanter.

"What the hell?" Marco leapt up. His bodyguard—whose name I'd finally overheard, Joey Ricci—lurched forward, hand automatically going to his holster, as if he could shoot down food poisoning in a standoff. In response, Cormac advanced.

"Eddie," Henry said quietly as he put a dessert by Eddie, "I made the stew—the same recipe you always like. We didn't have lamb. We used beef. Otherwise, it's the same." He gave Eddie a sharp look.

My heart thudded—what was Henry playing at? No one defied Eddie.

But Henry went on, his voice mellow and soothing. "I'll throw yours out, though." He smiled, adding so quietly that the rest of us barely heard, "I also made your favorite pound cake and butterscotch sauce."

Eddie grabbed his dessert spoon and scooped up a bite of the ice cream and sauce. He closed his eyes as he focused on the taste and moaned. "It's good, Henry. You always were the best cook."

I was taken aback. I'd seen Maxine and Henry serve Eddie and Rosita and Oliver during their visits in happier times, but I'd never heard either of the Carmichaels speak so personally to either of the McGees. None of them had hinted at a personal connection.

Though I'd come into the McGees' orbit three years before arriving on Trouble Island, all I'd learned of Eddie's background was the vague account everyone stuck to: he'd been an orphan, growing up at the Sisters of the Poor orphanage in Toledo. His mother was named Myra, which people only knew because he'd christened his yacht with that name. From the beginning of Prohibition, he'd made his fortune bootlegging, somehow evading capture and prosecution. The intervening ten or so years were skipped over.

"You gonna let one of *them* talk to you like that?" Marco said too loudly.

Eddie's eyes flew open, his hard gaze pressing into Marco. "Henry and Maxine have my respect. And you will treat them with respect, too."

Cormac stepped forward, glowering at Marco. In response, Joey pulled his revolver. Cormac's hand went to his own gun, and I had no doubt he'd be able to outshoot Joey. The room stiffened. I couldn't breathe.

Then, slowly, Marco nodded. The bodyguards receded to their spots. I exhaled, relieved.

But Henry looked calmer than I'd seen him all day, and gave Maxine a comforting look. The couple continued serving desserts while I gave Henry a little nod; he understood and gently took Maxine by the elbow and guided her from the dining room. I served the coffee. My head suddenly pounded—a sick headache, as my father used to call my "spells." I tried to ignore Dr. Aldridge's curious gaze. My head was made worse by Marco's boorish voice, recounting some anecdote, the specifics of which I tuned out. Claire laughed too loudly and too often at whatever Marco said.

Douglas looked both bored and boring. Disappointing, after all those swoony photos in *Photoplay* and *Picture Show*. Though it struck me that it had been a few years before I came to Trouble Island when I'd last seen those photos on the covers and the inside spreads. What had he been doing all this time?

The dining room felt suffocatingly small with Cormac lurking just behind Eddie, and Joey now leaning against the sideboard, and I wanted to tell him to get his elbow off of it. The sideboard was carved cherry, inlaid with birch and oak and other woods to create a gentle, intricate scene of a distant countryside. Maxine once told me—in an awed half whisper—that the sideboard had been imported from

China at great expense. All of the furnishings in the mansion are like this. Exotic, expensive, imported.

Even more irritating, Joey was ogling every move I made, giving me sideways smiles as if that was particularly charming. Acne dotted his forehead and cheeks, and his shoulders and chest were slight. Marco must have thought Eddie was not much of a threat to bring Joey along as bodyguard. On the other hand, the kid was quick on the draw, as he'd shown just moments before.

Finally, dinner concluded, and I began to clean up.

"Leave that for now," Eddie ordered. He pulled out a cigar, lit it, and waved a hand in a shooing gesture. "The men and I have business to discuss."

Claire's smile was charming enough, but also tight, and her eyes flashed with irritation. But she stood and flounced out of the room, winking at Douglas as she left. He didn't appear to notice her flirtatious effort.

I remained long enough to move a glass ashtray from a corner table to Eddie's side, then gladly made my exit. But just outside the dining room, a hand grabbed my waist. I twisted around, fists raising, an instinctive reaction.

Joey had followed me. He grinned. "Oh, darlin'," he said, "don't be like that. I know your type."

I dropped my hands, but they remained fisted. "You don't know anything about me."

"Sure I do," he said. "You're tired, so you've dropped your guard. I can hear the twang in your voice. Where you from? West Virginia? Eastern Kentucky?"

I gave him an appraising glance. I knew his type, too. I reckoned him to be eighteen, maybe nineteen, five or six years younger than me. About the age I was when I ran from my childhood home, determined to go to Chicago. Making it all the way to Toledo.

"I'm from none-of-your-damned-business southeast Ohio."

He lifted his eyebrows. "An Appalachian gal, putting on airs, getting above her raising. What're you running from?"

I sighed. I'd told myself, when I left the farm where I grew up, that I wasn't running *away*. I was running *toward* something better. Later, I realized how wrong I was. But in any case, I understood how a young punk like Joey could get caught up with the likes of Marco by being eager to believe gilded promises.

"I reckon same as you," I said, unleashing my childhood dialect. It was oddly relieving. "Mistakes. Despair."

Fright flashed in his eyes, as if I might actually know what, specifically, he'd hoped to shake himself free of. Joey was how I imagined Pony had been in his younger years—if I'd known him then. Pony had been much older than me. "Maybe someone you hurt." I paused. "Or killed, even if you din't mean to." That made him flinch, but he managed to hold on to his grin. Dispassionately, I studied his face: narrow jaw, high cheekbones, delicate chin, unruly dark hair, acned skin. Maybe not so much like Pony. He might stand a chance of aging into handsomeness, if he lived long enough.

I could have—probably should have—stopped, and yet, I pressed on. "Yeah, same as me, so I know how to deal—"

"Not the same! I'm from Missouri—"

"Ozarks." I shrugged. "Just another hillbilly. Listen, Hillbilly-from-the-Ozarks, you get handsy with me again, and I'll shoot you. Or have Cormac do it."

His cockeyed smile finally ran away from his face. "You wouldn't."

"You don't know what I might do."

I walked away, hoping he couldn't see how I trembled.

CHAPTER 8

I TREMBLED NOT because of Joey, but because Eddie had said *every-one* should gather in the music room after dinner. But Rosita, I was sure, would not come down.

I hurried into the music room to make sure the decanters were full of Canadian whisky, as Eddie would expect. I was surprised to see Claire in the room. I assumed she'd gone up to her room for the time being.

She'd already helped herself, but she held up her lowball cocktail glass, gave it a little shake to indicate she wanted more whisky. My hands still shook as I poured.

I sloshed amber liquid on top of Claire's slender, pale hand.

"Nervous?" she said.

"Oh, no, no," I stuttered. "I'm so sorry. I'll get a napkin . . ."

Claire licked the dot of whisky from the top of her hand, while giving me a wink. That was Claire, always straining to appear as alluring, as sexy, as her cousin Rosita—and spoiling the effect by trying too hard. "Aurelia—you are still going by Aurelia, right?"

The implication in her question—that I'd once gone by another name—startled me.

About a year after I met the McGees, Claire left Ohio to go to Hollywood to try to make it as an actress. I was so wrapped up in my troubles with Pony, my friendship with Rosita, that I nearly forgot about her until she showed up with the McGees on Trouble Island, a month or so after my own arrival. Thankfully, on her ensuing visits she never acted as though we knew one another, never questioned my new identity, even when she pulled me aside to privately beg to see Rosita. I assumed that Rosita had shared my cover story: I was Aurelia Escalante, a maid who'd worked for the McGees in Toledo, and my husband had died in a mob shooting. A grieving widow, I'd come here to work for the McGees in solitude as I mourned. It was a story that the few who'd heard it—the Carmichaels, Liam, Seamus, the occasional guest who asked where I was from—took at face value.

Rosita had promised me that only she, Cormac, and Eddie would ever know what I'd actually done. But Claire was her cousin, had been her best friend before I came along. After what I'd done, my demotion from friend to servant, could Rosita have needed a new confidante, brought Claire back from Hollywood? Would Rosita have told Claire what I'd done, why I'd been sent to Trouble Island?

Fear punched up like a fist into my throat, but I swallowed it back down. "Yes. I am Aurelia Escalante."

Claire's laugh was too loud, too sloppy. "Fine, I'll play along." Her grin implied: *for now.*

What if she had reason to reveal my real identity to the others? My colleagues would think less of me, but I could survive that. I'd spent most of my life knowing people thought little of me. But Cormac had said I didn't want Marco to know who I was. Why would that be?

I hurried to the dry bar, put the decanter of whisky back in its spot, then started to exit the room.

"Oh, *Aurelia*, stay, won't you?" Claire puffed out her lips in a pout that was meant to be charming, but just seemed petulant. "I don't like being alone, and who knows how long the boys will take." She gestured in the direction of the dining room.

Boys. As if they were youthful innocents discussing plans for a treehouse club.

I wanted away from Claire as much as I wanted to check on Maxine and Henry. "I really ought to get back to work, so much to clean up in the kitchen—"

"Oh, work, work, work! Don't you ever tire of serving Rosita and Eddie?"

She'd always been like this, trying to get me to say something damning that she could later report back to Rosita—and no doubt embellish.

I almost made my escape into the hallway when Claire's next question stopped me. "So, where will you go after Marco gets the island?"

I stopped, gasped, turned to look at Claire. Her pitiless, rasping laugh made my teeth clench.

"Oh, darling, you didn't think this was a social call, did you? This is, as are all things with Eddie, business." Claire arched an eyebrow as she eyed me, and I suddenly felt as exposed as if I stood in a spotlight wearing only a slip. "Though I daresay Marco will be fine with keeping a little thing like you employed."

"But how will Marco get the island?" The question burst out of me. "Rosita would never agree to sell it—"

Claire laughed. "Of course she wouldn't—not on her own. But with a little pressure in just the right ways . . ." Suddenly she shivered, gestured at the dark fireplace on the other side of the baby grand piano. "Why isn't it lit?"

I flatly explained, as I would to any guest, "The fireplaces in this room and the dining room are for ambience. We stop using them after the last guests leave—which is at the end of September. However, we have increased the heat in the mansion, and it should be toasty by bedtime." "Toasty" was an exaggeration. But to me, the coal-fired furnace which generated heat through ducts and vents through the whole mansion still seemed a marvel, toasty or not. I pointedly eyed her bare arms and her decolletage, her sparkly silver sheath's neckline cut so low that her breasts were at risk of tumbling out. "Perhaps you brought a sweater?"

She had, after all, brought enough luggage for a month's stay, so surely she'd thought to tuck in a wrap of some kind, given it was mid-November in Lake Erie.

My implied admonishment only amused Claire. "And if this guest demands more ambience, as you so cleverly put it?"

Couldn't she hear the howling wind outside, discernible even over the voices of the "boys" in the next room and through the thick walls of the mansion? Or the lashing of sleet against the window? Would Claire really expect me or Liam or Seamus to go outside for wood just so she could enjoy a fire, which she'd probably abandon after ten minutes?

The answer was in her teasing smile. Yes. Yes, she would.

"Of course, I'd be glad to accommodate you."

Claire laughed. "Oh, Aurelia"—she put undue emphasis on my name—"*accommodating* as always—or should I say more cowed than ever?"

I bristled at her description, but before I could settle on a reply, someone gave my rump a firm slap.

I jumped, whirled, ready to smack Joey, but it was Marco grinning at me, blowing cigar smoke in my face.

Marco waggled his eyebrows at Eddie, who was entering the room after him. "Does she come with the island?"

Marco chose the leather chair next to the table beside Claire. Eddie sat on one side of the couch, while Dr. Aldridge sat on the other side.

Douglas crossed to the baby grand piano. His lips pinched a cigarette. He sat on the bench, stared at the keys. Did he mean to play? The piano had been off-limits, Rosita's orders, after she came to the island permanently. Occasionally, I'd hear a few twinkly notes plucked out by guests, and if I was with Rosita when those came tra-la-la-ling up the stairs, I'd observe her stiffen, imagine her brow furrowing behind the veil. I'd have to run down to the music room, apologize that the piano was out of tune and not to be played, and then close the keyboard cover.

As Douglas plucked at the keys, I grabbed an ashtray and hurried it over to the piano, walking awkwardly behind the couch to avoid Marco. His ample, doughy face took on a pout.

I held the ashtray under Douglas's cigarette just in time for the ash to fall. He had begun to play a slow waltz. He paused to put his cigarette on the ashtray and give me an amused grin. His cheeks dimpled adorably, he winked, and a blush rose to my cheeks. Well, no wonder ladies everywhere swooned over Douglas Johnson. Maybe he wasn't as dull as I first thought.

"We're going to need something snappier for our film, Dougie," Claire said, a hint of jealousy in her tone.

Film? I wondered briefly, but then my focus turned to escaping the room. Joey came in, filling the arched doorway. He was bigger than he at first seemed. His gaze stalked me as I whisked past him to the sideboard, about to exit through the other doorway.

"Hold it!" Eddie snapped. "I meant it when I said we would all gather in this room after dinner. Cormac has gone to fetch the rest of the staff—"

As if on cue, Cormac entered and stood near Eddie. Though I tried to ignore him, Cormac stared at me, a half smile twisting his mouth, taking pleasure in making me uncomfortable.

Seamus, Liam, Maxine, and Henry all entered, lining up, practically at attention. Henry was the only one who slumped, weary from the day's labor, and I wished he'd sit, but I knew his pride wouldn't allow it. Maxine trembled and for a moment I thought she, too, was simply worried but then I saw her casting an uncharacteristically hard glance at Dr. Aldridge. He caught her gaze and looked away. I made a mental note of the silent exchange.

"Mr. McGee, the casino is set up as you asked," Liam said, as if Eddie was expecting a staff report.

Seamus gave him a little shake of the head. He'd read the room and knew something bigger was in play.

Indeed, Eddie said, "We are missing only one person." He looked at me. "You will go fetch her."

I squared my shoulders. "I cannot do that," I said.

Douglas hit a jarring note in his piece and stopped playing. The room grew still as if all the air had been sucked out of it.

"And why is that?" Eddie asked in a tone of practiced reasonableness—a tone that warned of imminent danger. He made a fluttering motion with his hands. "Has my wife suddenly flitted away like a bird?"

"Rosita is not someone who is *fetched*. She made it clear that she did not intend to come down tonight—"

I stopped as we all heard footsteps tapping down the hall.

Rosita, with each approaching step making a liar out of me.

CHAPTER 9

ROSITA, STILL SWATHED from head to toe in this morning's black dress and veil, stood as still as the water fountain goddess on the front lawn. Her signature perfume—jasmine—wafted around her, gently tickling my nose, stirring memories of happier times. She hadn't worn that perfume since she'd come here, and I wondered at her choice to do so now. A subtle way to taunt Eddie with all that they'd lost?

It was impossible to know where her gaze landed, but all eyes were on her.

Eddie—eager even after their earlier encounters, about to stand, but forcing himself back into his seat. Claire and Douglas—nervous and excited. Maxine and Henry—concerned. Seamus and Liam—surprised. Cormac—sneering, as usual. Dr. Aldridge—anxious. Marco—curious. Joey—indifferent.

It would be the last time we'd all be together. Alive.

"Oh, Rosita, how I've missed you—" Claire started, jumping up from her chair. For the first time since arriving, she didn't seem like she was acting. "It's been, oh, how long—"

"Shut up, Claire," Eddie snapped. She sat down, cowed.

He straightened his tie. "Rosita, I've come to give you what you asked for on our way here to bury our son. A divorce. But on one condition. You will turn the island over to me. I will pay you handsomely—"

Marco exclaimed, "You said this was your property, Eddie. That you could sell it to me, free and clear—"

"You want to sell this island—*my* island—where our son is buried? To his *killer*?" Rosita asked. Each word like cracking ice, each shard driving into my heart. Though Rosita had revealed earlier that day that she believed Marco was responsible for Oliver's death, I mourned anew the boy's loss, and, yes, perhaps selfishly, chafed with hurt that in all the times I'd tended to her over the past year, Rosita had never told me the circumstances of Oliver's death.

"It was never my idea to have him buried here," Eddie said. "We can have Oliver and your grandparents moved to a cemetery in Toledo. Where I can visit, too."

Rosita snorted at that, indicating her doubt that Eddie would ever bother doing so.

Eddie ignored that and went on. "And Douglas is working on a grand new script, a picture show that will star you and Claire as the Sweetheart Cousins."

Rosita turned toward Douglas. I imagined the cutting look, hidden by her veil, with which she regarded him. "What's changed your mind about Claire and me? Remember that before I met Eddie, Claire and I begged you to take us with you to Hollywood? And you said—"

"I wrongly said that your talent isn't big enough for Hollywood," Douglas said. "I'm sorry I said that. I've changed my mind. After—the tragedy—everyone will ..."

"Find me interesting? The tragic mother, emerged after a year of mourning—"

Claire clutched at Rosita. "Yes, and I'll be there right beside you—"

Eddie cut in, "It's a new start for you, and I'm funding it—"

"Being a star was never really my dream. It was just a means to an end."

"Right. To escape your crappy life," Eddie said bitterly. He jerked a thumb at Claire. "To rescue her."

Claire turned bright red, shame and fear flooding her face. I knew those emotions.

But all Rosita ever told me about her and Claire's childhoods was that, sure, they'd grown up poor in Toledo.

I realized then, based on Claire's reaction, not Eddie's words—for I knew he lied easily—that she'd been hiding her own past from me.

But then, I'd kept certain truths of my own hidden from her. From Pony. From everyone.

Now Rosita shook her veiled head. "No. I married you because I loved you." She emphasized "loved"—past tense. Even the shadows in the corners seemed to withdraw in discomfort. Why did they have to have this conversation in front of all of us? "Until you let our son get killed."

Eddie's lips tightened in a thin, cruel line. "We can't get him back. Forget the movie if you like, but take what I'm offering. Find a different island to hide away from the world."

Rosita asked flatly, "Why do you want to sell my island, Eddie? And to a rival?"

"I want out of bootlegging," Eddie said. "I'm using the capital to move into, ah, other businesses."

"He thinks Prohibition won't last," Marco said with a little chuckle, as if he could lighten the mood. "Crazy, I say—for all the talk, the politicians will be too embarrassed to end it. But I'm offering a great price—"

Something felt off to me. Eddie should have plenty of money from bootlegging. If he wanted out, couldn't he just quit?

Unless he'd already tried to get into one of those other businesses—heroin, prostitution, gambling—and had overextended. Or taken a loan, or made a deal with someone that was beyond his means?

"I don't care," Rosita said. She turned so she was facing Eddie, and though her veil remained lowered, I could feel her eyes boring into him, burning with hatred. "You have ruined the island for me. Coming back here. Bringing this . . . this swine with you. But I'm not selling it."

Marco jumped up. "Look, I know you're still mad about your kid, but I ain't the one who pulled the trigger, and I wouldn't'a gone for Eddie if I'd'a known the boy was with him—"

Cold crept over my skin. Marco had put a hit out on Eddie. Poor sweet Oliver must have died in the crossfire.

"And if you'd been a fit mother," Eddie said to Rosita, "instead of hungover after firing yet another nanny, I wouldn't have had to take him with me—"

"I wouldn't have fired the nanny or been hungover if you hadn't been screwing her—"

"I told you, we weren't screwing!" Eddie shouted. Then he cleared his throat, turned to Dr. Aldridge. "Are you making note of this—this—"

Dr. Aldridge turned red, but nodded as he cleared his throat and jerked at his burgundy bow tie. "Paranoia? Yes. Noted."

I gaped at the doctor. I was wary of him, given my history with him, but I always thought he was fond of Rosita.

Eddie switched his regard to Marco, and stated with satisfaction, "Rosita will turn the island over."

I wanted to scream. In that moment, I hated Eddie, Marco, Dr. Aldridge. I hated Rosita. All four of them, for being more concerned about their own desires and conflicts than about an innocent little boy.

"Look, doll, you can take the easy way—the stardom I'm willing to set up for you. Or just take the money and start over by yourself elsewhere. If you don't, if you try to stand in my way, well, you'd have to be insane. That's a fact that Dr. Aldridge here is happy to attest to. With Claire and Douglas as witnesses. Or sure, do it your way—the hard way.

Dig in your heels, and I won't have a choice but to make sure you're truly locked away." Eddie gave Rosita a cold smile. "And then my attorneys can make a case that an insane dame can't control property. It becomes mine to, ah, manage for you—and I'll sell it anyway. Either way, easy or hard, the island becomes mine, and I'm selling it to Marco."

Claire dropped her head. Douglas stared at his hands, at rest on the piano keys.

Dr. Aldridge tugged at his bow tie as if it was choking him. "I'm sorry," he started.

But Marco muttered something, an indistinct mumble to most of us, but Eddie must have heard clearly enough, for he was up on his feet in an instant, fists on his hips, leaning over Marco. Joey moved closer to his boss, and Cormac tensed.

"What was that?" Eddie snarled. "What the hell did you just say?"

Marco turned bright red but glared up at Eddie. "I said, wouldn't it just be easier to kill her? Then you'd inherit—" He stuttered to a stop and shrank back. Even blustering Marco knew he'd gone too far, as Eddie's face blazed with fury.

I looked at the Carmichaels, as if they might know what to do to stem the evening's horrid direction. But Maxine looked as though she might faint, and even Henry—who'd been so adept at soothing Eddie just moments before—looked aghast. Suddenly, Rosita laughed with bitter amusement. "Oh, you foolish toad. Eddie would never kill me." Was she only trying to defuse the tension, or did she really believe that? I wondered. Eddie saw murder as a tool of expediency, easily wielded against those he no longer needed. But from his reaction to Marco, he must still care about Rosita.

She went on. "And anyway, the answer is no. No, I will not agree to be in Douglas's film. The Sweetheart Cousins days are behind me. Nor will Dr. Aldridge or anyone else declare me insane. I will keep my island. And eventually, Eddie, you will give me my divorce." She paused, and I could sense a thin smile curling her lips behind her veil. "Because I have something you want more than any money you can get for this island."

Eddie's tight, red face suddenly fell and drained of color. For the first time in all the years I've known him, he looked scared. I did not know what Rosita referred to—but he clearly had an idea. From the flick of a worried frown on Cormac's face, so did he. Everyone else looked confused—except Seamus. He was expressionless, as he had been through the last agonizing minutes, observing as if from afar.

Rosita turned, started to leave the room, but Eddie grabbed her elbow, poked his gun in her ribs. "One song, sweetheart. None of us have heard you sing in so long."

"Oh, you'll kill me after all, if I don't sing? In front of all these witnesses?"

"Wouldn't it be a shame if my gun went off accidentally—as all these witnesses would attest," Eddie said. Well, so much for my brief hope that Eddie still had sentiment for Rosita. Apparently, he just didn't want Marco to be the one who killed her. "Not a person here who would say otherwise—if they know what's good for them. And Marco's right, I'd get the island free and clear, no need for me to lose money for a divorce." He shook Rosita. "Or to worry about what you've found."

"Oh, you don't think I was foolish enough to keep what I found all to myself, do you?"

At that, Eddie glared at me. Everyone else stared at me, too. It made sense that she would have told me about whatever she had found—who else had she talked to in the past year?

No one—as far as I knew.

And yet, I had no idea what she was referring to.

Rosita jerked her arm from Eddie's grasp. "All right, Eddie, I'll sing. Just for you. Not because I'm afraid of you. But because I want to." She strode over to the piano.

Claire jumped up. "What do you want to sing, Rosie?" It startled me to hear the old nickname again. "How about 'Yes, We Have No Bananas,' or 'Toot, Toot, Tootsie'?"

Ridiculous, cheery songs. Yet their unique stylings had made the cousins famous—at least in Toledo speakeasies.

Rosita shook her head. "I think instead—'Always.'"

I drew in a sharp breath. She'd often sung the ballad for Oliver, as a lullaby. The chorus echoed in my head: *I'll be loving you, Always. With a love that's true, Always . . .*

Eddie's eyes suddenly shone with sorrow. Rosita had made a purposefully pitiless choice. Perhaps, by dwelling on her sorrow for the past year, she'd gotten used to the pain. Eddie had pushed it back, to the point he could make this callous deal with Marco. But now, she'd again ripped open the hurt.

Rosita regarded Douglas. He struck a soft chord.

And then Rosita slowly lifted her veil. We all saw her face for the first time in more than a year. Everyone inhaled at once, so that it seemed the very mansion was gasping.

I pushed my glasses up on my nose, desiring to get as clear a view of Rosita as possible.

She looked exactly as I remembered her from the day of Oliver's burial. Her once bright cobalt eyes turned to gray ice, underscored by dark circles. Her lips pressed together in a thin, pale line, making the distinctive beauty mark above the left side of her lip more prominent. Her skin was dull, with a grayish cast.

Tears sprang to my eyes from surprised relief at seeing her face again. In the far reaches of my mind a worry had crouched that all along I'd served a specter.

Rosita's voice slowly lifted—rough, not as strong and clear as we all remembered—but sure. And for a moment I was back, back in the Century Club in Toledo, back to the night more than three years before, when I first met the McGees.

CHAPTER 10

I RAN AWAY from home in southeast Ohio—there, already an old maid at eighteen—hoping to be *free*. I'd wanted to go to Chicago and become a secretary but made it as far as Toledo before I realized I had enough money—saved from tending to an elderly lady, whose family paid me a dollar a week—to either get to Chicago or have a few good meals. I'd been foolish, not considering when I ran away that I had no abilities beyond the homemaking skills required for a farmer's wife, no formal education beyond eighth grade, augmented by everything I'd been able to soak up from reading every book (most of them twice) in the small Carnegie library in our county's seat.

I tried to get a job as a secretary or waitress or housemaid, but I was either too young, or inexperienced, or poorly spoken with my Appalachian accent (as one potential boss told me) for such work. I took the first job I was offered, selling cigars and cigarettes at the Century Club speakeasy, and felt lucky to have it, even if it meant keeping a forced smile in place while dodging handsy men.

Soon, I met Pony at the Century Club. He was the first person, besides my little brother, who made me laugh. The first man who'd shown interest in me, other than the boys Mama had pushed me toward back home, and he didn't care if I could cook or sew or clean. I thought that meant he was interested in me—for me. Plus, he was the first man to call me "pretty."

He was worldly. Full of big talk and promises. Filled my head with the hope that maybe, with his help, I'd get to see the world.

Naïvely, I didn't wonder why he wasn't already married or dating, why the other women at the club ignored him or gave him smirking, skeptical looks. I believed the big-fish tales he wove, and married him just months after meeting him, pushing aside my uneasiness when I asked him what he did for a living.

Pony was scrawny, with a long bony nose, and clammy hands, and, I found out later, was nearly twice my age. But he wasn't handsy. He was respectful, even shy at first. He made me feel pretty. Special. He described his apartment in sparkling terms—it was on a trolley line and had a full bathroom and kitchen. (I stayed in a boardinghouse, sharing a room with three other girls, with one bathroom on our floor, and no access to a kitchen.) And he had a good, steady job at the Hocking Glass Company, which he seemed to like. He tipped me well enough without seeming to expect anything untoward in return, and I'd been saving those tips, still hoping to get to Chicago. But then we started going out, and one thing led to another, and I became pregnant, and so we married.

Two weeks later, I miscarried.

I was heartbroken when my body cramped and expelled a rush of blood and matter. Pony didn't help me clean up myself or the mess. Just stared in disgust, then said, *You'll be all right if I go out?* and didn't wait for my answer.

Soon I realized Pony was relieved, and I wondered if he might release me from our marriage, but I was too timid to bring it up. The little bit of money I'd had when we married was gone, and I had no access to his.

I did my best to make sure a good, hot meal awaited him each night, though he mocked my "down-home cooking," as he called it. I never resisted his desires. And I discovered the most wonderous place I'd ever seen: the Toledo Public Library, just a quick walk or trolley ride down from our apartment building. I'd loved reading the books available to me back home. But this library offered an exhilarating, overwhelming treasure of books, and in them, I found refuge.

A half year into our marriage, Pony was restless, hating the apartment he'd once described as "great," refusing to let me work at the speakeasy, yet resenting the cost of anything that wasn't liquor.

What Pony wanted from me: unquestioning admiration. If my eyes betrayed me with a flicker of anything less, the price was his hand striking me. If he was frustrated that he wasn't progressing as quickly as he thought he deserved in Eddie's organization, he took it out on me. I became, as he put it, "a ball and chain."

A sentiment not much different from what Mama used to say of me. "A noose around my neck," she'd called both me and my brother, but more often me.

I began to fear for my life. I understood, vaguely, that Pony was caught up in a side business as a goon who could make me "disappear."

Then one fateful night, Pony said, "Put on your best dress, and let's go to the Century Club." His unusually chipper voice alarmed me. He was up to something.

My eyes strayed toward the book I was eager to finish reading, *The Circular Staircase* by Mary Roberts Rinehart.

Before I could say anything, Pony scowled. "What, waste Friday night in this dump?" But then he shifted to his best effort at a charming smile, as if he was convincing me, as if I had a choice. "C'mon, doll, let me take you out and show you off."

In the smoky, dim Century Club, I soon understood why Pony really wanted to come: Eddie McGee. I recognized the gangster's mug from a recent newspaper article; he was accused of setting up an assault on rival gang leader Marco Guiffre, which had resulted in the deaths of two alleged gang members, and of three bystanders. But there was no proof. McGee, one of the wealthiest men in Toledo, maintained the fiction that he'd made his wealth in the shipping industry, and that he now dealt in "insurance."

I sat at a tiny table, miserably crowded between two women I didn't know, trying to make small talk and appear chipper, sipping what was purveyed as the Century Club's special—supposedly whisky with a sugar cube and a dash of lemon juice, but it really tasted like watered-down, sugared turpentine. It felt strange to be in my old place of employment, however brief it had been. I thought I might see some of the other girls I'd worked with, or the bartenders or bouncers. But everyone was new. Turnover is high in places like that, which somehow made me melancholy. I'd wanted to break all ties when I ran away, but I guess I wanted some bonds after all. Maybe that's why I'd fallen so quickly for Pony. My gaze strayed toward him, but he was completely ignoring me as he anxiously lurked on the edge of a crowd of men gathered around Eddie. Pony looked like a puppy wanting to break into the ring of big dogs.

Then the already dim lights darkened even more. Three Black men came on a small stage, taking their places at an upright piano, a drum set, and a bass. I smiled, recognizing them. What a world I lived in, where musicians had the stable jobs. They played a few jazzy tunes, and I was relieved that their music gave me an excuse to not talk; I could gaze at the stage, take cautious sips of my cocktail, and nod along to the music's rhythm.

But after a few tunes, Eddie suddenly hopped up on the stage. I was astonished. Was the great gangster going to sing? The whole joint went still and quiet. He grinned widely, holding the crowd in his thrall for a moment, and then grabbed a microphone and announced, "The Sweetheart Cousins are back!"

The crowd, apparently knowing what this meant, or at least that it was a good idea to cater to Eddie, broke into raucous applause and cheers, and two glamorous, gorgeous women, wearing sparkling dresses that were little more than slips, their hair perfectly coiffed in matching dos, took the stage.

Cousins, but at first I thought that they looked like twins. I soon noted, though, that one had a beauty mark, and somehow, though her movements were more refined, exuded a hold on the crowd that the other simply lacked.

Rosita McGee, Eddie's wife.

And Claire Byrne, Rosita's cousin.

They went through a set of easy up-tunes. But then Claire's voice started to sound scratchy. Rosita whispered something to her, and Claire gave a little wave and trotted, unsteadily, off the stage. I wondered if she'd had a bit too much of the club's specialty.

"She'll be back," Rosita said.

I sat up straighter, stared at her, unable to look away as goose bumps rose all over my skin. On its own, without being watered down by Claire, Rosita's voice was like a balm of honey, pouring over me, promising comfort I didn't even know I needed.

"But first, a song I love, a tune from the vaudeville days, 'I'm Always Chasing Rainbows,'" Rosita said, and then began singing: *"At the end of the rainbow there's happiness, And to find it how often I've tried, But my life is a race just a wild goose chase, And my dreams have all been denied. Why have I always been a failure? What can the reason be? I wonder if the world's to blame, I wonder if it could be me?"*

My heart rose so swiftly to my throat that I put my fist to my mouth, as if I might have to punch it back down. I'd heard the song before by another performer on that very stage, but never sung like this with such . . . knowing. And longing.

A knowing and longing I'd felt, too.

Did this woman, Rosita, the wife of powerful, wealthy Eddie McGee, also feel this way? Tears welled in my eyes.

And then she saw me, staring at her. Our eyes locked. I felt, for the first time, that I'd met a kindred soul.

Pony must have noticed my reaction, for suddenly he was beside me, shooing the woman next to me away, and roughly whispering, *"What are you doing? Don't act crazy!"*

I ignored him as Rosita gently segued into the chorus. The band stopped playing, the musicians sensing that her voice was all this part of the song needed.

I'm always chasing rainbows, watching clouds drifting by. My schemes are just like all my dreams, ending in the sky . . .

As Rosita finished singing, tears slicked my cheeks. Pony growled at me to go clean up, to not embarrass him, but I paid no attention as Rosita signaled for the band to break and announced to the breathless crowd, "Claire and I will be back!"

Pony jerked my arm, forcing me to stand up. And suddenly, there she was, Rosita McGee, right beside us.

She, too, ignored Pony. "Excuse me, miss," she said. "Are you all right?"

"She's fine—right? Honey?" Pony pinched my elbow.

I jerked my arm away. Rosita was not concerned about Pony; she thought I could hold my own with him. I liked that. It made me think maybe I could. And I saw a flash of admiration in her eyes as I pulled from him. She liked my bit of spunk.

"I am fine," I said, "it's just your song—it—it—" I wasn't sure how to explain that it made me think of the dreams I'd had just the year before when I'd run from home. That the way she sang it made me realize I'd only been running away, not toward something. So I just finished lamely, "—it reminded me of home."

To my surprise, Rosita asked with genuine curiosity, "Where's that?"

"Southeast Ohio. Nowhere important." The way she'd sung it, I couldn't help but wonder what the song meant to her. So the question burst out of me: "Is that what you were thinking of? Home? You seemed somewhere else when you sang. I think that's why it took me back—"

"That's nonsense, doll," Pony said. "But ma'am, it's good to meet you, and uh, before you womenfolk get to gabbing, I'd love an introduction to your husband—I did some, ah, work for one of his men, over on Third—"

That took me by surprise. He hadn't told me this. But then, he'd been coming home late, sometimes after midnight. And he had given me a more generous grocery allowance, and told me to get better cuts of meat for supper. I'd only asked him about it once. He'd backhanded me, and when my nose bled, told me that's what I got for being nosy, and then cackled like he'd just made the cleverest joke.

Pony went on, "We came here tonight 'cause I was hoping to meet him, but, ah, it's hard to get—" He stopped, stared longingly over at Eddie's table, then jumped a little, straightening his shoulders like he was already a good soldier, for Eddie was making his way over to us.

I almost laughed at Pony. Couldn't he see that Eddie didn't notice him, or me? That Eddie's smoldering gaze, the hint of a tender smile on his otherwise cruel slash of a mouth, was only for Rosita?

But Rosita either didn't notice or was purposefully ignoring Eddie, for she kept her gaze on me. Her voice was thoughtful, as if an idea had just occurred to her and she was turning it over carefully. "I'll tell you about it sometime," she said. "If you'll come back to my shows—"

I looked down. I wanted to say no, to admit that I hadn't wanted to come that night, that I didn't want to come back here again, or have anything to do with the McGees. My stomach twisted, and I felt cold, even as hot bile threatened to come up in my mouth. Falling in with the McGees would only bring trouble, a voice warned. But was it my voice, or all the voices that had wanted to pin me down back home?

I like to believe that what I said next wasn't because I knew the beating I'd get from Pony if I ruined this chance for him.

That instead it was in defiance of those past voices.

Or better yet, that I was speaking up for something I suddenly, desperately knew I'd needed but never really had all of my life.

A friend.

I looked back up at Rosita, and said, "Yes—I'd love that."

"I'm Rosita McGee," she said, holding out her hand to me, offering a wry smile as if she knew introducing herself, unnecessary as it was, was a private joke we shared.

Even knowing that Eddie McGee was a gangster, I didn't really understand then the danger that I was walking right into by smiling, accepting her handshake, and saying, "And I'm Susan Walker."

CHAPTER 11

AFTER ROSITA FINISHED singing "Always," the room shimmered with silence. My eyes stung as I glanced at Eddie. His face was twisted, as if she'd physically struck him.

Surely, I thought, she'd see the grief that distorted his expression. She'd pull him from the room, or he would reach out to her and she'd go with him, willingly, somewhere else in this vast mansion to work out, if not their differences, then a plan for going forward, even if that meant separately. Wasn't she the least bit curious about why he needed the money from selling the island to Marco? Wasn't he the least bit interested in how she'd dealt with long, lonely hours, tormented by their son's death?

But just as Eddie opened his mouth, Rosita turned to me.

For the first time in more than a year, Rosita's eyes locked on mine. I could not glance away. Her gaze held me, forced me to see the emotion that passed over her face as she regarded me.

Hatred.

I gasped as she re-donned her veil. She glided from the room.

We all froze in her wake, staring through the empty archway for a long moment after she was gone.

I was the first to move, and my gaze turned as if of its own volition toward Seamus. He was already looking at me, his eyes touching
me gently, as if searching with care for wounds and bruises. And
though in that moment my hurts were invisible, my eyes welled at
his concern, at his soft gaze, so unlike Rosita's moments before. So
unlike, I suddenly grasped, how anyone had looked at me in years.

I gave him a slight nod, trying to communicate that I was *fine, just
fine*. But the gesture was enough to make my tears start to overflow.

I, too, hurried from the music room.

BY THE TIME I returned to the kitchen, I'd tamped down my emotions, and my eyes were dry. I focused on washing up the cooking
dishes. I was drying the last saucepan when Maxine entered with a
tray stacked high and rattling with plates, glasses, and silverware.

Weariness draped like a mantle over her shoulders. As soon as I
took the tray from her, she staggered to a chair and sat down.

Breathlessly she started, "Give me a minute and I'll—"

"I can take care of the dishes," I said. "Make up for not helping
you this morning."

"Where were you? We were worried about you. It's not like you
to miss your duties."

I blushed as I refilled the sink with hot water. Oh, the joys of a
water tower out back, modern plumbing, and the water heater and
furnace in the mechanicals room. Such luxury in Rosita's mansion.

I added dish soap, grabbed a greasy dish, and began scrubbing, the
cuts and nicks in the palms of my hands stinging in the hot water. I
should have let it cool, but I considered the minor pain part of my
punishment for neglecting the Carmichaels.

I'd gotten the scrapes after falling as I ran from the dock to the
mansion that morning. I'd startled Seamus as he came around the
bend, gaping at me in my swimsuit, soaked and shivering and moan-
ing in pain and fear, on all fours on the gravel path. He had helped

me up, quickly taken off his hunting jacket and draped it over my shoulders.

And for a moment, I had been tempted to lean into his strong shoulders, to sob out that I'd seen the *Myra* with the flag indicating that Eddie was on board, to confess my fear for what that might mean for Rosita. For me. For if she was taken from the island, if she withdrew her protection of me ...

But then he asked why I was in my swimsuit, why I had been in the frigid lake, why I was so upset. Without answering, I broke away from him, kept running.

I've often wondered what might have happened if instead of dashing to the mansion, to Rosita, I'd stayed with him. Answered his questions. Asked one of my own: What was he doing heading to the southwest dock so early in the morning, when he was needed at the mansion to help Henry?

Had I made those choices, instead of running to Rosita, would everything have turned out differently?

I was briefly tempted to confess all the details of the morning to Maxine. Instead, I said, "I was out for a walk." That was true. Just not the whole of it. If Pony had taught me one thing, it was how to segment the truth.

"Well, those chores still need doing," Maxine said. "The chandeliers need a polish, the furniture covered."

"We can't do any of that until Mr. McGee and his guests leave," I said.

We exchanged anxious looks. When would that be? The weather was already colder and icier than expected. A rogue storm could force Eddie, Marco, Claire—all of them—to stay here for weeks. Maybe, if a storm was really bad and the lake froze over, until next spring.

Fear gripped my heart at the notion of being stuck all winter on this island with Eddie and his coterie.

Impulsively, I grabbed a dish towel, dried my hands, grasped

Maxine's arm. "We could leave," I said. "In the morning. I—I know how to run boats, at least good enough to get us from here to Toledo. I can tell Henry is not doing well. He's been so weak and tired lately. He needs to get to a hospital—"

Maxine's eyes widened as she stared at me as if I had suddenly turned into a wild animal. I was scaring her, I realized, and I let go of her arm. "Henry and I—we can never leave. We made a deal—" She stopped, as if catching herself in the middle of a terrible confession.

"But why? If it means the difference between Henry getting help . . . I have some money hidden away . . ."

Maxine just shook her head. I sighed and went back to the dishes, but I was not ready to relinquish my concern. "Dr. Aldridge is here. Maybe he should examine Henry—"

"No," Maxine said, her voice turned so cold that I barely recognized it as hers. "I will not let that—that quack near my Henry." Maxine glanced pointedly at the wall clock. It was nearly ten, a half hour past my appointed time to take up Rosita's cup of tea and shortbread. "Listen, I can take care of the rest of these while you tend to Rosita—"

"She can wait," I snapped. Maxine looked hurt. I softened my tone. "Besides, the others will need you—"

Maxine gave a short laugh. "Claire has already gone up to bed. She wanted to go to the casino, which is where the men, except Henry, are, but Eddie dismissed her." She put on a gruff expression and lowered her voice in mimicry of Eddie. "'That's no place for a woman.'"

I looked at her in surprise. She'd always been so deferential to the McGees. Then, suddenly, we burst out laughing. Our mirth, after such a long day, was a relief.

When our laughter quieted, I said, "Let me take care of the dishes. You go check on Henry and get some rest."

Maxine gave me a grateful smile and then left. I plunged back into dishwashing, focusing on the clink of glasses and dishes to distract me from the whoops coming from the casino, and from thinking of the hatred that Rosita had directed at me. Surely I'd imagined it, spooked by this shocking surprise visit from Eddie and his entourage, by Cormac's vague but terrifying threats.

Jazz music floated down the hall from the casino. Someone had started up the Victrola. I hummed along, transported back to freer, happier times. When I'd first met Pony and thought we were in love. When we'd entered the glamorous, dangerous sphere of Eddie and Rosita and thought the world would be ours . . .

When I finished, I checked the time on the wall clock; now, it was a little past eleven.

I assembled a tray for Rosita, turned to leave, and saw that the kitchen door was open. Had Maxine left it ajar? Or had we not closed it after toting in the dishes? If so, anyone on this level—which meant everyone in the mansion except Claire and Rosita—could have overheard our conversation about my having money and my desire to leave the island. Heat rose in my face, but I shook my head to clear it.

Paranoia.

Dr. Aldridge's word flitted like a ghost through my thoughts.

I banished it from my mind and left with the tray of shortbread and tea.

As I CLIMBED the three flights of stairs to Rosita's suite, I considered that flash of hatred toward me that I thought I'd seen in Rosita's eyes.

Maybe I had imagined it, this odd reaction toward me, right after singing Oliver's lullaby. I thought back to all the times after I'd come to Trouble Island that I had tended to Oliver in his nursery in the evenings when the McGees were visiting and had guests to entertain. Rosita always seemed delighted to find us happily playing with his building blocks, or me reading him a story.

Another book? she'd tease. *You'll turn him into a bookworm like you!*

I'd watch as she'd sing him a lullaby and get him settled in his bed. Then we'd quietly visit in the sitting area until Eddie came up. She'd tell me silly stories from her day, or gossip—it was like old times. Almost. Except more than ever, I only listened. I had nothing to tell her from my long days of serving guests, helping the Carmichaels.

She never asked how I was doing. But then, she never brought up Pony. It was almost like that horrific night had never happened. Like I'd always been here, on Trouble Island. Like we were still friends.

I cherished those moments of normalcy.

They stopped after Oliver's death.

Memories flashed before me from the last time the *Myra* came with its blue flag hoisted, a year before.

Another surprise visit, especially since they'd just been here at the close of the regular season, weeks before. A frisson of worry chilled me as a deckhand lowered the plank, then disappeared. For long moments, no one came on deck. Then concern turned to shock as Rosita emerged, garbed in a black dress and veil, followed closely by Eddie in a dark suit and Claire in a black dress. Shock then became horror as four men carried a small casket.

A shriek flew from my mouth as I realized—*Oliver*.

I stumbled. Henry caught my arm to keep me from falling.

We cast our eyes down as Rosita and Eddie proceeded by us, then Claire, and finally Eddie's men with the tiny coffin.

After that, Rosita barricaded herself in her suite. She barely spoke to me, and I figured she'd put up a wall to protect herself from dissolving into grief.

But now, I thought as I finished my ascent, it was time for that wall to come down.

I knocked on Rosita's door. The knob turned from the inside, I waited a moment, and then I entered. I didn't see Rosita; she must have scurried away after unlocking the door. I took the tray to the dining table.

I went over to Largo's cage and gave her a piece of crumbled shortbread. A rare treat of human food, but her feathers were partly ruffled, so I knew she was feeling the stress in the mansion.

Then, heart thudding, I turned, determined to find Rosita.

But even as I turned, Rosita came out of her bedroom. "Susan."

I'd stopped being Susan on the morning I came to Trouble Island. Susan, the girl who'd run away from Copperhead Holler, believing she could leave her troubles there and find excitement, glamour, a new life. Susan, who'd run into the arms of a snake named Pony.

For a moment, I convinced myself that Rosita was using my old, given name out of sentiment. That I could reason with her.

"You said you had something on Eddie, that he'd want more than money—"

"I'm not discussing that with you," Rosita said coldly.

"But it's dangerous to play games with Eddie. We could still leave! I've found something—a treasure—and I've hidden it away under the lighthouse dock. It's enough that we could both start over. Take the Carmichaels and Largo, too. You said the island is ruined for you because of Eddie and Marco—"

Rosita cut off my wishful thinking with a barking laugh. "And because of you, Susan. Seeing you here, day after day, has tainted this place for me. I thought keeping you here would punish you, but it's only punished me."

I gasped. "I don't understand. Why haven't you talked to me about how you feel? We used to talk—I confided in you, about everything—" I hesitated, trying to gulp back my sobs, but also because guilt panged in me. I hadn't confided *everything* to her, though she'd given me plenty of chances. I went on. "—about Pony anyway, and to learn tonight about how Oliver died was so awful—" I was weary, and confused, and my words kept gushing. "And Cormac has told me that I must get you to agree to Eddie's terms or he will tell Marco who I really am and then my life will be in danger—"

"Stop!" Rosita snapped. "Did you think there would be no consequences for anyone else but you after you shot Pony? Beyond you, getting to hide here? Eddie had to arrange for Pony's body to be disposed of."

I shuddered, remembering how I'd glanced into our parlor where I'd shot Pony, thinking I'd see his body still on the rug, a fine floral wool tapestry that the McGees had bought us for Christmas, his blood staining the blue background, mingling with the red flowers. But I saw only the bare floor—Pony and the rug, gone. Our furniture looking somehow tawdry without the rug.

"A neighbor—some German lady—heard the shot. She was sitting on her porch and saw you run out of your house. Called the police. I convinced Eddie to buy her silence."

That information was new to me. The night was such a blur. I hadn't noticed dear old Mrs. Schmitt; I had just stumbled through the dark, desperate to get to the West End neighborhood. To Rosita. Nearly getting hit by an automobile. Someone screaming after me. Slipping on the rain-slicked streets. Panicked, breathless, horrified by what I'd done. Yet—relieved.

Rosita, comforting me, getting me to change into one of her robes, bringing me tea. Sipping the soothing beverage in her dressing room, hearing her and Eddie argue in the adjacent bedroom, but not making out distinct words.

"Eddie asked Cormac, who was still on the force, to have someone else blamed for Pony's death—someone in Guiffre's organization. Get back at Marco for past troubles." Rosita laughed bitterly. "So Cormac did. He chose Nelson Davison—not realizing this was Marco's wife's nephew. Nelson went to prison several months after you came here. Marco probably would have let that go—after all, Marco had taken down several of Eddie's men. The right bribes, and Nelson would be out in a year—two years tops. But a half year in, Nelson was stabbed to death in a prison fight. Marco decided to take revenge and set up a shooting of Eddie. No idea who the rat was who let it slip where Eddie would be that morning. But—"

Rosita paused, her voice finally catching. "But Oliver was with him that morning. So you see, don't you, the chain of events you set off when you lost your temper and shot your husband? Nelson's murder? Marco's desire for revenge? The attempt on Eddie's life? An attempt gone wrong, that took my precious son's life?"

Her eyes narrowed on me. Her voice shook. "Why couldn't you just take getting smacked, now and again, like a good little wife?"

I stumbled backward, realizing that I hadn't imagined the glint in her eyes earlier that evening. She did hate me because of Oliver's death.

A death that she blamed on me.

CHAPTER 12

I FLED FROM Rosita's suite. As I ran out of the stairway door into the second-floor hallway, I nearly collided with Claire, staggering out of the bathroom as if the island were a rocking ship on the lake.

Quickly, I shoved my fingers under my glasses and dashed my tears as Claire wobbled to a stop. Her eyebrows popped up and she stared at me, glassy-eyed. "Oh! Are you all right? Has Rosita been mean again—"

The smell of whisky wafted on her breath. Yet she sounded genuinely concerned, and I remembered that there were plenty of times when Rosita could be too sharp with her cousin, could bring her to tears with a barb.

"I'm just weary," I said. "Good night, Claire."

I waited as she opened the door to her guest room, the room next to mine, and staggered inside. When her door clicked shut, I entered my bedroom, closed my door, collapsed into the sitting chair, and stared around.

Over the past year and a half, I'd personalized my room. I'd moved the furniture so that the sitting chair faced the door to the veranda. I didn't need much storage. I'd brought one suitcase I'd hurriedly stuffed with clothing, and I'd been issued two maid's dresses. So I'd taken out the bureau and replaced it with a small writing desk and chair pulled from elsewhere in the mansion. I fitted one side of the large wardrobe with shelves for books I borrowed from the library.

On my desk, I'd arranged a few items I had collected on the shore of the island. Rocks. Feathers. I had two photos side by side in a silver frame: one of me and Oliver. One of me and Levi—my younger brother—from when we were children, on our parents' southeastern Ohio buckwheat farm.

I'd left behind all my other photos, even my wedding photos—well, perhaps especially those. I'd never asked what happened to the items in our rented house in Toledo after I'd been whisked away.

It would only take a few minutes to pack. In my suitcase, I could easily fit the items I'd brought, the feathers and rocks, a few mementos, my bird-watching diary. The maid's uniforms I'd leave behind.

I went to my desk and opened my bird-watching diary. I wrote the day's date—November 18, 1931—and made note of the birds I'd observed while spying for Rosita. Common and red-throated loons. Herring and ring-billed gulls.

Then I stared at the small bell hanging over my desk. The bell was attached to a cord, which ran up the wall, through a small hole in the floorboards, and up the wall in Rosita's bedroom to a lever alongside her bedside table.

Why couldn't you just take getting smacked, now and again, like a good little wife . . .

The words twisted knifelike in my mind, and my temple throbbed.

I jerked open the desk drawer, pulled out my scissors, and cut the cord. The bell dropped with a ding onto my desk.

For a moment, I indulged in the notion of her regretting her harsh words, ringing for me so I'd dash upstairs so she could beg my forgiveness, worrying when I didn't immediately respond as usual.

Well, now I wouldn't hear her summons. And, I promised myself, I wouldn't give in to the temptation to check on her.

I went outside onto the veranda.

I liked the numbing cold. I savored having to myself the enchanting view of moonlight glazing the water's surface. The waves crashed loudly on the rocky shore, a sign that the lake was more restless than usual. The wind drove snow into my face. This squall was a surprise, but the weather on Lake Erie—the most dangerous of all the Great Lakes—could change in an instant, especially in colder months. Soon Lake Erie would freeze over, thick enough for people to take automobiles from the distant Ohio shore onto the lake for ice fishing or take out iceboats—narrow vessels on large skate-like blades, like the one abandoned by the lighthouse dock—across the ice.

And yet, I thought of my swimsuit, now dry on the back of my chair, and imagined waiting until the first light of dawn, then grabbing my suit and running down to the lighthouse cottage by the southwest dock.

As I stared at the lake, I wished that I could leave right then, but navigating at night in this weather in a speedboat would be foolhardy. Yet I stood transfixed by the lake's breathtaking, deadly beauty, each wave a shivering pinprick of time, together forming a mirror of sparkling eternity, reflecting back to me my isolation.

I prayed that the storm would pass by morning. If I left at dawn, I'd have a good chance of making it to the north shore of Ohio in an hour. I could run down to the dock with my suitcase in the morning, quickly retrieve the lockbox, change into my dry clothes, and then take the boat.

The five hundred dollars or so I'd get for the bullion I had stashed under the dock would be more than enough for a train ticket, or even an automobile. Then I'd head south. I knew just where I wanted to go.

And this time, I'd use all I'd learned since running away from Copperhead Holler five years before. This time, I'd be smart in starting over. Third time lucky.

I went back inside and shut the veranda door. The room was

already several degrees colder, just from the few minutes I'd left the door open.

I knelt by my bed and pulled out my suitcase. The one item I'd left in it rattled. I opened the suitcase and plucked out the cigar box.

It had been my father's—a simple cedar box, hinged lid with a clasp, engraved on the bottom *Escalante Cigars, New Orleans*. Inside the lid was a painted picture of a lady in a wide-brimmed hat, trimmed with a black ribbon and a pink silk flower. She had a delicate face— petite features, curly brown hair, bow mouth, blue eyes topped by thin eyebrows. She wore a V-neck blue blouse, modestly covering her round, soft shoulders, but showing just enough decolletage to suggest that all of her would be just as soft and curvy. Nothing like me—with my thick wavy dark hair, wide mouth, dark brown eyes and glasses, bushy eyebrows, taller and broader of frame than most women, with shoulders made strong and square first by farm labor and then by swimming. Above her picture was the name "Aurelia," a cigar brand.

But to me, *Aurelia* was the woman in the picture. A properly beautiful lady, leading a genteel, sophisticated life. A persona and life I instantly longed for, far from the family farm I was growing up on when, at fourteen, I found it on my father's workbench in the shed, tucked away under a mess of hammers and screwdrivers, the box used to hold nails and screws. I was helping Papa with some repair on the farm; I don't remember what now. Levi, ten at the time, had just been diagnosed with epilepsy and my parents had decided that meant he had to always stay close to one of us, but couldn't do any- thing too strenuous.

I was fascinated by the cigar box, its provenance as mysterious as Aurelia herself. My father never smoked. So when and where did he get this box? I knew he used to make occasional fishing trip vacations to Florida with his brother, though he hadn't done that in years, after my mother declared such trips too extravagant— meaning she did not like being left alone on the farm with her kids. Even before Levi's diagnosis, we both knew we were great burdens to her.

I couldn't imagine where else Papa might have gotten a box of cigars. I knew that my mother would have been enraged by it, especially with the picture of a soft, delicate lady, when my mother was all hard angles and furrowed lines. I loved that Papa had kept the box as a treasure, even if just for nails and such, where Mama would never venture. It told me he had a hidden side far more intriguing than suggested by his grim, resolute silence around my mother, my brother, and me.

After a while Mama said I had to be a lady, that I could no longer help Papa with men's work, or go fishing with Papa and Levi. Both Levi and I were banned from swimming down at the river. I needed to act presentable, she said, try to be nice to the son of the preacher at the little church we attended. Mama saw this as an excellent match.

But I had not taken a fancy to the boy. I dreamed of flying far, far and wide, away from that farm. Of exploring exotic places like New Orleans or islands in the Caribbean or cities in Europe or even the Far East. Places I'd read about in books I got from the library and secreted away—my parents would not have approved of such books—just as Papa hid away his cigar box.

One Sunday, Papa took Mama's side, and I cried myself to sleep that night, then woke up from a nightmare of being locked in a cellar that slowly crumbled in on me. I snuck out to the shed, found the box, dumped its contents in an old oil can, then hid the box in my bedroom. My father never said anything about missing it. I began to fill it with fanciful items. A ribbon. A pearl button, fallen from a well-off townie-girl's sweater at church.

On Trouble Island, I added the items that I'd pilfered—paltry compared to the bullion I'd found, but why not take them with me?

That night, I opened the box and added in the feathers and rocks from my desk. From inside the desk drawer: a sapphire clasp earring, a hatpin with the face of an angel, a handkerchief. Bits shed from the women I thought of as sophisticated. Genteel. Superior to me.

Maybe collecting those things made me a magpie.

But if so, I was a magpie who gathered items that represented a different future.

A soft knock came at my door.

I sighed. *Claire.* I had no interest in seeing her, but neither did I wish to anger her.

I opened the door to Seamus.

CHAPTER 13

"Oh," I said. "I—I guess you've come for your coat?"

For a moment, Seamus looked perplexed, and then his expression shifted to amusement. A smile tweaked the corners of his mouth, and his dark brown eyes twinkled.

The man was about to laugh at me. I thought that I ought to be irritated but instead, I became flummoxed. My pulse drummed in my ears.

Seamus broke into a grin. "Well, a storm has whipped up, so yes, I'd like my coat." His expression suddenly turned serious. "But I was coming to check on you. That encounter with Rosita. It was . . . brutal."

My eyes prickled. "Let me get your coat, before someone sees you."

Seamus's laugh was sharp, critical, and that made my eyes water even more. "With all that's gone on today, that's what you're worried about? That someone might think I'm, ah, visiting your room? Does that really matter?" He sounded disappointed in me. Though I suddenly longed to grab him and pull him into my room, I pressed my lips together into a prim, taut line that would have pleased Mama.

I whirled around, grabbed his coat, then thrust it at him. I didn't regard him as he took it, but he let his fingertips unnecessarily touch my hand. A thrilling shock went through me, and I involuntarily trembled. I wished for him to drop the damned coat, shut the door behind him, then pull me to him.

But he turned, about to leave.

"Rosita told me it was my fault. Oliver's dying," I blurted. "Just now, when I brought her evening snack to her—" Seamus faced me, his expression almost pitying. I forced myself to go on. "I—I—made a choice, and it ricocheted, and that led to a shoot-out between Eddie's and Marco's gangs—" My voice strangled on the sob I tried to choke back. My mother's words clawed up from my buried past. From when I was Susan. *You don't deserve to live . . . it should have been you . . .* "And Oliver was caught in the crossfire—"

"Oh, Aurelia, that wasn't your fault," Seamus said. "Rosita was just so emotional tonight—"

He stopped, as if realizing he'd said too much. Was he just comforting me, or did he truly know something about the events around Oliver's death? For a moment, I thought I saw a dropping of the guardedness that he'd worn like an opaque mask ever since he arrived. But then his expression closed again.

A frostiness overtook my earlier emotion. "This morning, you were supposed to be helping Henry with shutting down the fountain and outbuildings for the winter," I said. Come to think of it, so was Liam, but he, too, hadn't shown up for his duties. I pushed aside that realization for the time being. I needed—wanted—to focus on Seamus for now. "But you were hurrying down to the southwest dock."

I looked at Seamus's red-and-black-checked hunting jacket, noted that he gripped it so hard that his knuckles were white and the hairs stood up on his fingers. I should, I thought, be alarmed. I was challenging this man, who was so much bigger and stronger than me, and who was blocking the exit from my bedroom. And yet, I felt nothing but curious, and calm.

I met his dark gaze as I asked, "Why were you heading there? Did you know that the *Myra* would be arriving today?"

"Why were *you* at the dock?"

"Swimming. As usual." My tone was defiant, yet my resolve was loosening. I thought of the treasure I'd found and then tied up below the dock. Had Seamus seen me do so? Or even Liam?

"But later than usual—"

"Oh, so you've been noticing what time I swim?"

He gave a cockeyed grin, but his grip on the coat didn't lighten. "I've sure been noticing *you*."

I ignored the comment. I wouldn't let him distract me—and yet, I felt heat rising in my cheeks. "Were you checking that the flag would be up?" I gasped. "Wait, did you want to warn Rosita? Did you . . . did you know Marco would be coming, too?"

What if he was working for Marco? Or in league with Eddie beyond just being a bodyguard, intent on manipulating Rosita? Or had been concocting some plot with Rosita, who, I assumed, only noticed him from her veranda and overheard his name. But she'd used it so easily, so casually that morning . . . Or what if he and Liam were plotting something together? Liam, who was quiet and goofy and easy to dismiss, yet he hadn't been at his appointed duties that morning, either. None of us, except the Carmichaels, had been.

Confusion and weariness made my head spin and I stumbled backward, ramming into my bed.

Seamus dropped his coat, reached out to steady me. A delicious shiver coursed through my body, and I knew what I wanted.

I knew he wanted the same thing, but would not, despite his occasional teasing remarks, do as I suddenly desired: encircle me in his arms, kiss me.

Suddenly, I was weary of being demure, waiting for what I wanted, instead of grasping it for myself.

In the morning, I'd be gone.

But at that moment, I wanted Seamus.

I pulled from him just long enough to shut my bedroom door.

I pressed my lips to his. For a moment he was unresponsive, and my heart gave a sickening twist. Maybe I'd misread his signs . . .

And then he responded, eagerly.

I grasped him, pulled us to my bed.

CHAPTER 14

THE NEXT MORNING, I woke to screams.

I bolted up in my bed, disoriented. The cawing cry seemed surreal. At first my fuzzy brain offered up the explanation of a lingering nightmare, seeping into my initial moments of awakening. I had had nightmares often when I arrived at Trouble Island—sometimes the one from childhood of the cellar caving in on me, sometimes that I was back with Pony and couldn't escape him, sometimes that I was trapped underwater and couldn't find my way to the surface.

But that morning, I didn't have the rapid heartbeat, the dry mouth, that usually accompanied my nightmares.

The scream stopped. Silence pulsed in its wake. I blinked in the soft gray light sifting through the curtains, trying to regain my waking senses.

I fumbled for my glasses on the bedside table. At some point, Seamus had gently pulled them from my face, then thoughtfully put them by the table lamp. I knew Seamus wasn't in my room anymore, but I put on my glasses and glanced around as if wishing for him would make him reappear. I savored traces of him—wrinkled sheets and the lingering scents of his Chesterfield cigarettes, of his body.

I smiled at the delicious memory of the night before. Being with Seamus had been so different than with Pony, the only other man I'd ever slept with. Seamus was slow, languid, gentle. With him, I was a wilder, freer version of myself. Not Susan, not Aurelia. Just *me*.

But I didn't know who Seamus really was. I was fairly sure that, although he was in Eddie's employ, he was not on Eddie's side. He could be an operative for Marco, or for another gang. He could be an agent for the Bureau of Prohibition. Given my past, none of these options boded well for my future—alone or with Seamus.

"Rosita!" The name was clear; I knew then it was Eddie crying out. Someone pounded on my door. "Where the hell is Rosita?"

I shivered, realized I was naked. I glanced at the bedside clock: 9:45 A.M. I did a double take. It had been years since I'd slept so late.

I quickly pulled on my bathrobe, opened my bedroom door and saw Eddie pacing up and down the hallway. He, too, was in a bathrobe, barefoot, his hair hanging in greasy strands. As soon as he spotted me, I recoiled. His eyes were wild, his manner frantic. He was before me in an instant.

"Where is she? Where the hell is Rosita?"

"I'm sure she's upstairs as usual."

"I went upstairs. Knocked. Called. She wouldn't come to her door."

Eddie slicked back his hair, and in that gesture, I saw how fearsomely his hand trembled. "I found this under my door when I woke up this morning." He reached into his robe pocket, pulled out a folded piece of cream stationery, and held it out to me.

I took the paper, unfolded it, and studied it. This note was not written on the cream letter paper that had Rosita's initials—*RMB*, R for Rosita, the *M* the largest letter for McGee, B for Byrne, her maiden name—embossed in gold at the top. She'd used that stationery in Toledo, and since arriving here to give me written orders if she didn't feel like talking with me. A request for a meal, or a book. Never anything personal, not even a simple "thank you."

But this note was written on a piece of paper with a ragged edge, clearly torn from a book.

Her red diary.

And this note, though simple, *was* personal.

Eddie—Come see me in my chambers. Please. Rosita.

Most of the note was written in her neat, block print. Her signature—Rosita—was a scrawl, illegible other than the big dramatic *R*. How unlike her to reverse her desire to see Eddie. How unlike her to ever say, or write, "please."

"I only saw it fifteen minutes or so ago," Eddie mused. "I hurried up but she didn't come to the door. No sounds from inside—except that goddamn bird!"

I glanced back down at the note. Her printing would be easy enough to imitate by someone who knew her well. As would the dramatic *R* and the squiggle that represented the rest of her name.

Of the people in the mansion, the ones who could easily replicate her writing would be the people who'd known her a long time before Trouble Island: Claire, the Carmichaels. Douglas. Even Eddie. Yes, and me.

But I knew I'd done no such thing, and why would any of the others want to? To torment Eddie? That was a dangerous game. If Eddie had done so, was he setting up some kind of ruse?

I handed the note back to him. Not having seen Eddie since Oliver's burial, I'd forgotten how exhausting the McGees could be, by turns fawning over one another, and then a short time later, getting into raging arguments. Wearily—and foolishly—I allowed myself a cruel jab.

"Rosita made it clear yesterday that she doesn't want anything to do with you. She's probably just ignoring you—"

"Is this some game you two are playing?" Eddie grabbed my shoulders and began shaking me so hard that my head bobbled. "Is she in there, laughing at me? So help me God, if she is—"

Perhaps I'd already had enough of the McGees' and Marco's drama.

Or maybe I was emboldened by having finally claimed something I wanted, just for me—the night with Seamus.

In any case, I lifted my heel, and stomped down as hard as I could on Eddie's foot. He yelped—more startled than hurt—but the shock was enough for him to loosen his grasp. I brought my fists up between his arms, and jerked my forearms wide, breaking his hold on me.

"Mrs. McGee isn't in Aurelia's room."

We both turned at the sound of Seamus's voice. He stood in the hallway, holding a tray with two cups of coffee and a plate of toast. I blushed, realizing he'd been planning all along to come back to my room. He put the tray on a decorative table that was against the wall between my bedroom and the one Claire now occupied, a table that held a vase of flowers in the regular season. Then he slowly put his hand to his hip, right by a holster that held his gun.

As a bodyguard, Seamus was always armed, but his gesture made it clear. He meant for Eddie to let me be.

Eddie's face turned a bright red. My heart raced, as I feared that Eddie would draw his own gun or summon Cormac. But then the door next to mine opened, and Claire stumbled out. She had on a floral silk robe, but she hadn't bothered with slippers. Her hair was tied up in a scarf that covered her forehead down to her eyebrows and matched her robe.

"What's going on?" she asked, her voice slushy.

"Claire, return to your room," Seamus ordered.

She puffed her lips into a pout at Seamus. "But I heard something about Rosita being missing—"

Eddie whirled around to her. "Or maybe she's in your room? Did you see her after we left the music room?"

Claire recoiled. "N-no," she said. "I—I came straight back to my room."

I thought back, remembered briefly seeing Claire, who'd been staggeringly drunk, coming out of the bathroom. It was midmorning now; could she still be hungover? But then, she'd taken the decanter of whisky from the music room before coming up. Maybe she'd kept drinking by herself all through the night.

"Enough!" I exclaimed. "I will be given a few moments to change into proper clothes. And then we will proceed to Rosita's quarters. You'll all see—she is just fine."

CHAPTER 15

MINUTES LATER, WHEN Rosita hadn't answered our knocks and cries, I nudged in front of Eddie, unlocked and opened the door. I stumbled as he shouldered past me, into Rosita's suite.

Her jasmine perfume lingered in the room. Largo, sensing our presence, squawked under the cloth of her cage. It was well past her morning feeding. I rushed to the cage, pulled aside the cloth. Annoyance rose in me; Largo's water dish was dry, her seed bowl empty. Couldn't Rosita tend to her son's bird for once?

But Rosita wasn't in the sitting area.

I ran to the bedroom, calling her name. She wasn't in there, or the bathroom.

A cracking sound made me jump, and I hurried back to the sitting area. Eddie was kicking at the door to the room that had been Oliver's nursery.

"Eddie, stop—" I lurched forward, but Seamus caught me by my arm.

"Do you have a key?" Seamus asked.

I shook my head. "Only Rosita—"

Eddie gave the door another kick, and another. Each crack to the wood made my heart thud, my eyes sting. God, how far from sane the McGees had fallen since the death of their son.

Finally, the door splintered enough for Eddie to step into the nursery.

I suppose he expected to find Rosita, sitting on the bed, draped in her veil.

Instead, Eddie dropped to his knees, whimpering. In spite of everything, my heart went out to the man.

But in the next instant, he leapt up, came back into the sitting room, charging at me, eyes bulging. "You! You've helped her hide away somewhere in this mansion, on the island!"

"I haven't!" I cried. "Rosita was angry at me last night. The last time I saw her was in here—" I waved my hands, as if trying to conjure her from a shadowy corner of the suite. "That was after midnight." I looked desperately around the room. "There—there might be a clue as to where she's gone—"

Eddie smirked, and Seamus looked skeptical.

"She—she had her red diary out yesterday morning."

Both men just stared at me, Eddie with derision, but Seamus as if he suddenly wondered if the woman he'd slept with the night before had lost her marbles.

"She used to write in it all the time," I said, "but not since coming here. Maybe if we found it—"

"You'd better hope we find *her*," said Eddie, his voice a scratchy growl, "or I will be telling Marco about who you really are."

My face flamed, and I avoided looking at Seamus, who I was sure must be staring at me with alarm.

I squared my shoulders. "I'm sure we'll find her," I said, "and she'll be glad to confirm I had nothing to do with her disappearing act." After the previous night's encounter, I wasn't sure about that at all. But by God, I thought, when we found her, she'd better tell the truth—I had nothing to do with her sick game of hide-and-seek—or I'd shake her until her teeth rattled. "And I'm going to look for that red diary."

"Goddamn it, I don't care about the diary—"

"If we find it, we can compare the handwriting in the diary to the note you think Rosita left you, so we can be sure it was from her—"

"She left me the goddamn note! And I recognize her handwriting!"

"Aurelia makes a good point," Seamus said. "How long has it been since you've seen her handwriting?"

Eddie scowled.

"And she might have left another note," Seamus added, "directing you to meet her elsewhere."

"Rosita wouldn't lead me on such a wild goose chase . . ." Eddie spluttered to a stop. His face reddened. He knew—we all knew—that yes, she would.

"I'll search the bedroom and bathroom. I need to get water for Largo anyway—" I started. But Eddie and Seamus weren't listening. They were already searching tables and bookshelves.

I uncovered Largo's cage and opened the door. Largo flew out, then landed on my shoulder. I gave her head a scratch, then pulled out her water dish and went to the bedroom.

I filled the dish at the sink, put it on the counter. Largo hopped down, began drinking. I checked the wardrobe and drawers and did not find the red leather diary, but it also did not appear that any of Rosita's clothes were missing. I looked on the top shelf, where the suitcase she'd come with a year before was stowed. It was still there.

I thought of my own small suitcase, how I'd tucked away my secrets in the cigar box. Maybe Rosita had done the same. I pulled down her suitcase and toted it to the bed.

Out in the parlor, I heard the men talking. "How did you come to be in my employ?" Eddie was asking Seamus.

Interesting question. I'd once assumed that Eddie hired everyone directly, but as I grew closer to Rosita, I'd quickly learned that the lower level of bodyguards or enforcers or collectors—men like Pony—reported up to lieutenants.

The few times men at Pony's level came over to our bungalow, he bragged about how he hung out with "the big boss," as if there was a friendship there. Once, one of the men had told him if he knew what was best for him, he'd stop bragging so damned much—Eddie wouldn't like it if it got back to him. As I brought in snacks for their poker game, Pony punched the man. The man, much bigger than Pony, had clutched his nose, blood oozing between his fingers, and I could see in the man's eyes that he wanted to kill my husband. Pony had that effect on people.

As the man narrowed his eyes on me, I realized that he wouldn't kill Pony only because of my friendship with Rosita. The man left. Pony had swaggered around for the rest of the night.

The men never came back to play poker. The other men's wives or girlfriends or mistresses no longer asked me to spend time with them.

I opened Rosita's suitcase. It was empty. Only her jasmine scent, transferred from her clothes to the burgundy velvet lining of the suitcase, lingered. Clothes that she'd once brought with her to all sorts of exotic places—Key Largo, New York, Bermuda, New Orleans. Sometimes, when we were friends and confidantes, she'd tell me about them on long, lazy afternoons by the pool at the McGees' Toledo mansion. She'd speak of them as if traveling was silly, as if leaving one's home at all was senseless and the places were boring. But her descriptions, disparaging as they were, made my head giddy with desire. Such adventures were why—well, one reason—I'd run from my home in southeast Ohio to begin with.

"Got to be friends with one of your men," Seamus was saying. "Boris Stefka."

I recognized the name and stiffened, on alert. Boris was the lieutenant that Pony had reported up to—and wanted to replace.

"Your friend?" Eddie's voice held suspicion.

"Met him on my beat."

Sudden tension from the other room crept into the bedroom. I snapped shut Rosita's empty suitcase and carried it to the wardrobe.

"You were a cop," Eddie said flatly.

Seamus didn't hesitate. "Yep. This pays better. I'd wager your man Cormac would agree."

Eddie laughed, or at least made a sound that for him approximated a laugh.

Then my gaze caught the handle and pull rope that had once been tethered to the bell in my bedroom. I imagined Rosita pulling on the handle. Feeling the slack in the rope. The rope falling to the tabletop. The image of my end of the rope after I'd severed it the night before flashed across my mind. The cut neat. Even. Purposeful.

Had she cried out? Felt hurt? Betrayed? What if someone had come up here, threatened her? And she'd tried to ring for help? She could have been signaling for me, as she had done so many times before, but not so I'd fetch a book or a cup of tea. So I'd help her.

You thought—as usual—of no one but yourself, your own selfish desires . . .

Mama's voice again.

A logical, cooler part of myself pointed out that Rosita wouldn't have taken the time to so neatly wind up the rope if under assault. And neither would an assailant.

"Did you find anything?"

I jumped and turned at the sound of Seamus's voice.

Well yes, I'd found the neatly coiled bell rope. But he meant the diary I'd referenced, or anything that would give us a clue to Rosita's whereabouts. So I just shook my head.

"We didn't either."

I cleared my throat. "We should talk to the others. See what they know—or if Rosita is elsewhere in the mansion. After last night—"

"Coming to the music room last night might have given her a sense of breaking free. Of wanting to go out into the rest of the house?"

"Maybe," I said. Though that didn't seem like Rosita. She was so determined to stay in her room, in her mansion, on her island. But Eddie's appearance had already forced revelations from Rosita. I had no idea what she might do next.

I clucked my tongue and Largo flew to my shoulder. "Good girl," I muttered. "Good girl, good girl," Largo repeated.

If only, I thought, Largo could tell us what had happened. Or repeat something unusual that she'd heard.

But Largo only repeated what she heard in the moment. I wondered what it would be like to be a creature like Largo, unburdened by memory or wondering about the future, without worry over ramifications of whatever was happening around you.

The sound of kicking made us both jump, and Largo cry out. We rushed to the sitting room. Eddie was finishing off the rest of the nursery door, making it easy to duck in and out.

Seamus gave me an apologetic look and followed Eddie through the opening. I couldn't bear to watch them enter the nursery. I eased Largo back into her cage.

I meant to stay in the sitting room, out of respect for Rosita. After Oliver's death, she'd had the nursery locked up with an unspoken rule that nobody was ever to enter.

But curiosity finally propelled me to step in after all.

The room was as I remembered it from the one summer that Oliver and I had been here on the island together. I'd witnessed Rosita tuck him in many nights, as I tidied the suite. Largo's cage had been in the corner. There was a twin-sized bed, a dresser, a mirror. A small child-sized desk and chair, where he liked to draw and color. The desk was just in front of the window overlooking the tennis courts and swimming pool. A wardrobe with his clothes. A tufted chair in front of a bookshelf filled with children's books—*Five Children and It, Anne of Green Gables, The Wonderful Wizard of Oz*— books from Rosita's childhood, all too advanced for Oliver, but she seemed to take comfort in reading them aloud as he sat in her lap, even after he dozed off.

Before I met Rosita, I used to think that anyone with a childhood rich enough to include their own books could have no worries, no sorrow.

I felt wetness on my cheeks, swiped them, but yet the tears fell unbidden. Seamus put a gentle hand on my shoulder. I glanced at him, saw the concern in his face, the question in his expression about whether or not I was okay. That just made me cry harder.

Not so much from the sense of Oliver's ghost—I would have welcomed that. But at the feeling there was no presence of him at all.

Eddie's eyes darted wildly from spot to spot. But not from chasing memories, I realized. He was searching for something, something more than Rosita's diary or another note.

He turned toward us, his face pale but devoid of all sorrow. He looked hard and cruel again, like stone. "We're going to check the rest of the mansion. We'll get Cormac to help. I don't want the others to know yet—"

"Claire knows," I said.

Eddie shrugged. "She's probably out cold again. I'll have Cormac gather everyone in the library. We'll sort out a search of the mansion and, if need be, of the island." He gave me a hard look. "Oh—and you will bring me the key to the suite."

I wanted to ask him *why* he wanted the key—but the answer came to me. He wanted to be able to search again on his own. He believed that Rosita had hidden something—whatever she had on him—in the suite.

"But I need to come up here to tend to Largo," I said.

"Just take the damned bird with you back to your room!"

Eddie turned, left his son's old nursery.

"Hurry up," Eddie barked from the sitting area.

As I followed Seamus out, I gazed around the nursery, my heart trembling with sorrow at all the loss it represented. Then a spot on the dresser caught my attention, and I froze.

Of course the men hadn't noticed it. They did not spend their days cleaning, in between cooking and tending to others.

In the thick coat of dust on the dresser top, there was a smear. A fresh swipe of an arm, or a hand, or a sleeve dragging through the dust. In its wake was clean mahogany wood. Not enough time had passed since it had been made to allow even a fine film of dust to resettle in the spot.

Someone—Rosita? Or someone who had forced their way into the suite, made her unlock the nursery?—had been in here very recently. I would come back here and look more closely.

But I had to give the key back to Eddie.

Luckily, I knew how to pick a lock, at least a simple one. Pony had at least given me that.

CHAPTER 16

WITH LARGO SETTLED in my bedroom, I rushed downstairs to the library where almost everyone was seated at the long mahogany table, except Joey, who had taken position behind his boss. Marco was smoking another cigar and mindlessly letting ashes drop on the table, though there was an ashtray right by him.

The library was my sanctuary. I loved the way the light was quiet and gray, even on bright days with the draperies pulled open. The comfortable leather-bound wing chairs. The framed maps decorating the few bare stretches of wall: one of the world, another of Lake Erie. Here and there amongst the maps were family photos—Claire and Rosita's paternal grandparents, Claire and Rosita as children. My favorite photo is of Rosita and her grandfather. She's proudly holding a fishing pole with a walleye dangling from the hook, and her grandfather is right behind her, both of them grinning widely.

There was a sliding ladder to get to the books on the top shelves by the ceiling. So many books. When not working, the two pleasures I allowed myself on Trouble Island were swimming in the lake, usually by the southwest dock, and reading in here. To see these rough men in my sacred space was jarring.

Eddie gave me a pointed look from his seat at the head of the table. I brought him the key to Rosita's suite, then sat between Maxine and Seamus. I tried to catch Maxine's eyes but she pointedly ignored me, still rattled from the night before when I'd suggested she and Henry run away with me. The rest of the staff and Eddie's entourage sat down the length of the table.

The only people not in the library were Rosita and Cormac.

"What the hell is going on, Eddie?" Marco snarled. His hair was a tangled mess, his silk robe open low enough to reveal his hairy chest and a thick scar running from his sternum up to his chest that looked like it was from a knife fight. His eyes were bleary.

"Rosita is missing," Eddie said.

Gasps and murmurs arose. I made quick note of everyone's reactions. Either everyone besides me and Seamus was surprised, or there were some good actors around the table—and the only good actor there was Douglas. Tears sprang to Claire's eyes. Douglas looked shocked. Liam began whistling in such a soft monotone that it was barely perceptible, and slightly rocking back and forth, something he did when upset. Maxine and Henry shared a shocked look, and Henry put his arm around his wife. Dr. Aldridge shook his head. Even Joey arched an eyebrow.

"What the hell?" Marco said. "You bring me all the way out here, makin' promises about how Rosita will give up the island without a fight, and now the broad is gone?"

Eddie gave Marco a forced smile. "Don't worry—we'll find the bitch. She's not getting away with some stupid game to try to ruin our deal."

At that, Marco's lips curled in a pleased grin, either unaware of or uncaring about the awkward tension among everyone else. Maxine's eyes widened, and Henry squeezed her hand. Liam fell silent, while Claire and Douglas exchanged alarmed glances. Dr. Aldridge stared down, I held back a snort. Did they really think Eddie was going to act a gentleman if Rosita didn't go along with his demands?

"Cormac is searching all the rooms now—" Eddie started.

"That's why you made us come down here at an indecent hour, not even properly dressed, so Cormac can toss our rooms?" Claire asked.

"So Cormac can see if Rosita is hiding in any of the rooms—or the kitchen, the casino, or elsewhere."

"If she's not in the mansion," Joey said, his grin showing he thought he was about to be clever, "did she run off in the storm? Throw herself into the lake?"

His boss gave the boy a hard look, and Joey's smile dissolved while he shrank back toward the wall. Joey would have to learn his place, and quickly, if he was going to survive in the world of men like Marco and Eddie.

Eddie turned to Henry. "The other buildings—they're all locked up?"

Henry nodded. "The pool house. The storage buildings by the north and west docks. The storage sheds by the tennis courts and by the gardens."

Locking those made sense, especially as the dock storage buildings often held bootleg, fuel for the boats, and at least one case of dynamite leftover from the blasting of the hard rock to form the basement for the mansion.

"You're the only one who has a full set of keys to the mansion, the buildings?"

Henry frowned slightly. "Well, and you—"

"No," Eddie snapped. "I gave them to Rosita the last time I was here."

Flung them at her in an argument after Oliver's burial, I recollected. I was in the suite, setting out a snack and drinks, when Rosita demanded a divorce, and Eddie said he'd never give her one. Then she demanded the keys to her mansion, and he'd thrown them at her, narrowly missing her head. They'd hit the wall. Again, the words he'd shouted at her echoed in my mind: *Don't try my patience. If I have to force you to come back to me, you'll be sorry* . . .

"They're not in her suite, so I think she took them with her."

"You can look in those places but you won't find her there," Claire said, her voice raspy. She blinked back tears and cleared her throat. "When we were kids, we loved to come here every summer to spend a few weeks with our grandfather. Well, Rosita did." She gave a sentimental laugh. "I just loved to be with her, wanted to follow her around everywhere—she had that pull even as a kid, you know?"

She looked directly at Douglas. "*You* know."

He gave a little nod, dropped his head.

"And she loved the lighthouse, the cottage. They aren't locked up, are they?"

Henry shook his head.

Eddie gave an impatient wave. "So what, you think she's hiding there?"

"Maybe. But there are other places, too. A small cave, for one thing, near the north dock."

Liam stopped rocking. His eyes widened. Eddie gave him a withering look.

What is that about?

Claire stood and moved to a hand-drawn map of the island, hanging on the wall near the library's entry. She pointed to faint lines crisscrossing it. "Rosita made this map as a kid. She'd learned the shortcut paths our grandfather had cleared across the island. She knew all the hiding spots on the island—the cave near the north dock, other small caves, coves on the edge of the lake."

"Those would be overgrown by now," Joey said derisively.

Claire gave him a hard look. "But she'd remember them."

"Do you?" Eddie asked.

Claire's shoulders slumped. "Barely."

"But Rosita told me you and she visited for two weeks every summer," I said.

Claire cocked an eyebrow and smirked. "That's what you talked about out by the pool? This damned island?"

We talked about a lot of things, out by the pool at the McGees' Toledo house, or in the cool sitting room of the mansion, or on the back porch. Or often we didn't talk. Rosita caught me staring one afternoon with both longing and trepidation at the pool, and asked if I was afraid of water. No, I told her, I used to love to swim. I couldn't bring myself to tell her why I'd lost that love. She encouraged me— taunted me, really—until I jumped in. Almost immediately, trepidation slid away as I sluiced through the water. I rediscovered my love of swimming. After that, Rosita encouraged me to swim in the pool whenever I wanted, weather permitting. She found great amusement in watching me swim back and forth.

"Maybe you know all her hiding spots, and just aren't saying," Claire added. All eyes turned to me, questioning.

I pushed the memory of swimming in the pool, of Rosita encouraging me, aside. I shook my head. "She wasn't that specific, only said the island was a magical place to her." My heart panged as I recollected her saying that my presence here had ruined the island for her. "But surely, with the map—"

"You will remember Rosita's spots," Eddie snapped, as if he could force Claire into recollection.

Claire sighed. "Okay, the lighthouse. A cave on the northeastern side, near the north dock." At that, Liam stiffened and stared at Claire.

I noted his reaction.

"Any number of rock formations, trees—"

Marco groaned. "This is ridiculous."

"Anyone going out there best be careful," Henry said.

"A little snow won't hurt us," Joey said.

"No, but there's a black bear that I sighted a few weeks ago while I was out. I think she got stuck here as a cub last winter and somehow never left with the rest of her family."

"There are bears on this island?" Dr. Aldridge spluttered.

"Not usually," Henry said. "But sometimes in the winter, after the lake freezes, if their hibernation is disturbed they might cross from Canada, seeking a new resting spot, and stop on the island—"

"Yes," Liam said. "Especially long ago when the Erie Indians lived in this part of the world, animals would cross on the frozen lake. Humans, too. I've found arrowheads, and also a few artifacts from Civil War soldiers escaping combat, and also items that I think are from runaway slaves—"

"Some of your people?" Marco chuckled, looking at Henry and Maxine. No one laughed along with him.

Eddie glared at Henry. "There was a bear on this island, while I had guests here? Why didn't you shoot it?"

"The guests rarely walk the main path, and never go off of it. They stay in the mansion, on the grounds, and the bear wasn't aggressive. She was probably confused after waking up this past spring, and I'm hoping this winter she'll leave on the ice—"

"No one gives a damn, just shoot it if you see it," Eddie said.

Cormac entered the library. He shook his head.

Eddie's face slackened for a moment.

"Right," Eddie finally said. "So we're going to divide into search parties—"

"Boss," Cormac said. It was a shock to hear him interrupt Eddie. "What if Mrs. McGee left? In one of the speedboats."

"She doesn't know how to drive them, and she's afraid of the lake. She's here—somewhere on this island!"

Eddie's voice strained with the frantic need to believe what he said. But as we looked at one another, I could see in everyone else's eyes that they thought Cormac's explanation was much more likely.

My heart sped.

I wish I could say it was due to concern for Rosita, out on the dangerous, icy lake. And it was, in part.

But I also knew that if we didn't find Rosita, or some evidence that I had had nothing to do with her leaving, then Eddie would likely tell everyone who I was, what brought me to Trouble Island.

For if Rosita blamed my murdering Pony as the catalyst of events that led to Oliver's death, then so, too, would Marco blame me for being the root cause of his nephew's death.

He'd have Joey shoot me.

Or do it himself.

With everyone alert and looking for Rosita, I had no chance to escape for the time being.

I had to find Rosita.

CHAPTER 17

HENRY, LIAM, AND Seamus went to search the locked buildings. I watched them leave the mansion, worried for Henry, who looked tired, already wishing I could be alone again with Seamus, and wishing to question Liam. Seamus had been heading to the southwest dock instead of helping Henry the morning before, for reasons I had yet to understand, though I was determined I would uncover them. But where had Liam been when he was supposed to help Henry? Maybe there was an innocent explanation; Liam always struck me as glib, an unlikely conspirator.

But then, I'd been shocked by Rosita's revelations and conduct over the past twenty-four hours. And I'd shocked myself with my own behavior. At this point, I wasn't sure anyone was as they seemed—or as I'd assumed.

Cormac and Douglas left to search the *Myra* and the property around the house. Maxine was dispatched to cook breakfast, while Marco sat in the library, playing cards with Dr. Aldridge, who was left to entertain Marco after complaining that he'd been sick lately and couldn't be out in the cold. Joey stayed behind to keep a watchful eye on things.

That left Eddie, Claire, and me. He'd ordered us to go with him to the lighthouse and cottage. He didn't say it aloud, but I think he believed that if Rosita was in either place, Claire or I would be able to reason with her to come back to the mansion and sort things out.

As we trudged along the perimeter path, only able to see a few feet ahead in the swirling snow, I pushed back a surge of excitement at the prospect of finally going into the lighthouse. I'd casually brought up the notion once to Rosita, who'd abruptly snapped that it was dangerous. Off-limits.

I'd heeded her warning, not out of fear, but out of respect. But she'd never said I should keep out of the adjacent cottage, and on a surprisingly cold summer morning last year, I found myself drawn to the tiny residence. I gave the door a try, and finding it unlocked, went inside. For a long moment, I peered into the dark shadowy corners as if the ghost of Micah Byrne—Claire and Rosita's grandfather—might emerge. I sat in the rickety chair, opening and closing the rolltop desk, as if disturbing an old expense ledger, now falling to pieces, and the spiderwebs might be enough to call his spirit forth.

I wanted to know what it was like for him, on the island. What Rosita had really been like as a girl.

But the only spirits I ever thought I saw or heard on the island turned out to be the shadows of bird wings on the water, or the creak of tree limbs moving in the wind. My ghosts were conjured by my memories.

Finally we came around the curve of the path and the gray stone lighthouse emerged, itself like a specter in the shimmering white. My eyes were immediately drawn to the top, where the Fresnel lens was mounted, though of course the light had been dark for years. Once, shortly after I arrived on Trouble Island, when I was swimming in the lake and became weary and nearly overwhelmed by waves, I thought I saw it flashing.

The door to the lighthouse squealed on its hinges as Eddie opened it. Eddie produced the flashlight. A scurrying sound followed by a high-pitched squeal prompted a similar yelp from Claire.

"For God's sake, it's just mice. Doesn't this bring back great childhood memories?" Eddie asked nastily.

"Grandfather kept the lighthouse spotless," Claire said, and she put her hand over her nose. Even in the cold, the air was dank.

"Marco's right—this ought to be burned to the ground," Eddie said, and began ascending the metal stairs, his shoes clanking on each step.

Claire gave a small whimper—whether from the smell or Eddie's callous comment, I wasn't sure. She looked at me wide-eyed. "What if there are bats?"

"There probably aren't," I said reassuringly. "And if there are, they're sleeping, right? During the day?" I nodded at the handrail. "We should hold on."

I followed Claire, and as we wound on and on, level after level, past small dirty windows, I began to shiver in my brown-and-burgundy plaid coat, made of thin wool, envying Eddie's heavier wool coat and Claire's full-length fur. At least that was a warmer choice than her blue coat with the fox collar. As Eddie had pressured us to hurry up and begin our search, I hadn't had the presence of mind to grab my gloves, and with each grip of the cold metal railing, I feared the flesh of my palm would freeze against it. Cold though I was, sweat pooled in my armpits and slicked the back of my neck.

At first I told myself that my symptoms were simply because this dizzying trudge up the stairs was harder than swimming.

But as we climbed on and on, the cylinder becoming narrower as we ascended, the gray stone closed in on me. I found it hard to breathe and my heart pounded. Panic threatened to overwhelm me.

I thought of Micah Byrne climbing these stairs each day to ensure the lighthouse lamp was perpetually fueled and burning. Especially after his wife died. What would it be like, I wondered, to live on this island all alone, year-round?

Back in Toledo, Rosita talked often of this island, about how much her grandfather loved it. She'd promised, several times, that she'd arrange for me and Pony to come visit—or maybe just me—and I told her no, Pony would be too furious if only I could come. (How ironic, then, that I am here because of—well, technically, because of what I did to him—but really, because of who he was.) For a time, she stopped talking about the island, and I knew she would never arrange that visit. But eventually, she couldn't help but talk about the island, about how much her grandfather loved it. I told her once how odd I found his desire for only one tiny spot in the world, how I wished to travel widely, see as many places as I possibly could. She'd laughed and said, *You're not the sort of person who is strong enough, brave enough, to travel the world*. That had hurt.

Now I wondered if she'd said that because she wanted to keep me tethered to her. More than that, I wished I hadn't waited for her help to escape and start anew. I wished I hadn't felt so sorry and beholden to her after Oliver's death.

And then my mind turned again to Rosita saying the night before that Eddie had ruined the island for her, both by returning and by bringing Marco with him. That she had something on Eddie. Would she really leave the island, taking with her whatever she had? Hoping to ruin Eddie?

Claire moaned. "Why the hell did our grandfather have to be fascinated with lighthouses?"

"Tell me about your grandfather," I said, my words coming out in puffing gasps. I wanted to distract her—and me. I wasn't sure how far we'd climbed—halfway? Two-thirds? "All Rosita ever told me was how much he loved living here."

"Oh, she didn't mention how upset our grandmother was about coming? But Grandfather prevailed, of course. How the hell would I know why he was fascinated by lighthouses?" Claire gave a breathless, bitter laugh. "And Rosita loved it, too. I only came along because I tagged after her everywhere."

"There weren't things you loved about it? Especially in summer?"

"You mean the relentless mosquitos? Sweating at night, unable to sleep in that stuffy cottage? Swimming off the dock was okay, though Rosita hated swimming—too many tales of shipwrecks from our grandfather, which I happily ignored by sticking by our grandmother's side. The fishing and hiking and bird-watching they did, or the adventures and making paths and exploring in the woods Rosita insisted I do with her?" Claire shook her head. "I hated that. But we came every year until we were sixteen. By then, we were of courting age, and our grandmother had been gone for two years. And our grandfather stayed here for four more years after that, alone, without visitors."

I shuddered at the notion, but Claire gave a small laugh at my reaction.

"Grandpa loved being alone. A recluse. Rosita is a lot like him. And he was proud that the Trouble Island lighthouse was legendary among those who use the Great Lakes. Proud that he kept the lamp burning. Then one night, a regular ship that passed by noticed the light was not burning. The captain and a few crew came ashore to investigate."

My heart clenched in anticipation of what she'd say next.

"They found my grandfather in the lighthouse, you know. Up in the lantern room. It was determined he'd died of a heart attack."

I startled. Rosita had not told me this, maybe because of my comment that I found his dedication to be odd. "And no one took up his post?"

"The Canadian government decommissioned the lighthouse," Claire said. "The lighthouses on all the nearby islands had been upgraded, and ships had developed better onboard navigation. There's a reason this godforsaken hunk of rock is called Trouble Island. So many ships used to slam into its rocky shoreline in fog and storms."

And then it had outlived its usefulness. Now, it was just a structure, and yet I felt sorry for the lighthouse. And for Micah.

Finally, we reached the main gallery.

Breathing heavily, Claire leaned against the wall near a stack of crates labeled as fuel, swatting at a spiderweb just above her head. Eddie was feverishly opening and slamming shut the small drawers of a desk.

"She's not in the desk, Eddie," Claire said with amusement in her voice.

"Goddamn it, I know that. I'm looking for something else—"

Claire and I exchanged looks. I saw that she thought as I did—he was looking for whatever Rosita had mentioned the night before. A sorrowful shadow passed over Claire's face.

Again demure, she said, "Of course, I'm sorry, Eddie. This is all making my head spin." I thought I saw anger in her eyes, but the expression flashed by so quickly that I wasn't sure.

Eddie slammed a drawer shut and began climbing a narrow spiral staircase in the middle of the gallery. I instinctively followed. If Rosita was up there, hunched down in the lantern room, I didn't want her to confront him alone.

I took ahold of the railing and started my shaking ascent. One spiral turn later, I was with Eddie in the topmost level, which was encased in thick glass windows. I wavered as if I were on a boat deck on choppy waters at the blurry sight of swirling ice and snow through the window. I focused on the Fresnel lens, circling it, fascinated by how its panes enclosed where the lantern would burn, by the gears that would turn the lens, send its light, reflected from the flame within it, strobing across the churning gray waters of Lake Erie.

Rosita was not up there. Eddie stood, his arms crossed, his chest heaving from the effort to climb up.

But I circled a second time, a third time, enchanted by the lighthouse mechanism. This lantern room was where Micah Byrne had died.

On my next round, I paused by a telescope still set up in front of one of the glass panes. I wondered if Micah had gazed through the telescope in his final moments. What his view had been. I put my right eye to the lens, saw nothing but a blur of white. I tried to focus the telescope but did not succeed in making the snowflakes come in any clearer. My thoughts stretched across time back to him. *I hope it was a view you loved. A clear day, the waves rising and falling gently, the loons wheeling . . .*

And then I saw a flash. I jumped back, nearly toppling the telescope, but catching it in time. My hands shook even as I steadied the telescope. That flash—it was as if the orb had come to life, strobing just for me. A warning? Encouragement?

I pressed my eyes shut. When I opened my eyes again, the orb was dark and still—as it had been all along. And Eddie was gone.

The next level down, I saw that only Claire was waiting for me. Eddie was already descending the stairs.

"Go on," Claire said. "I need a moment." She gave me a wavering smile. "Memories."

I nodded and followed Eddie down. Soon I heard Claire's footsteps right behind me.

As we exited the lighthouse door, my head spun. From the twirling descent. The swirling snow. The illusion—I firmly told myself of course it was my imagination—that the lighthouse orb had flashed just for me.

Henry was waiting for us just inside the lighthouse door.

His breath was labored, his words slow, but his message was clear. "The speedboat at the north dock—it's gone. The ropes have been cut."

CHAPTER 18

"YOU GOTTA BE wrong!" Eddie roared.

Henry gave Eddie a hard look, then pulled out his beloved Banjo lighter and a cigarette and offered it to Eddie, who took it with hands that I suspected shook as much from being upset as from the cold. Henry lit the cigarette, then took out one for himself. Eddie still breathed hard, his nostrils flaring, but he was calming down.

"You know I'm not, Eddie," Henry said. "You know I don't make mistakes like that."

There was a clear bond between these two men. I was fascinated, and curious. I glanced at Claire, hoping to read in her expression whether she was as surprised as I was by how Henry spoke so directly to Eddie, by how Eddie accepted his candor. But she was sniffling and rubbing her hands together, apparently not listening at all.

"And you know I need to see for myself, see if there is some clue to Rosita's disappearance," Eddie said. "We'll take this speed-boat around—"

"Not safe enough for all four of us, not in this weather," Henry said. Under the force of the intensifying wind, the lake was wild and choppy.

Claire groaned. "Oh, please take me and drop me off at the mansion."

I frowned. Henry was out of breath, unsteady. "Henry should go with—"

"It's fine," Henry said.

I longed to go with Eddie and Claire because I wanted to see for myself the cut rope. Would I be able to sense, after all this time of serving her, if Rosita had been the one to cut the rope? I shivered, not just from the cold, but also from thinking of the rope I'd cut between the bell in my room and the handle in hers.

But I could not bring myself to leave Henry to trudge back to the mansion alone. He seemed so tired, weakened even as we all walked carefully on the icy ground down to the southwest dock. How different the lake was this morning, just twenty-four hours since I'd swum and seen the *Myra* approaching. I wouldn't dare get in the frigid, choppy water, even in my modified suit.

And yet I thought longingly of the treasure I'd found the day before, tying it up under the dock. My heart panged. What if it had somehow loosed itself? But I'd tightly secured the fishing net—hadn't I?

"All right, get in," Eddie gruffly ordered Claire as we stepped onto the dock. It swayed from the force of the lake. The water wasn't quite frozen.

Eddie didn't even bother to offer Claire a hand as she struggled to get into the boat. "Not a strong woman," Henry said to me quietly. "Like you and Rosita. Losing a husband, losing a child."

Eddie got in next. Then Henry knelt on the dock and began unwinding one of the ropes from its cleat, and I did the same at the other cleat. A pang of guilt washed over me, as cold and relentless as the wind. Henry and Maxine—everyone except Rosita, Eddie, and Cormac—thought I was a sad widow, a role I'd played for over a year.

What would the others think if they learned I'd made myself a widow by killing Pony?

After we finished, Eddie furiously yanked the starter rope, then finally got the engine started and took off, the boat chopping up and down on the rough waves.

As they disappeared into the whirling snow, I said cautiously, "Henry, you're sure the ropes were cut on the boat on the north dock?"

He gave me a sharp look. "Yes. All three."

"I believe you, just—why wouldn't Rosita unloop the ropes?" Cutting through thick cotton rope would take more time, more effort.

"Maybe," Henry said, "because a cut rope makes it clear the ropes didn't just come undone. It was intentional—by her or someone else. I never knew Rosita to be impulsive. At least not at first, back in Toledo."

As we worked on figure-eighting the ropes back in place on the dock cleats, I thought again of my treasure tied up below, and gazed at the water, where the speedboat had just been. Would Eddie or someone bring it back?

Desperation suddenly clawed through my heart, up my throat, at the notion that they might not. The boat could remain tied up at the north dock. If so, when the time came, I'd have to get my treasure out from under this dock, dry off, and trek across the island to the speedboat. Not far in good weather, but if I was chilled, and the weather was fierce, it would be miserable and long. And would increase the chance of someone seeing me as I tried to make my escape.

After Henry and I finished securing the ropes, we climbed the slope in silence, and soon entered the thicket of trees just yards from the lighthouse, following the shortcut Claire had brought me and Eddie on earlier. The path was a blur of white and gray. As I breathed in the cold and focused on Henry in front of me, I wondered if taking the perimeter path would have been wiser. It was longer, more exposed to the cold and wind, but offered fewer risks of tripping on a tree root or rock.

Yet, there was beauty in the frozen limbs and dizzying twirls of snow, in the bright red winterberries popping out in the underbrush in contrast against the white-limned branches and bark, in the smell of the snow and pines and fusty leaves and dirt, in the rare trill and chirp of woodland creatures and birds.

Soon my thoughts whirled like the snow.

I imagined Rosita in the early hours, making her way to the north dock, knowing the shortcuts even better than Claire would have. Getting in the boat. Pulling out a knife. Cutting the rope. I thought of the bell rope I'd cut in my room. Of how the rope up in Rosita's bedroom had been left purposefully coiled like a nest.

I felt certain she'd meant for me to notice the carefully wound rope, so I'd know she'd been aware that I'd cut the tie to the bell in my room. Likewise, she'd wanted whoever went to the north dock to see those ropes had been cut.

Both of us literally, and figuratively, cutting ties.

And then my thoughts drifted back to what Henry had said minutes before.

I cleared my throat. "How did you and Maxine end up working for Eddie and Rosita?"

Henry gave me a sharp look, assessing. For the next silent moments, I thought that would be my only answer. Finally, he said, "Eddie and I met years ago on a Lake Erie freighter, the S.S. *Martin,* Eddie a deckhand, me the second cook."

Henry fell silent, as if he was considering how much more to tell me. Then he shrugged. "Eventually, we went to work for Eddie and Rosita in their Toledo mansion. We got paid well. We were treated well. I didn't have to take any shift I could get, and made enough that Maxine didn't have to take in washing or mending."

That was it? He'd just told me so much more about his past than either he or Maxine had ever alluded to, and yet he'd skipped over so much—how had he and Eddie become friends on the freighter? How had they reconnected, and why did the Carmichaels—such a sweet couple—throw their lot in with gangster Eddie?

As I was considering how to best nudge Henry to share more, a crashing sound made us both stop. Henry said softly, "Stay still." Henry's words wafted back to me on the wind as he slowly lifted his shotgun.

A black bear emerged onto the path, just a hundred feet or so in front of us. She rose on her hind legs. She looked emaciated.

My huffing exhale, my pounding heart, suddenly seemed dangerously loud.

I braced myself for the crack of Henry's shotgun, for the horrific crash of the bear falling to the cold, hard earth.

But Henry remained still.

Finally, the bear went down on all four paws and lumbered away into the woods.

We waited in silence. Despite the cold, sweat ran down my neck, pooled in my armpits, beaded on my upper lip.

Henry moved forward cautiously but kept his gun at the ready.

"Bears were hunted out of existence in Ohio about eighty years ago," Henry said. "Some still live in the Canadian woods, though." He gave me a look. "I wonder if she knows she can leave when the lake freezes again. Or if she's been stuck here so long that she's afraid to leave. She's in the wrong place, at the wrong time."

I looked away from him, down at my dark boots rising and falling in the snow. I wondered if, when he talked about the bear, he was really talking about me. Or about all of us.

"Anyway, I don't want to shoot her if I don't have to. She deserves a chance to escape," he said.

We didn't talk the rest of the way back.

A SHORT WHILE later in the mansion's foyer, we had barely started to shed our coats and warm up when Eddie stormed in and said yes, the ropes had been cut at the north dock; the speedboat was gone. He'd found no clues.

"But it could be a trick," Eddie said. "It's the kind of thing Rosita would do, to taunt me."

So over the next two days, even as the weather worsened into a mix of sleet and snow, Eddie made all of us—except Marco and Joey—resume our search so long as it was daylight. The same places, over and over: the *Myra,* the spots on the island where Claire and Rosita had played as children, throughout the mansion. Eddie seemed to believe Rosita was shifting from spot to spot on the island, like a wraith, and we just needed to catch her at the right moment.

Sometimes, I'd think I felt Seamus's gaze upon me, and sure enough, when I'd glance his way, I'd catch him looking at me with concern or curiosity. We'd exchange quick flashes of smiles and I longed to get him alone to ask him what he thought of what was going on, or better yet, ask him nothing at all, but just pull him to me as I had the night after Eddie and his entourage arrived.

At night, Henry, Maxine, and I cooked and served up meals that would have been tasty, if anyone had been focused on pleasure, but that were miserable under the pall of Eddie's obsessive fury. Instead we ate only out of need and in exhaustion: Eddie, Marco, Cormac, Joey, Douglas, Dr. Aldridge, and Claire in the dining room. Maxine, Henry, Seamus, Liam, and myself in the kitchen. After dinner, Douglas played jazzy tunes, but with a flatness that showed his heart wasn't in it.

It was clear to me, to all of us, that Rosita was not on the island. Only Eddie insisted she had to be on the island somewhere, that she was just hiding.

CHAPTER 19

AFTER THE FIRST long day of searching, of tense silences, of Eddie's outbursts, I should have fallen into an exhausted slumber. But that night, I could not sleep. I kept imagining Rosita in the north dock boat, after she cut the rope. Pulling the start line to the motor. Heading north, because we'd all be less likely to see her boat going in that direction.

I wondered what she'd packed, what she'd brought with her. I longed to sneak up to her suite, to assess what might be missing, but during the day, I was afraid of being caught by the ever-watchful Eddie or Cormac.

Maybe I could sneak upstairs at night? I got out of bed, pulled on my robe, tiptoed past Largo's cage so as not to disturb her, and stepped out into the hallway. Joey and Douglas were whispering about something, just outside Douglas's door. Joey was smirking, and Douglas looked alarmed. Neither man seemed to notice me, but I quickly went into the bathroom so that if they had seen me, they'd think I only needed to use the facilities.

A few minutes later, they were still in the hallway. I returned to my room and stared out through the glass of the veranda door. Pinpricks of moonlight sparkled on the lake's surface. I wondered, had Rosita glanced back at the island that had once been her sanctuary and then her self-imposed internment? Did she intend to return someday? Or was she leaving forever?

Or would the rollicking, freezing lake overtake her boat—and then her?

For a moment an image popped into my mind: Rosita floating in the slushy cold water, her arms and legs spread out, her dark hair fanning in the water. And then her sinking, down, down, down, to the bottom of Lake Erie.

To join the bones of other lost wayfarers, of other sunken vessels.

The image was too overwhelming. My face burned and my heart raced, and I went out onto the veranda. The cold, bracing air slapped me, and I leaned into the wind as I stared down at dark Lake Erie.

I recollected the first time I dove into Lake Erie, just a few weeks after coming to Trouble Island. I went early down to the southwest dock, just at sunrise, before the first guests of the season would awake, before I would be needed to help Maxine. At that point, I was only cordial with the other staff, and I was so disappointed that Rosita had not come with the guests. I'd thought she would come as soon as possible to check on me.

I shed my dress and plunged in wearing only my underclothes. But in my shame and despair, I didn't want to swim.

I wanted to drown. For what I had done.

Not just to Pony, but for all of my sins, even before I met him.

And so, I let myself sink, sink, sink. I willed myself to open my mouth, let it fill with water, let the water go into my lungs.

I wanted to swallow as much of the lake as I could, and for the lake in turn to swallow me whole.

I thought as I sank: *I'm not Susan. Or Aurelia. I'm nobody. I deserve to be . . . nobody.*

Then I saw them. Shimmering. Eyeless. Mouthless.

Logic admonished me: a trick of light and shadow. Or just water snakes, seen from an odd angle. But my heart knew otherwise: they were there, three silhouettes in a paper-doll chain, holding one another's fingerless hands. I thought: *This, at last, is the punishment I deserve.* But even mouthless, the silhouettes yelled at me: *It is not time. You have not earned us back.*

And then a loon dove into the water, scooped up a whitefish.

I kicked hard, swam to the surface. That was the first time I saw the lighthouse flash at me, a beacon reassuring me, luring me back to land. Even though I knew it was a trick of my imagination, I followed that light and finally flopped onto a stretch of the island's rocky shore, as if the lake had spat me back out. I sat there, weeping and shaking and cursing at the lake. At myself.

I tried again and again until one day I realized I no longer wanted to drown in that sea of saltless tears.

Instead, I'd come once again to love swimming. The sluicing of water over my limbs. The feeling of moving smoothly, elegantly, powerfully.

I did not see the silhouettes again. After a while, I stopped looking for them.

Swimming saved me; so did learning the island's birds and plants and rhythms and natural order and seasons. I'd grown up on a farm, and so thought I knew nature. But that was nature bent to man's will. Away from the mansion, the island was nature untamed.

The sound of an engine brought me back to the moment. I watched a speedboat pull up to the main dock on the other side from the *Myra*. A figure stood, carrying something, and crossed to the *Myra*.

Rosita?

But no, I could see that the figure was male. Spry movements eliminated Eddie, Henry, Marco, and Dr. Aldridge. I'd just seen Joey and Douglas in the hallway.

That left Cormac, Seamus, or Liam.

What was he carrying, and from where, and why was it going onto the *Myra*?

Not whisky. The items were too small, and the heavy crates of glass bottles required several men to carry them.

I withdrew into the shadows and quietly shut the veranda door. I pulled on my coat, hat, gloves, boots, and opened my bedroom door just a crack.

The hallway was empty.

As quietly as I could, I crept down the stairs to the foyer, then slipped out the front door. Every step I took down the slick walkway felt just on the precipice of a fall. Under the moonlight, the topiary animals seemed strange rather than charming, and I fancied they were real animals who had somehow been caught on the island and transformed into its vegetation, stuck forever on this lonely, frozen dot of earth.

At the bottom, the bear seemed to lunge toward me with its scratchy, twiggy paws, and I shrank back as if the actual bear had emerged from the woods. I skidded a little, and nearly cried out, but I caught myself just in time, remaining both upright and silent. Then I ducked down and stared at the dock, the *Myra* on one side, a speedboat on the other. The lake was choppy enough that both boats rocked to and fro. The *Myra* hummed quietly, a light on in its cockpit.

For a few moments, I didn't see anyone. Then a figure emerged from the yacht, and I heard a barely perceptible whistle, caught and consumed by the wind.

Liam.

It struck me that Eddie had sent only Liam and Cormac to search the *Myra* or the north dock for Rosita.

I watched him leap from yacht to dock to speedboat, pick up two small items, then return to the yacht. He repeated the journey multiple times. My thigh muscles ached and cramped in my crouching position, and my body stiffened with the cold. I longed to stand and stretch, but I dared not. I didn't want Liam to know I was spying on him. And so I remained still, leaning into the bristly topiary bear long enough that I could imagine myself freezing to it.

Finally, Liam started up the speedboat and pulled away, heading around the east bend of the island, which meant he was returning to the north dock. I waited until the sound of the boat faded and then I stood up, my joints aching and creaking.

I went as quickly as I dared on the slippery ground down to the dock, my heart pounding, fearful of being caught, but also wondering if Rosita was being held on the *Myra.* If so, then what was Liam carrying to the yacht from the speedboat?

On the dock, I paused just long enough to look back at the mansion to see if any figures stood on the veranda, staring at me. Had Liam noticed me up there earlier, watching him? No, I thought, not Liam. He was always too caught in his own world.

I stepped onto the *Myra,* only my second time on the yacht, the first being when it had borne me to the island. The feelings I'd had that morning—of self-loathing, despair, desperation—whirled around me, like ghosts of emotion. I shook off the feelings—no time for wallowing—and quickly assessed the deck of the yacht: engine at back, a closed bin that doubled as seat and storage for ropes and so on, additional bench seats under which were tucked life preservers.

In the wheelhouse itself, I took in the steering wheel, the instrumentation panel, the captain's chairs. Nothing of interest, except a floor hatch was left open. I looked around quickly and found a flashlight, then carefully went down the steps into the small hold.

No one was down there, and I was both relieved and disappointed. What would I have done, had I found Rosita either dead or alive?

What I did find was stacks of lockboxes, just like the one I'd found on the shore.

I took in the sight, needing a moment to overcome the shock of realizing that my lockbox wasn't a treasure left behind years ago in a romantic story of shipwrecks and rescue. It was just one piece of

Eddie's loot, fallen in transport to some hiding place. I thought of Liam's reaction to the mention of a cave near the north dock; was that where these boxes had been kept? And now Liam was moving them?

This had to be at Eddie's behest. My guess: the lockboxes held bullion, jewels, and money, and Eddie had been having it stashed on the island during the bootlegging runs—a clever way to hide his income from both his legal and illegal businesses. And he wanted the treasure off the island before Marco took it over.

I longed to grab one of the lockboxes, crack it open to confirm the contents, but what if Liam came back with another load and caught me in the act?

I hurried off the yacht, then scampered through the cold darkness toward the mansion and my room.

THE NEXT DAY, the snow finally abated. There was light in the sky. The air had slightly warmed; the lake, calmed. I stayed alert for a chance to go to the north dock, or question Liam, but I was kept too busy, either helping Maxine or searching the lighthouse and cottage again. I did find excuses to stay near Liam, though, and overheard him say to Eddie that the lake on the north side of the island was freezing along the shore, and the speedboat could not remain docked there.

Eddie had roughly jerked Liam into the library, away from everyone else, to continue the conversation.

Later that afternoon—again going to the lighthouse cottage in case Rosita might pop up there—I saw that the speedboat had been returned to the southwest dock.

I realized Rosita was not coming back. She was not going to set me free; she was never going to do that. I knew that now. And there was no reason for Eddie to keep me alive. Sooner or later, he'd remember what a nuisance I'd been—as Rosita had so cruelly put it—and get rid of me.

So after the second day of searching, I entered my bedroom limp with exhaustion. As my door clicked to, I wanted to fall into bed, stop my head spinning not from emotion, but from numbness. The searching and the tension of the past two days had drained me.

But I sat on the edge of my bed and reviewed the plan that had been percolating in the back of my mind all day.

I would pack a small bag.

At first light, I would go to the lighthouse cottage, put on my swimming suit. I'd dive below the southwest dock, retrieve my lock-box of treasure. Change back into dry clothes. And then I'd get in the speedboat, and I would leave.

It had been years since I last prayed, and more years the time before that—all the way back in my childhood. Prayer did not come easily or naturally to me.

But I knelt before my bed and prayed for courage, and for the weather to remain clear. Then I hunkered down to pull out my suitcase. But just as I grasped its handle, I jumped at a soft, light knock on my door. Ignoring whoever it was might cause a stir, so I quickly pushed my suitcase back under my bed and went to the door.

Seamus. Warmth rushed through me, followed quickly by sorrow. I would not ever see him again.

And yet, I smiled when he held out a plate with a sandwich on it. I stepped back and let him in.

"You didn't eat much—really, at all, tonight," he said.

I took the plate, put it on my desk. "Thank you," I said.

Seamus stepped forward, put his arms around me, pulled me to him, gave me a long, lingering kiss. Even as I leaned into him, his touch so comforting after the last few cold, brutal days, I knew that if he stayed the night, I wouldn't leave.

I put my hands on his chest and pushed lightly. "I'm exhausted. I just need to sleep—"

Seamus released me and stepped back.

"I understand. Just eat that sandwich before you go to sleep. You're going to waste away. Promise?"

I choked up and could not speak. I nodded and shut the door, looked around my room. My suitcase was only partially under the bed. Had he seen it?

I shook my head at myself. I couldn't do anything about that now. I wasn't hungry, but my hands shook, and I wanted to be strong the next morning. I took a few bites of the sandwich, and then I ravenously tore into it. In minutes, the sandwich was gone.

Largo, asleep in her cage, stirred, then resettled.

I pulled out my suitcase and packed, leaving behind the fancy dress I'd brought, opting for practical clothes. I hesitated for a moment, but then I tucked in my Escalante cigar box and my bird-watching notebook. I didn't want to forget Trouble Island entirely.

I put my suitcase, coat, hat, and gloves on top of my bed, then donned the clothes I'd wear. I went to Largo's cage and whispered, *"You'll be fine, pretty girl. Maxine will take care of you."* I pulled open the draperies over the veranda door and turned off my bedside lamp. I sat on the edge of my bed, staring out into the flat darkness, unable to see the sky or the lake. All I saw was flat gray darkness. I was determined to stay awake, to watch for the darkness ceding to the paleness of dawn. But just in case, I set my bedside alarm clock.

Either way, I'd wake up just before sunrise. Then I would put my plan into action. And, at last, be free.

I FELL ASLEEP after all. I dreamed of the shadow people in the water—Pony. My father and my brother. And now a fourth one joined them, a tinier figure.

Oliver.

I jerked awake, gasping for air as if I had been held underwater. I pushed aside the disturbing dream, glanced at my bedside clock. 5:30 A.M. on Saturday, November 21. I looked out the window. Still dark, but the night was softening. I considered going to the kitchen to retrieve the flashlight kept in one of the drawers, but decided I didn't want to risk disturbing anyone. I resolved that I could pick my way to the dock in the night if I stuck to the perimeter path. By the time I got to the dock, dawn would have commenced.

I put on my coat, hat, and gloves. Picked up my suitcase. I left my door unlocked so that Maxine could eventually come into my room and take over Largo's care. Then quietly, carefully, I crept out of the mansion.

I left my suitcase in the cottage, changed into my homemade full-body bathing suit and swim cap, already shivering. I held a sheathed fishing knife, also retrieved from the cottage.

Out on the dock, I noted that the snow had stopped and mist roiled over the land and the lake. Loons dove, seeking whitefish that resurface in November's cooler water. I took a minute to observe the birds I'd come to love. My heart panged. I'd miss them. But it was time to go.

I glanced at the speedboat. Yes, I reassured myself, I could navigate it to the north shore of Ohio. All I had to do first was get my lockbox.

I took a deep breath, held it. Dove into the lake.

The shock of slicing into the cold, churning waves was brutal. I knew I had about two minutes before I'd need to come up for air, about ten—maybe twelve—before cold would numb my limbs and hypothermia would start setting in. Yet I also knew that in Lake Erie, two minutes can be an eternity—and so can even one second. That's one of the funny things I've learned, besides birds' names and habits, from living on this island. Eternity can fit into any sliver of measured time.

I counted each heartbeat as a second's worth of time and swam downward. I needed just another minute to get to the lockbox. I didn't care that it was just like all the others in the hold on the *Myra*. It held enough value for me to start over.

But the lockbox was gone.

How could that be? It had been there the morning I swam here with Seamus. Had my nervousness at leaving, the chaos since Eddie's arrival, the bitter cold, all addled my brain so that I was looking in the wrong place?

I turned in the water and saw her.

Bare feet. White nightgown.

Her face bloated and her arms floating out as if grasping for fish, for water snakes, for *me*. The dead woman's mouth and eyes open but already partly nibbled away. One rope looped around her neck, another around her ankles, securing her to the dock beam.

I gasped, swallowed water.

Flailed, instinctively backstroking away from the dead woman.

Away from Rosita.

Swam back, back, back . . .

CHAPTER 20

I swam to the surface as fast as I could, my arms churning, my legs thrashing, then pulled myself up the ladder on the side of the dock, flopping onto the snowy surface like a fish suddenly cast from the lake. My stomach turned. I scrambled to my knees just in time, grabbing one of the dock posts, and then retched into the icy water.

I wish I could record that my first instinct after I finally sat up was to forget all my plans, to run back to the mansion to report having found Rosita's body lashed to the piling. But thus far I have recorded everything as clearly and honestly as I can remember it, so I will continue to do so now, and confess: even as her bloated, distorted face floated before me in my mind's eye, a cold, calculating part of my mind separated from the part that was in shock, an odd separating of the conscious I'd only experienced twice before—first with my brother and later with Pony.

What would likely happen when I returned to report my discovery of Rosita's corpse flashed before me: Eddie's rage, the sorrow that I knew the others—at least Claire and Douglas, and Maxine and Henry—would feel.

There would be questions: Why did I go swimming on such a morning?

There would be accusations: Had I killed Rosita? Left her there for some foul reason? Had a sudden stab of guilt that led me to report her death?

So yes, I was willing, in that panicked moment, to forget about Rosita and my missing treasure and the Carmichaels and Largo.

I crawled to the other side of the dock, where the boat was tied up, and slid from the edge into the boat, sitting with a thud on the fore bench, in enough of a panic that I thought after a moment to catch my breath, I'd unspool the ropes from the deck cleats, start the motor, head south to Toledo, without my treasure, or my dry clothes, or my glasses, or my suitcase.

But water sloshed around my feet. An axe, surely the source of several narrow gouges in the bottom of the boat, was embedded in the aft floor. Once powered up and running, the boat might get a half mile before it took on water and began to sink.

Someone—the same person who had murdered Rosita?—had sabotaged the boat.

I knew I couldn't take the *Myra*; Cormac had that boat's keys.

So the only choices now before me were to hide somewhere on the island.

Or go back to the mansion. And either tell everyone that I'd found Rosita, or pretend I hadn't.

I ran as fast as I could, feeling as though my full-body swimming suit was fusing into my skin as it froze.

I HADN'T CONSCIOUSLY chosen the shortcut that Claire had shown us a few days before, but I was soon thrashing through the woods, branches on the trees whipping into my face when I didn't shove them out of my way in time, tripping over my numbing feet, feeling the pressure of sticks but not yet feeling pain because my feet were so frozen.

Then I stumbled. Over a large log, I thought. I fell face-first into the frozen ground, my hand flying to my face to protect my glasses, feeling my goggles. Twigs scratched at my cheeks. The thought flitted briefly past—my glasses, and shoes, and warm dry clothes and coat were still just inside the lighthouse cottage's door.

I pushed myself up, looked again, and saw that I'd tripped over a body. A man. Face down. The back of his head was bloody.

I grunted with effort as I rolled him over, then gasped when I saw the face of Pony. Or what was left of it.

He'd been mauled, his left shirt sleeve and arm ripped apart, the left side of his face clawed. And yet it seemed to me a grin froze on the intact, right side of his face. That cockeyed grin he always had before backhanding me. His gun lay near him.

My breath froze in my lungs. My heart pumped wildly. All sound seemed to fall away. I shook from far more than the cold, so hard that I feared my bones would unknit themselves.

Possibilities swirled in my mind: I hadn't really killed him after all. Rosita and Eddie had let me believe he was dead.

The reasonable part of my mind lectured: *No. You killed him. Then you shook his dead body as if you could stir some remnant of life in him, undo what you'd done, just as you're shaking this man now.*

I let go of the man. This was not Pony. This was Joey.

He'd been attacked by the bear, or killed by a human—I thought of Douglas and the fraught, whispered conversation he and Joey had had in the hallway the night before. And then Joey had been left for the bear to maul.

I stood and resumed my staggering race back to Rosita's mansion.

THE NEXT PASSAGE of time remains to this day a blur. Perhaps it will always be a blur. Perhaps that is a blessing.

I recollect coming around the curve to the mansion, though this time it did not rise clear and stately before me. It was an impression, a ghost of itself under the muted gray sky, as snow started falling again. I stumbled up the steps, past the tarp-covered goddess fountain, the snow-covered animal topiaries, to the front door, and found it unlocked.

I heaved it open, sliding across the black-and-white tile, and for a panicked moment in the silent vestibule, its warm air taking my breath away, I had the thought that I was alone, that everyone had disappeared from the mansion. That I'd drowned after all in my attempt to take my life in the cold waters of Lake Erie after coming to Trouble Island, that I'd been wandering ever since in a nightmare purgatory of my own devising.

But then I heard voices from the dining room—Eddie and Marco, loud and boisterous. Claire's tittering laugh. The clinking of spoon and fork on glass and china. From the music room, a jazzy tune on the piano—Douglas, already called upon to entertain Eddie and his entourage, even at breakfast.

I burst into the dining room, and everyone went quiet and stared at me. I realized that I must look a sight in my swimming suit and goggles.

The piano music stopped, and Douglas—probably curious about why everyone had stopped talking in the dining room—entered, then came to an abrupt halt at the sight of me. His cigarette trembled between his lips, ash tumbling to the carpet like gray snow.

Numbly, I pulled the goggles from my face. My voice was oddly clear and steady as I spoke. "I went swimming by the southwest dock. Rosita is under it. Dead. She's been tied up there. I ran back on the shortcut. Joey was there. Dead. Attacked by someone or by the bear—"

My knees buckled. Sparkles drizzled before my eyes. I watched them, wide-eyed with wonder that it was suddenly snowing inside the mansion. Then my vision turned gray, a high-pitched hum pierced my mind, and I collapsed to the floor.

MY NEXT CLEAR memory is of being in Henry's and Maxine's quarters. I was warm and dry and felt clean and smelled of castile soap;

I must have showered in the staff's communal bathroom. My hair was damp, but my fingers combed through it smoothly, so it was wet with clean water, rather than lake water. I sat in one of their two wing chairs, constructed from plain oak but amply upholstered with blue wool, my feet up on the matching footstool. In the past, I'd imagined that the Carmichaels brought this furniture, and the tiny dining table with two mismatched wooden chairs, from their home, though I'd never asked.

I held a cup of hot tea, but I just stared at its surface. The chamomile scent was soothing, and stirred memories of my mother's herbal teas, a rare *good* recollection, and tears sprang to my eyes. Around my wrists, I saw the ruffled cuffs of one of Maxine's housecoats, a simple pink floral cotton, well-worn and soft. The quilt from their bed was draped around my shoulders.

I stared down at the quilt's pattern: brown-framed squares, tan background, with four shapes like an abstract four-fingered paw jutting from a tiny square in the middle. Simple, yet mesmerizing, but not a pattern I'd seen in the quilts made by my grandmother and mother.

"Aurelia?" Maxine's tone was probing, yet gentle, as if she was calling me back from a great distance.

My eyes drifted up and, though her face was blurry since I wasn't wearing my glasses, I could tell her expression was vexed.

I looked away from her and spotted the fuzzy outline of my full-body swimming suit heaped in the corner, like a skin I had shed. I wondered where my glasses were.

"Oh, honey," Maxine said. She pulled the other footstool before me. "I know your feet must be in misery. They were bleeding when Henry helped you down here."

Henry had helped me down? I didn't remember that.

She lifted the quilt, baring my feet. She shook her head. "There are still twigs and briars in your soles. I'll need to dab on liniment after they're out and it will sting a bit, but you don't want your feet to get infected—"

"I can clean my own feet." My voice was hoarse.

"Nonsense," Maxine said. She reached behind her to the dresser for tweezers and a small bowl. She tugged out a thorn. I flinched. "It will go faster if you sit still," she said as she dropped the thorn into the bowl. It made a tiny plink.

I stared past her at the dresser, focusing on the few framed black-and-white photos, one depicting younger versions of Maxine and Henry. A sepia-toned photo showed a clapboard house with a large wraparound porch and a sharply slanting roof. Twenty or so people, from a baby to an old woman in the middle, filled the porch, their images now faded and ghostly.

I held back a sharp inhale from the sting of the liniment that Maxine gently dabbed on my feet. When I breathed again, my stomach roiled at the coppery scent of my blood mixed with the tang of the salve. The images of Rosita, of Joey, filled my mind again. I swallowed back the bitter saliva that suddenly rose in my mouth.

"Close your eyes," Maxine said. "Focus on a good memory."

I obeyed, my mind numbly pushing past the images of Rosita and Joey, settling at first into grayness, which ceded with surprising swiftness to an image of Levi. He was seven, I was eleven, and it was a sunny Saturday morning in August, and we were with Papa in his canoe out on Possum Run, a wide creek that ran rapidly and fed into the Ohio River south of us. Mama would be angry at our lazing about, and at me especially, a girl doing boy things, when she needed my help canning tomatoes. But I didn't want to be in that suffocating kitchen with her. I wanted to be out with my daddy and my little brother, bobbing up and down in the clear, wide creek, the cry of birds above us, and chitters of small critters in the woods on the banks on either side of us . . .

"Aurelia?" Seamus's gently probing voice brought me back.

I opened my eyes. Maxine had finished tending my wounds and had moved on to fastening a button onto one of Henry's shirts.

Seamus stepped forward, holding my glasses out to me. I briefly wondered where he'd found them, and then I abstractedly recalled leaving them in the cottage. I put them on, and then spotted my shoes were on the floor by the bed, a selection of my clothes folded neatly on the end of the bed. My heart warmed with gratitude. Maxine must have gone to my bedroom, picked clothing out for me. I thought vaguely, then, of my coat, hat, and gloves, and wondered where they were.

Seamus's voice trembled as he said, "Eddie wants you upstairs in the library."

CHAPTER 21

SEAMUS WAITED OUTSIDE the Carmichaels' room while Maxine helped me shed the warm comfort of her nightgown and quilt. I changed into my pants and blouse, wincing as I forced my sore feet into my shoes.

Maxine gave me a worried look as I started to leave.

"I'll be fine," I reassured her.

But I wasn't so sure. My stomach churned, my head buzzed, as Seamus and I lingered in the hallway. He quietly explained what had happened after I burst into the dining room: Seamus, Cormac, Liam, and Eddie had gone down to the southwest dock. He had dived off, found Rosita as I described. With a knife, he'd sliced the ropes that bound her and brought her body up to the surface, laying her out on the dock. Eddie had stared down at her for a long time, quiet, and said simply, *Yes, this is Rosita.*

While Eddie kept watch over Rosita's body, Seamus changed back into dry clothes in a back room in the cottage, while Liam and Cormac found an old stretcher. The four men had borne Rosita back to the pool house. Eddie, Cormac, and Liam kept watch over her body, while Seamus went inside to find Henry, who'd unlocked the pool house.

Seamus went on to explain that he, Liam, and Cormac went back for Joey's body and transported him to the pool house as well.

When he finished his explanation, he gestured that I should precede him up the stairs to the main floor but didn't touch me or look at me. He was not just reeling from the morning's events. He was upset with me.

I was surprised at how that stung me. But as we ascended the stairs, I pushed aside that emotion and braced myself to face Eddie.

Eddie sat quietly, again at the head of the long table in the library. His gaze swept over the tips of his steepled fingers and seemed to land on the bookshelf, boring through the volumes of Austen and the Brontës and Eliot and Verne, traveling to even more distant places than in those fictions.

I'd like to think he was remembering lovelier times with Rosita, when they were first courting, or wed, or building this mansion.

Cormac stood at the opposite end of the table. Marco sat on one side. Quietly, Seamus took a seat opposite him.

Cormac pulled the chair back at his end of the table, gestured exaggeratedly for me to sit.

I sat, clasping my hands on the table, focusing on Eddie. My stomach growled; in response, my face flamed. It seemed indecent to be hungry—a need of the living—after discovering Rosita and Joey brutally killed.

"What were you doing down by the dock this early morning?" Cormac asked.

"Taking my usual morning swim," I said.

"Even in this weather?"

"I've made a full-body swimming suit," I answered. "I was wearing it when I came in to tell everyone—" My explanation faltered as

I glanced at Eddie, as still and frozen as he'd been when I'd entered the library. Did he even hear what we were saying?

Cormac turned to Seamus. "Well?"

"It's true," Seamus said. "She does like to swim. I've seen her."

I cleared my throat. "So we've established that I like to swim. So?"

"So you are the most comfortable of any of us with the lake. The most likely to be at ease underwater, tying up Mrs. McGee," Cormac said.

"I didn't kill her," I said wearily. Of course I was being blamed; I knew I would be. "Why would I? She saved my life after—" I stopped.

Cormac gave a curt nod to Seamus, the cue for Seamus to reach under the table and produce my suitcase. He put it on the table.

Oh. I deduced that after finding Rosita, he'd gone into the cottage to change, spotted my clothes, glasses, and suitcase. In the blur of that horrible morning, I forgot that I'd brought the suitcase.

Seeing it must have made him realize that I'd been intent on leaving without telling him my plans, and this hurt him. My eyes prickled at the notion that he cared that much about me.

I half rose from my seat, stretching my hand forward. "I'd like that back. I just used it to bring my swimming suit . . ."

I stuttered to a stop as Cormac gave Seamus a pointed look. Seamus clicked the latches, opening my suitcase to reveal my clothes, cigar box, and my bird-watching notebook.

"You were planning on leaving this morning, weren't you?" Cormac asked. "Taking the speedboat."

I nodded, miserably.

"And for some reason you went into the water—"

"I just—just wanted one last swim—"

"One last swim? In that freezing water? Or were you tying up Rosita's body—"

"From the body's condition," Seamus said quietly, "Rosita has been under the dock almost as long as she's been missing."

"Fine," Cormac said. "Maybe you wanted to release her, so she'd never be found—"

"I just wanted one last swim!" I said. What I'd really wanted was my lockbox, but I wasn't about to admit that. "And besides, if I killed her, why would I tie her up to be found? I'm the only one who swam there, the only one who would find her—"

I stopped, realizing that whoever killed her might have tied her up knowing that sooner or later I'd swim there and find her remains.

Perhaps someone who had seen me find the lockbox and tie it under the dock. One of my coworkers? One of them could have later told Eddie or a member of his entourage, reasoning that I'd surely want it because I was planning to run.

My head was pounding. I couldn't sort out who to trust, or who might be working together. So my only option was to trust no one.

My stomach ached at that. I'd grown to care about the Carmichaels and Liam. And in just a few months, I'd become attached to Seamus.

"Goddamn it, why do I have to listen to this?" Marco leapt up.

"You don't have to," Cormac said, his voice as tight as a thread pulled too taut. "But staff comes with the island, so you might want to know what you're buying."

My throat tightened as if a clammy hand had closed around it. We—the Carmichaels, Liam, and myself—were just part of the transaction, like tea towels and vases and the rest of the mansion's contents. I glanced at Seamus, who gave a tiny shake of his head: this was not the time to protest.

Marco leapt up. "All I wanna know is, does Eddie inherit the island, with the old lady offed?"

Cormac was by Marco in a blink, grabbing his arm and bending it back. Terror flooded Marco's face as if he was just now realizing that he was without his bodyguard.

"Mind your manners," Cormac snapped.

"Mind *your* manners, Cormac." Eddie finally spoke. He was still staring into the distance, so riveted that it seemed we might have imagined his voice. "We want Marco to only say nice things about us when this is all over."

Cormac released Marco's arm. "Yes, boss."

Eddie turned his cold gaze on his rival. "Yes, I inherit the island. The mansion. The contents. It was in her will."

The back of my neck prickled. It was in Eddie's financial interest for Rosita to be dead. And for her body to be found, to prove she was dead and not just missing.

Marco grinned. "Good thing there are no obstacles in the way of the sale."

I blanched at that. Rosita—an obstacle. It was also in Marco's financial interest for Rosita to be dead, her body found.

"But you know, word's gonna get around that your old lady died here. Folks might think it's jinxed. May be less likely to come here for me, the way they did for you. Plus coming here has cost me a bodyguard, and I'm gonna have to pay off his family to keep their yaps trapped. So I'm thinking a lower price—"

Eddie clapped his hand down, hard, on Marco's shoulder. "Or maybe a higher price?"

Marco frowned. "I'm not offering a penny more—"

Cormac pulled back his jacket, rested his hand on his holster. "You thinking maybe we can find another buyer, boss? One who won't whine about what's happened here?"

Marco's ruddy face blanched. "My—my men will be here in a few days, if I don't return—"

Eddie grinned, his mouth stretching like a snake's about to surround its prey. "I'm sure they'd be so sad to learn that you fell in the lake. And unlike my *old lady*, no one tied your body up to be found."

"I'll . . . pay whatever price you ask."

"Oh no, the original price is fine." Eddie patted Marco on the shoulder convivially. "Cormac, take his gun."

"What?" Marco started to protest. "But without Joey—"

"You'll be fine," Eddie said. "Cormac is going to gather all the other guns, too."

Marco pulled out his gun, handed it over. Cormac gave Seamus an impatient look, and Seamus, too, handed over his gun.

Who else was armed? Henry, with his rifle. Liam. Maybe Dr. Aldridge and Douglas. In any case, soon the only ones with guns would be Eddie and Cormac.

Eddie turned his gaze on me. "So, what to do about my wife's killer."

"I have an idea, boss," Cormac said.

The blood drained from my face.

Eddie chuckled. "Cormac, you have got to learn to think with more finesse. No, we need Rosita's killer alive, for her to turn herself in."

The realization struck me, just as surely as if Cormac or Eddie had hit me, that Rosita might be a recluse, and Marco and his wife might take over the island, but eventually—at their summer gatherings, their parties, there would be questions.

Whatever happened to Rosita McGee?

Where did she go?

She's not back in Toledo with Eddie, so . . .

And Eddie did not like questions about his business or life.

Eddie grinned at me. "You didn't really think you could get away with murder, did you?"

Oh, but I had once. Or so I thought. Why not blame me?

I clenched my jaw. "I didn't kill Rosita."

Eddie smacked his hands down on the table and leaned forward. For a mad moment, I thought he might clamber across the table to me. "Neither did I, doll."

"Then we should find out who did." Seamus's voice was calm. "I will get the doctor. He can examine the bodies. Maybe answer the questions about whether Rosita was already dead at the time she was lashed under the dock, or if she died of drowning. He might even be able to discern a few details about Joey's death."

"I'm coming, too." Eddie stood. "So's Aurelia. Could be seeing the bodies again might jog her memory for details."

A large shrieking cry filtered into the room. Everyone looked around, startled. *Largo.* I had nearly forgotten her. Up in my room, hungry by now, confused, lonely.

Eddie jumped up. "What is that infernal racket—"

"It's Largo," I said. "She needs tending."

"It'd be easier just to strangle her," Marco muttered.

I wasn't sure if he meant the bird, or me.

Eddie waved me away. "Go. Seamus, follow her, make sure she doesn't try to run again."

CHAPTER 22

SEAMUS WAS CLOSE behind me as I rushed out of the library.

I stopped so suddenly, he nearly smacked into me. "Are you really going to follow me on Eddie's orders?" I hissed.

He lifted his eyebrows. "I don't have much of a choice in this situation."

I started shaking. "You didn't say anything at all to defend me. Coward!"

"It's not cowardly to be afraid of snakes. Or men like Eddie," Seamus said, his voice suddenly hard. I'd gone too far, calling him a coward, and I wanted to snatch back the word, beg his forgiveness, but I stared at him stubbornly. "It's wise. And I didn't defend you because I don't know what happened to Rosita."

My breath hitched in my chest as if he'd smacked me in the stomach. "You think I could do that? Kill her?"

The muscles in Seamus's jaw tightened. "I don't really know you at all, Aurelia."

I'd been such a fool, thinking that what we'd shared was more than desire, that it portended anything beyond a night of pleasure.

He held my suitcase out to me. I took it, and for a moment our fingertips brushed. A desire to let that touch linger rose in me, but he abruptly stepped back.

"I'll let Eddie know you are on your way up to your room," he said, then turned quickly.

The suitcase suddenly felt like it weighed a hundred pounds. My whole body ached. But I started toward the staircase, blinking tears away.

Claire, though, popped out of the music room, teetering. She propped herself up with one hand on a display table that held an exquisite porcelain vase. In the other, she held an empty highball glass. She already reeked of whisky. I glanced at the grandfather clock at the end of the vestibule. It was nine in the morning.

Her eyes were watery. "It's true, then? You found Rosita dead?"

"Yes," I said impatiently. "Did you think I'd made it up?"

I immediately regretted my harsh words. The cousins had been close. I'd witnessed how much Claire adored, even worshipped, Rosita.

But in the next moment, Claire gave me a lopsided grin. She shook the empty glass in front of me. "Decanter's empty in the music room. You need to refill it."

I simply said, "No."

She looked down at my suitcase in my hand, then studied me quizzically, her eyebrows arched. "Why—you goin' somewhere in this weather? Got something better to do?"

"Because I don't want to," I said.

At that, Claire's mouth dropped, and I walked away from her gaping stare.

Upstairs, I put my suitcase on the floor beside my desk, promised Largo seedcakes later, then donned my coat, boots, and hat.

When I came downstairs to the vestibule, Claire was gone, but Seamus and Dr. Aldridge were ready and standing to the side by the door, each carrying old-fashioned kerosene lanterns. Henry must have gotten them out of the basement storage room. The pool house was not on the mansion's electric generator, and in the swirl of the snow, light would not filter through the pool house skylights.

I joined them, my gaze drawing to Seamus. "Why are you going?"

The guarded stillness of Seamus's eyes cracked my heart. "I was a medic in the war," he said. "I know a few things about wounds and injuries and death." He cocked an eyebrow. "Cormac wanted to come, but I thought it might be better if I did."

He did want to watch out for me a bit.

"So what is he doing?"

"Keeping an eye on Marco," Seamus said. A glimmer of amusement brightened his eyes. "His favorite duty, I'm sure."

In spite of the chaos around us, and the gruesomeness that awaited us, a slight smile brushed my lips.

Then we stepped outside into a blast of snow and icy wind. Winter had reasserted itself with revitalized force.

Earlier that morning, the door for leaving in fairly calm, safe weather had opened a crack. Now it was slammed shut.

THE POOL HOUSE is bigger than the entire bungalow I'd shared with Pony in Toledo. It's divided in half, one side for women, another for men, a door for each side. On both sides, its walls are lined with narrow cupboards, in front of which are benches.

The last time I'd been inside was at the end of summer, after the season's last guests had left, to help Maxine give both sides a deep cleaning before closing up the pool house for the winter. In the heat of summer, I'd hear laughter and chatter pouring from the building, and find myself longing to again be a part of that seemingly carefree, glittering world.

On that cold November morning, as I entered the women's side of the pool house with Seamus, Eddie, and Dr. Aldridge, the two coal oil lamps provided scant, flickering light that made shadows twitch from corners. Each bench held a sheet-covered human form. Joey and Rosita.

The air was cold and dank. I tried to inhale, and for a panicked moment, it felt as impossible to breathe as if I were underwater. I could hear my heart thudding.

Seamus put his hand on my arm. *"Focus on your breath,"* he whispered, and nodded at the white fog of our breaths exhaling in the cold, mingling. My heart calmed. Then he held his lamp out to me and asked more loudly, "Could you hold this up for us?"

I nodded.

Eddie moved to a corner, leaning against the walls, as if trying to shrink from the light.

Dr. Aldridge put his lamp on a table that once held stacks of fluffy white towels, then moved to the larger of the two bodies. Seamus pulled back the cover, revealing Joey's mauled body.

"From the spacing of the cuts, this was the bear Henry was worried about," Dr. Aldridge said. "Either Joey antagonized it, or the bear found him after he was dead."

Then Dr. Aldridge pointed to a stain of blood spreading in a circular pattern on Joey's pants leg, on the top of his right thigh. "I need to see the wound."

Seamus got a pocketknife out of his pants pocket, then slit the cloth, revealing Joey's thigh. There was a deep jagged gash, still fresh, the blood only congealed because of the cold, but still a shiny red.

Seamus wiped off the knife with a handkerchief. "A wound like this is from a knife. A slash this deep would come from a bigger, sharper blade. Whatever it was, it hit an artery. Joey would have bled out in minutes."

The light trembled in my hand but I willed my grasp to still. "I came to the southwest dock on the circular path, but after I found Rosita, I returned to the mansion on the shortcut Claire showed us.

Joey was out of sight from the circular path at the dock, but close. He had to have been killed before I took that path."

Dr. Aldridge said, "I didn't observe blood on your swimming attire when you came into the dining room. Seamus, you gathered her clothes. Was there blood on them?"

"No," Seamus said.

"An attack like this would have created a lot of blood spatter, impossible for it not to get on the killer," Dr. Aldridge said.

Relief coursed through me. Did Eddie and Seamus understand what Dr. Aldridge was saying? I couldn't have been the one who killed Joey.

"When he was attacked, he must have fought back," I said slowly. "But I didn't hear any arguments or cries of distress. How long, after an attack like this, would it be before he died?"

"It would take five minutes or so for him to bleed out," Dr. Aldridge said.

"So he had to be killed at least a half hour before I came nearby on the path."

"When did you near the southwest dock?" Seamus asked.

"About a quarter to seven," I said.

"So at the latest, Joey was killed at a quarter after six," the doctor said. "Maybe earlier, but not much earlier, because of the freshness of the leg wound."

I looked from the wound to Joey's shredded sleeves. Did someone emerge from the woods, surprise Joey? Or was the attacker someone who was with him?

In any case, I envisioned him falling, then staggering to his feet, either to try to get away from the other person, or to go after them. He reaches for his gun, maybe gets off a shot, but if so, his aim must have gone wide, for no one has been shot. Because he's bleeding so profusely, and in such pain, he drops his gun, falls to the ground on top of it. Sometime later, the bear crosses his path.

Seamus pulled the sheet over Joey. "We can confirm he was attacked, and probably died from the thigh wound. It wasn't an accident or a run-in with the bear." He shook his head. "But that doesn't get us any closer to narrowing down who or why."

My heart clenched as I stared at Rosita's sheet-covered body. The image arose of her body, tied up, mutilated by time, the lake, and its creatures, her nightgown floating in the water. Her torso, face, arms all bloated and milky like the underbelly of a fish, her eyes gone, part of her lip missing, her dark hair floating. I didn't want to look again, to see her like that.

But I didn't want Eddie to uncover her. Nor did I want Seamus or Dr. Aldridge to do so, who barely knew her.

I slowly peeled back the sheet. Part of me deliriously hoped that somehow she had reverted to look as she once did: beautiful, intact, smoothly carved as porcelain.

She was as I'd seen her underwater, though now her hair lay in two thick strands over her shoulders. I grabbed a handkerchief from my coat pocket and quickly laid it over her eyes.

Bile rose from my stomach to my mouth, and I felt as though I was again in the lake, swallowing the water, and I suppressed a gag, putting a hand to my throat.

I heard "Aurelia!" from a distance, as if I were underwater, and Seamus were on land, above the surface, calling my name.

I wanted to pull my gaze from the wrinkled, white, bloated flesh of her hands, her feet, her face, but I could not look away. I'd seen flesh like this before, waterlogged. I shook my head to clear the old memory.

Dr. Aldridge pointed to her neck, her ankles. Where the ropes had been were mottled red-and-purple lines. But there was something else—the beginning of a cut in her neck, on the right side.

"Help me turn her," Dr. Aldridge said to Seamus. They gently rolled her corpse to the side. My hand shook as I held the lantern high. The garish light illuminated a slashing from the right front of her slender neck, around the side, just to the back.

Rosita's neck had been cut before she was lowered into the water.

"A slash like this would leave blood, enough that it would be hard to clean up," Seamus said. "Surely she would have cried out, someone would have heard if it had happened inside. She must have been murdered somewhere out on the island. By now, finding the exact spot will be impossible."

As Seamus and Dr. Aldridge returned Rosita to her back, I pulled my gaze back to the bloated flesh. "She's been in the water for at least two days. Maybe since sometime in the late hours of Wednesday night, or early Thursday morning," I heard myself saying, my voice distant and flat. "But like Joey she would have bled out quickly. At least she didn't drown." Relief surged through me. I could not imagine a worse way to die.

Suddenly Eddie grabbed my arm, whirled me around. I nearly dropped the lantern as he shook me. "How do you know?" His coldness had broken, and he was screaming. "That she's been down there—that it's been two days? How can you know that?"

I couldn't give him the full truth. I'd never told anyone since leaving my childhood home in southeast Ohio. Certainly not Pony. Not even Rosita, in our closest days. I could barely whisper the truth to myself, though the truth whispered itself to me night after night.

I offered a partial truth. "I—I've seen a person before, a few days after they drowned. They looked like, like—"

"Like Rosita!" Anguish twisted Eddie's voice, his emotion at last coming out. His spittle hit my face as he screamed, but I dared not flinch or look away.

"Yes," I said, my voice raspy. "But if she'd been alive when she was tied up, her hands free, she would have been grabbing for anything, the dock posts, the rope at her neck." I looked at Dr. Aldridge. "Even after being in the water, wouldn't we see scratches at her neck, splinters under her nails?"

"Yes," he said quietly. "Warm water would decompose a body more quickly, but in this cold water, this is the expected state. Blood from the gash in her neck would have drawn the fish to her, speeding up the process, and—"

Seamus cleared his throat pointedly. Dr. Aldridge quieted. Eddie released me, turned away.

Eddie shuddered, but there was relief in his voice. "She didn't drown. She . . . she always feared drowning. I used to tease her about that, about wanting to be on an island, when she wasn't a good swimmer. And she'd say I didn't understand, the fear keeping her on the island was part of the appeal . . . She was right. I didn't understand . . ."

Eddie watched as Dr. Aldridge pulled the sheet back over Rosita.

"She was already dead, you know," Eddie said wretchedly. "She died of a broken heart over a year ago."

CHAPTER 23

EDDIE'S WORDS REVERBERATED in my head as I hurried away from the pool house and toward the mansion, a gray silhouette behind a white curtain of snow. I lowered my head, forcing myself forward against the wind.

This was an early winter storm, so surely it was a temporary squall. But my heart clenched at the possibility that it might rage on long enough that the *Myra* would be locked in by freezing water around the perimeter of the island.

I moved as quickly as my weary legs would allow, as if I could outrun the image of Rosita's corpse, the terrible tone of Eddie's voice. He was right. Rosita had been hot-tempered, mercurial, even conniving. But she'd also had a zest for life, a fierce love for those she held dear.

After Oliver died, she was different. Cold. Remote. Hard.

The warmth of the vestibule hit me as I entered, making me catch my breath. My glasses fogged up. I shut the door behind me, tucked my gloves in my coat pocket, took off my glasses, wiped the wetness—snow and tears—from my face.

Upstairs in my room, Largo squawked loudly. I opened her cage and gestured to my shoulder. She flew several times around the room before perching on my shoulder. She butted her head into my cheek, and I gave her a gentle stroke.

I muttered, "Pretty girl."

"Pretty girl," she said back.

In spite of everything, that made me smile as always.

As I petted her, though, my gaze darted as if compelled to the bell from Rosita's room, its cut rope.

Seamus had pointed out that Rosita was most likely killed outside of the mansion. And yet . . . why go to the trouble of taking her outside? Why not shoot her, leave the gun by her hand? Force her to take an overdose of her Veronal? Dose her tea or her food? After all, I'd left her tray outside her suite.

The cutting of her neck suggested action in the heat of the moment. Not a calculated killing.

But then—why the dramatic staging? Why not just dump her body in the lake? Weigh it down so it wouldn't rise again?

Because someone wanted to set you up as the killer.

I'd already sorted out that both Eddie and Marco had financial motives, as Rosita's death made the sale of the island easier.

But Eddie wouldn't kill Rosita himself. He'd have Cormac do it. Or Marco would have had Joey dispatch her.

Either Cormac or Joey would have needed help to tie up Rosita's body.

Would Cormac have asked Joey? And then kill him so he couldn't blab later?

Or, more likely, Cormac would have gotten help from one of Eddie's other hired hands.

Liam or Seamus.

Who might Joey have asked for help? I thought back to the tense exchange I'd witnessed in the hallway between Joey and Douglas. Would Douglas have been so angered that Rosita wasn't willing to help him with his movie that he would have helped Joey?

Or might Douglas himself have killed Rosita, then asked Joey for help with tying up Rosita's body?

My stomach turned at these thoughts, especially about Seamus.

But I had to look at the facts.

And the most likely killer was Cormac; the most likely accomplice, Seamus.

He could have witnessed me finding that treasure, tying it up under the dock. I'd been so focused on my supposedly lucky haul that I might not have noticed him. After all, I'd been startled by his presence on the path that morning as I ran back to the mansion, to Rosita. And though we'd exchanged flirtatious glances in the past few months, it was only after Eddie's arrival that he'd started paying more serious attention to me. Bringing me that sandwich. And he'd found my suitcase so easily in the cottage. Maybe he'd been keeping an eye on me, guessed that I'd try to leave. He could have followed me, watched as I discovered Rosita's body.

But then I remembered that first night in the music room, when Rosita said she had something to ruin Eddie. Everyone looked shocked—except Seamus. His expression had been carefully blank.

What if he was working with Rosita?

What if Seamus was a Fed? Working for the Bureau of Prohibition?

In Eddie's world, we were always wary of newcomers, who could be undercover cops trying to find anything to bring down a major gang like Eddie's, make a name for themselves. Or who could be informants for the government, or even for other gangs.

I'd seen Pony come home bloody and high on not just drugs or alcohol, but also from the excitement of being one of the goons who punished anyone thought to be disloyal. He'd grin and say, *We roughed him up good.* It always turned my stomach, made me want to run away from him, but where would I have gone? I knew I couldn't go back home to the farm where I grew up in southeast Ohio. And as I discovered shortly after arriving in Toledo, I didn't have skills that were in demand. I didn't have any money. So I thought I had no choice but to keep my expression carefully blank and tend to Pony's wounds, wondering if the other guy had even survived the altercation. My guess was that he hadn't.

On the other hand, Seamus could be a Fed who'd flipped to work the other side. After all, Cormac had been a cop. Feds could be bought, too.

In the world of men like Eddie and Marco, allegiances were as murky as the lake when dirt stirred at the shore. Constantly shifting like its surface.

Sorrow gripped me as I returned Largo to her cage. I needed to remember that I couldn't trust anyone on the island until I knew what had really happened to Rosita and Joey.

I didn't mind so much that I couldn't trust Eddie and his entourage. But I also couldn't trust Seamus or Liam, or Maxine or Henry. People I cared about—yet knew very little about.

I petted Largo one more time before I closed her door.

"We're all alone, pretty girl," I said.

"Pretty girl," she squawked.

This time, I didn't smile. I blinked back tears.

Then sternly told myself that I had work to do.

I TUCKED SEVERAL extra hairpins in my hair. I needed to go back up to the suite, pick my way in. See if I could spot Rosita's coat, hat, shoes. If they were missing, that would tell me that she'd left the mansion of her own volition, perhaps to meet someone. Or it might mean that at least whoever had forced her to leave had been thoughtful enough to let her cover up. And after killing her, the murderer could have tossed the items in the lake.

While I was up there, I'd search the dresser in Oliver's nursery. Maybe I'd get really lucky and find whatever it was she'd hidden away that would incriminate Eddie. If I could discover that Seamus really was an undercover Fed, we could find a way to work together.

I could be free at last.

And maybe, maybe Seamus and I . . .

But I couldn't allow myself the luxury of such fantasies. Flights of fancy had gotten me into enough trouble in the past.

And even if somehow we did end up together, I'd have to live with hiding from him the truth that I'd killed my first husband. If Seamus was who I wanted him to be, who I hoped he was, he wouldn't be able to just overlook that.

CHAPTER 24

I STEPPED OUT of my room and walked softly toward the stairway to the third floor.

But then I heard the front door burst open, the frenzied voices of Seamus and Henry.

"We need the doctor!"

I rushed to the top of the sweeping staircase and saw Seamus and Henry entering, a whirl of snow and wind behind them. Henry was bowed over, leaning into Seamus.

I rushed to fetch Dr. Aldridge from his room.

He didn't answer my knock or calls at first. It was only when I began pounding on the door that the doctor finally opened it an inch. He was disheveled and clearly did not want me to see inside. Bleary-eyed though he was, he seemed to understand the gravity of the situation. He emerged after a few moments with his medical bag.

We found Seamus and the Carmichaels in their room, Seamus kneeling before Henry, trying to ease a shoe from Henry's foot. He'd already taken one off, and I noted that its sole was pulling away from the rest of the sodden shoe.

"Been meaning to cobble these back together before winter," Henry said. "But this storm whipped up outta nowhere."

"His feet are swelling pretty badly," Seamus said quietly.

Maxine nodded, tears springing to her eyes.

"I just need a few minutes." Henry started shivering. "I want to help to dig her grave."

As Seamus finished working off the shoe, I had to fight back a gasp at how darkened and swollen Henry's foot was, nearly twice as thick as it should be.

Dr. Aldridge cleared his throat. "That's frostbite. I can help—"

Maxine leapt up. "No!" Her voice and chin trembled. "We don't need your help!"

Dr. Aldridge did not seem surprised by Maxine's outcry. How had the Carmichaels and the doctor known one another, I wondered, and why did Maxine so bitterly dislike the man?

"Your husband needs medical attention, and I'm the only doctor available. It's important to treat the frostbite properly—"

"Maxine, he's right," Seamus said gently. "I saw men with frostbite in the war. We don't want Henry to lose his toes, or worse."

"Darlin', I'm already gimped up enough," Henry said, and held up his maimed hand.

Maxine dropped her head and sighed. She moved to the chair next to Henry.

Dr. Aldridge cleared his throat. "Get some damp and warm but not hot cloths," he told me. "He needs to warm up and have bed rest."

Seamus put a comforting hand on Henry's shoulder. "We'll finish the grave. And Liam and I will finish the coffin."

I hurried to the kitchen and prepared wet, lukewarm cloths and a tray of hot tea and shortbread. By the time I returned to the Carmichaels' room, Dr. Aldridge and Seamus were gone, and Henry was dressed in clean, dry clothes, settled back into his chair, his outer clothes already put away. Maxine was spreading the tan-and-brown quilt over his lap. She quickly finished and grabbed the cloths from the tray and wrapped them around his feet.

"Why do you dislike and distrust the doctor so much?" I blurted out.

At that, Maxine's face closed, as surely as a slammed door, as it had when she said she and Henry could never leave. She and Henry exchanged a look. "That's a story for another time," she said firmly.

I knew they'd prefer I'd let the matter drop, but I had more questions. Equally difficult ones. I'd need to ease into them.

I touched the beautiful quilt draped over Henry, studying again the mesmerizing pattern of abstract paws. "This quilt," I said. "It's so lovely. My mother and grandmother made quilts, but nothing like this. Did you make this or inherit it from your mother?"

Maxine looked at Henry, who nodded. *With this, we can trust her.*

"I made it with my mother when I was a little girl. It's based on her grandmother's memory of a quilt she saw hanging outside a cottage on a clothesline," Maxine said.

I regarded her, confused. There seemed to be unspoken import to what she was saying, but I didn't understand. Maxine smiled gently. "Back in 1852. As my grandmother—and others from the plantation in Alabama—came north."

Oh. Maxine's ancestors and Henry's, too, would have been slaves. Maxine was saying that her grandmother came north to escape to freedom on the Underground Railroad.

Maxine pointed at the design inside the square. "This is a bear paw. It meant, follow the bear tracks north toward Canada. Stay away from the main road."

"There was . . . a code?" I asked with wonderment. "In the quilt that she saw?"

Maxine nodded. "In many quilts. A log cabin meant you could find safe, hidden shelter. Flying geese meant, follow the northerly direction of the geese in spring."

I traced my fingers along the fine stitching. "What a treasure," I said, honored that they'd chosen it to warm me earlier that day.

I cleared my throat. "The night Rosita went missing, the last time anyone but me saw her was around ten P.M. That's when she left the music room. You and I, Maxine, came down here to clean up, and you left around half past ten. Do you remember what we talked about?" *I know how to run boats, at least good enough to get us from here to Toledo. And I have some money. We can all start over . . .*

Now Maxine directly met my gaze. "I do remember," she said.

"Did you see anyone when you left the kitchen?"

Maxine shook her head. I cut my eyes quickly to Henry, and back to Maxine. Honesty and openness filled their expressions. "Or tell anyone what I said?"

She again shook her head.

Had Maxine somehow found out that my money was in fact a treasure? Did she know where it was? Know I'd seek it before leaving?

What if they had some reason for wanting Rosita to be dead?

I glanced around their room as an awful idea cracked open, doused me with its horridness. Could my lockbox be here?

Or the murder weapon that had pierced Rosita's slender neck? Joey's thigh? There were plenty of knives in the kitchen, knives that Henry kept well-sharpened.

Henry started dozing off. Maxine took his cigarette from him, tamped it out, returned his lighter to his pocket. Then she gently worked on switching the cloths on his feet.

I pressed on, forcing my voice to remain steady. "I last saw Rosita shortly after midnight. I saw Claire briefly after that. When did the men leave the casino?"

Maxine moved to the chair across the tiny table from me. "That's about when Henry came back to our room."

"Did you hear anything at all in the hallway? Any details you can recollect, even if they don't seem important, might be worthwhile."

"Well," Maxine said, "we heard Liam and Seamus coming back to their rooms. Seamus was helping Liam. He was rambling on about how he loved a woman, but she didn't love him back, he feared—someone from his past fancy archaeological digs, we reckoned. Although, I did see him eyeing Claire, and looking a mite jealous when she poured her attention onto Douglas." She shook her head. "That boy sounded pitiful. But Seamus helped him back to his room—then went on to his. That was just before two."

My cheeks brightened as I took another sip of my tea. Seamus hadn't gone on to his room; he'd come to mine. And he'd managed to quietly go up the stairs without making enough noise to alert the Carmichaels.

"And the rest?"

"We heard them about two thirty," Maxine said. "Well, I did. Henry was fast asleep and I'd drifted off, but they made enough of a racket that I stirred and looked at the clock." She nodded toward the Big Ben alarm clock on their bedside table.

"So leaving the casino would have been Eddie, Cormac, Marco, Joey, Dr. Aldridge, and Douglas?"

Maxine snorted. "They sounded like a pack of drunken dogs. Probably at least three of them. Maybe all six. Though Douglas didn't seem too keen to go to the casino, so he might have slipped by quietly."

I'd gleaned all I could from Maxine. On the night Rosita went missing, everyone had been to bed by shortly after two thirty—unless, of course, one or two of the men leaving the casino hadn't gone directly to bed. Had instead gone upstairs to Rosita's suite.

By then, I'd cut the rope between the bell in my bedroom and the handle in Rosita's. She could not have rung for help. And I'd been so enraptured by Seamus, I would not have heard the tread of footsteps from the second to the third floor, or the door to the stairwell, right by my room, opening.

Had Seamus sincerely followed his desire in coming to my room?

Or had he merely played the role of distractor for me as his criminal partner crept up the steps?

I took a deep breath. "I know we all believe Rosita stayed in her suite for the past year. But if she were going to leave the mansion, it would be through the kitchen door." Anyone looking out the front of the mansion could easily spot her, but the trees behind the mansion were allowed to grow as a way to obscure the water tower. It would be easier to sneak away through that exit. "And I'm guessing if you can hear goings-on in the casino on the other end of the hall, you could hear if someone came or went through the kitchen door? It squeaks a great deal."

"We always lock that door at night. And it locks automatically if it shuts behind you."

I nodded. I'd gone out that door a few times when I first arrived, forgetting to prop the door with a brick, then found myself locked out and having to traipse around to the front door. Embarrassing.

"Only someone with a full set of keys could come back in from the outside. So yes, technically, Rosita could have left, then come back. Only she and Henry have full sets of keys to the mansion."

CHAPTER 25

I STEPPED OUT into the hallway, about to quietly head back up to Rosita's suite to pick the lock. But I glanced down the hallway. This was a chance to search Liam's and Seamus's rooms.

For my missing lockbox—unless, if Liam was the culprit, he might simply return it to the stash on the *Myra*.

For a murder weapon.

Additionally, in Seamus's case, something that would tell me whether or not he was a Fed. A Bureau of Prohibition badge, tucked in a drawer? Under a loose floorboard?

Hesitancy slithered over my skin like a snake. I'd lived for the past year and a half blithely unaware of why the Carmichaels and Liam were on Trouble Island, for the past few months not knowing much about Seamus except that he attracted me as surely and steadily as the waves surged on the shoreline.

And now, in just a few days, I saw them all as possible murderers.

I chose to go first to Liam's room, partly because I found the notion of considering Seamus as a killer to be too heartbreaking, but mostly because I was still curious about Liam's absence from his duties on the morning Eddie arrived and wanted more information about the lockboxes he'd been moving onto the *Myra*. Could either be connected to Rosita going missing—and then turning up murdered?

His cot was perfectly made up, the dresser top holding only a hairbrush and a cup with a toothbrush. I reckoned that in the dresser drawers, I'd find his underclothes and socks all perfectly folded and lined up, and in the wardrobe, his shirts and pants on hangers arranged by color. There were three hooks on the wall; one held a bathrobe, the other a rain jacket, and the third was empty—reserved, I guessed, for the coat he was currently wearing outside.

There were no photos or knickknacks, but there was a bookshelf filled with titles all pertaining to ancient history or archaeology. Another bookshelf next to it held an array of items labeled with handwritten notes: on the bottom shelf, fossils of shells and teeth in rocks—brachiopods, mastodon tooth; on the middle shelf, bits from long-ago lives—an arrowhead, a hollow tube identified as a ceremonial pipe; on the top shelf, shards of pottery, a stone hook, and a polished stone roughly oval in shape, with a hole pierced at the edge. An ancient pendant?

But what really caught my eye were the handwritten notes. The letters were carefully formed, almost like typeset lettering, and I thought of the note that Rosita had supposedly left for Eddie. Was the lettering similar, or was that my imagination? And if I took one of the notes, how long would it be before Liam noticed it missing? I wasn't sure how I'd get the note, supposedly from Rosalita, to compare the handwriting, but I reached for the note that was beside the pendant—

"Please don't touch anything."

At the same time that I jumped at Liam's voice, I closed my hand in a fist, crumpling the note. I jammed my hands in my pockets, turned, and expected to see Liam scowling, but his expression was as quietly bland as usual.

"I'm glad to see you're interested in my work," Liam said. He took off his hat, placed it neatly on the end of his bed, and removed his coat, which he put on the empty hook. His fine, blond hair matted to his head, and his face was flushed from windburn. "Usually people seem bored when I start to tell them about the interesting things I find in my digs."

Did Liam really believe I'd come into his room out of sudden curiosity about his interest in archaeology? He had told us that he was an archaeologist, and he was excavating artifacts from ancient people who had once lived here. He sometimes went on at length about the tools he found, the methods of digging he used. We all listened politely enough, but I'd dismissed the notion of Liam as an archaeologist as a fantasy of his. Why in the world would Eddie want an archaeologist in his employ, and why would an archaeologist want to be beholden to Eddie? But now, seeing the carefully displayed collection, I realized that Liam was interested in archaeology. I still questioned whether he really had been an archaeologist before coming here. People, after all, can believe all kinds of things about themselves, no matter if they're objectively true.

"Actually, I came in because I—I thought I heard a scampering sound," I lied. "We can't have mice in the mansion."

Liam looked alarmed and glanced protectively at the shelf behind me. "Oh no, I can't have them knocking anything off!"

My cheeks started to flush. Maybe if he saw the pendant note missing, he'd think a mouse had knocked it to the floor. I imagined Liam desperately looking for the note under the bed or dresser and felt a pang of guilt. "I'll have Henry set some mousetraps," I said. "Um, Liam, are you doing all right?"

He turned his gaze to me, a confounded look in his eyes. "Well, I am cold, and I need to go to the bathroom, which is why I came inside."

I smiled a little at Liam's usual literal interpretation. "I just meant, the past few days have been so shocking. Rosita's death, of course, but even before that, the surprise arrival of Eddie and everyone else."

Liam's expression remained blank. And then, as if realizing what he was supposed to say, he stated flatly, "Oh yes. That was quite unexpected."

I nodded, even as I thought, *Not unexpected to Liam.* How had he known Eddie would arrive a few days ago? A message delivered by one of the last guests? Had he been away from his duties that morning because he was preparing the lockboxes for transfer?

My skin prickled as the hairs on my neck and arms went up. I wanted out of that room. "You know, I think I'll go get those mousetraps myself—" I started.

Then Claire's screaming voice carried from the top floor.

"Eddie, please stop!"

UPSTAIRS, I STOOD panting in the second-floor hallway after sprinting up two long flights of stairs.

Claire was still screaming at Eddie in her room. Drawers slammed. Douglas and Dr. Aldridge had come out of their rooms and stared. But they didn't make a move to Claire's door.

Cowards, I thought, and gave them a withering look.

Or maybe, since they were unarmed and Eddie was not, they were just cautious.

But I couldn't stand to hear Claire's pleading cries. I'd wailed like that with Pony. And even before that, in my childhood home. I knew what it felt like to dissolve into feral fear and yet have enough of my humanity left to realize that no one was coming to save me. The heartbreaking feeling of betrayal, of hopelessness.

Suddenly, Claire was silent. And I knew that was worse.

I rushed into her bedroom.

Eddie had slammed her against the wall, both hands around her throat. Her feet dangled off the ground by a few inches. She stared at him, her eyes bugging. She gagged, an awful gurgling sound, the tip of her tongue darting in and out.

I knew, too, what that felt like. The sudden, choking inability to breathe. The hopeless gasps at trying anyway. Seeing the eyes of the person who you thought cared about you, cold and cruel, as they tried to choke the life out of you.

"Eddie," I said quietly, "let Claire go."

My eyes darted around for something, anything, that could serve as a weapon, startle him enough to make him release her. His gun was in his holster, and as soon as he released her, he'd probably grab it and shoot me.

Yet slowly my hand closed around the heavy bronze stem of a bedside lamp. Claire's eyes shifted to me and I shook my head, not wanting the change in her focus to draw his attention, ruin the moment's surprise I had on my side. She looked back at him.

"She's too loud," Eddie said.

"Just let her go." I stepped forward, feeling the taut pull of the lamp's cord.

Eddie pressed harder. Claire gagged.

"Eddie," I said. "Do you really want to have to explain her death? She may not be famous yet in Hollywood, but she's known."

"She can go over the boat's side. Like Joey."

"The more bodies, the more questions," I said. "Besides, what if she's Rosita's killer? Don't you want to wait, exact justice later? Wouldn't that be more satisfying?"

Claire struggled to shake her head, but that just made her gag harder.

I was about to pull the lamp the rest of the way from the wall, when Eddie suddenly let Claire go. She collapsed. Quickly, I pushed the lamp back to its spot on the side table. Eddie looked amused as Claire scrabbled away from him.

I helped her up, sat with her on the edge of the bed, put my arm around her.

She opened her mouth and I expected her to protest that of course she hadn't killed her cousin. But, her voice sounding like she'd swallowed thorns, she said, "All my beautiful things, he's ruin-ing them."

That was what she cared about? I pulled my arm away. Scattered all over the floor were her clothes, jewelry, perfume bottles.

Eddie shrugged. "Half of this was on the floor before I came in."

"What are you looking for?" I asked.

"Murder weapon," he said.

I frowned. If he'd killed Rosita and Joey—or had Cormac do so—he wouldn't look for the weapon. He'd just stick to the plan to pin the murder on me. It was almost hard to believe that he had not orchestrated their murders. But perhaps that was just my bias, and he really was interested in finding the true killers?

Then he said, "And something else." For just a moment, his expression softened into a hint of vulnerability. "The note Rosita wrote me."

The last thing she'd written, the note she'd left for him to come see her.

Then his face rearranged back into its usual composition of hard planes and deep scowls. "Someone had the nerve to come into my room and take it."

But he'd have kept his room locked, since he had a room key.

I must not be, I thought, *the only skilled lockpick in the mansion.*

If he was telling the truth, why would someone risk coming to his room, taking the note?

Unless that someone thought Eddie had gotten from Rosita whatever evidence she had against him.

Seamus.

Or maybe Eddie was using the pretense of a stolen note, of look-ing for a weapon, to find that evidence.

"I can help you," I said suddenly. Distrust flashed across his eyes. I felt Claire turn, look at me. "Search, I mean. I'm also interested in finding the murder weapon." After all, if we found it in someone else's possession, that would clear me as a murderer. And yet, my stomach turned at the possibility it could be one of my workmates. "And it will go much faster if you have someone helping," I went on. "Or, you could call in Cormac to help. Of course, that will just delay digging Rosita's grave. With the earth frozen, it might be impossible. Her body would then also have to go into the lake—and then there goes your evidence she's dead and not missing—or just be left out to freeze in the pool house. Let's hope the bear or small creatures—mice, chipmunks—"

Claire shuddered as Eddie snapped at me, "Enough! Take her and the others downstairs to the library. Tell Marco I said keep an eye on them. If they try to leave, shoot them." He grinned. "Just enough to maim them, of course."

Claire stopped suddenly in the doorway, said in her scratchy voice, "Why are you trusting her? What if she finds what you're looking for and doesn't tell you?"

I wanted to smack Claire for bringing this up, but she'd had enough hurt inflicted on her. I'd gone over the edge before, and I didn't want to be that person again.

"We will search each room together," I said. "I'm sure Eddie is wily enough to keep an eye on me. Right, Eddie?"

He puffed his chest up. He was thinking this dame, his dead wife's little friend, couldn't pull anything over on him. I'd learned so much from Rosita—including how to flatter at just the right time, with just the right pressure.

CHAPTER 26

BY THE TIME night fell, Eddie and I had gone through all the rooms in the mansion. All the bedrooms on the second floor, except his. He'd balked at searching Cormac's room, until, my heart beating at my boldness, I said, "Who can you trust, Eddie? Really trust?"

I felt like a snake of doubt, with my slithering, quiet question. But it worked. We searched Cormac's room, too.

And mine. I stood aside, keeping a watchful eye as Eddie went through my few things. When he was done, I felt like they were all tainted, although he didn't toss them around as he had Claire's items.

"Shouldn't we search Rosita's suite?" I'd asked.

"*Our* suite. And we already did. She couldn't take the note back from me after she was dead, now could she?" Eddie'd sneered as he said this. "And the murderer wouldn't leave the weapon there."

But searching for that note, and maybe even for the weapon, was pretense. He was really looking for whatever she had on him, and he'd already searched that room.

I was looking for that as well, plus my lockbox, the murder weapon, Rosita's keys. If someone had forced her out the back, they'd have needed those keys to get back in the mansion without alerting anyone.

We didn't find any of that.

At the end of our fruitless efforts, we parted without saying anything to one another.

I went directly to the kitchen and put together a simple meal of roasted chicken, mashed potatoes, and green beans, and for dessert, a bread pudding.

My workmates were quiet as they ate: Henry ashen, Maxine gazing at him with worry, Liam and Seamus exhausted. They'd come in several hours before from the outside and went right to work on Rosita's coffin under Henry's supervision in the storage and furnace room. I'd stepped in the room long enough to look at it while they cleaned up for dinner. It was simple, rough-hewn, but appeared airtight, and it was nearly done.

I carried trays of food up to the dining room for Eddie and the others. All of them were quiet as well, even Marco and Claire. The only conversation was at the beginning of dinner.

"It's done?" Eddie asked.

"Yes, sir." The exhaustion in Cormac's voice matched his weary expression. "Covered over with tarp. Snow is coming down hard."

Eddie gestured at an empty chair at the dining table, inviting Cormac to sit next to him for dinner. But I saw a wariness in Eddie's gaze as he regarded Cormac. I'd planted a seed of doubt in Eddie about his right-hand man.

After that, no one spoke. Each clink of spoon on bowl that I made, serving up potatoes and gravy, or sound of chewing and swallowing, seemed amplified in the cold silence.

Sounds drifted up from the basement below us: the rhythmic banging of a hammer. The faint yet steady grind of a saw through wood. Liam and Seamus finishing Rosita's coffin. Against the background of those sounds, the smacks and slurps of eating became grotesque. Cold and snowing though it was, I wished that I could be outside instead, hearing the whoosh of the wind, the occasional stirring of birds and animals, the constant thrum of the waves on the lake.

Eddie pulled out a cigar and lit it. I grabbed an ashtray and put it beside him. "Get me a whisky," he ordered. Then he looked at Douglas. "And you—go play something!"

Douglas strode to the adjoining music room. Within moments, a jazzy tune drifted into the dining room. But his playing was flat, rote. The usually snappy music rendered lifeless seemed almost worse than the sounds of coffin-making that it was meant to cover.

AN HOUR LATER, I was alone in the kitchen, cleaning dishes and cooking pans. Eddie and his entourage were all still upstairs. As I dried the pieces of silver and put them on the tray, already laden with china plates and crystal, I suddenly realized that other than the sounds of my own movements, the clink of silver, the kitchen was utterly silent.

A chill came over me as the silence took on significance. The hammering and sawing had stopped. Rosita's makeshift coffin, rough-hewn and unpolished though it was, was done.

I sat down, hard, on a kitchen chair. My body trembled. I wanted my workmates to come into the kitchen where we could comfort one another.

And yet . . . I didn't want them to come into the kitchen at all. If I discovered that one, or more, of them was guilty of Rosita's and Joey's murders, could I bear it? Bring myself to expose them as killers, knowing the fate they'd meet? And some would say that my penance on Trouble Island was not sufficient for killing Pony. For my past sins. My own conscience told me so on many a troubled, sleepless night.

Since coming to Trouble Island, I thought I'd been alone, so all alone.

But I had not. I'd been with Henry and Maxine and Liam through all of it, and with Seamus in the past few months. They had all been my true companions on Trouble Island, and I'd been too caught up in my guilt over what I'd done, too sorrowful over what I'd lost, too eager for Rosita's approval, to see it.

I'd been a fool. I'd betrayed them by working with Eddie to search their quarters earlier. I wanted to seek them out, beg their forgiveness, and be accepted again in their embrace.

For a wild moment, I wanted to run upstairs and confess to Eddie that yes, yes, I'd killed Rosita. Tied up her body, just out of cruelty. That I'd encountered Joey wandering through the mansion, that he began asking too many questions about why I was leaving and where I was going, and so I'd lured him outside, and then surprise attacked him with—what? A fishing knife I'd found in the cottage, the same one I'd used to kill Rosita?

I shook my head. Too many holes in that story, too many questions. And if I confessed, how would I know I was saving the Carmichaels, or Liam, or Seamus? Most likely, I'd be saving Eddie and Cormac or one of the others who'd come with them.

My ruminations were broken by the sounds of Marco and Eddie and Cormac coming down to the casino. Music started up on the record player—a different jaunty tune than Douglas had been playing. I waited until they sounded settled in, laughing at something, and then I picked up the heavy tray of china, crystal, and silver, and went upstairs.

CHAPTER 27

"AURELIA? IS THAT you?" Claire singsonged into the dining room from the music room. After hearing Eddie, Cormac, Dr. Aldridge, and Marco come down to the casino, I'd assumed that Douglas and Claire had gone up to their rooms.

I sighed. I just wanted to put away the dinnerware and then go to bed, though I knew I wouldn't sleep well. My head was spinning.

Claire persisted, "Aurelia! Come in here."

In the music room, Claire and Douglas sat on the couch close to each other, but not in a romantic way.

"Aurelia!" Claire exclaimed enthusiastically, as if she hadn't already called my name twice. "You can help us sort this out."

Douglas frowned, the lines startling in his usually smooth, handsome face. "Claire, I don't think we need to involve—"

"Oh, nonsense! Aurelia knew Rosita better than anyone, didn't you?"

I shifted uncomfortably from foot to foot. "I thought so, but—"

"Great! I think Rosita would love it if we threw a party in her memory, once we're back in Toledo." Claire plucked at Douglas's shirtsleeve. "Dougie will be quite the draw. We can do a few songs,

say how Rosita was eager to be in a movie with us before her un-
timely death—"

I sank down on the chair across from them. "But she wasn't. She—"

"Oh, no one needs to know that, Aurelia. It's all about how things
appear. The story we tell. So she was eager to be in our movie, and
now we're doing it—" Claire paused to switch her face from ani-
mated to morose. She forced tears and gave a big, fake sniffle. "In her
honor!" She immediately re-brightened. "Isn't that a brilliant idea?"

"No." The word, leaden with disgust, fell from my lips.

Douglas arched an eyebrow and gave me a half smile. "I knew I
liked you."

Claire flopped back against the couch, rolled her eyes. "Well,
Aurelia, thousands of girls would be jealous to know that the great
Douglas Johnson likes you."

Douglas snorted. "The *once*-great Douglas Johnson."

"Right!" Claire swatted his arm. "Which is why we needed Rosita's star power. But now that she's dead, why not use the moment—oh,
everyone will be so sorrowful!—to get some attention. Get in the
newspapers. Get noticed. Then Hollywood will have to give us a
chance."

I stared at her, dumbfounded. This was crass, even for Claire,
who'd never hesitated to ride Rosita's coattails in real life. Now she
would use Rosita's death for her gain if she could.

But I also realized that Claire's and Douglas's need for Rosita's
star power gave them powerful alibis. Unless one of them, incensed
that she'd sworn she wouldn't be in Douglas's film, killed her in a
moment of fury?

"And where will you have this attention-seeking shindig?" I
asked. "At Mr. McGee's Toledo mansion? I hardly think he'll agree
to that."

Claire crossed her arms over her stomach, rolling out her lower
lip like a petulant child. "But he promised. That's why he brought us
here, to lure Rosita back to her real life, so she'd give up the island

to Marco. You know, he's told me that Eddie's in way over his head financially with some heavy loans."

That confirmed what I'd overheard between Eddie and Marco, and I wanted to see if I could pry more details from Claire, but Douglas sighed. "Can't we just put aside our worries about the film for now? Remember Rosita as she was before—before—"

Tears—real ones, I noted—sprang to his eyes. I knew what he meant. Before Oliver.

Though, he was an actor.

Eddie hadn't said anything about a service for Rosita. Would he just have her put in the ground, no words spoken? Sorrow welled up and stuck in my throat. I should at least gather some winterberry and evergreen stems to make an arrangement for Rosita's gravesite.

I looked back at Douglas. "You're right. I only knew her a few years, but the two of you grew up with her. Someone should say a eulogy for her."

Claire's eyes widened. "Eddie hasn't requested that. What if he doesn't want—"

"To hell with that! It's only right. Claire, you could—"

"Oh, I just couldn't!" Another honking sniffle, more fake tears.

"What about you, Douglas? After all, you're used to—"

"What, acting?" he snapped. "I don't have to act. I loved Rosita."

"Well, as a friend," Claire said.

"Yes," Douglas said. "As a friend."

I focused on Douglas, asking softly, "What was she like?" Rosita had only rarely referenced her childhood. When she did, it was to talk about Trouble Island.

Douglas stared off. "She was quirky. Imaginative. She loved games of mystery—not just hide-and-seek, but also games she made up. And she was obsessed with this island. Talked about it all of the time, even when we were little."

Claire snorted. "Ain't that the truth! I came with Rosita because otherwise we'd spend the summer apart. And Grandfather was nice enough. But this island—it's always given me the creeps. Too remote. But she loved hiking in the woods. Making all those trails. Clearing them with Grandfather. Helping him take care of the lighthouse. Listening to his stories for hours about the island's history and shipwrecks. Which made her terrified of the lake itself, and yet she loved the stories and the island." Claire was teary-eyed again. This time, I thought, genuinely.

"Did you ever come here, Douglas?" I knew he hadn't as an adult. That would have made the gossip columns. "As a child?"

For the first time since he arrived, Douglas laughed, a lovely deep laugh, yet tinged with bitterness. "I would have loved to. Begged to, once. But no. Even though we were all on the wrong side of the tracks, my family was too low even for the Byrnes."

The biography I'd read of Douglas Johnson in the fan magazines was that he'd grown up modestly, yes, but as the son of a Methodist preacher, an only child, whose mother had died when he was young. Why wouldn't Claire and Rosita's parents have wanted him along?

Claire rolled her eyes again. "Yes, yes," she said in a mimicking tone, as if she'd heard this before, "Rosita's parents and mine were awful, awful people, even though they were very involved in the Catholic church in our neighborhood. And they didn't want the son of the neighborhood drunk—especially a boy—coming with us to the island."

"I thought your father was—"

"A preacher, beloved by his flock, raising his only son on his own after his wife tragically died in childbirth?" Now Douglas's voice took on a mocking strain. "Don't believe everything you read in the celebrity rags, kid," he said. He lit a cigarette, took a drag, crossed his legs, and gave me that trademark smile, complete with a twinkle in his eyes.

"What was the truth, then?"

"Why does it matter?"

"Well, she's a curious one, aren't you, Aurelia?" Claire said. "She was always asking us questions about our childhood, or Trouble Island, or what we thought about this or that, back when she and Rosita were friends, and she'd hang out by the pool." She smirked. "Irritated them to no end when I'd interrupt. I think that's why Rosita sent me off to Hollywood in the first place."

Douglas arched an eyebrow, gave me a curious look, and I realized he didn't know anything about me other than the same story everyone had been given for my presence on the island.

I cleared my throat, choosing my words carefully. I, too, had been telling tidied versions of my truth. At what point, I wondered, did cleaned-up truth become a wholly different truth—and thus a lie? But I wasn't about to confess my whole past to this man—or to Claire.

"I met Claire and Rosita at their first Sweetheart Cousins comeback performance. That was—" I paused, choking up on the memory of Oliver.

"About a year after Oliver was born," Claire jumped in, with no compunction. Disgust rose in me. Even when she'd come with Eddie and Rosita to the island to bury Oliver, she'd looked bored most of the time. Did she feel no sorrow for her nephew's death? "Eddie thought even then that if Rosita could rise to fame, that would be a path for him to eventually go legit." She shrugged. "That's what he wanted for Oliver." She gave me a hard look. "Did you know he blamed you for Rosita changing her mind about going back into performance?"

I frowned at her. "But Rosita told me that she didn't want that life. She wanted a quiet life—"

"And what about what I wanted, huh?" Claire exclaimed. "You took my place as her confidante, and encouraged her in this silly notion of a quiet life, which meant she wasn't willing to perform with me—"

"She and Eddie footed the bill for you to go to Hollywood!" I snapped.

Claire recoiled, hurt flashing across her face, and I immediately regretted my comment. About a year after Pony and I got caught up with the McGees, we were at their house for a Christmas party. Claire had gotten outrageously drunk, dancing around, flirting, laughing, and when other partygoers started to become uncomfortable and distance themselves from her, she'd opened Largo's cage. The bird, a Christmas gift for Oliver that Eddie had disapproved of, had flown out and escaped the house; little Oliver, then a few months shy of three, had run out after the bird. I'd spotted him darting outside, and I ran out after him, grabbing him just as he was about to get hit by an automobile zooming up the circular driveway. I'd carried the wailing toddler back inside, and somehow one of Eddie's men recaptured Largo.

Within a few weeks, Rosita had Largo's wings clipped. And then she sent Claire off to Hollywood to make it on her own, telling me she'd put her cousin in touch with their childhood friend Douglas Johnson, the heartthrob famous actor. That was the first time I learned that Rosita and Claire knew Douglas.

But, come to think of it, I hadn't heard much about Douglas in the press since then. A younger actor, Curtis Langly, had risen to prominence in the heartthrob magazines.

For the first time, I wondered if Claire arriving in Hollywood on the McGees' dime and wanting help from Douglas had any connection to Douglas's fading from popularity. No, surely it was coincidence.

"Well," Claire said, "my first trip to Hollywood didn't work out swell, but now, with Eddie's backing, even without Rosita, we can make a comeback." She leaned toward Douglas, twirled one of his dark curls in her index finger.

He swatted her hand as if it were a fly. "Or in your case, you can just make it for the first time," he said. "Unless what you really want is to again be a Girl Friday for producers and directors?"

Claire looked down, sipped her drink. So that's what she'd done with her time in Hollywood, before coming back after Oliver's death. I felt sorry for Claire, and decided to steer the conversation back to Douglas. I asked him, "So how did you become friends with Rosita and Claire, then?"

But Claire jumped in. "Remember how I said Rosita loved adventures, in the woods here? Well, she was no different in Toledo. She'd convince me to go along with her, to run off from our houses. But she was too wild for most of the kids in the neighborhood. She'd concoct some game—looking for pirate's treasure, like she said could be found on this damned island—though we never found any."

I shifted in my chair, as if its contours were making me uncomfortable, but the lockbox and its contents flashed before my eyes— followed by the image of Rosita's body.

"Or that we were on a safari. Or trekking up Kilimanjaro." Claire laughed. "Never mind that our streets in Toledo are as flat as pancakes."

"Rosita did have a grand imagination," Douglas said. "One day, she and Claire found me in the middle of a street fight."

And rescued him. I could see that. Rosita had commented once to me that she always had a soft spot for lost causes—a notion that made me uncomfortable then as it did now. I'd wanted to be her friend, not a pet project. Maybe Douglas had felt the same way.

A thin smile tweaked Douglas's lips. "Oh, I can see you're thinking what most people would—jumping to the conclusion that I needed rescuing. No. It was the other kid who did. I'd learned how to give a beating by getting plenty of them from my father. And the kid had called me—well, it didn't matter what he called me—I wasn't going to stand for it."

"I thought we should go back home," Claire said, "but Rosita jumped into the fray."

Now tears glistened in Douglas's eyes. "Rosita grabbed me by the collar, pulled me from the kid, and slapped me—hard. She shouted at me—'Stop being a bully!'" He chuckled. "From that moment, I knew we'd be friends."

My eyebrows went up. "That made you like her?"

Douglas nodded. "She was . . . a force."

Claire went to the sideboard to refill her glass with whisky. "Only Rosita could pull that off." She took a sip, and twirled, pointed at Douglas, her hand shaking. "She was smitten with you." She turned to me, mimicked Rosita's lower register. "After that, it was always, 'We have to go see Douglas. Douglas will love the new game I've come up with! I've saved some biscuits for Douglas . . .'"

"You stayed close until Eddie came along and stole Rosita's heart?" I said to Douglas.

"It wasn't like that. Rosita and I were good friends. She understood me. And I understood her. At least, I thought I did, until I heard she was marrying Eddie. I never understood what she saw—" He shook his head. "Not jealousy. Concern. Eventually, I went on—found my own way in Hollywood. We all just drifted apart."

Had they, though? Or had they remained close, and Eddie had not liked that?

"No, you drifted away," Claire said. "And after all she did for us!" She looked at me. "She got us gigs, the 'Sweetheart Cousins,' so we could leave my parents' house—" Claire paused, a look of terror passing over her face. I wondered what horrors had driven the cousins away. "—and have our own apartment. Our independence. It was going brilliantly, until Dougie here abandoned us!"

"I went to Hollywood," he said flatly. "I told everyone I was going. It wasn't a secret. And besides, by then Rosita was dating Eddie."

"And Dougie became a big famous star and forgot about us!"

"I wrote—"

"To Rosita!"

He didn't try to deny it. "Yes, for a while, and then, well, life got busy."

"Busy?" Claire snorted. "Rosita told me you wrote to her that you had to cut things off. Your career couldn't afford being associated openly with a man like Eddie, a man in his business." She looked at me. "He meant bootlegger. Gangster. Mob. Thug. Too many people getting killed in the streets in the crossfire." Her voice had gone slushy, and was teetering toward resentful.

I said, "But you came to Trouble Island with Claire, hoping to get Rosita to start a new life in a film with you after all." If Douglas thought so negatively about Eddie, he surely didn't come just as a favor to him. "What changed?"

"I felt really badly about Oliver. I should have reached out, but I didn't."

Claire and I exchanged looks. We understood that sure, Douglas would have felt badly about Oliver, but that also wasn't his reason for coming on this visit.

And then something quick flashed in Claire's eyes, something she wanted me to understand. Our gaze held for a second, but I couldn't pick up on what she was trying to tell me, and a twitch of a frown crossed my brow. Claire looked down, disappointed.

Douglas cleared his throat. "And then Eddie reached out to me. He sent a, ah, representative to tell me that he needed my help, he said, to get Rosita to let go of the island, to get back to her original love of performance."

Something didn't sit right with me. How long had it been since I'd seen Douglas in the movie magazines? Mentioned as top billing in a film? Even before I'd come to Trouble Island, I'd stopped seeing his name plastered across the covers of the magazines.

"He needed your help? Or you needed his?" I asked.

"Look, I have been taking a bit of a break, it's true. For personal reasons. But I'm ready to get back, and yes, I could use Eddie's help, just as he could use ours. What of it? We needed Rosita's help—" He stopped, blanching, realizing the grotesqueness of what he'd just implied. That they'd only come for selfish reasons, not out of any genuine concern for Rosita.

Claire snorted. "Aurelia is just trying to save her own skin, asking all these questions, trying to dig up something to put the blame on anyone but her. But we're in the clear, right? Because why would we want Rosita out of the picture? We needed her to get a fresh start in Hollywood."

Unlike Douglas, Claire didn't appear to have any shame at her admission that needing to use Rosita was her big alibi.

"Rosita also turned you both down flat, in front of everyone, that first night," I said. "I saw how upset both of you were. And anger is a powerful motivator. It can lead someone to—"

Claire sneered, and I stuttered to a stop. I wondered—did she know? How anger and fear and self-defense had led me to kill my own husband? Had Rosita told her? Rosita swore she never told anyone. But then, Claire had been her confidante before I came along. Maybe after I came to Trouble Island, Claire had become her confidante once again, until Oliver's death.

I pressed on. "It can lead someone to do . . . the unthinkable. Did either of you go up to Rosita's suite, any time after midnight the first night you were here?"

Claire barked out a laugh. "What, you think we snuck up? Forced her out of her suite, and brutally killed her? Strapped up her body in such a cruel way?" She plucked at Douglas's hair again. "That's not our way, is it, Dougie? We'd have poisoned her, made it look like suicide."

Douglas recoiled, and both of us inhaled sharply.

Claire rolled her eyes. "Oh come on, I don't mean that. But no, we didn't kill her. Or at least, I didn't. How about you, Dougie?"

Douglas dropped his head to his hands. "Of course not."

"I was thinking," I said, "more along the lines that you might have gone up there, either together or separately, to plead your case about being in the film. Might have overheard someone else in her suite? Maybe someone you've been afraid to mention?"

Douglas looked up, shook his head. "No. I went straight to my room after we all left the casino. I was exhausted, and in any case, I wouldn't bother pleading with Rosita. It wouldn't have made a difference. Once she made her mind up about something, she didn't budge."

Claire stared down into her glass, swishing around the liquid. "And you saw me as I was coming out of the bathroom. I was a bit drunk, and ill, and went to bed after that. Slept through the night until Eddie woke us up."

Yes, I had seen her, and I could believe she was so drunk that she'd passed out in her room. Yet her tone was so uncustomarily meek that it raised the hair on the back of my neck.

Suddenly, Maxine burst into the music room, panicked and out of breath. "I—I'm looking for the doctor. He's not in the casino—it's Henry! He just fell to the floor, saying his heart was seizing up. He needs help!"

CHAPTER 28

I FOUND DR. Aldridge sprawled across his bed, snoring, still fully clothed in his suit and shoes and tie, smelling of alcohol. A bottle of pills—Veronal—were knocked over on the end table. The pills were scattered around a small silver-framed photo. A quick glance revealed a photo of a young man who resembled Dr. Aldridge, along with a young woman and two small boys. The doctor's son, daughter-in-law, grandsons?

Curious—the doctor had never referenced a family of his own—but that didn't matter in the moment. I shook him, shouted his name. When he finally came around and sat up, he was so glassy-eyed that I wasn't sure he saw me, though his gaze was directed right at me.

"If you want to redeem yourself for whatever you've done to make the Carmichaels hate you," I said, "now is the time. Henry needs you!"

Shock passed over his face. He wobbled to his feet and grabbed his medical bag.

Minutes later, Dr. Aldridge hovered over Henry, who lay still on the bed in the Carmichaels' room. Though the doctor was glassy-eyed as he leaned over Henry, his hands were perfectly steady as he put a stethoscope to Henry's chest.

Henry lay back, his eyes closed. Maxine sat on the edge of the bed, her hands intertwined with his, her expression pinched with worry, yet also suffused with devotion.

This, I thought, is what love looks like. Quiet, tender, and true, even in the hardest of times.

Finally, Dr. Aldridge straightened. "His heart rate is irregular. But not as alarming as it could be. He needs plenty of bed rest." He regarded Maxine. "You said he complained of chest pain?"

"I'm still here," Henry muttered. "And yes. Felt like someone reached in and grabbed my heart and gave it a good squeeze. Or a bad squeeze." I'd been blinking back tears ever since I'd come into the room, but now I held back a smile. Henry still had his sense of humor—that had to be a good sign, I told myself.

"But it still hurts?" the doctor asked.

"Yes."

"I can give you morphine for the pain, and a sedative, Veronal."

"No, no," Maxine said, shaking her head. "I don't want Henry taking anything like that."

Dr. Aldridge gave Maxine a tired look. "Mrs. Carmichael. The treatment I'm suggesting is the standard protocol. It's what any doctor would recommend."

Henry gave Maxine's hand a squeeze. "It will be all right. I want to take it."

Maxine sighed. Then gave a curt nod.

The doctor put his stethoscope back in his leather bag and removed a bottle of morphine and a syringe.

IN THE KITCHEN a short time later, Maxine sat at the table, shifting restlessly in her chair. We heard Eddie, Marco, and Cormac in the casino, laughing and gabbing, the record player on full blast, unaware of the drama playing out just down the hall.

I thought about letting Eddie know. He had history with Henry, seemed to care about him. And Seamus and Liam. But they were likely sound asleep after a long, hard day, and there was nothing they could do for Henry or Maxine.

"I should be with Henry," Maxine said.

"He's asleep," I reminded her. He'd drifted off quickly after the drugs were administered, and Dr. Aldridge had left. Maxine had pulled the Underground Railroad quilt smoothly up to Henry's chin. Then she'd sat down next to him and I knew she'd stay like that all night, disregarding her own needs. I'd nagged her until she came with me to the kitchen, where I'd then insisted she sit down while I made her a ham sandwich. She'd barely nibbled the corners.

I got out a plate and filled it with pieces of Henry's shortbread, one of the few items he baked.

Sure enough, as I sat down, Maxine pushed away the sandwich, picked up a piece of shortbread, and took a bite.

She gave me an appraising look. "I doubt you've eaten today, either."

I had to smile at that. Maxine was always watching out for me. I helped myself to a piece of Henry's shortbread, too. It was buttery and delicious, melting in my mouth.

After we finished our treats, I said, "I'm glad you let Dr. Aldridge help Henry."

"You're still wondering why I don't like him, aren't you?" Maxine said.

I nodded.

"Well, we had a daughter of our own." Maxine stared off into the distance, looking sorrowful. Like she was staring at a different time and place. I thought of the photos on the dresser in the Carmichaels' room. "Ada. She was sweet—but too trusting. Got involved with the wrong people." She looked back at me, her dark eyes suddenly turning hard. "Got hurt—beaten up badly, and started taking morphine for the pain. But then she got addicted. Rosita set her up to go see Dr. Aldridge. We were so grateful at first. But he prescribed heroin and, sure, that got Ada off the morphine, but the heroin was worse. She couldn't think, couldn't do anything except pine for her next fix.

"We didn't have enough savings to spend on a countryside clinic for her to get off the drugs—and anyway, we knew that they wouldn't take people like Ada," Maxine said. A rare tinge of bitterness tightened her voice. I understood what she meant. People who weren't white. "She just got worse and worse. Ended up thrown in jail for, well, selling herself to men on the streets." Maxine shook her head, tears springing to her eyes. "I never hated her for it, though she always said I judged her. I could see what pain she was in. Henry finally went to Eddie, asked if there was any way he could help us."

Maxine sighed. "You know, I didn't like it when Henry got us to work for the McGees. I knew that Eddie and Henry had a special bond, from being on that freighter. But up until then, we weren't involved with anything more than cooking, cleaning, Henry sometimes helping with the landscaping. Anyway, Eddie told Henry he needed him to go into a bank, make a scene. Didn't say why. Henry swears he didn't know the whole plot. Just that Eddie promised he'd get Ada out of jail and down to Alabama to be with my sister. And we reckoned that would be as good as—maybe better than—a fancy clinic." Maxine took another sip of her tea, then stared into her cup as she said, "We butted heads all the time, my sister and me. She didn't like that I'd come up north, away from our family. And she's more stubborn than a mule who doesn't want to go backward. But if anyone could set Ada straight, it would be her. So, Henry agreed."

Maxine put her cup back down. "So Henry went into the bank, made a scene. Didn't know, he swore, that Eddie had men ready to rush in a side door while the guards and manager were distracted by Henry, to rob the bank. I guess Eddie was desperate for money for one of his deals. But it went wrong. One of the bank employees had a gun, started shooting, took out two of Eddie's men before another of Eddie's men took out the bank employee. Then Eddie's men fled, and Henry was arrested. Blamed for the bank employee's death, the deaths of Eddie's men, who were identified in the newspapers as innocent customers. Didn't matter that Henry didn't even have a gun."

Tears coursed down Maxine's face as she relived the ordeal. "Henry would have been executed for that bank robbery. I thought I'd lose both my daughter and my husband. There was an attorney who wanted to take Henry's case—get him to testify against Eddie. Henry said no. He knew that going up against Eddie would be a death sentence—and besides, he was loyal to Eddie. But then the charges were suddenly dropped against Henry. Our daughter was released. A reward for our years of service. For Henry not testifying against Eddie. But in exchange, we had to come here. Cut off our ties from our daughter and everyone else." Maxine shook her head. "I reckon Eddie didn't trust us not to turn on him in the future. Our deal with him was a life sentence. But it saved our daughter."

I turned this information over in my head. It would have been easier for Eddie to have just had Henry and Maxine, even their daughter, killed, and it was curious to me that he had at least enough conscience to find a different way for them. "When did all of this happen?"

Maxine wiped away her tears. "Seven years ago."

Nineteen twenty-four. Three years before I met Rosita. So that was why she'd never mentioned them.

"And Ada? You haven't heard from her, from your sister, all this time?" I asked softly.

Maxine's face softened. "A photo came to the McGees' house in Toledo, from my sister in Alabama. Of her and my Ada. Rosita brought it to me here. I still have it." The framed picture on the dresser in their room. "Ada wrote on the back—*I am here. All is well.*"

Maxine swallowed hard. "And that's what I cling to." She reached up, gently grazed my cheek with her fingertips. "In some ways you remind me of Ada. Trusting. Eager to taste all of life's flavors. Even those that the world would deny women, especially women of lesser means."

CHAPTER 29

MAXINE'S WORDS PLAYED over in my mind after I went upstairs.

I was impatient to finally slide back upstairs and search Rosita's suite, but not while Eddie, Cormac, and Marco were in the casino. What if they came up while I was going up the stairs?

I decided I'd have time to luxuriate in a hot bath. I locked the bathroom door. I was generous with the castile soap, making plenty of bubbly foam. It felt good to scrape the stink and grime of the day off my skin. As I soaked, I reviewed what I'd learned from Claire and Douglas about their childhoods with Rosita—how gratefully and fondly Douglas saw her, how Claire had admired her and been in awe of her. But yet, they'd wanted to use her for her connections and Eddie's money and influence: in Claire's case, to gain a foothold in Hollywood; in Douglas's, to regain one.

I could understand Claire needing all the help she could get. She was talented, but not in a breakout way. She'd worked in studio secretarial pools and had had a few minor film roles.

But Douglas had been a major star. Why had he lost his foothold?

In either case, it seemed they'd had every reason to want her alive and well—and yet, she'd turned them down flat, in front of everyone.

Could they have gone to her that first night, after the scene in the music room, begged her to take Eddie's offer, to help them? Then, when she turned them down again—and she would have done so cruelly—killed her out of anger?

Then there was Maxine and Henry. Eddie had come, wanting to wrest the island away from Rosita. And then what would have happened to the Carmichaels? Maybe they thought Eddie might release them from the island, set it up so they could go be with Maxine's sister and Ada in Alabama? Maybe they'd gone to Rosita to plead with her to take the deal. Maybe she'd spurned them, and then in frustration and anger, they had killed her.

On the other hand, Rosita had indicated that first night that she had information that could ruin Eddie. If she succeeded, wouldn't that be good for Maxine and Henry and Ada? For Claire and Douglas? Free of Eddie, she could keep her island and still help them all. Except no, even in prison, Eddie would find a way to pull strings to control all those lives.

I still hadn't worked out motivations for Liam, Dr. Aldridge, or Seamus. Yet, I knew that Liam was moving those lockboxes for Eddie. How had the one I'd found gotten so far from where the lot was probably stored, near the north dock? Had Liam been holding some back for himself, lost track of the one I'd found? Did Rosita somehow know?

And Dr. Aldridge, who the Carmichaels didn't like or trust for good reason, had been coming here regularly to check on Rosita at Eddie's behest. Had Rosita given him some reason to want her gone?

As for Seamus . . . if he was a Fed, he'd have no reason to want Rosita gone. But if he was a Fed who'd flipped to serving either Eddie or Marco, he might. Either man might demand he prove his loyalty by taking out Rosita.

I shook my head, not wanting to believe that Seamus was capable of murder. I didn't want to believe that about any of them, either, except Eddie or Marco. It made more sense that one of them, or their henchmen, were behind Rosita's killing, and that something had gone awry and led to Joey's killing.

All I knew for sure was that whoever had killed Rosita needed the world to know that Rosita was dead. Otherwise, why not let her body sink to the bottom of the lake? And they wanted me to find her, making it likely I'd be accused of the murder. Whoever it was knew I'd had a lockbox below the dock, that I'd try to retrieve it when I panicked and decided to leave the island.

And I knew one other thing: how fragile our existences all were, dependent on Eddie and Rosita and their fraught relationship.

BACK IN MY room, I donned my nightgown and tended to Largo.

Then I listened for telltale sounds of the men. Could I risk creeping up to the suite, to see if there was something hidden in Oliver's nursery?

I was starting to doubt my own memory. Maybe in the chaos of the morning, I'd imagined the swipe in the dust on the dresser?

I needed to know. And now that I was alone, away from others, with no activities to distract me, my head spun, and the image of Rosita floated before me. Not the beautiful, charming Rosita I had known. Or even the figure in black from head to toe. But the bloated, pale corpse, seemingly reaching for me with her turgid arms . . .

I pinned my damp hair back with hairpins. Pony had shown me how to use such a pin to pick a lock. He'd wanted me to get into Eddie's office at the Toledo mansion.

You're there all the time with Rosita. I need you to look for something.

I can't do that to them. They've been good to us.

But I had done it. I'd been too afraid of Pony not to.

Rosita caught me in the attempt, and I'd begged her not to tell Eddie.

Now I wondered what I'd say to Eddie if he caught me trying to get into the suite.

I could say that I wanted to pick out a dress for Rosita. She'd brought a few that weren't black mourning clothes, almost as if she anticipated someday being able to bring herself to circulate among the living enrobed in something other than the garb of the bereaved.

I'd say that I knew we couldn't dress her for burial, but at least a lovely dress would be with her. I could say that yes, I should have thought of asking him, but I was so brokenhearted and frazzled that it hadn't crossed my mind.

You always are so clever, Susan, wriggling your way out of trouble . . .

Rosita's voice, from the night I'd killed Pony?

Or my mother's, from before?

I told the voices to hush, and quietly left my room.

I MOVED QUIETLY in my soft-soled slippers, climbing the stairs to the suite. My heart panged for all the times I'd ascended those steps, eager to see Rosita, yet chafing to be free of Trouble Island, of my past. At the same time cherishing my time with Rosita, cool and remote though she was. Thinking Rosita was the one true friend I'd ever had.

I knelt, pulled a bobby pin from my hair, and slowly inserted it into the lock, trying to remember what Pony had told me to do next.

But then I heard a crash from inside the suite, followed quickly by Seamus exclaiming "Damn it!"

I started to run back down to my bedroom, but anger filled my chest. I had slept with him, trusted him. And yet I didn't know who he really was. What he might know of my past. I needed answers to those questions.

I knew the suite's contents and layout in intimate detail. On the small table next to the settee, there was a tall slender pewter vase. If I got in and moved fast enough, I could grab that vase before Seamus even spotted me.

I fell to my knees in front of the door as if in supplication to Rosita's former lodging and pressed up on each pin in the lock. As I pressed up the final one, I held my breath and turned the doorknob. Exhaled as it gave and the door cracked open a sliver.

I poked my hairpin back into my bun and slipped inside. The ruined door to Oliver's nursery was open. I saw Seamus just inside the nursery, his back to me.

I quietly moved to the side table, grabbed the pewter vase.

Suddenly, Seamus pivoted, stepped out of the nursery, holding a small pistol. Relief and amusement broke over his face, which made me want to throw the vase at him. I was weary of being taken for granted, seen as either at fault for events beyond my control or as ineffectual.

"Put the vase down, Aurelia. No matter how good your arm is, a bullet is faster—"

"You'd shoot me?" I asked, putting on my best petulant-Claire voice. Coming from me, though, it sounded snide.

"Well, no, but I'm just saying if you're ever in a confrontation, have a weapon that can help you—"

I threw the vase, hard, aiming for his head. The vase instead hit the arm of the hand holding his pistol. He dropped the gun, which landed without going off.

I eyed the pistol, started toward it, but he picked it up before I could get to it. He tucked it under his belt, behind his left hip.

I cocked an eyebrow. "I thought you all had to hand over your guns to Cormac. That he searched your rooms to double-check?"

"Cormac is not as clever as he makes people believe. And besides— this is a small pistol. A stocking pistol, because women prefer it."

"Oh yes. God forbid we use real guns. Our delicate hands would probably snap off."

At that, Seamus merely raised his eyebrows.

"I used to hunt and target shoot with my father and my—" I shook my head. This was not the time for reminiscences. "What are you doing in here?" I snapped. "Are you a Fed?"

Amusement turned to alarm on Seamus's face as he rushed past me to the door, pulling it and turning the inside lock.

So, yes. His action confirmed what I suspected. I wasn't sure whether to feel relieved or alarmed.

If he'd flipped, or was working both sides, he was dangerous. And if he hadn't, if he truly still adhered to the rule of law, and he found out I'd killed Pony, no matter how understandable my motivation, he'd want to haul me in, too.

Seamus's past kindnesses toward the Carmichaels, his gentle way with me a few nights before, rushed back through my mind. I gambled that he was still on the side of the law.

"You were working with Rosita," I said in a near whisper. "To take down Eddie."

Seamus nodded. He came close to me. The heat of his body brushed my skin. My pulse quickened and my face bloomed. I wanted to fall forward into his chest. But I forced myself to keep my stance rigid, my gaze steady. "I was trying to convince her to, yes."

"Bureau of Prohibition?" I asked.

He hesitated. Then nodded again.

"You couldn't have been working alone."

"No. There's . . . a mole in the organization."

"Claire?"

Seamus gave a short, barking laugh at that notion.

So, I thought, an unhappy wife of one of Eddie's well-heeled associates—narrowing the identity of the mole down to at least a dozen or so women.

"I can't say, and it doesn't matter who. What matters is that our mole saw how unhappy, miserable, and angry Rosita was—rumors of Eddie's affair with their nanny—and how Rosita wanted out of her marriage, but safely."

I understood that. Divorcing was difficult, and if you were married to a man who believed he owned you, who thought that violence was the easier way to settle conflict . . . I shuddered. I didn't have to know who the mole was to understand her situation.

"At our direction, our mole tentatively approached Rosita. This was several months before Oliver died," Seamus said. "At the same time, I went undercover and worked my way into Eddie's organization."

This would have been after I'd come to Trouble Island, after Pony.

"Rosita picked up on what our mole was offering—at first without directly saying it—and then agreed yes—she would turn over information she had on Eddie, but she needed time, she said."

I sorted through the women I'd known, women I'd seen here on the island, who I'd served. They made a mosaic of brunettes and blondes, long arms and slender legs, chic hairstyles and elegant clothing, sophisticated laughs designed to show they were above actually being amused by anything, lilting voices gossiping about nothing and everything all at once.

I couldn't imagine any of them as agents for the bureau.

But then, they probably couldn't imagine me as a killer—and yet, when pushed, I'd become one.

And if I'd been offered the opportunity to get away from Pony, serving as an agent for the bureau, to double-cross the McGees, would I have?

Yes. Yes, I would have—if I knew Rosita wanted out, too.

If she hadn't wanted out? I wasn't sure.

"But then, tragically, Oliver died. And Rosita came here, locked herself away. We didn't count on that. And we didn't count on you. An effective guardian of Rosita's privacy, if ever there was one."

I flashed back on several women who'd asked—even insisted— they must see Rosita. Offer sympathy. Condolences. I'd rebuffed them all, been proud to do so, to protect Rosita.

I shuffled backward from Seamus. "So when that didn't work—they sent you as the season for visitors was ending. To woo me? The pathetic widow who had hidden herself away on the island to serve Rosita McGee. To see if I could convince her to turn her information over to you? Or, if not, to see if I could get it from her and turn it over?"

A pained look crossed Seamus's face. "To convince you to let me talk directly to Rosita, yes. But not to woo you. That was . . . unexpected."

"And if you'd convinced me, what would I have gotten in exchange?"

"What you've wanted all along," Seamus said. "Freedom. From any charges against you in your husband's death. From the McGees. A fresh start."

My heart, my breath stilled. The room went cold around me. He knew who I was all along, what I had done. Rosita must have told him about me, before Oliver's death. But why?

Or had she revealed my truth to someone else, who'd informed Seamus?

My head spun, considering the possibilities, but I made myself focus on what mattered most in that moment: that the truth about my past had gotten back to Seamus.

That he was a Fed.

That he was willing to use my past as leverage to get me to do what the Feds wanted: testify against Eddie, share what I'd learned through Pony and Rosita about how his organization worked, in exchange for amnesty.

I forced myself to inhale. Drawing in breath made me shudder, like I was hearing footfalls in the dark too close behind me.

"Then I got word through our mole that Eddie would be coming. There was chatter of an alliance brewing between Eddie and, of all people, Marco. We got the date, and the information that Eddie and Cormac were coming to take Rosita away. If Eddie succeeded, then all our efforts would have been in vain."

I stared at him as I put together the pieces. "So that morning, you were on the path because you were following me. You—everyone—knew I went swimming down by the southwest dock. You—you wanted to make sure I'd see the *Myra,* knew I'd run to Rosita—"

Seamus made an apologetic expression. "Yes. If you weren't by the dock or in a place to see it, I was going to call for you, get your attention, so you'd see the yacht. I hoped knowing that Eddie was coming would make Rosita frightened enough to finally agree she'd work with me."

"But that's not how she reacted."

"No. It wasn't."

Instead, she'd kept following her own mysterious scheme, until she was murdered.

I swallowed hard, though the inside of my mouth was dry. If Seamus feared that Rosita would reveal his identity to Eddie, would he have killed her?

No, I thought, surely not. Not if he was still on the side of the law.

Seamus sighed. "If Rosita wanted to flip on him, that was her chance. To have you send for me even as he came ashore. To give me whatever she had on him." He gestured behind him toward Oliver's nursery. "I was hoping I'd find it hidden away in there. Something I saw when you and I and Eddie were up here made me think someone had been in the room recently."

He'd seen the smudge on the dresser in Oliver's nursery, too.

There was no point in trying to keep him from looking. "Well, come on," I said. "Help me move the dresser."

As we walked to Oliver's nursery, I wondered if we'd find nothing at all. Or the evidence Rosita supposedly had against Eddie.

I thought I should tell him about the lockbox I'd found, about Liam moving dozens more lockboxes like it to the *Myra.*

And yet, I held back the truth. I still wasn't entirely convinced I should trust him.

FIRST WE OPENED drawers. All we found was Oliver's clothing, still neatly folded. My throat caught at the sight, at the faint scent of castile soap. I was heartbroken by knowing that my self-protective action against Pony had eventually led to other actions that resulted in Oliver's death.

We tugged the smudged dresser away from the wall. The thick plaster wall was intact. But then I glanced down at the wooden floor and spotted two cuts thicker than the lines between the rest of the planks, which had been mitered and fitted so carefully.

"We need a screwdriver, or the claw end of a hammer—" Seamus started.

I shook my head. "We don't want to risk being seen going to the basement to fetch a tool."

I knelt and went to work with my thumbnail as an impromptu screwdriver to loosen a drawer handle, and then used the drawer handle to pry at the floor panel.

"Clever," Seamus said, admiration in his voice.

I smiled to myself, even as I focused on the panel. Finally, it popped up. I stared in shock at a metal lockbox. Just like all the others.

Seamus knelt, pulled out the box. It was unlocked. I held my breath as he opened it.

Nothing was in there—except, caught in the corner, a small shred of paper, as if the box had been overstuffed with documents, and in someone's haste to remove them, a piece caught and tore off.

Seamus gave the shred of paper an irritated flick. "Whatever was in here has been moved."

We both stood. The question was—had the scrap been from papers Rosita had to condemn Eddie? Had she moved them? Or had someone else found them? Then destroyed them, or kept them to use against Eddie? Or, if Eddie had found them, why had he gone on such a rampage to look for them? As a way to cover the truth, to play some game I didn't yet understand?

I sank down on the edge of the bed, suddenly weary from all the questions spinning in my head. I asked Seamus, "You hoped that I'd alert Rosita to Eddie's arrival. That that would be enough to scare her into finally giving you whatever she has—had—on Eddie. Then what? You'd take him on? And everyone he brought with him?"

"I didn't expect a whole entourage. Or Marco and Joey."

"Just Eddie and Cormac."

Seamus nodded.

"And you thought you could manage them?"

Seamus gave a rueful smile. "The information I had was that just Eddie and Cormac would be coming. I figured that you, the Carmichaels, and Liam wouldn't stand in my way. I was confident I could take out Cormac, and then handle Eddie. But I wasn't counting on a full entourage—including Marco and his goon." His smile dropped. "Or thinking that Rosita would be murdered."

"But that's not how it played out," I said. "Rosita didn't send me to fetch you."

"Yes. And I knew that our whole scheme had unraveled. I would not be able to get to Rosita through you. She would not come to me directly."

"So then what did you plan to do?"

"Wait them out," Seamus said. "Observe. Hope that she wouldn't reveal who I am. Eventually, leave when it was safe. Report back in."

"And if Eddie had succeeded in convincing Rosita to turn the island over to Marco, or if he'd forced her to leave with him, then what? Same thing? Leave? Report back in?"

Seamus nodded.

"Trouble Island is in Canada, so how does that work?"

Seamus chuckled. "Lots of bureaucracy. But our governments

work together. Alcohol may be legal in Canada, but it is still prohibited in the U.S., and the Canadian government doesn't want American gangsters causing trouble in their towns and cities."

I turned over all he'd revealed to me. If he really was a Fed who hadn't flipped, surely he would have feared Rosita might reveal to Eddie and the other gangsters who he really was. That would have given Seamus a powerful motivation to kill her.

And he would want her body to be found, so his bosses would know that Rosita was no longer a possible witness to flip.

Then I thought, what if he feared I might reveal his identity? Wouldn't he want me dead, too? But he could have killed me already, if that was the case. Made up some story to justify shooting me.

He could have killed me the night we made love.

I didn't dismiss the possibility that he'd come to my room to distract me while an accomplice snared Rosita from her suite. Killed her. Left her for me to find.

Then it occurred to me that just as he might fear I'd reveal his identity, I should fear that he could reveal mine to Marco. And if Marco knew I was the catalyst, as Rosita had put it, for his nephew taking the fall for Pony's death, then I'd be in danger with Marco and Joey.

But so far, Seamus hadn't exposed me. He hadn't even threatened to. And moments before, his sorrowful expression seemed sincere. I hoped—I had to believe—that it was.

I wanted to believe he was who he said he was. But my ability to trust my instincts, already damaged when I arrived on Trouble Island, had been obliterated over the last few days.

Softly, I said, "If you really are a Fed, here for the purposes you've described, and I am no longer useful in getting Rosita to turn on Eddie, then that means eventually—"

"You can still be a useful witness. And your circumstances with Pony, from what's been said, were brutal enough that any sentence would be minimal, or dismissed. Then eventually, you could be free."

Free. Such a simple word, yet a nearly impossible attainment. I could cooperate with Seamus, with the bureau. They could make all kinds of pretty promises. And, oh, I was tempted to tell him yes, yes, I'd love his help.

After all, I'd never sought Eddie's world. I'd gotten caught up in it because of Pony, and then more deeply ensnared because of my relationship with Rosita. Because of how that relationship ensured Pony's rise in Eddie's gang. I'd heard of people like me—wives, lovers of his goons, the goons themselves—simply "disappearing."

If I trusted Seamus, would I really be free? Or would he, too, betray me?

Even if he didn't, I'd never truly be *free.* Incarcerated, Eddie would remain a dangerous, powerful man. Sooner or later—either personally or through someone like Cormac—he would come after me. If Eddie died, whoever took over his gang might blame me, come after me. And then there was Marco. His nephew-in-law had taken the fall for killing Pony and ended up dying in prison. If Marco knew, he'd seek vengeance. Or someone in his gang would.

From so many angles, I was doomed to live my life—however much was left of it—always nervously looking over my shoulder.

"Aurelia? Are you all right?"

Seamus's voice gently pulled me back to the moment. He took my hands, pulled me to my feet, brought my fingertips to his lips. Even in our impossible situation, with all its fraught uncertainty, desire unknotted itself from deep in my core and released itself into my limbs, my groin, my veins.

The thought curled through my mind and escaped my lips as a moan: Maybe I couldn't be free forever. But I could be deliciously free in the moment.

As I had a few nights before, I pulled him to me, pressed my lips, my body, to his.

He pulled back.

"I'm not sure I trust you," he said, his voice husky.

Frankly, that he had doubts thrilled me. I'd always been the girl everyone thought of as awkward, credulous, naïve. Easy to dismiss.

To be, just for a moment, a woman of intrigue—well. I kissed him again, my tongue exploring his tender and delicious lips and mouth.

QUIETLY, WE HURRIED down to my bedroom.

We undressed one another, Largo squawking at our frantic movements. Her sounds made us giggle, then clap our hands over each other's mouths. We didn't want anyone to come to my door to investigate.

Seamus carefully took my glasses from my face and put them on the bureau. Then he began kissing the palm of my hand, working his way up my arm to my shoulder. The need to muffle my moans only heightened the sensations. Seamus moved to my breasts and then my mouth and I returned his kisses until he worked his way down my stomach, and then I couldn't help but gasp out loud, realizing where his lips would go next. Hoping for them to.

He lifted me onto my bed and began kissing me in ways I'd never been kissed before, sending my mind and soul out of the reality of the room, of the mansion, of the island, into a realm of only sensation and bliss. Then, I gave to him the gift he'd given me.

At last, we lay side by side, staring into each other's faces, awed at the bliss we'd just created for one another.

I traced my fingertips over his chest and found a divot near his left shoulder blade that I hadn't noticed the first time we made love.

"From the war?" I ventured.

Seamus looked away. "It was a long time ago—"

"I want to know—need to know—about you—" Tears sprang to my eyes. A feeling came over me that this was the only chance I'd have to learn about his past.

"Hey!" he said, putting his hand to my face. "There's plenty of time—after all of this is over—after—" He paused, and in his hesitation I could see that he was making the same calculations about our future that I'd already made.

His eyes suddenly glistened. But he cleared his throat and gave me the life story I'd asked for. "My life was pretty simple," he whispered, twirling a strand of my hair. "Grew up a farm boy in Nebraska. Met a girl from the farm next door." He smiled, a distant look drawing him from my bedroom, and my chest panged with jealousy. "We married in October 1916—I was eighteen and she was sixteen." He shook his head at the impossible hope of youth. "But I wanted to do the right thing, so I went off with the army." He kissed my fingertips and pressed them to his battle scar. "I became a medic, worked in a field hospital. Buried too many men. Near the end, I was shot by a sniper, but fortunately not a great one. My shoulder healed. I went home, knew I could inherit my father's farm someday, but I—" This time, as his voice trailed off, his faraway look turned from sentiment to sorrow. "I just couldn't dig in dirt day after day. We moved to Kansas City, and I took a job as a cop, but what I really wanted to do was become a doctor. To help people live. She had our son. And then one day . . ."

My heart fell, and I immediately regretted the pang of jealousy.

He took a deep breath and went on. "One day, she was out with our son. He was in a stroller. An automobile came flying up onto the sidewalk. Ran over them both."

I gasped, horrified.

"The man driving the automobile lost control because he was dying. He was a mobster and had been shot by a mobster in a rival gang." Seamus's gaze hardened. "There was—is—no enforcement of Prohibition in Kansas City. Or in many other places. Powerful men find the loopholes or just ignore the law altogether. I wanted to be part of something that brought back control—" His voice waned. "I should have stayed on that farm where Julie wanted to stay, and then they would have been safe . . ."

Julie. What a pretty name. He still loved and missed her. I did not envy that or Julie's horrid fate. But I did envy being cherished—and cherishing—as they clearly had.

I wanted to ask why he would engage in a fight he saw as futile. Bringing down Eddie would not bring back his wife or son. Nor would it fill the hole in Seamus's heart and soul. Only moving forward, one step at a time, would do that.

But I had run away to fill a hole in my own heart and soul. Then, for a time with Pony, I'd thrown myself into lawlessness and wild living, and that hadn't worked either. Over the past year, I'd come to realize that all I could do to set myself free of past haunts was, again, move forward. Believing Rosita would help me take those steps, then pity for her loss, kept me on Trouble Island. Now I knew she would never have helped me. That I had to, somehow, free myself. Or die trying.

"You shouldn't blame yourself," I said. "Heartache can find us anywhere, without us doing anything wrong—"

Seamus stopped my philosophizing by running a finger down my nose. Just that light touch stirred me. "Where did you come from, Aurelia Escalante," he said, "that gave you heartache?"

"A small farm in Ohio," I said.

He laughed softly.

"No, it's true. I was a farmgirl in Ohio and I—I—" I stuttered to a stop.

I'd never told anyone my full story. Not Pony. Or Rosita. Or Maxine. I could barely admit it to myself. The wound of it still festered deep within me, scarring my very soul.

And maybe that wound was what really had kept me stuck with Pony. Then stuck on Trouble Island. Maybe, I thought, confessing it was what I really needed to set myself free.

I forced out a laugh. "I was just bored. Wanted to see what life could offer in the big city. Got all the way to Toledo—and ended up in over my head."

Seamus's eyes shuttered with disappointment. He knew I was not exactly lying, but neither was I telling him the truth. And yet, he pulled me to him.

I melted into his arms, eager to make love again, to escape for a while the realities of my past and of the island, and go into timeless, pleasurable bliss.

CHAPTER 30

WHEN I STIRRED awake, I was warm and cozy and happy. I smiled at the memory of the night before.

But then I saw that Seamus was gone. He'd moved my glasses to my end table and pulled open the veranda door drapes so that as I awoke, I could see fuzzy striations of pink and bruised-purple and blue-gray in the sky. I put on my glasses, and the markings became more distinct. I pulled on my robe and moved to the veranda, staring out at the slushy movement of the frigid lake. A thick layer of snow covered the lawn and topiaries and bushes, turning them into indistinguishable lumps.

This was the morning of Rosita's burial. I told myself to focus on that and turned from the window.

Then something on the bureau—where Seamus had left my glasses the night before—caught my eye.

His small stocking gun.

He'd left it for me. A sign of trust.

And a clue that he was wary of what was to come.

AN HOUR LATER, wind and snow swirled around us in the small cemetery as if the island itself wanted to bind us up in this cruel weather and sling us far away. There was no sound beyond the wind. Even the familiar *shush-shush* of the lake's waves had silenced, and that silence was more frightening than any sounds of crashing water. It meant that the water was freezing along the shoreline.

We'd divided ourselves on either side of the neatly dug grave. Rosita's coffin sat on planks crossing the grave. Under the coffin were two straps, their ends lying out on the ground.

Now Oliver's mother would lie at rest next to him on one side, his great-grandparents on the other.

I stood with Seamus, Liam, Maxine, and Henry on one side. Maxine and I had fussed at Henry not to come out in this cold—so hard on any of us but especially on him—but he'd insisted. At least he'd agreed that he would be bundled up in his coat and hat and the Underground Railroad quilt and would sit in a chair. Liam and Seamus had carried him out on that kitchen chair. He tried to light a cigarette, but what with the wind and the snow and his trembling fingers, he gave up, tucked away his smokes and his Banjo lighter.

On the other side of the grave stood Douglas, Dr. Aldridge, Claire, Eddie, Cormac—and even Marco, who nervously eyed Oliver's grave, fidgeting, as if finally the import of his actions was weighing on him, as if the little boy might rise up to haunt him. Or maybe he was nervous without Joey there and feared that Eddie's emotions from the loss of his wife and son might overtake him, and he might take his grief and anger out on Marco.

But Eddie's expression was stony, as hard and immovable as the face of the winged angel statue on top of Oliver's headstone.

He stared at Rosita's coffin, the snow accumulating on its plain, rough-hewn top. All of us were miserable in the slanting lashes of sleety snow.

But none of us dared say a word. We were waiting for Eddie.

Finally, he spoke. His voice was the even monotone of someone who knew they must say something, and desperately wished they didn't have to. "I will say a few words. And then each of you will also do so in turn."

We glanced at each other, knowing it was not a request. It was an order.

Eddie cleared his throat. "We had our troubles. I guess most husbands and wives do. But I loved her. If our son had lived—" Cormac offered a steadying hand to Eddie's elbow, but Eddie swatted it away. "Maybe things would have been different."

I looked past Eddie and the others to Oliver's gravestone.

"It was a duty and—an honor—to do her bidding from time to time," Cormac said.

I studied the bronze statue of an angel with her up-reached hands releasing a dove heavenward. Something still felt off to me.

"I was glad to care for her," Dr. Aldridge said.

"I, uh, I didn't know her well, but I'm sure she was a good wife, and, uh, mother," Marco said. I heard his boots crunch as he shifted uncomfortably from foot to foot. "A real looker, that's for sure, and, uh—"

I suppressed a groan and a shake of my head. How grotesque could he be?

"She was my best friend in childhood," Douglas said quickly, stopping Marco from saying more.

"Mine too," Claire said. "Like a sister." She sniffled, the first person to show actual emotion.

I was numb, from the cold and wind and snow. From the surreal horror of the situation.

The eulogy-giving, such as it was, came around to our side of the grave. Maxine and Henry commented on how she was always lovely to them, Seamus that he was sure she was a fine person.

Liam's voice was the one that caught my attention. I expected him to say something in his usual flat tone, something bland like everyone else, but his voice shook. I pulled my gaze from the bronze angel statue atop Oliver's gravestone and regarded him. Tears ran down his face. "Before—before Oliver's death, she—she was always kind about how much I liked to go on about my archaeological findings here. I remember showing Oliver arrowheads I'd found, and pottery shards, and . . ." Liam stuttered to a stop. Eddie glared across the grave at Liam.

I looked again at Oliver's gravestone, thinking about the boy, imagining yes, Liam would have gone on and on about arrowheads and such—sometimes he did so during staff dinner breaks in the kitchen—and then it hit me, what bothered me about the marker at Oliver's grave. The dove that the angel had been holding in her outstretched hand was missing.

On the morning of Eddie's arrival, when I'd briefly stared out Rosita's bedroom window, I hadn't seen anything amiss. Later, when we were looking for Rosita and I'd gazed out that window, I'd sensed something off but hadn't identified it.

So the dove must have disappeared the same night as Rosita had, the night of Eddie's arrival.

That dove, with its sharply carved beak and wings, could have served as a murder weapon just as well as a knife. The slashes on Rosita's neck, Joey's thigh, flashed before me. The image of the dove, red blood smeared on its beak or wings, hovered in my mind's eye as surely as if a bloody bird had arisen from the depths of Rosita's grave—

"Aurelia?" Seamus grabbed my arm. I was dizzy, swaying.

"I'm sorry," I said. Everyone was staring at me. I was the only one who hadn't spoken so far. I took a deep breath.

I wanted to say Rosita was my friend, but was she? She'd helped me, yet she'd also entrapped me, used me, and I'd come to realize that even before she blamed me as the catalyst for Oliver's death, she'd used me as someone to look down on, to make her feel superior.

The truth sputtered out of me, the only truth that I could bring myself to say. "I'm sorry that she lost her son and suffered so. That she was killed and left in such a horrible state."

I stared into the dark empty grave, swiftly filling with snow. I pushed my hand deeper in my coat pocket, wrapping my hand around the gun Seamus had given me. I wasn't sure why I brought it with me, except that I felt my doom closing in on me as surely and swiftly as the cold hard earth would soon come down on Rosita's coffin.

"All right," Eddie said roughly, "let's wrap this up—"

"Wait—that's it?" Claire cried. "No prayer, no music, just plunk her in the ground?"

Eddie sighed. "You want to say something else?"

"We at least need a hymn!" she said.

"All right, go on."

Claire looked startled, like she was trying to think of something to sing. Then she began singing "Amazing Grace," warbling, off-key. No one joined in—no one tried to. By the time she got to ". . . was blind, but now I see," we were all staring at the ground. She took a deep breath as if to start the second verse, but Douglas mercifully put an arm around her, and said, "Thank you, Claire, that was lovely."

"Oh, thank you, Dougie," she said, and tried to snuggle closer. This time, he did not rebuff her.

"All right, men, you all know what to do."

Cormac, Douglas, Liam, and Seamus each took hold of one of the strap ends, carefully lifted the coffin. Eddie gestured to me to come help him, and we pulled away the planks. Then we stepped aside as the four men lowered Rosita's coffin into the grave.

For a moment we all stared into the grave. Maxine stepped first to the snow-covered soil mounded nearby, grabbing two handfuls. She tossed in one, then gave the other handful to Henry. Seamus helped Henry to his feet, and Henry tossed in his soil. After Henry was back in his chair, we each took a turn—Liam and then Seamus and me, even Cormac and Marco, followed by Claire and Douglas and Dr. Aldridge, and at last Eddie.

"Douglas, Seamus, get Henry inside," Eddie said. "Everyone else can go, too. Liam and Cormac and I will finish up."

I frowned. Surely he didn't mean that he would be part of putting the earth back over his wife? I couldn't imagine him dirtying his good leather gloves or wool coat. Liam looked scared. Seamus and I exchanged worried looks. But we all did as ordered.

Once inside the mansion, I lagged behind, as the Carmichaels, with the help of Seamus and Douglas, went downstairs, and Claire, Marco, and Dr. Aldridge went to the music room.

I started up the stairs.

"You're not joining us?" Claire called after me.

"Stomach trouble." I put my hand to my stomach and bent a bit as if cramping.

"You mean women's troubles." Marco chuckled.

I rushed up to the third-floor suite. Seamus and I had not bothered to lock it when we'd left the night before. I shut the door behind me and locked it.

I rushed to Rosita's bedroom. I knelt on the floor before the window overlooking the small cemetery and pushed up the window slowly to minimize squeaks. Cold wind rushed in, swirled with sleety snow into the room. From this vantage, it was even more apparent that this was the front end of the big storm that Henry had predicted.

But the voices below carried up to me.

"Listen, this storm is going to kick in and freeze in the *Myra,*" Cormac said. "How much have you gotten on?"

"About two-thirds, I think. If I could use the speedboat, it'd all be moved by now. It's a lot harder, wheelbarrow loads in this weather. Maybe you can come back for it—"

"I can't come back for it after Marco takes possession of the island, and I need it all!" Eddie roared. "Get it in the hold. We're leaving tomorrow. Before we're stuck here."

"I can get it all moved, if I have an extra day—"

"Or extra help," Eddie said.

Eddie must have given Cormac a meaningful look. I heard him

groan, then say, "It would be quicker to bring the *Myra* around to the north dock—"

"And have everyone wonder why—and where—it's moved?" Eddie snapped. "Plus, the north dock isn't equipped for the *Myra*. You'll help Liam finish up."

"But Cormac's always with you, Mr. McGee, and no one ever notices me not being around," Liam said. "Won't they wonder if Cormac isn't with you?"

I wondered, did Liam just feel uncomfortable at the notion of being alone with Cormac? Or was there something he was trying to hide from Eddie and Cormac?

Eddie wondered, too. "What, did Rosita get you to hide away whatever she had on me? At your precious dig?"

"No, I don't know what she had, and I wouldn't have helped her. I just wonder, what if someone asks you about Cormac?"

"Let them wonder," Eddie said. "They're not going to bother me with questions—"

"Well, Rosita's little maid might—" Cormac said.

"Don't worry. We're going to take care of her anyway."

I felt my throat close as if choking hands grasped it. I knew exactly what that meant.

"Get the grave filled in. Then finish the transfer. We'll leave tomorrow with Marco, Claire, Douglas, Dr. Aldridge."

I wondered if taking the time to bury Rosita had been a show just to buy time to transfer those lockboxes.

"And me?" Liam said.

"Sure, of course, and you. We'll say your father wants you back."

I frowned at that. Who was Liam's father? And then I felt sorry for Liam as Cormac laughed cruelly, implying that Liam's father wouldn't want him at all.

"And . . . and Seamus, and the Carmichaels, and Aurelia will be left alone here?"

"Sure, kid," Eddie said. "We'll leave them alone for the winter."

I knew what was inferred even if Liam didn't read between the lines. As soon as it was safe to come back, Eddie would send some men to take the rest of us out.

Douglas and Claire would get their movie.

Liam would get whatever he wanted—back into archaeology, I guess.

And the murders of Rosita and Joey would be covered over. Eddie really didn't care who had killed them—which told me that the killers were probably him and Cormac. The most obvious suspects after all.

I closed the window, slowly, quietly, praying it wouldn't squeak and draw their attention. Stayed low to get to the bedroom door, though I didn't think they'd glance up to see me moving about.

I had to trust someone. Get help. Seamus. I had to fill him in, figure out a plan to save us, to stop Eddie and Cormac.

But just as I came out onto the second floor, I spotted Claire knocking on my bedroom door. She whirled around toward me.

"I'm freezing," she whined. "Wait, what were you doing up there?"

"I just needed a moment alone with my thoughts. About Rosita."

Something softened in Claire's eyes. But then her usual flat-eyed, ditzy expression returned. "Listen, the whole house has gone cold. We're going to die in this godforsaken mansion!"

CHAPTER 31

CLAIRE WAS RIGHT; the mansion was cold. Still, I wanted to tell Claire to think for herself and find the Carmichaels or Liam, who were responsible for the mansion's maintenance.

But Henry was supposed to be resting, Liam was moving contraband with Cormac, Seamus and Douglas were burying Rosita, and I didn't want to talk with Eddie.

"I'll look into it," I said, as if I knew anything about how the mansion's coal furnace and electrical system operated, other than that they were in a room in the basement.

Through chattering teeth, which I suspected she made clack together harder on purpose, Claire said, "Well, what am I supposed to do in the meantime?"

"Put on your fur," I snapped. "Or the blue coat. Or another. Or just put on all the clothes you brought! You'll be sweating like you're in a sauna in no time."

Claire looked a mix of surprised and hurt at my uncustomary comeback, and I admit it, I took satisfaction in that.

I WENT INTO my room long enough to put on an extra sweater and tossed another scarf over Largo's cage. Then I went down to the kitchen, where it was even chillier, and found that the electric light didn't switch on. I found the kitchen flashlight in its proper spot and went to the storage room, where I found the coal oil lanterns usually used for our work on the southwest and north docks.

Next, I went to the furnace room, lit the lanterns, and then stared helplessly at the furnace—a monstrous affair with a central section that looked like a silo, and numerous ducts coming out of its top and disappearing into the walls and ceiling.

On I went to the Carmichaels' room. Henry, eager to be useful, ignored Maxine's grumblings that he should remain in bed and listened to my ramblings about the heat and electricity. I gave Maxine an apologetic look as we helped Henry into an extra sweater, and offered him my elbow as we exited, as if we were accompanying one another to a ball and not the furnace room.

The light from the coal oil lanterns flickered from their spots on the floor, and I held the flashlight and directed its beam wherever Henry told me.

Finally, Henry explained, "This is an octopus gravity furnace. The ducts go up through the walls, to vents in the rooms." I knew about the vents, though I hadn't thought about the system that sent heat through them. "Hot air rises from the boiler, which is heated by the coal furnace, and goes through the ducts. The system was upgraded two years ago, to an automated Ironman thermostat, so no one has to constantly check the coal and how hot it's burning."

"It sounds complex," I said.

"Not really—but it can't function without a damper door." Henry pointed to an open rectangle at the bottom of the furnace. I turned my beam to the spot. The door was gone, gray ash heaped at the bottom. Then he pointed to a far wall. "We use a Delco generator for electricity for the mansion."

I nodded at that. Even in southeast Ohio, I'd heard of a few farm families well off enough for a Delco generator—basically, a private grid, given that rural areas were too far away from the grids that increasingly served bigger towns and cities. My family hadn't been one of the lucky few. We'd used coal oil lanterns and candlelight, a wood-burning stove, cellar, and fireplace.

"Look. The wiring in the generator has been cut. Even if I could fix it, the fuel cans are gone," Henry said.

I stared at the empty shelves which had once held the fuel cans. I didn't need to ask what had happened. Doors don't unscrew themselves, wires don't cut themselves, and fuel cans don't vanish on their own.

Someone had purposefully sabotaged the mansion's heating and electricity in the middle of the night, while the rest of us had been too caught up in Rosita's burial that morning to immediately notice.

BY NINE THAT night, we were all in the library, the room in the mansion with the largest fireplace.

Seamus, Douglas, Liam, and Cormac had split the firewood, mostly chopped from fallen trees on the island, stacked on a side porch. We used firewood in late spring and early fall in the library and the dining room to provide ambience for guests. Bedrooms and other rooms did not have fireplaces. They were all heated by the modern furnace—now sabotaged.

Meanwhile, Maxine and I moved food—meats, vegetables, and breads—from the freezer out to the pool house, where in this weather it would remain frozen. My stomach turned as we placed the carefully wrapped food, meant to get the staff through the winter, on the benches where Rosita and Joey had been.

Eddie succumbed to reason, after Henry and I explained the situation, and gave the pool house key to me so that we could lock the building, lest the bear or other animals tried to get in. Until the electricity was restored, I'd have to trudge out to the pool house to get food.

By the time we'd finished that task, Eddie had rounded up everyone who was still in the mansion—Cormac and Liam were still gone—and told them to bring clothing and bedding to settle down for the night in the library.

After Cormac and Liam returned at nightfall, Maxine and I served bread and cheese and cold cuts for dinner, then carried the dishes down to the kitchen to wash in the freezing water in the sink. We didn't complain. At least the water line to the mansion hadn't been sabotaged.

When we returned upstairs to the library, everyone was quiet, huddled in their chosen spots, even, at last, Marco and Claire, who had complained most bitterly about the inconvenience of the situation, yet had done nothing to make it more tolerable. Even Dr. Aldridge had helped Henry, Claire, and Marco move clothing and blankets to the library.

It could have been a jolly scene, all of us gathered in the library, warmed by the large fireplace, under blankets and bedding we'd gathered, chatting or reading by candle and kerosene light. Except we all knew that the furnace and Delco generator had been sabotaged, that one of us was the saboteur. In the eerie interplay of shadow and light, we cast glances at one another, askance, except Henry and the doctor, who dozed. Claire sat in a chair staring at the fire, drinking whisky. Maxine shared a settee with Henry, keeping an eye on him. I sat in a corner next to Largo's cage, and tried to read more of *The Circular Staircase,* but I was uncomfortably far from light and my eyes strained in the dimness, the words blurring gray. I held the book open in my lap but put my remaining energy toward murmuring at Largo to keep her calm. Eddie cursed as if personally affronted every time the poor bird made a peep, and she was, understandably, upset by the confusion and the cold.

Meanwhile, the gangsters all played poker at the library table—

silently, resolutely, as if forced at gunpoint. Eddie had insisted that they would play. And so they did, grimly, grunting if they had to say something—*pass, deal, fold.*

As I watched them playing, I thought about how Eddie meant to leave Seamus, Maxine, and Henry here, but if he did, it would ultimately be a death sentence for them. The house was already freezing cold.

I shivered. Had the temperature dipped low enough, long enough, that the water would freeze around the *Myra* overnight?

There would be no way to leave with the *Myra* and the one good speedboat frozen in. The only other vessel was the old iceboat, which needed repairs and required a fully frozen lake—months away—and a new sail. It would carry, at most, two people.

If that became the only option, I wondered: Would Eddie take Cormac, his loyal soldier, back to the mainland with him? Or Marco, with whom he'd made a deal, in order to avoid the gang war that would surely ensue if he returned without him?

Marco angrily tossed his cards to the table, grunting with disgust. I pressed my lips together to suppress a smile. Apparently, Eddie had had enough of catering to Marco's ego and had finally decided to play poker to his full ability. Eddie smirked at Marco.

"Goddamn it, why can't we just leave on your stupid yacht?" Marco groused.

I inhaled sharply as Eddie's smirk pinched into ire. Marco should have known better than to malign a proud possession of Eddie's—especially one named after his mother.

"Oh yeah?" Eddie twisted the word into a warning snarl. He took a sip of his whisky and then smacked his lips. "You wanna leave on the *Myra*? In the dark? In this weather?"

"Yes?" Marco stretched the word out like a hiss, as if torn between believing he was going to get his way and sensing that Eddie was about to rip into him. Fool. Marco should also have known that his fate would be the latter.

"Don't think that's wise," Eddie said.

"Well, if you don't wanna leave, just have one of your men take me back." Marco gestured widely to take in everyone from Henry to Cormac. "Or else my men will be coming soon—"

"Sure, sure, 'cause it's so easy to navigate Lake Erie in a storm. Huh. Maybe we should share a story with you before you get on my *stupid* yacht with one of my men," Eddie said blithely. Marco frowned. Henry sat up, instinctively alert, it seemed, to his boss demanding his attention.

Maxine looked annoyed at Eddie disturbing Henry's rest, but Henry grinned, pulled out his Banjo lighter and a cigarette. After he'd allowed himself several satisfying draws, he said, "We both served on the S.S. *Martin*. So small, it barely qualified as a freighter. But it was a good boat. I was the second cook."

"And I was a deckhand," Eddie said. "Signed up as soon as I broke free from the Sisters of the Poor orphanage." He took another swallow of whisky, crossed himself. "Nothing against those nuns. Donate to them every year—under the table, of course. Somehow they don't want it publicized that their most notorious student gives 'em a big chunk of change." He chuckled, as if their shame and hypocrisy were funny.

Cormac leaned forward. He spoke as if they'd all told this story before, and he knew his lines. "Right. And who was your deck boss?"

"Why, your dear old dad, my boy," Eddie said.

I lifted my eyebrows at this. The room was tight with tension, but I was intrigued. I'd never heard this connection before. Had Rosita been aware of it?

"Good man," Eddie went on. "And Henry was the best cook. Shoulda been the first cook but, you know." He gave Marco a sharp look. "Being one of *those* people . . ."

Henry shrugged. "Learned a lot. No one gave me a hard time, 'cause I was making their meals." He, too, cut a look at Marco. "Loved my job."

"Good at it, too," Eddie said. "That was part of the deal of being on a freighter. Sure, the work was hard, dangerous, you got a bunk bed and a locker and shared a room with a bunch of other men, but the grub? Top notch."

Henry nodded. "Freighter captain used to bring on his well-heeled buddies—"

"Some of 'em are mine now!" Eddie joshed.

"—just to marvel at the food we served up."

"Better 'n what you might get in a fine Chicago restaurant. Even New York, heard more than a few of 'em say."

Where were they going with this patter? The more light-hearted they acted, the more tense the room felt. I glanced around. Everyone else was feeling that, too. Even thick-headed Marco.

"Then came October 20, 1916," Cormac said. I turned to him in surprise. How oddly specific. "The day of the Black Friday storm."

Henry shook his head. "Came up all of a sudden. Like some monster at the bottom of the lake reached up its tentacles, grabbed the *Martin,* tossed it like a plaything amongst its slimy limbs."

"No warning," Eddie said. He wasn't mugging or grinning or chuckling now. His face went granite hard. "Oh, we felt the cold and wet, but the slam of wind, rising up out of nowhere, seemed to knock our freighter around like a twig boat." He turned his dark gaze on Marco. "You ever make a twig boat, Marco?" The gangster shrank back, turning pale. He didn't respond.

"Well, all the vessels on Lake Erie turned into twig boats that day. Biggest lake storm in history, and it came out of nowhere." Eddie leaned forward, keeping his eyes pinned on Marco. "So bad that the biggest freighter on the lake, the *Merida*—more than double our boat's size—"

"Three hundred sixty foot, more 'n thirty-two hundred tons," said Henry.

"—broke apart just like a twig boat. Lost all thirty-two crew to the bottom of the lake. Boat and men, what's left of them, still down there."

I shuddered, thinking of Rosita's state after a few days in the water. Marco remained still, eyes wide, as if terrified to react or move.

"Guess we were lucky," Eddie said. "We just lost ten good men that day."

"Including my father," Cormac stated flatly. "I don't remember him. The company didn't have the decency to send along a man to tell us." He paused, and then said, as if merely musing, "But I do remember this. My first memory. Eddie here brought the news. And some money to help us out. My mother, oh how she wailed. Though she was always grateful when Eddie came around."

"How is she doing?" Eddie asked.

"Well, thanks," said Cormac. "She sends her best."

"It still haunts me, how I grabbed for him, but he slipped away," Eddie said, still staring at Marco. "But I was too late. Nearly went overboard myself. Would've, if not for Henry."

"I was pushing a cart of meals to the officers' quarters when that storm came up," Henry said. "Lost the cart but got ahold of Eddie."

"Lost more than the cart," Eddie said.

Henry held up his maimed arm. "Yeah, damned winch broke free, whipped around so hard, it sliced through my forearm and hand." He shook his head. "Not sure what hurt worse—that ripping, or the doctor trying to patch me together. 'Course that had to wait until we came safely to shore. Lost part of my hand." He held up his left arm. A thick scar ran from the stumps of his lost pinkie and ring finger, and corded up his arm to his elbow. I shuddered. Henry gave Marco a stiff, grim wave. I glanced at Marco, who grimaced, pale and uncomfortable. Served him right.

Henry went on. "Yep. Captain spotted a lighthouse beacon and came ashore—"

"Here," Eddie said, his voice the softest I'd ever heard it.

"Only reason our freighter didn't go down like—"

The room fell silent, though even through the thick library walls we could hear the wind howling like an anguished animal circling the mansion.

The implications of the story they'd just shared settled over me like a shroud. Trouble Island's lighthouse—manned by Claire and Rosita's grandfather—had saved the lives of the men on the S.S. *Martin* during the worst storm in Lake Erie's history. Including Eddie and Henry.

Had he, I wondered, ever shared that story with Rosita? If so, had she shared it with Claire?

I looked at Claire. Her eyes were wide, her expression stricken. No, this was new to her, too.

Then I looked from Eddie to Henry to Cormac. I'd had no idea how closely bonded these men were.

Finally, Eddie broke the silence, his voice back to its usual gravely harshness. "Still wanna leave on my *stupid* yacht, Marco? In this storm?"

Marco whimpered. A mewl of a sound, but it was enough for Eddie. He grinned. "I didn't think so. All right, another round of—"

Suddenly Claire stood, shrugged off her fur. She took a long drink, emptying her glass, then slammed the glass down so hard on a side table that we all jumped. She staggered away from the fire. "God, it's hot in here. And I'm sick of watching you play poker like it's some genius game. The story was better—"

Cormac frowned. "It wasn't just a story, it was the truth—"

"Ah, the truth," Claire said, her voice edging toward a hysterical pitch. "Let's get at the truth, why don't we? One of us sabotaged the house, as if trying to force us all together so we'd have to confront one another, but here we are, trying to ignore what's been going on—"

"Claire, enough," Douglas said. He stood. "You need to settle down—"

"Anyone else want to try to shut me up?" Claire said.

"Yeah," Eddie snarled. "Maybe smack you into silence."

"I can think of another way to stifle her mouth," Marco said. He gave a foul chuckle and Cormac joined in.

"Oh, you don't want to hear from me? Then how about Miss Prim and Proper." Claire pointed to me. "Our very own Aurelia Escalante. Weren't you tasked with figuring out who killed Rosita? And Joey? We're all gathered here, against our will. Why don't you tell us what you've uncovered."

I focused on Largo's pretty feathers, teal and yellow and blue. This was a bird who was not meant to be here on this island in the cold north. In that moment, I felt more akin to Largo than I did to any human in the room.

"I haven't," I said softly.

"Speak up! We can't hear you! You must project more." She made her voice more sonorous, but then giggled. "That's what Rosita always told me."

"I said, I haven't uncovered the truth. Just more and more confusion. You're right, someone in this room—probably at least two people working together given how Rosita's body was left—killed Rosita and Joey. Most likely, the same people who sabotaged the mansion."

"Well, if Aurelia isn't going to lay out all the possibilities and motives, then I will!" She traipsed around the room, and then stopped behind Liam. She put a hand on his shoulder. "How about you, Liam? Tell us about the history of Trouble Island."

Even as Liam brightened, Eddie snarled, "No one cares. We're playing a game—"

Claire reached into the middle of the game, picked up cards and chips, and threw them up in the air. "Game's over!"

I held my breath, expecting Eddie to smack her after all. But he leaned back in his chair, staring at her. Maybe he was just curious, I thought, about what Claire was playing at.

"Fine. Go on, Liam," Eddie said.

Liam moved to stand in front of the fireplace, clasped his hands behind him as if he were delivering a lecture to a great hall. "Archaeological evidence shows Trouble Island was home to indigenous peoples between 500 BC and 1500 AD and became a stopover for escaped slaves and military runaways during the Civil War. I've found pottery ware, arrowheads, weaponry," Liam said, "at various spots around the island. Even human remains." He was alight, already caught up in sharing his enthusiasm, not realizing that somehow, Claire was about to play him for a fool. "I've cataloged it all." He looked at Marco, suddenly anxious. "It should be preserved, cared for, even after you take over the island. The McGees were good about that." He suddenly teared and choked up. "Especially Rosita. She said her grandfather would be pleased, that I was honoring the island—"

"When? When did she say this?" Eddie demanded.

Liam reddened. "Oh—oh—just one of the times you visited. Before, before, before—"

My heart clenched at his shamed face, at his stuttering. When he'd fall into this mode every now and then with me, the Carmichaels, and even Seamus for the short time he'd been here, we'd tell him to pause, take a deep breath, and help ease him out of it. There was no such kindness in the library that night.

"Before Oliver's death?" Claire said coldly. "How kind of her. But why don't you tell us how you really ended up here, Liam? That's so much more interesting than all your facts and details about a bunch of dead people from long ago. What about the three people you killed on your last dig, over in Egypt, before you came here?"

Liam staggered back so fast and hard that I feared he'd tumble into the fireplace. "Rosita told you?"

Eddie frowned. "How would she—"

"Oh, she listened much more than you ever thought, Eddie," Claire said. "Rosita overheard you talking to Liam's father—a senator." She looked around the room, satisfied by the surprised looks from everyone, including mine. All were shocked except Eddie, Cormac, and Marco. This was not news to them. "That's right. Senator Robert Watts of Ohio. I think he's been here several times, and not just to visit his son. Trading favors with Eddie—"

"I didn't know!" Liam cried out in anguish. "How the sand could shift so easily in the wind. I thought the supports over the dig site were strong enough, but . . ."

"And now here you are, hiding out, at Eddie's benevolence—and because your father demanded it," Claire said. "Doing his bidding. You must have wondered what would happen if Rosita ever decided to take down Eddie, work with the Feds. Then that benevolence, that partnership with your father, would no longer protect you. After all, two of the people who died were the sons of highly placed businessmen, who'd gone to visit you, trusting you—"

Liam dropped his head to his hands. "College friends."

"Yes. Eddie's paid dearly to cover up your negligence, to make sure their fathers think it was truly an unfortunate accident. Your life would have been over if they found out the truth."

"Claire, stop this!" Eddie roared. He looked at Liam, a rare look of sympathy flickering just for a moment over his face. "What is the point of—"

"I for one would like to hear," Marco said, smirking. "I find this entertaining. Better than being allowed to win at poker, or dry facts about Indians and cowards."

"And then there's Seamus," Claire said. My stomach knotted at the realization that she was going to say something about each of us. I glanced at Seamus. Could she know he was a Fed? But his face betrayed no expression, even as she ruffled the top of his head. "I was here with the last set of visitors, just after you came on. Caught you several times, staring up at Rosita's balcony. What did you do, breach the door past her little guardian—" At that, Claire gave me a snide look. "Get spurned? Or did she take you in her open arms? Awful lonely up there."

Seamus turned to Eddie, returned his furious glare with a calm, even gaze. "Nothing like that happened, I assure you."

For a moment, I thought Eddie might suddenly pull out his gun, or command Cormac, with a single glance, to shoot Seamus. My hand slowly eased toward my right boot, where I'd tucked the stocking gun. Could I shoot fast enough to take out Eddie and Cormac? And possibly Marco?

To protect Seamus?

To release us all from their terror?

And . . . would I?

I felt sickness rising in my stomach.

Claire moved from the table to stand before the Carmichaels. "And then there's the ever-sweet Carmichaels. Always serving. Doesn't it get tiring?"

"I've known Eddie since our freighter days," Henry said. "And he was good enough to hire us both."

"But you're stuck here on the island because Henry took the fall for a robbery, in exchange for keeping your daughter safe," Claire said. "If Rosita had agreed to give up the island, the island going to Marco, you might have a chance to convince Eddie to release you from your obligations here, to go to your daughter. But of course, she didn't agree."

Maxine shook her head. "We'd never hurt Rosita, and we couldn't—"

"Oh, because you're too old, too weak?" Claire said mockingly. "But with Joey's help—"

Henry started coughing, a great rattling sound that shook him.

Dr. Aldridge leapt to his feet. "For God's sake, Claire, enough, Henry needs to rest—"

"Ah, the ever-concerned doctor," Claire said. "Here to decree Rosita insane if she doesn't go along with selling the island—or maybe for something else? Because after the Carmichaels' daughter became sicker after coming to your clinic, Rosita slipped word to

Cormac—who was still on the force at the time—about the back-room, off-hour dealings you did to cover your own habits. And that led to the raid that shut down your clinic. No decent folks would go to you for treatment after that, and so you've been stuck, ever since, treating only Eddie's men."

Dr. Aldridge sank back down into his seat. "I ran a decent clinic. I'm sorry about the people who couldn't handle my treatments, but it wasn't fair I was shut down, and—"

"So you had a good reason for revenge."

"No, I didn't know Rosita was behind—" The doctor stopped, staring at Claire for a long moment. "I came here, after poor Oliver died, to check on her each month."

"At my request," Eddie interjected, then took a drag on his cigar.

Claire moved swiftly to stand behind Douglas. "And then there's Douglas."

Douglas blanched. "Claire, everyone knows that we needed Rosita to launch our film—"

"No, we need Eddie's money, which he would only provide if Rosita would agree to be in your film. Whatever it is. I've only heard ideas. Not a page of script or a note of song, but that's probably because you're still mourning the loss of your lover," Claire said.

"Oh, come on, man, good-looking chap like you, there are surely plenty of ladies to take her place," Marco said.

Claire laughed. "Ladies?"

"Claire, don't, I'm warning you—" Douglas started.

"Or what? You'll kill me, like maybe you killed Rosita, because you know she's the one who made sure Eddie had his connections out west let the word slip that it's not ladies you're interested in. Because she knew how heartbroken I was after I went to Hollywood and you didn't want to work with me and so you had my name blackballed as a no-talent hack," Claire said. "How perfect. She ended your career and your relationship with your, well, *friend,* because your friend—famous actor that he is—knew the two of you couldn't be caught together."

Oh, I thought. *The latest Hollywood heartthrob, Curtis Langly.*

"Eddie," Douglas said, "I resented Rosita for that, yes, but I really did come out here, with Claire, hoping she'd agree to make it possible to start over. In Hollywood. As friends."

"Goddamn, my wife and her friends are gonna be so disappointed," Marco said.

"Shut up," Eddie said.

"I'm not done," Claire said, though Eddie's comment had been directed at Marco. "Then there's the obvious, of course. Marco killing Rosita—well, having Joey do it—because it would be less complicated for Eddie to just inherit the island and confer it to him, than killing Joey, because God knows he was young and dumb and might blab—"

At that, Marco blanched. "I didn't!" He turned to Eddie. "I swear, I didn't."

"Or Eddie having Cormac kill Rosita for the same reason, Joey somehow finding out—or maybe helping Cormac. Then Cormac killing Joey—again, same reason," Claire said.

"Claire, just stop—" Eddie snarled.

"Oh, but there's just one person left. I've saved the best for last."

CHAPTER 32

MY GAZE DARTED to the door, my hand gripped the top of Largo's cage. How fast might Marco draw his gun? How fast could I run, and where would I go? I could grab my coat, run to the cottage, hide there, or find somewhere else to hide . . .

But no. This was a small island. They'd find me. My eyes pricked with tears as I also realized that Largo would quickly freeze to death. I understood now, from Claire's creeping smile, that in the time between my coming here and Rosita's coming here after Oliver, Rosita had again taken Claire in as confidante. And told her everything.

"And then there's Aurelia. Rosita's darling," Claire said. "Every time I'd come here, there you'd be, cowering in the corner, so unsure of yourself—until it was time to dash off to serve Rosita her breakfast, her lunch, whatever she needed. Do you know how often we laughed at you—me and the other women—for being such a mouse, scurrying off to see the cat, trusting time and again that you wouldn't be eaten. But of course you were, bit by bit."

I stared at her, numb.

"I told the others to pity you. I knew why you were really here, though they didn't. Eddie and Rosita and Cormac did such a great job covering for you. The poor widow of Pony Walker."

Marco startled, stared at me.

"Pony was killed in a mob shooting. Shot through the head. Dumped from a car onto the road—where he'd be oh-so-conveniently found. His wife—Susan Walker—supposedly running off, never to be seen again. Easier to arrange that, to pay off the Walkers' neighbors to keep their mouths shut, than to let the cops talk with Susan. God knows what Pony had told her, or what she'd share about Eddie's operations. But actually, she was sent here to recover, under the name Aurelia Escalante."

"Claire, stop, please—" My heart pounded harder.

"Because Susan was really the one who shot her husband. Marco's dear nephew Nelson took the fall—Cormac set that up, just like he set up the raid on Dr. Aldridge's practice. All so Susan could get away with killing her husband, but really to come here because Rosita wanted to keep her confidante, her pet, available on her island."

Marco leapt to his feet, drawing a gun. Seamus wasn't the only one who'd secreted a gun from Cormac's search. I wondered how many others might have done the same, then startled as Marco pointed his gun at me. "I knew Nelson wasn't to blame—he was with me and my wife at dinner that night. I figured it was someone in Eddie's gang, knew Cormac had set up Nelson to take the fall, but—" His aim turned to Eddie. "For *her*? You set up my nephew to take the fall over her?"

Eddie shrugged, unconcerned by Marco's threatening stance, as Cormac quietly rose and moved toward Marco, who was so intently glaring at Eddie that he didn't notice. "I wanted to have her killed, make it look like a murder-suicide, but Rosita wanted to protect her. And at the time, you and I were at war with each other, so—"

Cormac grabbed Marco's wrist, pulled it down, wrested Marco's gun from him. Marco winced, cried out, "Give me my gun back! Rosita's gone now, so—"

"Now's not the time," Eddie said quietly.

My heart raced—not the time to kill me, not just yet. I was still useful.

Cormac tucked Marco's gun into his waistband. Defeated, Marco sank down into his chair, turning his hateful gaze on me. Far worse were the looks of shock on the faces of Henry, Maxine, and Liam. I ventured a glance at Seamus. He was expressionless.

"Anyway," Claire said impatiently as if she'd merely been interrupted in conversation, "Aurelia knew that Rosita could reveal at any time to Marco who she really was, and Marco would have the, well, predictable reaction he just had."

"But Eddie knew, too, and could have revealed it," I said. Though I was trembling, white-hot anger rose in me toward Claire.

"Why would he? After all, Eddie wants Marco happy. Buying the island."

"Rosita told you all this?" I asked bitterly, knowing the answer.

Claire gave her tittering laugh. "Of course! After you were sent here, what was she supposed to do? Sit with her thoughts? No, she reclaimed me as her confidante, told me everything—"

I'd had enough. I jumped up, my fists clenched at my side, my shoulders tight to my body. Largo squawked and everyone stared at me. "Everything? Really? Did she tell you that after losing our first baby, I thought I'd never be able to get pregnant again? But then I did, and I thought I could be happy . . . until Pony was cut out of Eddie's organization. I never knew why. But he took his anger that he wasn't rising like he wanted in Eddie's organization out on me. He hit me—and I lost the baby."

"Oh, dames lose their litters now and again," Marco said. "And a man's got a right to discipline his woman, and you don't know getting swatted had anything to do—"

"It did." Dr. Aldridge spoke up. His voice was shaky, thin, but he gave Marco a harsh look. "I attended Susan—Aurelia here—multiple times at Rosita's request. And after she lost her baby. Susan had called Rosita for help. She was badly beaten, far worse than in the past."

Seamus's gaze flashed between sorrow for me and rage at Pony. Eddie gave me a slightly sympathetic look. Everyone else—except Marco and Cormac—looked horrified.

"Still didn't need to shoot him over that," Cormac said, giving me a look that said he thought I was an interfering dame. "Did you really think we was gonna cut him free and let him live? We knew he'd been talking to a rival." He stabbed Marco with his gaze, and Marco squirmed.

Had Pony been stupid enough to make plans to try to jump to Marco's gang?

It didn't matter now.

"I didn't shoot him over causing me to lose our baby," I said. "I shot him because of what he did to the canary Rosita sent to cheer me up—"

Eddie frowned. "I told her to cut you off after we got rid of Pony."

"But she didn't. She sent me the canary. I named her Dahlia. And that night, he got angry at me when he demanded I get Rosita to get you to bring him back, and I told him that wouldn't work, and he grabbed Dahlia out of her cage. And he squeezed the poor bird to death." My throat clenched, but I forced myself to go on. "And I couldn't . . . I just couldn't take it anymore . . . and his gun was on the end table and I just picked it up and I shot him."

I stared at my right hand as if it was a foreign thing with a will of its own. But no. I knew what I was doing.

I wanted to kill him.

The moments after I pulled that trigger flashed across my mind. The reverberating air. The sound of Pony crying out, then falling silent. My rushing out of the house, Mrs. Schmitt out on her front porch sweeping as she did every night, pausing to stare after me as I ran, ran, ran for Rosita. The only person I could think of going to.

I should have just grabbed any money or anything of value in the house and run toward Chicago as I'd planned. But my emotions were a swirl—horror, then relief, then horror at that sense of relief— and I missed Rosita and was still so dependent on her friendship.

She'd comforted me, told me she'd figure things out. She called for Dr. Aldridge, who came and gave me a double dose of Veronal. By the time I was coming around, Rosita, Eddie, and Oliver were out of their Toledo mansion. Only Cormac was there, gruffly ordering me about, taking me by my Toledo house one last time, then taking me to Trouble Island, where I've been ever since.

"Well, enough of Aurelia's sob story," Claire said, and gave a small, shaky laugh. "That's everyone, so who do we think the killers really are—"

"Not everyone," I snapped. "You've left yourself out."

Surprise flushed Claire's face, a satisfying sight. "Why would I kill my dear cousin Rosita? I needed her, after all, and of course I loved her, too—"

"Someone had to go up to Rosita's suite. And of everyone here, who would she most likely have let in? Her *dear cousin,* as you say. Her once and future confidante. Maybe you went to beg her to reconsider the movie with you and Douglas. Maybe she laughed at you." I paused. "Maybe you convinced her to walk again those paths you know so much about, the ones she'd once made you walk with her when you were children. And maybe jealousy finally took over. If she wasn't going to help you, after all these years of you being in her shadow, then why not get rid of her? Make it easier for Eddie to sell the island to Marco. You could cozy up to him, later, for influence and money."

At that, Claire blanched. "I wouldn't, I—"

"Oh, come on." My voice grew in both volume and coldness. "You enjoy toying with people, don't you?"

"Well, I certainly wouldn't have had the strength to tie her body up—"

"So, you got big, dumb Joey's help. Then stabbed him and left him for dead. And now you're assigning motives to everyone else."

Claire sank down into her chair. "You don't have any proof," she said petulantly, staring into her empty glass.

"Neither do you," I snapped.

Claire looked up at me then. "But I do know this. Rosita blamed you for Oliver's death. You set everything in motion, by killing Pony. She wished she'd never helped you. Wished she'd let Eddie have you killed as he'd wanted. She told me on the way over from Toledo. As she stood by Oliver's casket." Tears rose in Claire's eyes. "She never left his casket. Stood with it the whole way. And standing there, she told me she wanted you dead. But that she knew she couldn't bring herself to kill you. Couldn't bring herself to ask Eddie to get rid of you, because now she hated him, too. All she knew was that the worst thing that ever happened in her life was meeting you—"

Maxine stood, rushed over to Claire, put a hand on her arm. "Claire, please—"

Claire shook Maxine's hand free as if it were merely a pesky fly, and on she went, her cold voice sprinkling down on my head like ice shards, like the spitting ice and snow outside. "She told me that the only satisfaction she could imagine would be to keep you serving her as you had been over the past year, seeing the shame and guilt you carry in your expression, your shoulders, your eyes, seeing how torn you were between knowing what you'd done, that you didn't deserve freedom, and yet longing to pursue your fanciful dreams of traveling far and wide. Oh yes, she told me how you still talked about that with her, even after you came here. So, she would make you keep serving her, but not talk with you at all, and watch you slowly wither. And then, if you didn't kill yourself as you apparently wailed you wanted to after killing Pony, she'd eventually get Eddie to have you killed." Claire finally paused, long enough to take a breath. Long enough for her thin smile to again slowly creep across her face. "Because she hated you, Aurelia. To the bitter end, she hated you."

I gave my head a defiant toss. "I know she hated me. The last time I saw her alive, she made that clear." A lump rose in my throat, but I swallowed it back. "But I never hated her. And I didn't kill her."

CHAPTER 33

AFTER CLAIRE'S ROUND-ROBIN of accusations, we all became quiet and withdrawn.

We huddled under our blankets on couches and chairs or on spots on the floor.

I tried to stay awake, and I noticed Seamus and Cormac doing the same, eying one another mistrustfully.

I felt the weight of the small pistol that Seamus had given me pressing against my ankle. I wondered if this gun was the only one he held back, or if he'd secreted away another one. Or, for that matter, his badge or paperwork proving he was part of the bureau.

I kept turning over the possibility of running.

But where to run? I'd be found in the cottage or the lighthouse quickly enough. I'd freeze to death if I tried to hide outside on the island. The horrifying story that Eddie, Cormac, and Henry had shared earlier haunted me.

But the storm would surely abate. Maybe the speedboat would be too dangerous to take. But surely, once the lake calmed, the *Myra* would be safe enough.

Could I get to the *Myra* without being caught? Figure out how to start it up, run it?

I shook my head at myself. The speedboats had pull starts, simple cords. But the *Myra* would have an ignition key.

And that key would be securely kept by Cormac.

Shy of drugging him or killing him, I wasn't going to get the key from him.

The northern shore of Ohio now felt thousands of miles away instead of ten or so.

Eventually, my eyelids became leaden, and I fell asleep. When I jerked awake, uncertain what had startled me, the candles had burned out but most of the coal oil lamps were still going. The fire had died down. My first thought was that we—meaning me and Maxine—would have to fill the lamps, and add more wood to the fire, and soon.

But then my gaze drifted to Seamus. Light flickered across his handsome face. I longed to go to him and gently stir him awake and lead him upstairs. It would be colder up there, but we could make our own warmth and comfort.

I noted the others: Marco, head back, mouth open. Claire on the couch, Douglas and Eddie in their chairs, all sleeping.

Cormac and Liam were gone. They'd snuck out, I guessed, to keep transferring those lockboxes to the *Myra*. Through the window, the sky was still pitch-black. I closed my eyes, tried to will myself back to sleep.

But then I heard Maxine desperately whisper, *"Aurelia."* She was by Henry, her arm around his shoulder, her face clenched in a terrified expression. I quickly made my way over to them and immediately understood why she was so panicked—Henry's lips had a bluish cast to them, and he was short of breath.

"He's not responding to me!" Maxine cried out. The others stirred around us. I hurriedly looked around for the doctor—but he was also gone.

I RUSHED UP the stairs, hoping I'd find Dr. Aldridge in his room. Maybe he'd slipped up there, thinking he'd be more comfortable, if not warmer, in a bed? Or, if he were elsewhere, I could grab more of the medicine he had administered to Henry just two days before. Veronal and morphine, I recalled. But how much?

Dr. Aldridge was splayed across his bed, dressed as he had been the night before. The bed was made up. He hadn't crawled under the covers for warmth. His eyes were still open.

On the bedside table was an empty water glass. And a bottle of Veronal. Also empty. That photo of a young man and his family.

The room smelled of human waste. In a quick glance, I saw the dark stain on the doctor's pants at the crotch, on the bedspread. I put my hand to my mouth, stifling a gag.

Suicide? I looked again at the bedside table. No note, at least not in an obvious place.

But I didn't have time to indulge in theories. I had to help Henry.

I spotted the doctor's medical bag on the floor in front of the wardrobe. That was where his morphine should be—morphine he'd brought to sedate Rosita.

I dropped to my knees, opened the bag.

The bottle and syringe I'd seen him use earlier with Henry were gone. I pounded my fists to my knees in frustration. Then I jumped up, rushed back to the bedside table. Maybe the medicine was there. Maybe Dr. Aldridge hadn't brought the morphine just for Rosita. His flushed, bleary-eyed demeanor flashed before me. Maybe he'd been an addict.

There was no bottle or syringe on the table, or in its drawer.

But this time, I noticed that the doctor's shirt and jacket sleeves were pushed up on his right arm. There was a rusty red dash of dried blood on the inside of his wrist. A clumsy injection, odd for a doctor—

"Henry!"

Maxine's cry, as visceral as if her very soul was being rendered, echoed all the way up to me.

I stood and ran.

"You have to help us! Get us on the *Myra*, take us to Toledo for help," Maxine was crying as I rushed into the library. She was standing nearly against Eddie, her fists clenched as if she might start beating on his chest.

Eddie glanced over Maxine's head at me. "Where's the doctor?"

I gave a small shake of my head. "He's dead."

Several people gasped; I don't know who. My gaze was going between Maxine and Henry, her so frantic, him so quiet and still. I didn't have time for anyone else.

"Please, Eddie, listen to her," I started.

"We've worked for you for years," Maxine said. "Please."

"I'm sorry. We can't leave just yet," Eddie said.

Because of his damned precious cargo. The lockboxes Cormac and Liam were transporting onto the *Myra*. Even after revealing their shared story of terror on the freighter, money mattered more to Eddie than Henry did.

I rushed over to Seamus, standing in the corner. His arms went around me immediately, but it wasn't comfort I wanted. Still, I leaned into his embrace, taking the chance to whisper in his ear, "Cormac is occupied. We can take out Eddie now, maybe Marco too, worry about Cormac after we get Henry out to the *Myra*. I have the pistol you gave me and surely you—"

"I'm sorry. I can't leave while there's still a chance I can find whatever Rosita had—"

My body stiffened so quickly that Seamus stopped whispering. Disgust and anger rose in me. Seamus would pass on helping Henry for his chance to get incriminating evidence against Eddie. I wanted to shove him away from me. But doing so would draw attention. Better to make it look like I was simply seeking comfort from him.

I backed away slowly, but before I turned from him, I gave him a direct, cold stare. He looked sorrowful but gave his head a small shake.

"You have to help him, please, please!" Maxine was sobbing, now hitting Eddie's chest.

"You gonna take talk like that from—" Marco started.

"Shut up!" Eddie snapped.

"Maxine, stop. Come here." Henry's voice was thin and reedy, a raveling thread between this life and the next.

I rushed over to Maxine, put my arm gently around her shoulder, and guided her back to her beloved. She kneeled before him. He put his trembling hand on her head, and she took his other hand in hers. I stepped back to give them space.

"It's all right," Henry said. "I've had a good life with you. And me being gone—this will free you." He glanced at Eddie, spoke a little louder. "Right, Eddie?"

Eddie's eyes glistened. But he cleared his throat. "Yes, Henry."

Henry looked back at Maxine. "So you will go. Have me buried. Go to our daughter."

I looked at Eddie. Though he was moved by Henry's imminent passing, he'd never set Maxine free. She knew too much, had seen too much.

Maxine was crying freely now and nodding at Henry.

"And it's better this way, because I have a confession. I killed Rosita."

"No!" Maxine cried out.

"Yes," Henry said. His eyes flicked to me ever so briefly, and my breath just stopped. "I was up late, unable to sleep the night after everyone arrived. I went up to the suite to talk with her, asked if she would please sell the island, talk with Eddie about letting us go to Alabama, but she laughed at me. I pushed her, and she fell back and hit her head. I knew she was dead. I went to get help and ran into Joey and promised him I'd pay him to help me move her." A coughing fit cut off Henry's words. After he regained his breath, his voice was raspy. "But I knew I could never pay him, so I got him outside a few days later, telling him I had money locked away in the lighthouse, and I killed him."

"What?" Marco roared and started toward Henry.

Eddie grabbed Marco's arm and shoved him to the couch. "So help me God, Marco, just stop."

Claire rushed over, fell to her knees by Henry's side. "No, Henry, you couldn't have. Forget everything I said last night. You love Rosita and—" She stopped on a gurgling sound, like something was caught in her throat. "—and she loved you." Tears streamed openly down her face.

"I know, honey," Henry said. Then he moved his hand to his wife's face.

"Come, everyone out, let's leave them with privacy," Douglas said. His voice came from another corner of the room. He moved to Claire, dragged her out of the library.

"But it's warmest in here—" Marco started, then stopped as Eddie glared at him.

They followed Claire and Douglas out to the vestibule, and then Seamus and I left, too.

"To the music room," Douglas said.

We followed him, finding seats in the frigid room.

He began playing something soft and simple and sweet, like a lullaby, his eyes closed. Whether to comfort Maxine and Henry, or to mask whatever words they might have to say to one another at the end, I've never been sure.

But as he played, I stared at Claire, the tears streaming down her face.

You love Rosita and—and she loved you . . .

What she'd just said, how she said it, echoed in my mind. Her emotion, so overwrought for Claire about the Carmichaels, struck me.

You love Rosita and—and she loved you . . .

That catch between the two ands.

Claire had been about to say, *You love Rosita and I love you.*

But it hit me all at once, not *I* as in Claire.

I as in Rosita.

CHAPTER 34

CLAIRE IS . . . ROSITA.

It seemed impossible, and yet, I couldn't shake the thought.

Maxine came into the music room only twenty minutes or so after we'd left her with Henry. *He's gone,* she'd said quietly. Tears streamed down her face, yet she looked numb.

She asked for me, Seamus, and Douglas to return to the library with her.

If Rosita has been pretending all along to be Claire, then someone murdered Claire and Joey. We've buried Claire . . .

Why hadn't I seen it? That "Claire" was really Rosita? I glanced back at the woman as I exited the music room. No, I still didn't see it. The two women were the same height, same coloring. But Claire was pudgier. Rosita had a beauty mark—easy to add, but impossible to completely cover up even with makeup. And after the rough night, any traces of makeup were worn from Claire's face. And beyond that, their voices were so different, their demeanors, their expressions and style of speaking . . .

I shook my head. Surely I was wrong.

In the library, Maxine knelt beside her husband, leaned over him, kissed him gently on his forehead. She pulled his beloved Banjo lighter from his pocket. Then insisted on overseeing Seamus and Douglas as they carefully covered Henry's body with a blanket, on following them out to the *Myra*. I helped Maxine put on a coat, then quickly donned mine, determined to go with her. I held her elbow; she did not shake me away.

Eddie promised that he would bring Maxine and Henry back to Toledo, that Henry would get a proper burial, that he would let Maxine free to go to her daughter.

I didn't believe him. Even in her shocked, numb state, I could see in Maxine's eyes that she did not believe him, either.

I also did not believe Henry's confession. Yes, I had considered why he and Maxine might have killed Rosita and Joey, and he had given an explanation for why he would have done so, but it was too convenient that he'd confessed only when he knew he was dying.

He knew that Eddie had kept me around only as a scapegoat. By confessing that he was the killer, he was saving me from having to be the scapegoat. Was that his motivation?

Or was he afraid I'd just keep digging for the truth about Rosita's and Joey's deaths? Did he know who really was guilty and he was trying to protect the person? Of course he'd protect Maxine. If he knew that Rosita was really alive, and pretending to be Claire, I imagined he would protect Rosita, too. After the revelations about his and Eddie's and Cormac's father's traumatic experiences on the S.S. *Martin* freighter, I could also see why he'd protect those men.

I made sure that Maxine was settled down in front of a newly built-up fire in the library. Claire—*or Rosita?*—promised me she'd keep an eye on her. I nodded but kept from making eye contact with her. Seamus and Douglas quietly settled back into the library, while Marco stared sulkily into the fireplace.

But why would Rosita allow us to believe she'd been murdered, knowing her cousin Claire was the real victim? Had Rosita killed Claire? Was it possible that Eddie was in on the ruse? Or—I thought back to that moment between Henry and Claire—*even Henry and Maxine?*

Eddie and I went up to Dr. Aldridge's room. I carried a coal oil lantern to light our way up the stairs; Eddie had a flashlight. The draperies were open, but the snow whirled so thickly outside that only thin light filtered into the room.

"You found him like this?" Eddie asked.

I nodded.

"You think he killed himself?" Eddie asked, staring at Dr. Aldridge splayed across the bed.

The scenario made it look like he had. But the injection mark on his arm, plus the missing vial of morphine, the syringe, made me wonder. Would he have injected himself, and then gone to the trouble to hide away the vial and syringe? Wouldn't a full bottle of Veronal be sufficient for suicide? Where was his note—or had he opted not to leave one? Had someone lured him upstairs and then killed him, tried to make it look like a suicide?

"I don't know," I answered flatly.

Eddie picked up the photo of the doctor's son's family from the side table. "His wife died just a few years after their only child was born." He put the photo face down on the doctor's chest, and briefly touched the old-fashioned bow tie. "I guess he never got over it. Numbed himself, lived in the past. Son left as soon as he was old enough. The doctor couldn't break free from it to move forward. But what kind of a man commits suicide?"

My heart suddenly beat hard, like a panicked bird trapped in a cage. I knew the answer to that. I'd witnessed it, been part of the reason, back home. That's why I'd run to Toledo, with every step pushing the images, and my own guilt, back, far back, in my mind, where I'd kept them hidden for years.

"Maybe Claire's words got to him last night," Eddie went on. "Felt guilty."

What did Eddie know about Claire really being Rosita?

"Dr. Aldridge did not strike me as someone who often felt guilt," I said carefully. "And Henry did not kill Rosita or Joey, either by himself or with help."

Eddie gave me an incredulous look. "You don't know that for certain," he said. "And Henry's confession gives you a way out—"

I whirled on him. "Because with that confession, you're going to take us all back with you on the *Myra*? Let Maxine and me roam free, out of your control?" Liam and Douglas would remain beholden to Eddie, in his employ. And Seamus would keep up his ruse as long as he could. As for Claire . . .

If Claire isn't Claire, but is Rosita playing Claire, why? To test Eddie? To help Seamus? Are they in on Rosita's ruse together? If not, how could he not recognize his own wife pretending to be her cousin? Or that Rosita's body was really Claire's?

But the bloated body, the grotesquely marred face, floated across my mind. Suddenly I was dizzy. Eddie caught me as I pitched forward, keeping me from falling on top of Dr. Aldridge's body. For that I was grateful, but I pulled my elbow from Eddie's grasp.

"Never mind what Claire said last night. It was cruel. Rosita wanted to give you another chance at life here on Trouble Island," Eddie said. "Henry's confessed. There are witnesses. Why can't you accept that as his dying gift? And no, you won't roam free, you will have to live under the conditions I set, but you'll live. And not just on this island."

I stared at him. "You wanted to just kill me after Pony. Why change your mind?"

"You've shown yourself to be a lot spunkier and more resourceful than you ever seemed before," Eddie said. "Getting rid of Pony did you some good. And me, too. He was a loose cannon. Sooner or later, he was going to mouth off to the wrong people. Undercover Feds try to get in my organization all the time." He arched an eyebrow at me. "Maybe you could be even more useful. A pretty little thing like you could help me root them out."

My face burned bright, both at his callous words about what I did to Pony, and out of fear. Did he suspect Seamus?

What if he already knows Seamus is a Fed? What kind of game might Eddie and Rosita be playing together?

Yet, Eddie was offering me protection in his gang, probably to become some gangster's moll. I turned Eddie's offer over in my mind. He was offering me a chance to live, but under his terms. I knew what it was like to live with a man like Pony, and I would not do so again. I would still not be free.

Dizziness threatened me again, pinpricks dancing in my field of vision, but I took a deep breath, then fought back a gag at the odors I inhaled, speaking as calmly as I could. "But now Marco knows I killed Pony, that I'm the reason his nephew was set up to take the fall for Pony's murder. He'll come after me—"

Eddie grinned, a rare expression. It made his face look like it was cracking in half. He leaned toward me, and said softly, "Don't worry about Marco, sweetheart. Cormac and I know how to handle him."

Oh. Eddie would take Marco's money for Trouble Island, sure. Use it to clear his debts. But Eddie would never let Marco live to enjoy the island where Oliver was buried, the island and mansion that were a wedding gift for Rosita in happier times . . .

Oh God. Rosita and Eddie really are in this together. Conspiring somehow to lure Marco here, get his money. Had Claire figured that out, and so they killed her? But why have Rosita pretend to be Claire? And could she really do that to someone she grew up with, someone she'd supposedly loved?

I shuddered, suddenly feeling like an insect caught in a murderous sticky web so large that I couldn't really see it.

Eddie mistook my trembling for queasiness. "Go downstairs, doll," he said. His sudden cloying kindness made my stomach knot. "This is no place for a lady."

I didn't understand what was going on around me, all the undercurrents and games. But I did understand that challenging Eddie would not help me break free of the snarling, grasping hold of the McGees. So I said, "Thank you. And thank you for your advice."

Eddie's eyebrows went up. "So you'll come, then? Back on the *Myra*? Trust me to work things out for you?"

Trust Eddie, this sudden change of heart toward me?

Never.

I just wanted out of the room, away from Eddie. So I nodded.

"Tell the others it was suicide," Eddie said. "That our best guess is we think he was overcome by guilt after Claire's little diatribe. Life poorly spent, all that." He actually chuckled. "Maybe that'll make her feel guilty." He paused, considering. "She was sure more overcome by Henry's death than I'd have guessed. She was never as close to the Carmichaels as Rosita."

Maybe Eddie doesn't know . . . Maybe not seeing her for more than a year, and his own anger at her, blurred his memory of the details and nuances of her face, her demeanor . . .

I shuddered at that sorrowful possibility as I rushed from Dr. Aldridge's room. But in the hallway, I paused. A light flickered from under the doorway to the bathroom. The door opened and Claire (*Rosita?*) stepped out, holding her own lantern.

I stared at her, at the light and shadow from her lantern dancing over her nearly perfect face. No, this had to be Claire. Just Claire. Where was the beauty mark, for one thing? Claire's face was clean, clear of makeup. If Rosita had merely dabbed on makeup to cover up her beauty mark, the mark would be evident. And Claire's voice, her heavier girth, dumpier demeanor—yes, I told myself. This was Claire. My confusion and exhaustion were making me imagine the impossible. Of course we'd buried Rosita.

Claire frowned at me for staring at her. "What?" she snapped. "I had to go to the bathroom."

CHAPTER 35

MY MIND WHIRLED. I needed proof that Claire was really Rosita, that the woman we'd buried was really Claire, before confronting Rosita to find out why she would pretend to be Claire.

Even while tending to Maxine, I was distracted, worrying over how I could find such proof, and what I would do once I found it.

"He's going to the strobing lights," she muttered, as she stared at Henry's Banjo lighter, flicking it now and again, as if the light might conjure him back to life. She didn't seem to notice the food or water I'd just brought her.

For a moment, I pushed the Rosita-Claire conundrum to the back of my mind, sat down by Maxine, and put my arm around her.

She offered a wobbly smile. "I nearly died in childbirth with Ada. I saw lights, pulsing on and off. Strobing. Like they wanted me to follow. Like the light from a lighthouse, leading a ship to safety. I didn't think that then, but after we came here, I thought that's what the strobing light was like. But it must not have been my time to leave this life, go on to the next."

Maxine tucked the lighter in her apron pocket, and closed her eyes. As I pulled the quilt over her, I recollected how I'd once thought

I'd seen those lights. I put the sustenance I'd brought her on a side table. It would be there for her when she awoke, but I hoped for now she'd drift off. Dream of better times in the past with her dear Henry and Ada.

After that, I fetched simple foods and drinks for everyone else. Sights—Douglas and Seamus taking the doctor's body to the *Myra*—and sounds—the wind gusting in the foyer as they came and went—were a humming background to my preoccupation: how to best handle my realization about Rosita.

After dark, Cormac and Liam returned, and they took in the news about Henry and Dr. Aldridge with the numbness of weary soldiers.

I understood their numbness.

Marco bellowed, "I thought we were leaving today," and as Cormac gave an almost imperceptible head shake, Eddie casually dismissed Marco. "We'll leave when the time is right." Even my own thought—*Oh, they still haven't finished moving the lockboxes*—seemed like it was happening outside of myself, in the chilly library.

That night, my mind whirled.

We were all again bedded down in the library, a few candles flickering. The wind howled outside, nearly overpowering the sounds of sleeping—snores and, in poor Maxine's case, moans.

I lay wide awake, staring at shadows, thinking back on how gleefully "Claire" had accused each person of Rosita's murder. It was obvious to me now that the real Claire would never have been that clever. How hurt expressions flitted quickly as the brush of a hummingbird wing across her face whenever Eddie had referred to Rosita's death in a callow way. How her gaze could not pull free from Oliver's gravestone at the burial.

They had to have made the switch late that first night. While the Carmichaels rested in their quarters. And the rest of the men played in the casino—except for Seamus. Who'd been with me, in my bedroom.

A chill ran over me with the prickling strides of a thousand ants as I thought about that next morning, Eddie going wild about Rosita being missing, and the woman coming out of Claire's room actually being Rosita. Acting as if she were Claire.

But why? To protect herself? And if so, why not seek Seamus's help? He'd already admitted to me that he was trying to work with Rosita.

What if Rosita and Claire switching roles had been preplanned between them? What if he'd been in on it? And what if I was naïve enough to believe that he really was on the up-and-up as a Fed?

I looked over at Seamus. I still wasn't sure I could trust him. But I decided to take a risk—a careful risk.

Fortunately, there was no one between us on the floor and he was positioned near the library door. I sidled over to him. He was deeply asleep. I allowed myself a moment, just a moment, to mourn what could only be a fantasy, never come to being in real life. Then I quietly pulled the stocking gun from my boot and poked the weapon into Seamus's ribs. I wanted to trust him, but doubt nibbled at that desire.

He stirred, then startled, turned to look at me, then realized I held the gun on him. His eyes grew wide.

"We're going to slip out of this room, quietly. If anyone stirs, we're just sneaking off for privacy," I whispered.

"But why—"

I pushed the gun harder into his ribs.

Out in the vestibule, I gestured to the stairs. Quietly, he ascended, with me right behind him. At the top of the stairs, he whispered, "Now what?"

I pointed to Claire's bedroom.

The door was locked. I knelt and used a hairpin to quickly release the flimsy lock. Seamus eyed me with a mix of amusement and admiration, and I shrugged.

We slipped in and I shut the door, locking it in case anyone had stirred and followed us. Even if someone else could pick a lock—I thought immediately of Cormac—this locked door rattling would buy us a little time to come up with an excuse for being in her room.

Inside the bedroom, Claire's shoes and clothes and jewelry were scattered over the floor, the bed, bureau, chair. Seamus faced me. He didn't say anything. His expression, in spite of the stocking gun I held on him, was patient.

I spoke quietly, sharing my theory—that Rosita and Claire had switched roles sometime that first night, and that either Rosita had had a hand in Claire's murder and continued pretending to be Claire for some reason, or that someone had murdered Claire thinking she was Rosita and again Rosita—perhaps to protect herself—had continued to pretend to be Claire.

He looked shocked. "But why switch?"

"I'm not sure. Maybe to be able to freely move around the mansion, hear what people say about her. Or to be able to move around whatever she has on Eddie."

"Then why wouldn't she have just come to me?"

I glanced at the gun I held. Seamus's wry expression told me he probably regretted giving it to me.

"Maybe, like me, she wasn't sure if she could trust you."

Seamus looked crestfallen. "Oh, Aurelia—"

"I don't know who to trust anymore. I can't sort out who is working with who, all the undercurrents and secrets—" I stopped, hearing the weariness in my voice and hating that I sounded that way. "Anyway, if Rosita has been playing Claire, maybe she moved whatever she had on Eddie from the floorboard under the dresser in Oliver's nursery to somewhere in here."

"Are you going to just hold my own gun on me while we—what?"

"Search for anything proving Claire is really Rosita. And if Rosita is staying in here, she's probably hidden away the proof she has against Eddie." I thought of her reference to it that first night, of the scrap of paper caught in the corner of the lockbox under the floorboard. "And I'm guessing that you know what that proof would be."

"Not specifically. But documents, double books maybe, that might show one set of income for taxes, another for actual accounting. And I do know that Eddie has been taking nearly half his payments from his customers and in the shakedowns his men do for him in the form of gold bullion and jewelry. This sidesteps having to deposit cash at the bank, and therefore pay taxes."

I forced my expression to remain still. I wasn't willing to share with Seamus what I knew about the lockboxes. Not until I was sure I could trust him. But when would that be? And after all I'd been through, would I ever be able to trust anyone again?

"So if he has these assets as payment instead of money, it would make sense to store them here, planning to sell later," I said as casually as possible. "And he is in desperate need of money, so he wants Rosita to sell the island to Marco, but he definitely doesn't want Marco to get his mitts on any of the gold or jewels. If, for now, it's legal for him to have them—"

"Wouldn't it be helpful to have a record of all the bullion and jewels—quantity, type, precise description—to match up to past sales, and when they start flooding the pawnshops again? Especially if the record matches the receipts of purchases made time and again at one specific pawnshop by known members of Eddie's organization."

I understood, and I nodded. All the Feds needed was the shop owner and a few members of Eddie's organization to flip; Liam's testimony would make the case almost ironclad.

I recollected that Pony had complained about all the buying and transporting he had to do, how menial it was; I thought he meant bootleg whisky and was confused why he would feel this was beneath him, since that's what he often said he loved—the challenge of pulling off a transfer or sale.

"Rosita has those records? How could she have kept track at the same time that she was—supposedly—staying in her suite? Oh!" It hit me. Liam would have kept those records for Eddie. He'd been on the island for years now, as long as the Carmichaels. I bet he'd been making the transfers, keeping Eddie's records since he arrived. How long ago had Rosita charmed Liam into making a duplicate set for her—or reporting the information to her so she could record it? Maybe shortly after meeting Liam. Before losing Oliver.

I thought back on Liam's face that first night she came down, the surprise, but almost immediately, a look of wonder, adoration. Rosita and Liam . . .

But she never left her suite . . . I shook my head. I didn't know what was true anymore of Rosita. At one time I'd have been certain that, as she vowed, she never left. But at one time I'd have also been certain that even after the trouble with Pony, after Oliver's death, we'd remained friends. That she was just distant because of grief. But I'd have been wrong.

The image of her red diary, out on her dining table the morning of Eddie's arrival, came to mind. Would she have really used the precious book in which she'd recorded Oliver's life as a ledger to track Eddie's financial shenanigans? Had she really become that hard-hearted?

But then I thought of the scrap of cream paper in the corner of the lockbox under the floorboard in Oliver's nursery.

Of how eager both Eddie and Seamus had been to find Rosita's red diary, after I mentioned I'd seen it out.

Slowly, I said, "You mentioned a mole."

Seamus nodded, an eyebrow cocked. He was interested, I could tell, in what I'd be able to piece together on my own.

I frowned, thinking of the women who came here during the warmer months. Wives, more often lovers, of men that Eddie wanted to coerce or repay. I'd assumed one of those women was the mole, desperate to break free. But maybe I only assumed that about those women because that was how I felt.

Which of the women came regularly? A few came more than once, but not regularly.

What about shy, awkward Liam, with his focus on his fossils and archaeological finds? I tried to imagine him talking smoothly to one of those women, in a way that wouldn't stand out.

And then it hit me. Of course. Only one person had regular access to Rosita besides me after she came here—a person who Eddie not only trusted, but who he'd sent on purpose to check on Rosita. "Dr. Aldridge," I whispered. "He was your mole!"

Seamus nodded. "He approached someone in the bureau. He wanted out of working for Eddie, wanted immunity and money and safety so he could reconnect with his family. A son who'd long ago left Ohio and wanted nothing to do with the doctor or his criminal connections. And . . . Dr. Aldridge was sick. Dying. Liver cancer. He just wanted protection for the final months of his life and for his family, so he could make amends."

Oh, how tragic, I thought. The doctor was dead before he could make that reconciliation. Was his death truly an accidental overdose, or had someone killed him because they figured out he was a mole for the Feds? Or, after Rosita's apparent death, had he panicked and foolishly tipped his hand to Eddie?

Nervously, I cleared my throat, but still spoke in a hushed tone. "Did either Liam or Dr. Aldridge know you're undercover?" If they had, and revealed that Seamus was a Fed, surely Eddie or Cormac would have taken out Seamus.

Unless, again, Seamus had flipped his loyalty to Eddie—in which case, I was a fool for trusting Seamus this much, even with a gun on him.

Seamus shook his head. "I was chosen to come here because I was new to Toledo. No one knew me."

"But you said before that the mole . . . Dr. Aldridge"—the realization that the loyal doctor had betrayed Eddie was still head-spinning to me—"told you that Rosita was possibly open to working with you."

"That's what Dr. Aldridge told one of my colleagues. The doctor and I never met before he came here a few days ago. Anyway, yes.

According to the doctor, Rosita had financial information that proved Eddie was guilty of tax evasion." Seamus grinned. "The assistant attorney general—a woman you'd like, Mabel Willebrandt—came up with the tactic of nabbing these criminals on tax evasion, since they often slip out of other charges."

"How did Dr. Aldridge know this? Surely Rosita didn't trust him with this?"

"He spotted that red diary of hers out on the table during one of his visits. She must have been lightheaded from the Veronal, gotten careless and left it out, and fell asleep. He reported that the first pages in the diary were ripped out—"

Oh! My heart panged at that—Rosita tearing out what she'd written about Oliver. Had she kept the pages? Burned or otherwise destroyed them?

"—but she'd carefully copied out Eddie's financial holdings. She must have done so just before coming to Trouble Island to bury their son."

How would she have gotten ahold of that information? But then I remembered that Rosita had caught me using a hairpin to try to pick the lock to Eddie's office back in Toledo. Pony had wanted me to get in, find anything he could use to go to another gang to get in their good graces. He was frustrated, felt he wasn't rising fast enough.

Rosita had caught me in the act. I didn't realize, until that conversation with Seamus, that she'd been observing how I did it. She'd just acted all horrified, and I told her that Pony was eager to pay off some gambling debts and he wanted me to bring home any cash I could find.

I feared that if I told her the truth, Eddie would have him killed. Little did I know that six months later, he'd push me so far, hurt me so much, that I'd kill him myself. If I'd have told the truth so that Eddie's thugs would kill Pony, I wouldn't have gotten into the mess that has me caught on this island.

Anyway, in that moment with Seamus, I was focused on the

important information—Rosita had accessed and copied out Eddie's records before coming here. And that meant she had planned all along to betray Eddie.

Combining the knowledge of what Eddie had reported of his income, with records of how much he'd spent to convert unreported cash to goods—the bullion and jewels hidden away on the island—would make a compelling argument that he was guilty of tax evasion.

Seamus had trusted me with what he knew. Sure, I held a gun on him—but I knew that I wouldn't bring myself to shoot him. And I was sure he knew that too. He could have powered it away from me at any time if he'd wanted to.

My head was pounding, but I forced myself to think. Seamus had gone wide-eyed when I referenced Rosita's red diary the morning Rosita was discovered missing and Seamus, Eddie, and I searched her suite for clues. Seamus must have been anxious to find the diary before Eddie did; no wonder Seamus had gone up to the suite a second time.

And Eddie must have been just as desperate to find what Rosita had on him. Did he know that she had copied out his original records? Had the doctor flipped his loyalty back to Eddie and told him, or was the doctor working both sides? Was that why the doctor was killed—if his death wasn't accidental or suicide?

Then I considered—if Seamus had flipped to Eddie, he probably already knew about the lockboxes. But if he hadn't, if he was on the up-and-up as a Fed, then this would be important information to him.

Finally, I said, "Remember the empty lockbox we found under the floorboard in Oliver's nursery?"

A frown flicked across Seamus's brow as he nodded.

"I found one the morning that Eddie arrived. Thought it was unique, and I spun up a story in my head about how I'd found a bit of lost treasure. It had bullion and some jewels in it." Tears pricked my eyes. I put my gun back in my boot and sank down on the edge of the messy bed. "And I thought maybe it was also a sign. Here was a treasure I could hide away, use later, to start over. So I tied it up in an old fishing net I found in the cottage, and secured it under the dock. The southwest dock."

Understanding dawned on Seamus's face. "And later when you found her—"

"The lockbox was gone." I spoke slowly, carefully sorting out my logic. "I thought maybe you'd seen me tie up the lockbox. After all, you were on the path that morning. Or I thought Liam could have seen me. Either of you could have then told the Carmichaels, or Eddie, or someone in his entourage—depending on who you were truly loyal to." I'd also told Rosita about the lockbox the morning Eddie and his entourage came to Trouble Island. But I didn't think she wouldn't have had time to retrieve it. The lockbox under the nursery floor, with the scrap of paper in the corner, had to be a different one. My head spun at all the permutations and possibilities.

Seamus nodded thoughtfully. "All right. You found a lockbox like the one under the floorboard. I'm not sure how that fits in with what I already know—"

"Because those were only two of probably hundreds of lockboxes," I said in a rush. "I saw Liam moving them into the hold in the *Myra*. Knowing Liam, he had to keep a careful record of all the lockboxes."

I thought of the archaeological finds and fossils I'd seen in Liam's room, how carefully he'd labeled each item. And I thought of how upset Liam had been after Rosita went missing, and then when her body was allegedly found. Well, we all were, but Liam usually kept his emotions under wraps, and he'd rocked back and forth at the news of her missing, and had been so emotional at her burial.

I went on. "I think Liam was working with Rosita. Before she locked herself away in the suite. And then, later, what if they were still working together, but through the doctor?"

"Dr. Aldridge never told anyone at the bureau that anything like that was going on," Seamus said.

"But he wouldn't, would he? If he'd decided to throw his allegiance to Rosita and Liam, if the three of them had decided they'd use the information they had to blackmail Eddie instead of helping your organization? All the bureau could give them would be promises of freedom from Eddie. Blackmail, though, could give them freedom and money to start over. But once Eddie arrived, especially with the doctor in tow, I could see Liam panicking, and killing Rosita—or the woman he thought was her. To keep her from telling Eddie that she'd been getting the records from him."

Seamus nodded. "Or maybe he confessed all to Eddie and Eddie ordered him to kill Rosita as part of his punishment—and to get her out of the way?"

"I don't believe Henry killed either her or Joey," I said.

"Neither do I," Seamus said. "And it's awfully convenient that Dr. Aldridge is dead now, too."

Could Liam have been behind all three deaths?

I gazed around the messy room.

"We can figure out confronting Liam later. First, we need to see if the papers are in here—but also if anything indicates Rosita has been posing as Claire. Then we can confront Rosita, try to sort out why she's posed as Claire, where she stands."

I could only think of one reason Rosita would have pretended to be Claire. Taking on Claire's role gave her protection. And Rosita, as Claire, could study people, listen in, ask questions, and try to figure out who her would-be killer, or killers, were.

Maybe, too, she'd hoped to just continue her life as Claire, either in Hollywood, or slipping away to live quietly, using grief as her reason to opt for a private life after all.

But how had Rosita so artfully pulled off appearing to be Claire?

I pondered as we searched, moving as quietly as we could through the items in the room, the drawers, corners, wardrobe, luggage.

Well, Rosita could easily have modulated her voice to mimic Claire. She was that talented as a vocalist. Their heights were similar, though Claire was a little shorter, more round-shouldered, and Rosita could have slumped to mimic Claire's posture. The difference in height wasn't enough to matter. Claire was thicker, chestier, but there were enough clothes here to create padding under other clothes.

But the lack of beauty mark? I didn't understand how that could be.

After going through all the items, we started looking for floorboards that appeared to have been modified. Finally, underneath the nightstand, we found the hiding spot.

There were no lockboxes or copies of financial records that would take down Eddie, and I could see the disappointment in Seamus's expression.

But stuffed in the hiding spot was Dr. Aldridge's medicine bag. In his bag: an empty morphine vial, a syringe, a ring filled with the mansion's keys, and a bronze dove.

From Oliver's grave.

That was all the proof I needed—this memento. Claire would not care about taking such a token. But Rosita—planning to leave the island as Claire, for reasons I didn't yet understand—would.

I studied the dove. There was no blood on its beak or the pointed tip of its wing. It was not the weapon that had murdered Claire or Joey. Just a sad keepsake.

I put the dove on top of the dresser.

CHAPTER 36

ROSITA HAD BEEN pretending to be Claire; Claire was the actual murder victim.

And Rosita had killed Dr. Aldridge with his own morphine.

I heard scratching outside the door, saw the knob turn. I turned, alarmed, and then the door swung open and in stepped the woman who still had the look, the demeanor, of Claire. I blinked, trying to see Rosita. I couldn't.

I would have doubted, but in one hand Rosita held a gun far more steadily than Claire would ever have, all while poking a hairpin back in the lock tucked behind her ear, giving me a smirking grin.

When she spoke it was lower, in Rosita's register. "You two aren't nearly as sneaky as you think." She closed the door behind her. "I see you've found my stash."

"Why?" The word crept out of me, a tremulous yet curious thing. "How?"

She looked at me with such hatred and disdain that I withered back into myself for a moment, again her guilty, cowed servant.

"During one of Dr. Aldridge's earliest monthly visits, I paid him handsomely to remove the beauty mark over my lip. There is only a faint scar," Rosita explained. "Unfortunately, last night in the candlelight, I got too close to him, and he noticed the scar, and realized the switch I must have made. After everyone was asleep, he said he wanted to talk with me.

"We came up here, and he confronted me. I told him it was for good reason. Soothed him, reassured him—I would reveal all to him soon. He got into a coughing fit—the cold of the mansion was getting to him. I got him some water. And put in half a bottle of my own Veronal. I rarely take it. It was enough to put him to sleep, and then another dose of his own medicine took care of the rest."

"All so he wouldn't talk?" Seamus asked.

"I wasn't done being Claire," Rosita said. "And I've hated him for what he did to the Carmichaels' daughter. Hated seeing him around the house, kowtowing to Eddie. Do you know what he said to me after Oliver died? I was holding my dead son in my arms and Dr. Aldridge said, *Comfort yourself that you're young and fertile. You can have another child if you want.* As if children are interchangeable."

I shared her outrage, and yet, was chilled that she could use the doctor and then kill him in cold blood.

I had a feeling that ever since Oliver—and maybe before, though not to the same degree—she'd been using all of us all along.

"You would leave the suite, and be Claire," I said, "and Claire would be you?"

"Yes. Ever since I came here after Oliver's death. She got a kick out of being cold and stiff toward you, hiding under my veil, wearing my mourning dress. With those clothes, and under strict orders from me to remain silent, she could pull it off. She loved being my confidante, loved seeing the hurt on your face and reporting it to me," Rosita said. "And I loved hearing about it. Seeing it myself at other times."

"But why did you do that?"

"I told Claire it was because I didn't want to talk to anyone else as Rosita, but I did want fresh air and to hear gossip and just pretend to be a regular person from time to time." She gave a wavery smile, but then quickly recomposed herself. "What I was really doing was gathering as much information as I could from other women, and a few men, about what was going on in Eddie's world. And, of course, visiting Liam, convincing him to help me. To get the records. To eventually pass on to you." She smirked at Seamus.

Suddenly he lunged, grabbed Rosita's arm, forcing her to drop the gun. He pinned her arm behind her back, snagged the gun from the floor in an easy swoop, and held it to her temple. "You're going to sit down now," he said, "very quietly."

Rosita complied, lowering into a side chair.

"How do you have a gun?" Seamus asked.

"I kept one hidden away in my suite. The night after Claire went missing, I went back up and got it. I've kept it on me since."

"And you took the records."

"Yes. And hid them elsewhere—outside the mansion. After what happened to her, after it was clear someone wanted to kill me, I knew I couldn't trust anyone."

"What happened with Claire?" I asked. "How did you switch?"

"She came up to my room that first night, after midnight."

After I'd seen Rosita, and she'd told me she blamed me for Oliver's death. After I'd seen Claire stumbling from the bathroom toward her room. Then what? I replayed the timeline in my head: I'd gone to my room, cut the rope, then been pleasantly surprised by Seamus. Claire must have gone up to Rosita's suite after I let Seamus in.

"She came up, I let her in," Rosita was saying. "She wanted to talk like old times. She'd had too much to drink and threw up on herself. I helped her clean up, put the rinsed but dirty dress in my laundry basket, helped her get dressed in one of my nightgowns. I was afraid she was going to throw up again, and she was getting too loud, so I told her to go back to her room. She said only if I'd come down too, and we could lie in bed beside each other like we did when we were kids, and chatter and giggle." Rosita rolled her eyes. "As if I was in the mood for girlish games. But I agreed, helping her down, hoping she'd just be quiet. I didn't want her to draw attention to the fact that she had come up to my suite. I was afraid she might say we'd switched roles before, and that might lead to Liam giving away that he and I had been meeting up, too. I wasn't ready for Eddie—for anyone—to know about the records I've been copying. She was still too loud so I convinced her to take a walk with me. Thought that might sober her up. She loaned me her fur and a pair of boots, put on her blue coat and another pair of boots, and we went for our walk.

"But we soon got into an argument. She whined that it was cold, that I wouldn't help her and Douglas, and why wouldn't I?"

For a moment, I thought Rosita was going to confess to having killed Claire, but she just looked sad for a second. Then she returned her face to its placid composure and went on. "I stormed off. Left her on the path. Wandered to the cemetery and took the dove, which I knew had broken off from the angel's outstretched hands. A storm last winter. From my window, I'd watched a large tree branch come down on it, break the dove. Then watched Henry clean up around the graves and put the dove in the angel's hand." For a moment, Rosita looked sorrowful. "Henry knew I'd want that, without having to ask me." Her expression abruptly reverted to coldness. "Anyway, I retrieved the dove, knowing then that I would leave, I would help you," she glanced at Seamus, "but I would take a part of the island with me forever."

She pressed her lips together for a moment. "I felt bad about the argument, went into Claire's bedroom, planning to wait for her. I waited up and then fell asleep—until I heard Eddie screaming, 'Where's Rosita?' That's when I knew something had gone very wrong with Claire."

"The note that drew him up to your suite—why did you write that?" Seamus asked.

Rosita shook her head. "I didn't. I learned later that Douglas had done so, hoping to get Eddie and Rosita—well, me—to talk. He told me this in confidence, thinking I was Claire."

"So you decided to pretend to be Claire because—"

"Because something had obviously happened to her! And later, she was found—murdered. Everyone thinking it was me. If I could be Claire, I could be safe. And I could try to figure out who would want to kill me."

"You could have come to me," Seamus said.

"Really? You could have flipped to Eddie's side like Cormac did years ago." She looked at me then, as if expecting me to also say she could have come to me.

And once, she could have. I would have protected her, as I believed she'd tried to protect me by having me sent here. But that first awful night of Eddie's arrival, I'd learned that Rosita actually hated me. Blamed me as the catalyst of her son's death. Wanted to punish me. Would I have protected her after that?

I wanted to believe so. But I wasn't sure.

I looked away from her.

"And the night that I accused everyone of having a motive to kill Rosita—they were all true, of course, except Seamus's. It was easy to convince people who knew me best, or thought they did"—her eyes flicked to me but I knew she also meant the Carmichaels— "that I was Claire. Because no one wanted *her* to be dead. But really, deep down, everyone but Liam—sweet, trusting Liam—could have a reason to kill me. Liam loved me—though I did not love him back. But I found him sweet. Useful, for gathering those records. And he trusted me to get him out of Eddie's clutches. That's all I told him— 'Make me copies of the records you're making Eddie, and I'll get you free. You can go back to your archaeology.'"

Had he believed her? Was there a chance she'd meant it?

But Seamus and I had just worked out the possibility that Liam had killed Claire, thinking she was Rosita. Seamus gave me a warn-ing look, and a tiny head shake.

He didn't want her to know just yet.

How awful. To be alive in a different guise, all the while knowing that most of the people around you had reason to want you dead.

"I can tell you where the records are," she said to Seamus, as plac-idly as if she was a librarian directing someone to files.

"Oh no," Seamus said. "You will take me to them."

He did not trust her.

"I'd like a coat," she said.

I grabbed the mink on the chair, checked the pockets, the lining. No stashed guns. Rosita snatched it from me. As she put it on, she rolled her eyes when I said to Seamus, "You need a coat, too—"

"I'll be fine," Seamus said. I understood. He didn't want to disturb anyone in the library for the sake of a coat.

I embraced him, for just a moment. "Be careful," I whispered. "Don't trust her."

"You stay up here until I'm back, all right? It will be safer."

I obeyed. I sat down on the edge of the bed, like a good girl.

CHAPTER 37

I SAT ON the edge of Claire's bed, shivering. There were so many of her clothes in a mess around me, but I could not bring myself to gather any to myself, or get under the covers. It felt like crawling into a dead woman's skin.

How had Rosita been able to do this? Maintain this for so many days? Did she care so little for her cousin? But no—she seemed to care for Claire. For Oliver. She still had emotion. And yet, she was so detached at times, too, as if she could manipulate her own mind into compartments to serve a deeper will.

I saw the faint fog of my own breath on the air.

What I knew so far: Liam had likely murdered Claire, thinking she was Rosita. Rosita had murdered Dr. Aldridge because he'd figured out her ruse. Rosita had been leaving her suite over the past year, swapping roles with Claire—and no one had caught on, no one knew except Liam, who had so far kept her confidence.

The records of the bullion and jewels were the documents that could help Seamus and his colleagues take down Eddie. Douglas had written a fake note to lure Eddie upstairs to Rosita's suite, apparently unaware of the drama unfolding with Rosita and Claire, assuming—as we all had—that Rosita had stayed in her suite for the night. But according to her, Claire had switched into one of Rosita's nightgowns, her dress being soiled. And Claire and Rosita had gone out on that first cold night for a walk, had an argument, and Rosita had returned ahead of Claire, then regretted the fight, and fell asleep in Claire's room while waiting for her to come back.

I wanted proof of Rosita's account. Claire's soiled dress should still be in Rosita's bathroom hamper—if Rosita had just told the truth.

I needed to see it.

I STOOD ON the suite's veranda, as Rosita and I had done several days before, but alone this time.

I'd checked, when I first rushed in, the laundry basket in Rosita's bathroom. Sure enough, at the very bottom, damp and smelling of mildew and sickly sweetness, was Claire's dress from that first night.

After shoving the soiled nightgown back down in the hamper, I'd rushed to the veranda, flung its door open. Not caring about the cold and icy snow swirling in. How poorly I was dressed for the weather, just in the same pants, and blouse, and boots I'd been in for the last several days. Immediately my breath stiffened, my face went numb.

But through the snow, I could see at the end of the main dock the *Myra,* where it had been for days. Its blue flag was still hoisted, but frozen in its drooped state. The yacht dipped up and down, just the slightest. The water might be freezing around it, but it could still make it away from the island, at least today. By tomorrow, it might not.

Then one shot shattered the cold silence into a thousand reverberating shards. And another shot.

I skidded backward, nearly losing my footing on the slick balcony floor.

I had to know. I whirled around, and ran down the stairs, and nearly made it to the front door, but in came Cormac and Rosita, snow whirling behind them.

Cormac looked irritated. But excitement danced in Rosita's expression. *Rosita's enjoying this, whatever game it is she's playing . . .*

My heart stopped. *Where is Seamus? Why is Rosita with Cormac?*

Cormac grabbed my arm, pinching so hard that I yelped. "Sorry about your boyfriend. But Claire told me some things that made it clear it had to be done. We had to protect Eddie."

An overwhelming punch of grief knocked the breath out of me. They had killed Seamus.

Pin prickles danced before my eyes, and all sound faded other than a high-pitched moan somewhere in my head.

I MUST HAVE passed out, then been carried by Cormac into the library, because the next thing I remember is sitting in that room, in a chair near the fire, and Maxine hovering over me, trying to get me to drink water.

I pushed the glass away, looked around the room. There was Liam. Marco, looking upset and confused as usual. Eddie. Douglas. Maxine, Cormac—and Rosita.

But then, I saw that Largo's cage was missing. My heart clenched. Yes, I'd lost Seamus. Joey, Henry, Dr. Aldridge, Claire were all dead, too. But the bird that had been Oliver's—that connection to Oliver—how could Rosita have allowed something to happen to Largo?

Then, faintly, I heard Largo's squawk. She was crying from the parlor at the far back of the mansion's first floor. At least she was alive—though stressed and cold.

"Since when do you take orders from Claire," Eddie was saying to Cormac.

No one knows Claire is really Rosita. Except me and Seamus, and he's dead. I wondered, did she mean to keep pretending to be Claire? If I went along with it, would I buy myself some time?

"She told me that Rosita had told her that she'd been working with Seamus, and that Seamus was a Fed. You'd have told me that we couldn't kill him. Not here. Too many questions from the bureau. That we'd have to flip him, or take care of him later," Cormac said. "But I didn't want to risk that. He wasn't the kind to flip, I could tell, and he wouldn't have waited to get the information to the bureau. I was protecting you, boss."

"Thanks," Eddie said, but his voice was thick with sarcasm. "Now I'll have to come up with a way to cover his death. Rosita's gone anyway, so he didn't have his star witness—"

"Claire told me that Rosita was getting Liam here to make copies of your, ah, records. That she was planning to hand those over to him. After you came here, Rosita changed her mind. But Rosita worried that Liam was also working directly with Seamus, that he'd give another set of the records to Seamus. So I thought if I got rid of Seamus, that was better than offing a senator's son—"

Eddie turned to Liam. "You were working behind my back, with a Fed?"

"No, no, it wasn't like that," Liam said, his voice quaking. I could tell he was lying, but poor Seamus wasn't around to contradict him. "Rosita asked me if I'd make copies of the records for her. She said she couldn't say why she needed them, but to just bring them to her at set times when she said. Claire would bring me notes, saying when to come up to the suite—"

Claire said, as Eddie glared at her, "I thought they were having a fling. Cute senator's son. I didn't know anything about the records or any of that. Getting back at you for all your flings. Broke Rosita's heart, you know."

Eddie's hand went to his holster as he whirled back toward Liam, who threw his hands up in a pleading, deferential gesture. "We didn't. I just brought the records, and I guess, I guess she hid them away."

"And you're telling me this now?" Eddie roared. "Instead of right away?"

"I wasn't sure who had murdered Rosita. I figured you and Cormac. I even thought it might be Seamus. Wouldn't he be angry if he knew she'd changed her mind about working with him?" Rosita said in Claire's nasal-toned voice. "Then I saw him and Aurelia go upstairs this morning. I went up after them, heard them in my room. I listened through the door, realized they were looking for the records."

A chill crept over my skin. How much had she overheard?

I shuddered. Maxine put a comforting hand on my arm, and I put my hand on hers. The warmth was soothing. Douglas looked at us, worry and confusion in his face. Marco stood with his arms crossed over his chest, unhappy with what was unfolding. This was, to him, supposed to be a simple weekend for making a transaction. Our emotions and reactions were varied, but we were united in this: Maxine, Marco, Douglas, and I were a hapless audience to this drama.

"But of course the records aren't in my room," Rosita said as Claire.

"Where are they?" Eddie demanded.

"I don't know. But I went downstairs, alerted Cormac that Seamus was looking for records to take you down, told him I'd get Seamus to come with me outside. I'd lead him down the perimeter path. Then Cormac could take care of the problem. I told Seamus I knew where the records are—but I don't, I really don't."

Marco stepped forward, said, "For God's sake, enough already. Why can't we just leave, and kill all of them—" He paused to give the woman who he thought was Claire a lascivious grin. "—except you, darling—and toss them from the *Myra*? If you want this sale to go through, Eddie—"

"I just said, it's going to be hard enough to cover Seamus's death. A senator's son? A movie star?"

"Well, the rest aren't important enough to keep around—" Marco started.

Rosita-as-Claire interrupted, "Liam has told me something else very useful, haven't you, Liam?"

Liam looked terrified.

"Liam told me he knows who killed the doctor," she said.

I balked at that. She'd confessed to me and to Seamus that she'd killed Dr. Aldridge so that she could keep pretending to be Claire.

"Who cares?" Eddie said.

Even Maxine, who'd hated Dr. Aldridge for good reason, looked taken aback.

"Because it was Marco. Because he knew the doctor had over-heard Marco and Joey talking about getting rid of Rosita, to make the sale easier, and figured out that Marco killed Joey to cover his tracks," Rosita-as-Claire said. "He told me he saw Dr. Aldridge and Marco leave the library, followed them upstairs, overheard the whole thing. Right, Liam?"

Liam nodded, looking confused. "That's, that's right." Why was he going along with her?

Eddie pulled out his gun, pointed it at Marco. In his remaining warped love of Rosita, and in anger, he would kill Marco. No matter that not coming back with a boss as big as Marco would trigger an-other gangland war between Eddie and whoever took over Marco's organization.

"What, no, no, I didn't—" Marco whimpered, holding his hands up in supplication. I'm ashamed to admit I found some satisfaction in that.

"Boss," Cormac said quietly, coming to the same realization. "If we don't want the Feds or a senator gunning for us, then we sure don't want a war with Marco's people—"

"I can handle that," Eddie snarled.

I'd had enough of these manipulations. And I didn't want more people—innocent people like Oliver—to die because of shoot-outs between Eddie's and Marco's gangs. "Do not shoot Marco," I said. "Not over Rosita's death. He didn't kill her. Neither did Henry, no matter his confession. In fact, no one did. You see, Claire is not Claire. She is really Rosita."

CHAPTER 38

EVERYONE LOOKED SHOCKED. But Eddie went as still as one of his precious labyrinth statues.

"Oh, now, Aurelia, you are so silly—" Rosita started in Claire's singsong.

"I can go get the evidence," I snapped. "From Claire's room. I'm sure no one will believe me that you confessed to both me and Seamus that you killed Dr. Aldridge, but I have evidence that you killed him. He quickly figured out your ruse, pretending to be Claire and letting everyone think Rosita was dead when it was really Claire. Because he removed your beauty mark almost a year ago so you and Claire could swap identities."

"No, no, this can't be true, we would have noticed, *I* would have noticed—" Eddie stammered to a stop.

Suddenly, Rosita sat down in a chair, with a weary sigh and a petulant pursing of her lips, an expression that wasn't quite like Rosita, nor like Claire, but a disconcerting mix of both identities. When she spoke, though, it was in Rosita's lower, reedier tone. "Oh, don't bother. Aurelia—clever little Aurelia—is right. But you didn't notice the switch, did you, Eddie? None of you did. Not just because of my own cleverness, or how much alike Claire and I look, or because I'd been covered by a veil, unseen by anyone but Claire for the past year, so you'd slowly—or maybe gladly—all begun to forget the small differences between the details of how we look. But because really, wasn't it going to be easier for all of you if I was dead?" She looked at Eddie, her gaze as sharp as a knife she'd like to drive into his heart. "Easiest of all for you—"

Eddie's eyes widened. "No, no, I came here hoping—"

"That what? I'd fall into your arms, let you sell my island to this monster?" She waved her hand dismissively toward Marco. She shook her head. "That's not going to happen."

"Oh yes, yes it will," Marco bellowed. "I came all this way—"

"Shut up!" Cormac snapped. "Or I will shoot you, whatever the fallout." He glared at me. "All right, if you're so clever, then tell us who killed Claire thinking she was Rosita—if it wasn't Henry or Marco? And don't say it was me or Eddie. Because it wasn't."

I dared not look at Liam. I didn't want Henry to be blamed, or anyone else for that matter, yet those fossils and artifacts lovingly arranged in his room came to my mind. He was so sincere. And so clueless. I wanted to tell him, *Run.* If Eddie had been willing to shoot Marco as Rosita's murderer, he'd do the same to Liam, never mind that his father is a senator. Eddie might even have the senator taken out.

My mouth gaped open. Nothing came out. I couldn't speak, couldn't breathe. My mind raced—*Say it was Henry, though that would break Maxine's heart. Or Seamus, already dead. Dr. Aldridge. Joey. Make something up,* I ordered myself. But my mind went gray.

"Apparently she's turned shy. Well, I overheard her and Seamus talking," Rosita said.

I wanted to shake my head, *no, no,* at her, keep her from saying what I feared would come next.

But there was no stopping Rosita when she'd decided something. And I could tell from her expression—so like the night she'd helped me after Pony—that she had not only made up her mind. She was thinking multiple steps ahead.

"Liam must have mistaken Claire for me that night and killed her. Left her body under the dock, where he knew Aurelia—or, shall we just drop the pretense, *Susan*—put one of Eddie's lockboxes, which she found on the shore. And Liam guessed, correctly, that she would panic at some point, try to leave, and first retrieve the lockbox. After all, the contents of each box are probably worth five hundred dollars." Rosita gave me a damning look. Then she switched the grip of her gaze to Liam. "But why did you want me found? And for that matter, why did you kill me?"

It was cruel, saying *me,* like she was a ghost. Liam already had a haunted look about him, and I understood that. He'd taken someone's life. I knew how that felt. We were not people who could take life cavalierly, like the Eddies and the Marcos and Cormacs of the world. Even with a reason that at least some would call understandable, I walked with shoulders drooped under a heavy mantle of guilt, even though I'd come to hate Pony. But I'd never learned his story, how he came to be the way he was. I could never get him to open up to me. And as cruel as he was later in our marriage, he'd made me laugh at the beginning. So there was still a spark of good in him.

So yes, I still felt guilt for Pony. For so much more, before Pony.

I feared Liam's motive would not be understandable, especially to Eddie. And, though he was also guilty of past deaths, I wanted Liam to evade Eddie. To think slickly.

For a moment, since his face was so stiff, implacable, I thought he might pull it off. Say in the same flat tone he'd lull into when he went on too much about a particular topic, *I didn't kill her . . . it was . . .* and then blame one of the others who have already died these past few days.

But Liam's face cracked so suddenly it was like a boulder had hit him square on. He crumpled to the floor. On his knees, he looked up at Rosita, and wailed her name, then, "I'm sorry, I'm sorry."

She knelt down on her knees before him, grabbed his chin, stared into his eyes. Her voice was as airy and cold as the outside. "Why did you kill me? Explain. Without blubbering."

She let go of his chin as if she were shaking off spit, but she did not release his gaze. And he had no will to look away. His sobs had stifled a bit, but each word pulled out of him with painful effort. "I was out, moving lockboxes for Mr. McGee that first night," Liam said. "On the path, near the main dock. I heard a sound, grabbed the shovel from my wheelbarrow. Realized it was a woman's voice— you, I thought."

"But Claire's voice is so different than my voice."

"We—we—hadn't talked in so long. You—she—was singing, warbly, off key. I figured from drinking, from the cold. She was wearing only her nightgown, no coat, no shoes. I asked where they were and she said she'd thrown them in the lake. She didn't need them, she didn't need anyone, she said, and she wanted to go skinny-dipping." Liam dropped his head in shame. "And then she came over, and grabbed my arms and said I should go skinny-dipping with her, and in the moonlight, at least, I was sure it was you." He paused and pointed at the right side of his upper lip. "You had—she had—the beauty mark."

"Makeup, Liam. Just makeup. She'd play with my makeup during the times we switched roles, and I went out among the guests as Claire. And she'd add that beauty mark, as a lark, as a joke. Put on my veil. She'd say in case that Susan comes in off schedule. She'd painted on the beauty mark that night in my bedroom. You're right, she was drunk, and putting on my makeup, all the while talking about Hollywood." Rosita glanced away for a moment. "She had . . . a bad time in her childhood home. I tried to protect her.

"That night, she became combative. She was angry that I wouldn't sell the island, go with her and Douglas to Hollywood. I tried to tell her that was their dream, not mine. And then she said—" Rosita paused to clear her throat. "—said it was time for me to get over Oliver. Let go of the island."

Rosita looked sorrowful for a moment. "I slapped her, ran back to the mansion. It was too much for me. By the time I was back, I decided to wait in her room for her return. I fell asleep, and well, Claire never came back." Her eyes hardened on Liam. "Because of you. Why?"

"I thought she was you. I was sure she was. And she was flirting with me—I think. And I—I said I'd always loved her, and we should take the yacht, and go away together. That we could leave the records with Dr. Aldridge and he could take them to the Feds."

At that, Eddie and Cormac looked genuinely shocked. They had no idea that they had a mole in their gang—what's more the quiet, putzy doctor. That's the problem with men like Eddie and Cormac. They take everyone else for granted, as if loyalty is owed to them.

"I said that we could take the lockboxes—"

"You were going to steal my woman and my money?" Eddie gave a harsh laugh at the preposterousness of Liam pulling off such a thing. And yes, it was preposterous. But the look on Liam's face was heartbreakingly sincere.

"—and run off together. But Rosita just laughed—I thought she was Rosita—and said, 'I've been working with Eddie this whole time, you silly boy.'" Liam stopped, cast his gaze downward. "I realized Rosita never cared about me. She was just using me to get what she needed to get back at you, Mr. McGee."

"But that was Claire," I said quietly. "She was drunk and had forgotten to be Rosita. Claire meant she'd been working with Eddie to come up with a scheme to convince Rosita to leave the island, turn it over to him to sell to Marco." *If only Seamus was here,* I thought. He could help calm Liam, get him to carefully parse his words.

My breath caught in my throat and my eyes stung. Seamus—shot down, his body left out on the icy, frozen land. I had to keep myself from glaring at Cormac. I wished I could hurt him and Rosita for what they'd done to Seamus. I wished I could properly bring his body back to the graveyard where his wife and son lay at rest.

I forced myself to refocus on Liam. "So you've been used, and confused, for a while now, Liam."

I turned to Eddie with a pleading glance, hoping against hope for pity for Liam. "He didn't understand, he's not fully responsible for his actions."

But Liam pressed on, his eyes foggy and distant, like he was back in the woods with Claire, thinking he was with Rosita. "And she said I was a fool to think she'd ever love me, and to let her go. I did, but it was cold and I wanted her to have my coat, and I stood up, and started to take it off, to give to her, but I must have scared her, made her think I was reaching for my gun. Out of her robe pocket, she pulled out a small pistol, aimed it at me, and, and, I swear it was instinct. I grabbed the shovel and hit her, and the front point sliced through her neck." He started sobbing, rocking. "I didn't know what to do. I couldn't just leave her there, and I was too scared to tell anyone. But I couldn't dump her in the lake, either. So I tied her up, took the lockbox. I thought sooner or later Aurelia would go swimming like she always did, find the body."

He looked up at Eddie. "I put the lockbox with the others. You have everything back, you'll have all of it—"

"What are these lockboxes?" Marco said. "What's he talking about? Eddie, the deal was everything on this island—everything conveyed in the sale, even the contents of the mansion. So if you were hiding something away that you're trying to take off now, you'd better—"

"Watch it, Marco," Cormac said. "Talk like that got Joey killed. Sure, Joey was a lot wilier than I gave him credit for. While we were searching for Rosita, he got away from me, out of sight. Even in winter it's impossible to see through the thick brambles. Followed Liam, saw he was moving goods. Later, Joey said we should take a walk early Saturday morning. Told me that he knew about the goods, and he wouldn't say anything to Marco, avoid a confrontation that could get ugly and lead to worse back home, so long as I'd agree to help him set up a heist of the boxes. We could fence it later, split the profits."

Marco looked outraged. So stupidly ambitious, so naïve of Joey to think he could pull off such a thing, could trust Cormac.

Cormac shrugged. "Asking me to betray my boss. I wasn't having it. He was a loose cannon. So I reached in for a handshake with one hand, and with the other, got out my knife—" He grabbed it from his belt sheath. It glinted in the light from the coal oil lanterns, the flickering candles.

Surprise and fear arose on everyone's faces except Liam's. He still looked torn up with emotion from his confession. Nor Eddie's face. He had a small smile as if he knew what was coming.

"And I slit his throat." Swiftly, Cormac moved behind Liam, held the knife to his throat.

Maxine exclaimed, as Rosita cried out, "No!"

And for a moment she looked panged. But she had to know what would happen to the person who'd thought he'd killed her once the truth came out. And sure enough, there it was, a flicker of a smile. She was enjoying this drama.

But Eddie gave a little shake of his head.

For a second I thought, *senator's son.* Even in vengeance, Eddie would not allow Cormac to harm a senator's son.

In the next instant, Eddie grabbed Rosita, pulled her up by the arm, shoved her away, at the same time that Cormac leapt aside.

Liam didn't move.

He just closed his eyes, knowing what was coming.

Eddie shot him in the forehead.

CHAPTER 39

FOR A LONG, terrible moment, the room reverberated from the gunshot.

Liam had fallen over on his side, and now his blood trailed from his forehead to the floor. I wanted to look away but couldn't.

A wail of outrage arose from Maxine. She started to rush toward Eddie, but thankfully Douglas grabbed her, held her back.

"No," Douglas pled with her. "You can't do anything for Liam, don't get yourself hurt or killed—"

"Why?" Maxine wailed. "My Henry is gone, and Seamus, and now Liam—soon we'll all be killed." Suddenly she grew silent. Then she narrowed her eyes on Eddie, her gaze full of hatred. "You," she said in a near whisper, "you are nothing more than a monster."

Marco started to say something, but Eddie held up a hand to silence him as Maxine's gaze turned to Rosita. "And you as well. A selfish monster. You want to blame everyone for poor Oliver's death? You should blame yourself." Her gaze shifted from Rosita to Eddie and back again. "You should blame each other. Your greed. Your selfishness. And your desire for vengeance. All of it has led only to more death. All of it dishonors sweet Oliver's memory."

At that, she slumped, as if finally saying her piece had drained her. Douglas let go of her arm, and she started to collapse, but I put my arms around her, and held her gently. She trembled.

For a moment, fury knotted Rosita's face, and I expected her to demand that Eddie punish Maxine. But then her expression smoothed into a cold calm. That was even more frightening than her fury. It meant she was calculating several moves ahead of where the rest of us were.

Eddie put his gun away.

"Well, how are you going to explain this to Liam's father?" Marco asked. No pity for the young man. He was disposable, just like Joey had been.

Eddie cleared his throat. "Easy enough. Just before we arrived, a maid who worked for us, Aurelia Escalante, got into a lover's quarrel with Liam. Turns out she was also Susan Walker, who was distraught after losing her husband. We took her in because she was Rosita's friend. We had no idea she'd killed her husband, until Maxine and Henry heard Aurelia screaming at poor Liam that she'd killed Pony, and she'd kill him, too. Rosita heard it, too, and finally came out of her room to try to calm Aurelia—poor, brave Rosita. But Aurelia shot and killed Liam—and ran off. They later found a confession and suicide note in her room, which we'll write up. And they witnessed her swimming out into the lake and drowning."

I swallowed hard. Death by drowning. Would they shoot me and throw me over, or just leave me in the middle of the lake to struggle until I finally succumbed?

A voice slithered up from the past, through cracks in the wall I usually kept up, cracks made from exhaustion: *Drowning is the fate you deserve.*

My eyes threatened to well over, my throat to close, as I pushed the voice back.

"And what about Seamus?" Marco asked.

"He tried to stop Aurelia, and she shot him, too. Henry died from the stress. Dr. Aldridge accidentally overdosed."

"Joey?"

"He fell overboard—tough passage on Lake Erie in this weather."

Marco lifted his eyebrows and chuckled, no longer upset about his bodyguard being killed. To men like Marco, those he sees as beneath him are interchangeable. Disposable. "You think of everything."

"Except what about Claire?" Rosita asked. Her expression was still, but I could see in her eyes, in the grim set of her mouth, that she was seething. The expressions, the tics, of the Rosita I had observed so closely in the past, came back to me.

"Oh, poor Claire went overboard with Joey. They were embracing when it happened. I'll send some men to have her exhumed later and make sure her body does go into the drink. I'll also have Oliver and your grandparents exhumed, but they'll be reburied in a Toledo cemetery. Where they should have been buried all along," Eddie said.

"And the rest of us?" Rosita snapped. "Me? Douglas? Maxine?"

She didn't even attempt to make an argument for sparing me.

"You'll all return with me and back up my story," Eddie said.

"And if we refuse?"

"Douglas won't. I'm giving him a shot at reestablishing his career. Maxine won't, because there is one person she cares about—her daughter, Ada. And she knows that I can, and will, make Ada's life a living hell if need be. Same for Maxine's sister."

Maxine pulled her face away from my chest, allowing my arms to stay around her. But she stared at Eddie. Her hatred for him was palpable. But I could also see in her face, and in Douglas's face, that Eddie was right. They would back up his story.

"And as for you, darling," Eddie said, giving Rosita a tight, hard smile, "you will comply. Or Cormac will shoot you." Cormac's hand moved to his revolver. "Another victim of Aurelia, here. Don't worry. You won't go overboard. You'll be buried next to our son. Or you can confirm the story I've created, come back, turn the island over to me, and you'll get everything you want. Divorce. Enough money to start over. With Douglas in Hollywood if you wish. Or all alone as you seem to prefer."

"Wouldn't it be easier to just kill her?" Marco asked.

Of course it would. But what Marco didn't understand was that, in his own way, Eddie still loved Rosita. That no matter what happened, he always would.

Suddenly, Rosita reached into the folds of her dress and whipped out a gun.

For a moment the room stiffened as she pointed her gun at Eddie. Cormac started to pull out his weapon, but Eddie held up a hand to stay him.

"Did you really think," Rosita said, "that I would not have a gun? That I would not bring one with me when we came to bury our son, that I would not find a hiding spot in the suite I spent every day in for more than a year? That I did not think about using it on myself every day?" She mimicked Marco's voice. "'Wouldn't it be easier to kill her?' That's what I thought each day—wouldn't it be easier to kill myself? But I could not bring myself to do it." For the first time since she'd arrived accompanying the body of her son for his burial, her voice cracked. "Goddamn it! I want to live!" The words came out as a strangled sound. "I want to go on living in spite of everything—"

"Oh, Rosita," Eddie said softly, and I knew to him the room and all of us in it had fallen aside. "You can. We can—"

"Not with you!" Rosita barked.

There were only two ways to be free of a man like Eddie—or Pony. The first was to die yourself.

The other way was to kill.

For just a second, I thought, *This is it: Rosita will kill Eddie.*

Cormac will kill Rosita in revenge.

None of them knew I had a stocking gun in my boot.

I gently let go of Maxine, preparing myself to swoop down, pull out my gun, and be ready, in the aftermath of Eddie and Rosita's deaths, to take out Cormac and Marco. I knew I had the necessary seconds to do it.

But *could* I do it? I told myself I could, but I was already trembling at the prospect.

Then Rosita sighed. "Oh, Eddie. Not every desire I have is for you."

Swiftly, she swung her arm and aimed at Marco. She didn't even look at him with the first shot, yet hit him square in the chest. He staggered back. His hands rose to his chest as his blood swiftly bloomed on his shirt, his mouth gaping open.

She waited for him to fall before she moved to him, staring down at him. He tried to cry out but the only sound he could emit was a gurgling gasp. He stared up at her.

Rosita hesitated just a second, but not with remorse or shock over what she'd done. She wanted him to see the hate in her eyes.

She held the gun steady, as Maxine cried out—*"No, no, child!"*—and I knew Maxine was thinking of Rosita's immortal soul. But Rosita's hands were steady, as still as the arms of the angel statue overlooking Oliver's grave, as she pulled the trigger a second time, shooting Marco directly in the face.

In the next moment, Cormac rushed up behind Rosita, grabbed her.

Rosita was so limp in Cormac's arms that it appeared she had finally taken the revenge she wanted, that she'd now give up. But I knew Rosita better than that. Knew her well enough to know that she wasn't done. She blamed Eddie and me for Oliver's death, just as much as she blamed Marco. She was calculating how to take us out, too.

Eddie had gone pale. "What have you done?" The words staggered out in stilted shock.

The corners of Rosita's mouth quirked up in a mocking smile. "I think it's obvious," she said flatly.

Cormac released her, shoved her toward Eddie. He picked up the gun that Rosita had dropped on Marco, wiped it with a handkerchief, pocketed it.

"I needed the money from the sale of the island—" Eddie started.

Rosita shrugged. "Right. Pay off debts to another gangster."

"Marco's gang—this will start a war—"

Her smile widened. "Exactly."

Eddie whirled around to me, Douglas, and Maxine. "You—you saw what happened. We'll all go back, and you will testify against her. That she was insane. That she killed Marco." His gaze focused on me. "You can live. Be free." Then he shifted his focus to Maxine. "You as well. Ada and your sister will be left alone." Next, to Douglas: "A fresh start for you. You never needed the Sweetheart Cousins before, you won't need them now, I'll be sure you're a star."

Cormac cleared his throat. "Boss, we can still take her out, you'll get the island, you can sell it to someone else, and we still have everything in the hold."

"Fine, kill me," Rosita said. "But Eddie, you won't get the island."

"Yes, it's in your will—"

"My old will. But after Oliver, before we came here to bury him, I had it changed. Upon my death, the island would go to Claire. I didn't tell her, of course. She might have been tempted to do away with me. A heaping dose of Veronal in my tea, perhaps," Rosita said.

"Claire's dead—"

"It still wouldn't convey to you, Eddie," Rosita said. "In case of Claire's death, it goes to the Sisters of the Poor. Your old orphanage. I'm guessing that not even you would take out the entire staff of the orphanage where you grew up. And are you really going to fight an orphanage for the inheritance that will give them a lovely property to sell—probably to another gangster, but so be it. So, you want me alive so I can at least sell you the island and you can offload it. Maybe to whoever takes over Marco's gang. Oh, but wait—there's also the matter of the records that Liam made for me. I'm guessing you still want those."

Eddie's eyes narrowed, mistrusting her. Rightfully so.

Rosita laughed bitterly. "You promised me a life of joy and everything I could dream of. I never dreamed of this. Of losing my son."

"*Our* son—"

"I will tell you where the records are," Rosita said. "But only if Aurelia stays here with us."

Alarm shot through me. I didn't want to drown, but I was also terrified of staying here. What was she up to?

"Why?"

"After you got here, Liam came up to my suite that night."

I frowned. Why hadn't Liam mentioned that in his confession? But Eddie just looked furious with jealousy and wasn't wondering the same thing.

"I told him to put my red diary with copies of your actual ledger, and the records he'd brought me, locked away in the rolltop desk that was my grandfather's."

I nearly gasped at that, but I restrained, not wanting attention.

Yet I knew that there was no key to the rolltop desk. The lock was broken.

"Great," Eddie sputtered. "We'll just take an axe to the goddamned desk—"

"Or maybe I told him to lock the books away in one of the cabinets. Or a footlocker. Or in one of the old cabinets up in the lighthouse." Rosita grinned. She was, even in this dire situation, enjoying taunting Eddie. "By the time you take an axe to everything, Eddie, the *Myra* might just be frozen in. So it's better if we retrieve the key. I'm sure once I see the key I'll remember . . ."

"Boss, she's up to something," Cormac said. "We can force Rosita to tell us where the records are, and off Aurelia on the boat. We need to get out of here before the storm gets worse and we're stuck here—"

"That's my point," Rosita said. "And, Eddie, you know you won't be able to force me."

Eddie clenched his jaw, said through gritted teeth, "So what do we have to give you so's you'll tell us where the goddamn key is?"

"Leave Aurelia here."

We all stared at her, shocked. I was not, by then, foolish enough to think she was making a play for saving me from being sent to drown overboard.

"Nope."

"Then you won't get the key—unless you want to swim in the lake to get it. I told Liam to put the key in a lockbox, and secure it deep under the lake by the southwest dock." She gave me a hard, flashing look.

The darkness started to crawl in on the edge of my vision. For a second I couldn't breathe. I knew that there was no lockbox down there, but that wasn't what shocked me so.

Was this tale of Rosita's just a coincidence to the fact I had tied up a lockbox?

Or would I discover that all along, Seamus hadn't flipped loyalty to Eddie or Marco—but to Rosita.

Oh what a striking, intriguing figure she must have made on the balcony, even under her mourning veil. Had Seamus slowly fallen for her? Gone to her as Liam had? Hadn't I seen something flash in her eyes—something jealous, something possessive, like the look that she'd just given me—the morning of Eddie's arrival when she asked about Seamus? And I'd been surprised she'd known his name.

Had Seamus and Rosita been making a plot for escape together all along? Then plans went awry? Had she then double-crossed him, too, setting him up for Cormac to kill?

"All right," Eddie was growling. "She can stay and dive for us—"

I wanted to scream *No!* but this at least bought me some time. I had a better chance this way than going on the *Myra,* even though I had no idea what Rosita was up to.

"Fine," I said.

"Oh, Aurelia, no—" Maxine started. But I gave a little shake of my head. Douglas put a comforting arm around her.

"Cormac and Douglas, get these two"—Eddie gestured roughly at Liam and Marco—"onto the *Myra.* I'll wait here with the women. Cormac, first frisk them to see if there are any more hidden guns."

I forced myself to look calm, keep breathing. I had the small stocking gun far down in my boot. There was a chance Cormac would miss it. I prayed that he would.

Thanks to the first bit of luck I'd had in years, Cormac found nothing.

He and Douglas went about removing Liam and Marco.

Maxine, Rosita, and I remained silent under Eddie's glaring eyes, his gun aimed at us.

But then Maxine spoke up. "Eddie, there are some items in my and Henry's room." Her voice cracked on her late husband's name. "Nothing to anyone else, but important to me—a quilt, some photos—"

Eddie shook his head. "Do you think I trust you to go to your room alone? And I'm sure as hell not leaving these two here while I go with you—or shepherding the three of you down."

My heart broke at the notion of Maxine having to leave behind her family photos, her precious quilt. "Maybe after Cormac and Douglas are done, Cormac could go down with Maxine—"

But again, Eddie shook his head. "Everyone will leave in what they're wearing, and whatever coat they have already brought up here."

Maxine started crying softly. Rosita moved toward her. Eddie tensed.

"Oh, for pity's sake," Rosita said. "I'm just giving her a hug. Is that all right?"

Eddie's stance softened, and he gave a curt nod of his head.

Rosita hurried over to Maxine and embraced her. She whispered something in Maxine's ear. As she let Maxine go, the older woman's expression was stricken, but Eddie didn't notice.

Soon, Cormac and Douglas returned.

"Now, take Maxine onto the *Myra*," Eddie said. "Wait for me."

Maxine looked at me, wide-eyed, and Douglas looked alarmed.

Me. Eddie intended for Rosita to take him to the records, for me to get the treasure for him. And then he'd kill both of us. Or he'd kill only me. I did not believe he could bring himself to kill Rosita under any circumstances.

Douglas and Maxine left, with Cormac right behind them, ready—and probably eager—to shoot at the least provocation.

That left just Eddie and Rosita and me in the library.

CHAPTER 40

FOR A LONG moment after their footsteps faded, after the feeling settled over us that we were the only ones still in the mansion, Eddie, Rosita, and I remained frozen in place. A tableau.

Rosita standing in front of the bookshelf sliding ladder.

Eddie in front of the fireplace, a barely flickering fire backlighting him.

Me, standing by the head of the table.

Eddie's gun was trained on Rosita. They stared at each other, as if I wasn't there, but I knew if I tried to run, or tried to attack Eddie, he'd shoot me in an instant. I was bearing witness to the McGees' final showdown.

"All right," Eddie said. "Let's get to the goddamned southwest dock."

FIFTEEN MINUTES LATER, we stood inside the old lighthouse cottage. On our way, I'd looked around desperately for Seamus, hoping against hope that maybe Cormac was mistaken, thinking he'd killed Seamus when instead he'd wounded him, left him for dead. We took the perimeter path, and I didn't see any sign of Seamus. He must have been shot on the shortcut path. What if the bear had found Seamus's body? I shook my head, trying to rid my mind of the image.

The lantern I'd carried illuminated the room, casting Eddie and Rosita in a shifting interplay of shadow and light. It was warmer inside the cottage, but cold enough that I could see our breath in the air.

Eddie still held his gun; he'd had it on us for our whole trek as we walked in front of him. We'd moved fast, and Eddie had worked up a sweat. He unbuttoned his coat, put his hat on a table. But never moved his aim from Rosita.

"Go on," Eddie said to me. "Get on your weird suit."

I stared at the suit I'd made so carefully, clasped in my gloved hands. Eddie had followed us upstairs to get our coats, and in my case, my swimming suit. I told him that if I froze to death, I wouldn't be able to get the lockbox for him.

The lockbox I knew wasn't there. I was just playing for time.

"We'll look the other way," he said with a crude chuckle.

I started to slowly unbutton my coat.

"I've thought of a way we can work things out," Rosita was saying to Eddie. "And we couldn't have the others here while we talked about it, and yes, you were right all along, it would have been easier to just kill her"—she jerked her chin toward me—"the root cause of Oliver's death." Her voice caught on her son's name. Eddie stared at her, belief flickering across his face, even after all this time. Fool. "The root, really, of all of our troubles." She moved closer to him. "Did I question anything before she came along? Before I foolishly let her—and her stupid husband Pony—into our lives?"

I turned around, staring at the pair.

"I was content before her, I will be again after her . . ." Rosita said, now coming up to Eddie so that their faces nearly touched, and suddenly he reached behind her, grabbed her hair, pulled her head back roughly, about to kiss her—and then he gasped, staggered back.

Red bloomed on his white shirt, around the sharp tip of the wing of the bronze dove from Oliver's grave.

She must have grabbed the dove from Claire's room, in that brief moment of my and Seamus's last embrace. Sentimentality? Knowing it would make a good weapon? Both?

Eddie dropped his gun, and it spun away from him. He lurched toward it, but Rosita cried out, ran at him again, stabbing him viciously, directly in the stomach.

He fell to the floor, grabbed his gun.

Quickly, I pulled the stocking gun from my boot, aimed it at him. He was shaking so badly that he could barely hold his gun.

"Shoot him!" Rosita screamed at me.

I started to lift the gun, my hand and arm shaking violently, and then let my arm fall to my side. Tears, silent but swift, ran down my cheeks. I was reacting not to the loss of Eddie—but at what we'd all become. What we'd done to one another.

I stared at Rosita, our eyes locked, her gaze blazing and commanding.

"Finish him off," Rosita said. "You've shot and killed a man before. What's another gangster dead?"

I shook my head. I'd shot Pony, yes, in pain and self-defense and in a heated moment. If I shot Eddie now, it would be a calculated move. A shot to prove to Rosita that I was on her side. A shot to use as a bargaining chip for my own life.

"Oh for God's sake, he's going to bleed out anyway. He will not come back from this, you can't save him, and why would you want to—"

"Rosita." Eddie said her name like a plaintive wail.

We both looked at him then. He'd managed to sit up, to aim his gun at Rosita. His arms were shaking. He was liable to pull the trigger without meaning to.

I expected she'd scream at me again. But she squared her shoulders and went still as the angel statue overlooking Oliver's grave. She held her palms out, with the bloody dove in them. She stared into Eddie's eyes.

And for just a split second, I considered waiting. Letting him shoot her. If he still had the energy to turn to shoot me, I could shoot him first. Self-defense—again.

I could run back to the mansion to grab Largo's cage. I could get on the *Myra,* somehow overcome Cormac, at least save myself and Maxine and Douglas.

If I was lucky, I might start over, all alone. I'd take Largo with me. Form a whole new identity. A backstory I'd make up for myself.

Suddenly, Rosita threw the dove at me. It hit me in the head, and I fell, dropping the stocking gun.

She squatted down to get it, even as Eddie fired at her.

But he was in too much pain to hold his aim, and his shot went wide, hitting the wall.

Rosita aimed at him, pulled the trigger once. The sound of that shot was still reverberating when she shot Eddie again. She pulled the trigger to shoot him a third time, but that time, there was a click indicating all the bullets were spent.

She tossed aside the stocking gun, then grabbed Eddie's gun, and I thought she was going to empty it into his body, too, or turn it on me.

Instead, she slipped the gun into her waistband.

"We have to hurry," she said.

I stared at her, still numb and in shock from all that had just transpired.

Rosita gave an impatient sigh. "If Eddie doesn't show up soon at the *Myra,* Cormac will come back," she said. "Douglas will probably help him—he has the most to gain from Eddie. But if they can see Eddie approaching the *Myra,* they'll think he's alive, coming to them. We're going to get him on the speedboat, propped up like he's driving the boat. You'll be in the boat, in your full-body swimming suit, hunkered down. As you approach the *Myra,* turn off the boat, tip it over. In these waves, that shouldn't be too hard.

"They'll see him go in, and think he's drowned and go on. Then you'll swim back toward the life ring from the dock. You can swim that far, in your suit, even in this weather, right?"

I considered, my head spinning as I considered this crazy plan, but I nodded.

"We'll put the life ring in the boat, tethered to the dock by a rope. You'll toss it out before you get around the curve to the *Myra,* so they don't see it from the boat. I'll be on the dock. Just grab the ring, and I'll pull you in."

"And why would you do that?" I asked flatly. "Why not just shoot me, do this yourself?"

She looked sad for a moment. But I wasn't sure if that was genuine emotion, or acting, just for me. After all, she'd convinced us she was Claire for not just the past few days, but for a whole year.

"Aurelia, you know I'm not a swimmer. And I will reward you for doing this—"

"There is no key, is there?" I said. "You know perfectly well where your records are. You—you planned all this—"

"On the spur of the moment," Rosita said. "I had to come up with something, didn't I?"

"Would you have turned the records over to Seamus? If Eddie hadn't shown up and created chaos?"

Rosita regarded me for a moment, and then said the first honest thing I believe I'd heard her say in a long time. She said, "I don't know. And you ought to be asking what we'll do after you've dumped Eddie and returned to the dock," she said. "The first night Eddie was here, after I left Claire in the woods but before I returned to the mansion, I hiked to the north dock and moved the speedboat to a well-hidden cove in case I needed to get away."

"So you did cut the ropes to that boat—"

"Quicker in the cold than untying the knots," Rosita said. "Anyway, you help me make everyone think Eddie drowned, and I—I will let go of my blame of you for Oliver's death. I should never have said what I did, that you were the catalyst—"

Oh, how I longed to believe her. My heart ached from sudden pangs of hope that she was, at last, being sincere.

"I was just so shaken, so upset by Eddie's arrival," Rosita said. "By him bringing that monster to my island. I'm sorry. I forgive you for any tiny part you had in Oliver's death. Do you forgive me?"

I nodded, though I was unsure whether either of us were any more forgivable than Eddie or Marco. And, she still had Eddie's gun. She could shoot me, take the north dock's speedboat, leave my body on the island.

"And then what? If I help you with this crazy plan, if we forgive each other?"

"I have some of my own bullion and jewels locked away securely in Toledo," Rosita said. "I used some of my own influence, and payoffs using the allowance Eddie gave me, to skim some of Eddie's loot. I will give some to you, so you can start over again. After all, we'll have to make up our own new identities so we can outrun Cormac, or Marco's men. We can't let anyone know we're alive. They'll never let us live after Marco's and Eddie's deaths."

My stomach turned. She was right about that.

I had no one back home. No one I'd connected with on Trouble Island other than Maxine, Henry, Liam, and Seamus—and only Maxine still lived. No hope for even a final goodbye with Seamus.

God, I prayed, *let Maxine somehow get reunited with her daughter, Ada.*

"What about Trouble Island?"

"After some time, I'll be presumed dead. And after all that's happened, this place means nothing to me anymore. It's just a bitter reminder of what was supposed to have been. I cannot live here in peace. As I told Eddie, it will go to the orphanage he grew up in."

"Why Eddie's orphanage? After you've come to hate him—"

She gazed down at her dead husband. "Oh, I don't hate him. I just knew that only one of us could live. And I wanted it to be me." She looked back up at me, and I was startled at the coldness in her eyes.

"And Largo?"

For just a split second, she hesitated, long enough for me to realize she'd forgotten about her son's bird.

And that reignited my doubt. Did she mean to help me? Or would she just kill me as soon as I returned from depositing Eddie?

But she was right—Cormac would come back soon. He could follow our steps in the snow to the cottage. Her plan might work. And after I got back from tipping Eddie's body in the lake, I would insist on warming up in the cottage. That might buy me a chance to get Eddie's gun from her.

"All right," I said. "I'm not sure this will work. But I'll do it."

CHAPTER 41

AT THE DOCK—WHERE I'd first seen the *Myra* approaching, where I'd hid the treasure I'd found, where I thought I'd found Rosita but had actually found Claire—I stood in my full-body swimming suit. I placed my goggles over the top of my glasses. Together, we'd dragged Eddie's body down to the dock, propped him up in the speedboat with wood from the side of the cottage. We buttoned up his thick coat, pulled his hat down over his eyes. From a distance, in the falling snow, it would be easy enough to assume that he was alive.

As Rosita had plotted, we'd tied the life preserver to a longer rope, and one end was lashed securely to the dock post. I got in the boat.

Our gazes locked for a moment, and now, looking back, I think I knew this was the last time I'd see her.

But she gave me a swift nod, somewhat impatient, hurrying me along.

I turned from her, pulled the cord for the motor, and after a few tries, it started up. I regarded the axe still wedged in the bottom of the boat, and calculated again that I could get around the bend and to the yacht, but not much farther before water began filling the boat.

I hunkered down, steered the boat with the tiller at the back of the boat.

As I came around the bend, water already coming into the hull, I tossed the life preserver into the water. The speedboat rocked side to side on the thrashing lake, already about to tip over. I just needed it to stay afloat, moving forward until I made it around the curve, until the *Myra* was in view for me, and the speedboat—and Eddie—were in view for those on the *Myra*.

Moments later, I was around the curve. My heart fell; no one was watching from the side of the yacht. But then I saw Cormac, waving anxiously at Eddie.

This was the moment, before Cormac got suspicious. A wave knocked the boat to the port side, almost all the way over, and I threw my weight to the side. That was enough. The boat did not capsize, but Eddie went overboard, and I slipped into the water.

The cold stunned me, the water pulled me down. I couldn't move. But then I came to my senses, kicked back up to the surface. I stayed behind the speedboat, watching the *Myra* through my goggles. Water was already freezing on the surface of the lenses. I forced my legs and arms to tread.

"Eddie!" I heard Cormac's desperate scream. The horrified anguish in his voice.

He turned to the interior of the yacht, crying out. "He went overboard! We have to—"

But another figure approached. A woman. Maxine.

A shot rang out.

Cormac fell.

And Maxine was holding something protectively in her right arm, like a baby. Then she lifted something with a tiny light in her left hand, bringing it toward the item in her right.

A man rushed to her, grabbed her—Douglas? But no, this man was too short to be Douglas. Too broad. And the man cried out, "Maxine! No!"

Seamus.

In an instant, hope surged with a new plan. I could get on the boat. Return for Rosita. Take down Eddie's organization. Maybe, just maybe, Seamus would not reveal me as Pony's killer. Maybe taking down Eddie would be enough for him, and after that, he'd leave behind the law, and we could be together after all.

I swam as fast as I could toward the *Myra,* water sloshing into my mouth every time I rolled to get a breath, gagging me, the force of the waves trying to push me backward, away from the yacht.

But on I plowed, and by the time I got there, a ladder had been lowered for me. Holding it at the top was Douglas.

I climbed up, flopped onto the deck, assessed.

There was Cormac, alive, but shot in the leg.

And Seamus. Shivering, his right arm bare. He'd ripped the sleeve from his shirt and made a tourniquet for his left arm, where he'd been shot earlier.

And Maxine.

Crying. Holding a bundle of five sticks of dynamite. And Henry's beloved Banjo lighter. She'd flick it, the wind would blow it out, but she'd flick it again. Eventually the lighter would run out of fluid. But all it would take was a split second for her to light the fuse, another few seconds for the fuse to burn down, and the blast would bring down the boat, and likely kill everyone on board.

I wanted to ask Seamus *how* . . . But there was no time to quiz him. I turned to Maxine.

"Maxine," I said carefully, gently. I held out my hand, which shook both from fear and coldness. "Why don't you hand me the lighter?"

"What are you doing here?" Maxine said, her voice stilted with shock. "Rosita said—she said if Eddie approached, that meant he'd killed both of you. That I should go to the bin—" She gestured with a nod toward a metal bin, opened, revealing a stack of tan bib-style life jackets. And something else that didn't belong there.

Fuel cells for the Delco generator. Maxine went on: "And get the gun and the dynamite—" She gazed down at the bundle she held in her arms.

"Why?" The question came out of me as a strangled cry.

"She said Eddie would never let me—any of us—out of his grip. That Ada would never be free. She whispered this to me when she came to say goodbye . . ."

I thought back to the moment when Rosita had said she needed to say goodbye to Maxine. My heart fell at the deception. At Rosita manipulating Maxine, who was out of her mind in grief over Henry, not thinking straight, worried about Ada.

Where had Rosita gotten another gun?

You don't think I have hiding spaces in my mansion?

The dynamite?

The old sticks left in the cottage. She'd only taken a few.

The fuel cells?

From the mansion's basement.

When had she placed these items in the bin of life preservers?

She'd had days and nights to do so, wandering freely as Claire. Maybe the same night—before "her" funeral—that she'd sabotaged the mansion.

It hit me.

Before I revealed her ruse showing that she was pretending to be Claire, Rosita had never meant to make it back to the mainland. If she couldn't have the island, her mansion, then rather than face a life under Eddie's control, she'd get on the *Myra* as Claire, and take her own life—and everyone else's—by blowing up the yacht midway between Trouble Island and the shore of Ohio.

And she'd meant for me to be on the yacht with her when she blew it up.

But once I'd shown that she was Rosita, that her cousin was the one buried on Trouble Island, Rosita had quickly calculated that if she could make the right moves, she could take out Eddie, get me on the boat, and have Maxine, who in her grief and fear wasn't in her right mind, take out me and everyone else.

Then Rosita would get to live after all and at last be alone on her precious Trouble Island. Free to calculate an explanation for why she'd survived and everyone else died.

Or free to leave and start over.

I only had seconds to talk Maxine back into being her practical self. I had to focus on the moment.

"But Eddie is gone now, Maxine."

"He has other men, he has Cormac—"

"Seamus will protect you."

Maxine laughed, a short, brutal choking sound, and glanced toward Seamus, struggling to hold Cormac down.

Douglas stepped forward. "Mrs. Carmichael, don't do this, to yourself, to us . . ."

"I'll be gone in an instant. Out of this pain," Maxine said flatly.

"But you don't really believe you'll be gone," I said softly. "You told me what you believed about the strobing light. The afterlife." A look of confusion rolled over Douglas's face but there was no time to explain. I focused on Maxine. "You believe in an afterlife, and how will you face yourself there, knowing you've killed all of us—"

"Knowing my Ada is free! As long as I'm alive, she's tied to this corruption, this evil, this ugliness—"

With a great grunt, Seamus slammed Cormac's head into the deck. But Cormac managed to fling Seamus off his back. Blood oozing down his forehead, into his eyes, Cormac staggered to his feet, pulled his gun on Maxine—

"No," I cried.

Maxine flicked the lighter, and held it close, so close to the dynamite. One staggered step, one jostle of the boat on the water's surface, and she could light it even if she didn't mean to. There would only be seconds before the fuse burnt down and the dynamite exploded.

My cry caught Cormac's attention, and he froze but didn't lower his gun. His gaze flicked to me, and I saw his eyes glistening with emotion. "Eddie—what happened?"

"Rosita killed him," I said flatly. "Just another gangster, gone."

He turned his gun's aim toward me.

Seamus rose up behind him. Staggering, hurting. For the briefest of moments, our eyes met, and in that sliver of time, the possibility of a life together flashed up in our gaze. Maybe the dream of getting off free and starting over with Seamus, away from gangs and lawmen and their chaos, could come true. But I also saw the determination in Seamus's eyes and knew it couldn't be. Seamus was a cop, first and foremost. If he let that part of himself go, he'd be betraying his dead wife and son. He couldn't do that. He would have to take me in as Pony's killer, as part of Eddie's organization.

"Henry would not want you to do this," I said to Maxine.

Maxine shook her head sadly. "Henry isn't here. And he thought that serving Eddie and Rosita would keep Ada safe—but she'll never be safe until all the connections are broken. With everyone here gone, Rosita told me, the gang will forget about Ada."

Cormac rushed toward her, and that was enough for Maxine. I grabbed for the dynamite, but I wasn't fast enough. Even as my hands touched the bundle, she lit a fuse.

"Seamus!" I screamed.

He stumbled toward us, and pulled Maxine from me, jerking her backward hard, so that now I held the dynamite with the burning fuse. I rushed toward the edge of the boat and caught Cormac out of the corner of my eye, about to shoot me. But Douglas suddenly tackled him from the side, and Cormac's gun went spinning out of his hand as the boat rocked.

I didn't have time to think or say anything or look at anyone. I threw the sparking bundle as far as I could from one side of the boat. I ran to the other side, and threw myself off of the *Myra,* as I'd longed to do just over a year before, on my way to Trouble Island.

I heard Seamus cry out my name as I went over.

I heard a faint explosion.

I hit the water with a smack.

I let myself sink, and then I began swimming underwater, away from the *Myra*.

I swam until my lungs began to burn and then I surfaced for just a moment to grab a sip of air. I heard in the distance behind me Seamus and Douglas calling my name. Ahead I saw the curve of the island.

I dipped under again, my arms straight ahead in glide position, my legs and feet beating rhythmically, kicking from the hips. I didn't want my arms to lift above the surface. I wanted them to think I'd drowned.

When I popped up again, I saw the dock—but I did not see the life preserver bobbing in the water. Or Rosita on the dock. I saw the life ring on the edge of the dock.

I went under again, swimming as fast as I could, up again for air, hearing the sound behind me of the *Myra,* and the voices calling to me. Seamus's most frantically of all.

Let me go.

I dove down, down, down, swimming downward, now dangerously far from the surface, but I didn't want the *Myra* to run me over, and I feared that Seamus—thank God he was alive, that he sounded in charge—would come to the southwest dock to search for me.

I swam and my lungs and heart felt like burning balloons on the cusp of bursting.

For a second, I saw them. The shadowy figures. Like a paper-doll chain, hand in hand, no definition to them, but there were five now. Father. Brother. Pony. Oliver.

Eddie.

They want me to join them.

Something bumped against me. A whitefish.

That meant I was too low under the surface.

I swam toward the shadowy figures, but they retreated.

As if luring me on.

Or—not wanting me to join them after all, for they disappeared.

Pressure built in my head, a hissing sound like a pressure cooker.

My lungs longed to convulse, my mouth wanted to open, to inhale.

Then I saw the sparkles. I was vaguely aware that I was no longer kicking. That I was going to drown.

And I did not panic. I felt oddly calm. At peace. I could just let go, be free in this way of all my panic and worry and foiled plots. Maybe, after running from the tragedy I'd experience in water in my childhood in southeast Ohio, this is what I'd been running to all along. Letting go of my life, after all, underwater . . .

But then a light strobed before me, in the murky water, ahead. It strobed again. My legs began moving as if of their own will. My mind wasn't willing anything. I kicked and moved toward the strobing light of the lighthouse.

Impossible, but I saw it, as I had once before.

My legs kept kicking, and my fingertips stretched so long and far in front of me that my arms felt like they might pop out of their sockets.

Finally my fingertips hit something hard—a support to the dock. I was under it. I popped up. I barely had my nose and mouth above water. I was freezing. Water, a semi-frozen slush, sloshed under the dock in waves and I caught a mouthful, gagged and spit. I inhaled as the slush receded from me, exhaled when the water came over my mouth and nose. I could not feel my body. But I forced myself to keep treading. Right by the spot where I'd put the treasure box. Where I'd found Claire's body, thinking I'd found Rosita.

I heard the *Myra* passing by. Seamus calling—"Aurelia!"—throaty and raw voiced.

But I would not let myself pop out. He had to think—they all had to think—I was dead.

Just let me go.

They had to think I was taken by the waves, by the lake.

"Goddamn it, are we going to get frozen in here for that stupid bitch? She's drowned! And I'll kill her anyway if not!" That was Cormac.

"Shut up!" said Douglas.

A cracking sound, a cry from Cormac. I imagined him bound up, Douglas cracking him on the head with the butt of a gun.

I focused on treading.

"Aurelia! Aurelia! I'm sorry!" Maxine cried.

"She'd come back to this dock, she's a good swimmer—" Seamus, disbelief and shock shaking his voice.

"We have to go. I'm sorry. But we have to." Douglas.

"Aurelia!" Another cry from Seamus.

And then the sound of the boat slowly leaving.

The voices fading.

Then nothing but the sound of the waves, no feeling but cold. Yet I kept treading.

And finally I could tread no more.

I sank under the water, but grabbed on to a dock post, and swung out from under the dock.

With bleary eyes through my goggles, the water on them quickly freezing, I gazed across the lake—toward the horizon, lost in the snow falling harder now. The *Myra* was gone. They could not see or hear me, nor I them.

My goggles froze over. I pulled them off and they fell from my numb fingers into the lake. I pulled myself up the ladder to the dock. I still had on my glasses but they quickly fogged over. Then I felt the dock surface and launched myself onto it like a fish being landed, heaving in great gasps of air.

I pulled off my glasses for a moment, wanting to be able to see at least shapes.

The first thing I noted was the life preserver and the neatly coiled rope.

Rosita had never meant to pull me in. She'd meant only to leave me to die in the explosion—or to drown.

Had she watched? Waited? Or left already? Gone back to the mansion?

But no. She'd have left from the north dock. Just like she said we would do.

I stumbled to my feet, willing myself to move, knowing I should get in the cottage, light a fire for warmth. But I stared at the top of the lighthouse, seeking that strobing light.

There was only snow.

I forced myself to climb the boat launch rise, keep going past the cottage, to the lighthouse, and in I went, climbing step after step, my lungs starting to burn as feeling returned to my limbs.

I got to the top at last and gazed through the telescope.

All I could see was snow. But then, for a moment, I thought I saw a shape like a boat, moving across the water.

Rosita.

She'd gotten to her hidden speedboat and was racing away.

In the next second I blinked and the dot was gone.

As I came down, something caught my eye. A piece of paneling pulled free.

I remembered when Rosita-as-Claire, Eddie, and I came here looking for Rosita. "Claire" had remained behind. This is where she must have left her red diary containing the information that would condemn Eddie. Rosita had come up long enough to get them.

Of course she'd want them. That way, if whoever took over Eddie's gang tried to hurt her, she had evidence she could hand over to the Feds. Evidence that would condemn those who worked most closely with him.

CHAPTER 42

I MOVED AS fast as I could, my thighs, arms, and chest burning, even as I shook from the cold, eager to get back to the mansion to warm up. I clenched my teeth to keep them from chattering, anxious that I might bite my tongue.

I feared if I paused for even an instant, my feet would fuse to the ground. I would freeze in place, as still as the broken angel overlooking Oliver's grave.

Finally, I pulled the front door open. Largo squawked from somewhere in the main floor. I knew I had to get her to warmth, too. I followed her cries, found her in her stand in the parlor.

I carried Largo in her cage to the library. I was desperate to get out of the swimming suit, but as I tried to pull it off, pulling down the shoulder, I sensed, rather than felt, my skin rip. I looked down; blood on my shoulder. The suit was frozen to me.

The fireplace glowed with only a few embers. I willed myself through the necessary steps to rebuild the fire. I stood before it, until water started to drip from me to the floor.

When finally the ice in my hair, on my face, on my lashes turned to water and dripped off, I peeled off the suit, and tossed it into a corner.

I stood fully naked before the fire for a few minutes before I realized that I could not feel my toes or the tips of my fingers.

Frostbite.

I recollected what Dr. Aldridge had said about treating the onset of frostbite for Henry.

I grabbed clothes—one of Seamus's shirts, a pair of my pants—and pulled them on. I heated the cast-iron pot, still half full of water, in the embers of the fireplace, then donned oven mitts to carry the hot water upstairs to the bathroom. Thank God, the pipes hadn't yet frozen in the mansion. I mixed hot water with cold, then lowered myself into the lukewarm water.

Water.

The last place I wanted to be was back in water.

But I had to thaw myself out slowly, reduce the risk of frostbite. I didn't have anyone here to amputate fingers or toes if they turned black and rancid, and I didn't want to perform surgery on myself. I could not bring myself to dunk under the water, so I lifted handfuls of water to my face, and made sure to douse my numb ears, too.

At last, I leaned back. Closed my eyes.

At first my mind was empty. Gray.

And then the full import of what I'd just done hit me. I'd succeeded in making Seamus—making everyone—believe I'd drowned.

I was alone. Truly alone.

I opened my eyes, stared at the tub water—now a brownish pink from my blood, from the sediment that had clung to my body.

My face was wet and I realized I was sobbing.

Not at the thought that Seamus, Maxine, Douglas, Cormac believed me dead. Or at the thought that Rosita surely did, too. Or even that she had hoped I was, as she pulled in the empty life preserver.

I sobbed over all that had led me over the years to this moment. The betrayals I'd committed, the betrayals I'd suffered.

I closed my eyes again and finally let myself replay what I'd never been able to confess to Pony, or Rosita, or Maxine, or Seamus.

Why I'd run from my childhood home in southeastern Ohio, all the way to Toledo, into the treacherous arms of Pony Walker. Why I remained tethered to him as if I deserved all the pain and terror he dealt me. Why I'd thought I deserved to remain imprisoned on Trouble Island.

IT WAS MID-AUGUST in 1923 and Mama's zinnias drooped on either side of the creaky wooden steps of our farmhouse. I sprinkled them with water I'd toted from the well, meant for our garden. A smack on the back of my head made me drop the can, whirl around.

Mama, of course, hissing: "What are you wasting your time on them for?" I'd started to say I hoped to make them pert again, maybe for a bouquet, but Mama wasn't in a bouquet mood. She never was.

The next morning, a Sunday, I was still fuming over that smack. The barn was already sweltering, and I was miserable and sweating. My brother, Levi, four years younger than me, was in a cheerful mood, though. Humming.

Levi was always cheerful.

As I finished milking a cow, I said, "Hey. Let's go down to the lake! We could go swimming . . ."

"What? We have church!"

"Well, I'm not going. It will be even hotter in there than in the barn." I gave Levi an impish grin. "Hotter 'n hell!"

He gasped, both at the notion of playing hooky from church and at my curse word. Plus, because of his epilepsy, he was timid. My parents hovered over him. Protective. I was protective, too, but I just wanted us to have a bit of fun. Just be free.

And I loved swimming. Papa had taught us both when we were kids. But since Levi's diagnosis, about the same time I became a "young lady," as Mama put it, we'd been forbidden from swimming.

Rebelliousness arose within me. "Come on!" I joshed him. And then Levi's face broke into the biggest grin I'd seen on him in a long while. The grin of a carefree twelve-year-old boy.

We ran down to the small river that ran behind our property, to a shady, still spot along the bank, good for swimming and fishing.

We stripped down to our underclothes. Levi sat on the bank, wiggling his toes up and down in the water. I took off my glasses and gave them to Levi to hold.

As I waded in, I wondered if I'd remember how to swim, but it all came back to me.

Oh, how I loved it. Gliding through the water, the sense of weightlessness if you got your limbs moving in just the right rhythm.

I popped back up, about to cajole Levi into the river. But even with my fuzzy vision, I saw he wasn't where I'd left him.

Then I heard him screaming out. "Susan!"

Looking back, I believe Levi wanted to show me he could do more than sit at the water's edge, holding my glasses. In that moment, though, I saw my little brother thrashing in the current, panicking.

I swam toward him. I popped up to spot him, but his head, neck, and shoulders were bent back, skyward. He should be able to breathe, to cry out, but he'd fallen silent. His body jerked.

He was having an epileptic fit in the river.

Desperately, I swam toward him. The next time I popped up, I didn't see him. I dove, swam, treaded water, searched for him, cried out for him, over and over.

But he was gone.

A year later, I found Papa in the barn. He'd shot himself in the head. But Mama said he'd died of a broken heart because I'd let Levi die.

Finally, several long, suffering years later, the day after I turned eighteen with no celebration or fanfare, I packed up what I could, including the Aurelia Escalante box from Papa's shop.

I began walking north toward Toledo. Toward freedom, I thought.

I didn't anticipate how hard it would be to make it on my own. I didn't anticipate Pony or Rosita.

I OPENED MY eyes again and stared into the tub water, as murky as the river had been. And as sorrow and guilt over Levi clutched my throat, I wondered if I should have drowned in the lake. If that would have been justice for all my sins. I contemplated finding a razor or knife to lance my wrists, then sinking under the water once more. With the lake starting to freeze, it could be months before Marco's men or Eddie's men or Seamus and men he worked with would come back to the island. Or maybe no one would come at all.

In the next moment, I heard Levi's voice, a faint whisper from the past: *No, Susan.*

I sat up straighter in the tub. Though I wouldn't know anything of it, I could not stand the thought of being found in this water, bloated like Claire had been under the dock. Or worse.

More importantly than that, with sudden ferocity I knew that I wanted to get off this island.

I wanted to live.

Largo's demanding squawks drifted up from downstairs.

I dried off, dressed in my bedroom in layers of stockings, pants, a shirt, a sweater. Wrapped a scarf around my neck.

And yet I still shivered.

I was burning with fever.

With that realization, I worked as quickly as I could, gathering food, water, firewood in the library. I pulled the divan before the fireplace.

The last thing I did before the fever and sickness took over was to put water and seedcakes in Largo's cage.

"Don't eat it all at once, pretty girl," I said, though I knew it was a hopeless request.

THE NEXT WEEK or so—I am not sure exactly how many days—passed in a feverish dreamlike blur.

I dozed in and out, sometimes sweating, sometimes chilling. I saw the bear, I was in the lake, I saw Pony and shot him again, I swam joyously, free and naked, but also swam half-frozen among the silhouettes of the dead—Oliver and Pony and Eddie and Levi, then they'd disappear and I'd be alone again in the gray slushing water, under the dock.

Sometimes I dreamt of Seamus, conjured scenes of us together, in the sunshine, in the yard of a tiny house in a small city, tending a garden, smiling over a small child in her playpen—ours! I knew these images to spring from a fevered wish for a different future, born of altered pasts for both of us. Impossible. Yet I reveled in my imaginings until they felt as real as memory, and gasped with sorrow when I'd come around and know they were only fantasy. Know that I must never see Seamus again if I was to start my life over again, free.

AT LAST MY fever broke.

I woke one morning to bright light coming in through the window. I was still weak, but I could move without every bit of bone feeling like it had been put in a wrench and twisted, without my very flesh crying out in pain against my clothing.

The room was cold; I'd let the fire burn out. I saw my breath in the air in the room. Alarmed, I checked on Largo. She had pulled into herself. She would not long survive this cold. I covered her cage with clothes.

I went to the window, opened the draperies, and stared out. Frost filled the window, cold seeping into the bones of the house. We were packed in by snow and ice.

It was, I calculated, early December. It would be two more

months or so before the lake would be frozen over deep enough for me to safely cross it by foot. And the crossing wouldn't be fast enough for Largo. She would freeze in her cage—if she didn't freeze inside.

I needed wood for the fireplace to keep us warm enough for two months. Food. A faster way to get us across the lake to the shore of Ohio. I needed a plan.

AGAIN, I GATHERED supplies: Largo's birdseed, tinned food, anything Maxine had canned, an old coal shovel and a rake leftover from before the furnace was automated. I remembered the bear and found a shotgun in the Carmichaels' old room.

I shoveled snow from the front door, then left the door wedged open with the shovel—I didn't want it to slam to in the wind and freeze shut while I was gone—and used the rake as a walking stick. I brought the shotgun with me.

Down at the southwest dock, I examined the iceboat. Its hull was in need of repairs, and there was no sail. No oars. But the seating bench and the frame for the sail were still intact. The blades on the bottom of the boat were in good enough shape. All those clothes piled in the library: I could fashion a sail. Years of helping my father in his workshop: I could repair the hull, make some oars.

Repaired, the iceboat would be large and sturdy enough for one woman, a few possessions, and her bird.

OVER THE NEXT weeks I fell into a daily rhythm. First, clear the front door. Bring in wood for the fireplace. After the mansion's pipes froze, I added the task of melting two pots of snow for water; one for drinking, one for cleaning myself and my eating utensils.

I took care of my bathroom needs outside, away from the house.

Outside, I wore Claire's fur over layers of clothing to stay warm, and Dr. Aldridge's fur hat. I ice-fished from the side of the docks, with a line and bits of bologna as bait, and then, after I caught a few fish, with fish guts. Usually, I didn't catch any fish, but when I did, I roasted the fish in the fireplace.

Soon the purple sandpipers I so loved to watch were gone, migrating on to the northern Atlantic. I missed watching them dart in and out on the shore, or float on the lake, huddled together to make a bobbing raft of their bodies.

Each time I went fishing, I held my breath as I tried to break through the ice with my rake handle. When I no longer could, that was a cause for celebrating and calculating: water freezes by the shore first, but by February, the whole lake should be frozen over.

Bit by bit, day by day, I repaired the iceboat, patching the hull with pieces of metal I pried from the now useless furnace, piecing together a sail, shaping wood into oars. I calculated the sail's dimensions from the iceboating book that had been Rosita and Claire's grandfather's.

On the day I estimated to be December 31, 1931, I finished repairing the hull. That night, I finished sewing my patchwork sail. I'd used thread and needle I'd found in Maxine's things, and I made sure to cut fabric from clothes from each of the people I'd known in my last days on the island: Rosita, Eddie, Maxine, Henry, Claire, Douglas, Seamus, Liam, even Marco and Joey and Dr. Aldridge. A patchwork of fear and hope, dreams and despair, love and hate.

I toasted myself with the remaining whisky in the music room decanter.

THE FOLLOWING MORNING, I went to the iceboat, and tied ropes to it, and looped the ropes over my shoulders, and began pulling the boat along the path, now tamped down with all the treks I'd made in the snow between the mansion and the southwest dock. Though the iceboat's blades made it easier to pull on the packed snow, it was still slow, hard labor.

Suddenly, the bear appeared on the path before me.

For just a second, we stared at each other. She was haggard. I wondered if I looked like another animal to her in Claire's fur and Dr. Aldridge's hat. My hand tightened on my shotgun. My heart clenched in fear.

And yet I felt sorry for her, too, even as she rose up on her hind legs, her dark eyes staring at me. She'd been stuck here all summer, imprisoned by the water until she sensed it would be safe to walk across the frozen lake.

I knelt slowly, knowing I'd shoot her if I had to, but praying I would not. I lowered my eyes. I could not back up with the iceboat harnessed to me. And if I tried to free myself from the boat, my movements might frighten her. Plus, I knew it would be foolish to run.

I relied on quietness. Even the sounds of the birds and small woodland creatures who lived on the island year-round hushed. I forced my breath to slow. Willed myself not to panic.

Then I heard her huff, and I chanced a glance up and watched her slowly lumber on. I waited until she was gone, until the sounds of birds and small creatures started up again, at first timidly, then in full-throated abandon.

On I pulled the iceboat, until at last I was back at the mansion. It was just narrow enough to haul into the entry. The blades scratched the beautiful black-and-white tile floor. But that no longer mattered. I wanted the boat inside, not iced over, until I was ready to use it.

That night, the wind howled and the ice lashed so fiercely outside that I feared the house would not withstand the assault.

The next morning, I could barely open the front door to clear it again. Ice had frozen over the dock, on the ground. I was glad I had gotten the iceboat into the house the day before. The sun was out but ice had encapsulated the topiary evergreen shapes leading down to the main dock, making the elephant and rhinoceros and giraffe look as though they were limned in crystal. They sparkled.

I thought, briefly, of searching for where Liam stored the lock-boxes of bullion and jewels for Eddie. He must have missed several. Surely I could find the cache using Rosita's hand-drawn maps from childhood.

But what if I got hurt, fell, froze? Slipped into the lake from the rockier northern side of Trouble Island? Drowned after all? Became another body at the bottom of the lake?

So I shook aside the temptation and closely studied the iceboating books that had belonged to Micah.

I went on a treasure hunt of my own from room to room—searching clothes and belongings left behind for money or anything of value I could find. I collected jewelry, tie tacks, cuff links, silverware, and yes, wallets and money, and put them in pillowcases. I filled my suitcase with some of my clothes and my Aurelia Escalante cigar box of trinkets.

I opened my bird book to the blank pages at the back and began to write my story. It's taken me three weeks to write this record.

I have just one more confession: yesterday when I went outside to clear the door and gather wood, I heard crackling from the direction of the cemetery. The hair rose on the back of my neck.

Had someone from the *Myra* returned to the island? Or had Rosita come back to search for me, one last surprise?

It's just the bear, I told myself, as I grabbed my shotgun and went out to investigate, even as I also thought, *And what will I do if it is Rosita?*

I wondered, would I at last tell her everything that I've written here, all that brought me to Toledo and into her world?

Would I be tempted to shoot her, out of anger and revenge?

Would I want to know why she'd come back to the island—a change of heart? Worry over me after all?

But then I realized that even wondering such about her meant I'd never really known her. To a great degree, Eddie had been right. Rosita, in the end, had cared only about herself. About some image of herself that she wanted to project. Had sweet Oliver lived, she would have been disappointed in him, as she ended up being disappointed in Claire and Douglas, in Eddie, in me. No one could ever have worshipped Rosita enough.

So if the sound came from Rosita, I knew I would not engage with her. I would take Largo and get away from her, whatever that required.

My heart expanded with relief.

The sound did not come from the bear, or from Rosita.

It was a pair of deer, a buck and a doe. They regarded me for a second, then dashed down to the shore, then trotted confidently across the iced-over lake. As I watched them disappear into the snow and mist, I knew that it was, at last, time to leave Trouble Island.

EPILOGUE

ONE LAST TIME, I am on Rosita's balcony. I gaze across the frozen lake at the point where it meets the surprisingly bright blue sky. Just beyond the horizon is the first stop of the journey I've planned, the shore of Ohio.

Over the past few weeks, I've attached the sail to the iceboat, and tested the vessel on the frozen lake.

Now I see the iceboat by the dock, awaiting me and Largo. The wind is right. All I need to do is collect Largo, who is in her cage, covered over with Maxine's Underground Railroad quilt, and go down to the dock. Get in the boat.

I have loaded it with food, my suitcase, my lockbox, my bird book. I have burned the rest of my clothes and any evidence I have ever been here. I've left the mess of the others' possessions in the library. Let anyone who comes here in the spring come up with their own stories, their own explanations. Let everyone think as Eddie wanted them to think—that Rosita and I are gone, lost to the lake.

But we will not be lost to the lake, Largo and I. And I sense that Rosita is not. I can only hope we will not cross paths again.

Once I'm in Ohio, I will sell all I can, take the money from that and from what I collected from the rooms for a train ticket—or if I get enough, for an automobile—and Largo and I will go to Key Largo. I will work, perhaps in a bar or restaurant. I will save. Eventually, I will have my own place. An inn with a restaurant.

Largo will have a place of honor. She might not be able to fly free with her clipped wings, but at least she'll be in a climate that suits her.

I will need another name. I would like to go by Maxine, but no. I will not have the name of anyone I knew before. I will come up with something altogether new.

I will start a new bird-watching notebook, but for birds on the furthest tip of Florida.

One night, at the fire circle outside behind my inn, where people gather for an evening to tell stories of their fishing exploits, I will not tamp out the fire. I will let it rise again.

In it, I will at last put my father's cigar box. And my bird book with the story of all that's happened on Trouble Island.

A funeral pyre for the past.

Now, I wonder, once Largo and I are out on the ice, the wind pushing us away from the island and toward our new life, will I look back? Take one last glimpse of Rosita's mansion on Trouble Island?

I will be tempted.

But I will not look back.

Instead, I will feel the mansion receding behind me, and I will think of how eventually the mansion will crumble into the earth, leaving only remnants for future people to wonder about. Because eventually, nature overtakes everything man-made.

The wind will push us on, and I will stare straight ahead across the frozen gray-and-white ice of Lake Erie.

Perhaps a goshawk will soar above us, gazing down, noting us as a peculiar dot sliding across the frozen lake, on and on, pushed by the wind, finally loosed from Trouble Island.

ACKNOWLEDGMENTS

THIS NOVEL WOULDN'T exist without the story of my Great Aunt Ruth-in-law, whose own life inspired my protagonist. Thank you to my husband, David; my sister-in-law Laura; and my brother-in-law Steve for being supportive of pulling from the family lore of their Great Aunt Ruth, who did what she had to do when her version of Pony crossed a boundary one time too many.

Likewise, this novel wouldn't exist without the history of Middle Island, the southernmost point of land in Canada, in the waters of Lake Erie. Middle Island is the inspiration for Trouble Island. Though Middle Island is now a conservation area that is not open to human visitors, it is part of an archipelago in Lake Erie, and is visible (with the help of binoculars) from nearby islands in Lake Erie near the north shore of Ohio.

This novel's setting and atmosphere grew from a long offseason weekend visit to one of those islands, South Bass. Thank you to my daughter Gwen for accompanying me, going on many hikes, helping me keep track of notes, taking photos, and spending lots of time looking through binoculars! And for keeping me from getting lost, which yes, I could do even on a small island. The visit included a long afternoon at the Put-in-Bay Library—Erie Islands Branch reviewing the archives of local newspapers and historical accounts. Finding stories of iceboats, daring lake rescues, and yes, bootlegging, all fortified this novel's plot.

Another wonderful resource that deeply informed this novel is the National Museum of the Great Lakes (nmgl.org) in Toledo, Ohio. A long visit to the museum's displays and its *Col. James M. Schoonmaker* freighter provided valuable details on lighthouses, shipwrecks, storms (particularly the 1916 Black Friday "perfect storm" on Lake Erie), life on freighters, bootlegging, and more. It's a beautiful, fascinating museum and I highly recommend visiting. Thank you to Gwen and David for accompanying me and being just as enthusiastic about the exhibit as I was.

While novelists spend many hours working alone, novels are the result of community. First, I must thank the members of my amazing writing tribe, all of whom I count as dear friends: the "Cute City Bitches" Katrina Kittle, Erin Flanagan, Christina Consolino, and Meredith Doench. (And a special shout-out to Kelly H., Erin's sister, for generously letting the CCBs retreat several times a year to her lovely house so we can write, write, write as well as encourage one another in our literary endeavors.) A special thank-you to fellow writers and dear friends Heather Webber, Jessica Strawser, Kristina McBride. You all never fail to cheer me on and cheer me up, and I'm ever grateful. Extra shout-outs and hugs to David, Erin, and Christina for being my beta readers for *Trouble Island*; your insights helped me make sense of the story.

A huge thank-you to my publishing team. All of you inspire me to work on being a better writer, every day! From The Book Group: Elisabeth Weed for initial feedback and my agent, Nicole Cunningham, for a thorough review of initial drafts and for illuminating conversations. From Minotaur Books: Catherine Richards, my editor, for insightful direction and always helping me serve the story; Kelly Stone and Kelley Ragland for shepherding the novel through its final stages; copy editor Christina MacDonald for polishing the manuscript; and publicist Sarah Melnyk and marketing manager Stephen Erickson for their dedicated, tireless efforts to make sure *Trouble Island* reaches readers.

Finally, I must thank my dear, dear family: my husband, David, and our daughters, Katherine and Gwen. Your belief in and support of me over the years makes my life a true joy. Endless love and hugs right back at you.

David Short

Sharon Short is the author of sixteen published books. Her newest, *Trouble Island,* is historical suspense inspired by bootlegging and family history. Sharon is a contributing editor to *Writer's Digest,* for which she writes the column, Level Up Your Writing (Life) and teaches for Writer's Digest University. She is also a three-time recipient of the Individual Excellence Award in Literary Arts from the Ohio Arts Council and has been a John E. Nance Writer-in-Residence at the Thurber House in Columbus, Ohio. Sharon currently serves as president of the Midwest Chapter of Mystery Writers of America. As Jess Montgomery, she writes the historical Kinship Series mysteries, which are set in the 1920s and inspired by Ohio's true first female sheriff. When not writing, Sharon enjoys spending time with family and friends, reading, swimming, and occasionally hiking.